The Adler Chronicles

The Story of Phil Adler

By Hal Aetus

Contents

Dedication

My first thanks go to Pheagle Adler, a fellow bald eagle fanboy I met through the furry fandom. This book grew out of a commission request by Pheagle sometime around 2019. Pheagle is known in the fandom for transformation art of his primary character, Phil Adler, who often transforms while he is playing football, much to the demise of his uniforms and the shock of the crowd. Pheagle wanted a novel-length story about Pheagle's background, and he wasn't in a hurry, so I accepted the challenge. As usual, once the project got rolling, I couldn't just settle for a short story and the plot grew to a full-length novel.

I set to it by first reading up on pro football player lore and found a lovely little book by Tommy McDonald titled *They Pay Me to Catch Footballs*. Tommy played for the Philadelphia Eagles 1957-1963, in a similar position to the fictitious Phil Adler, and went on to a distinguished career with multiple teams. Though dated, the book provided a rare insight into the dedication and personal motivation it takes to stick with the sport and make it to the pros. I tried to bring some of Tommy into the character of Phil and I hope it reflects well upon him.

Secondly, but perhaps more importantly, I want to thank my love, my husbird, Colin Stuart, for patiently putting up with my obsession with authoring and drawing, which has led to many dull weekends and evenings for him while I sat planted at my desk. Colin is the love of my life and, I think, the only one that truly understands me. Love you, honeybird.

Thirdly, thank you to Victor for kindly allowing Pheagle and me to incorporate his red-tailed hawk character into the story. Victor has been a positive influence in the furry fandom for many years, volunteering on staff for Midwest Furfest every year since I've known him. It was great fun to include him as a key character in the book and bring more of his character to life.

Thank you also to my beta-readers who provided excellent feedback. These include Barnibu, Hauke Basilisk, Trisha Owler, and Doc Flareon. Special thanks also to Victor Redtail, a real-life best friend to Pheagle, who was willing to be placed in the story as Phil Adler's adopted brother. And thanks to Hornbuckle, who provided artistic inspiration for the team logo for the Pennsylvania Baldies. Thank you also to Ahab for their suggestion on league naming.

Foreword (by Pheagle Adler)

I have known Aetus for about a decade, having first met at Anthrocon, a furry convention in Pittsburgh, Pennsylvania. Our mutual love of the majestic bald eagle and all things avian quickly cemented our friendship.

I am a huge fan of transformation, so when I first learned of Aetus' first novel, *The Sky Calls*, I was intrigued. In 2019, I purchased a copy from Amazon and brought it to the next convention for him to sign. Even though I was busy for most of the weekend, I read the whole thing in a matter of days. I felt a strong connection to the characters, and the story touched me in ways others haven't. It brought a fantasy I'd only previously dreamed about to life.

In fact, I enjoyed the book so much that I wondered if he'd be willing to write something more personal, perhaps something featuring my fursona, Phil "Pheagle" Adler, a football-playing anthropomorphic were-eagle. While Aetus doesn't really watch sports, he's a wild bird vet with a plethora of knowledge of avian biology and I knew I could help him with any football terminology where necessary.

I don't know if it was his fascination with the subject, the challenge of writing about werebirds and football, or just our friendship that drove him to accept my request–maybe all three! But over the past three-and-a-half years, Aetus proved his dedication to accuracy and detail. He even surprised me with what he learned about my favorite NFL football team, the Philadelphia Eagles!

Even now, looking at the finished product, I can hardly believe my eyes. An entire novel about Pheagle! It still seems like a dream. I don't want to give too much away, so I'll just say that this book will appeal to a wide range of people–not just my fellow furries, but fans of transformation, football, birds, and another fourth subject that has mass appeal (it's too important to the plot to mention here). There's plenty of conflict to keep every reader satisfied. I hope you all enjoy the ride as much as I have!

--Pheagle Adler

Maps & Figures

PENNSYLVANIA
NORTH
10 MILES
SUSQUEHANNOCK
STATE FOREST
BOONETECH
BLOOMSBURG
CATAWISSA
SUNBURY
BOONEDOCKS
BALD EAGLE
STATE FOREST
GRAMPS'
CABIN
APPALACHIAN MTNS.
SUSQUEHANNA RIVER
PHILADELPHIA
HOME OF THE PENNSYLVANIA
"BALD EAGLES"

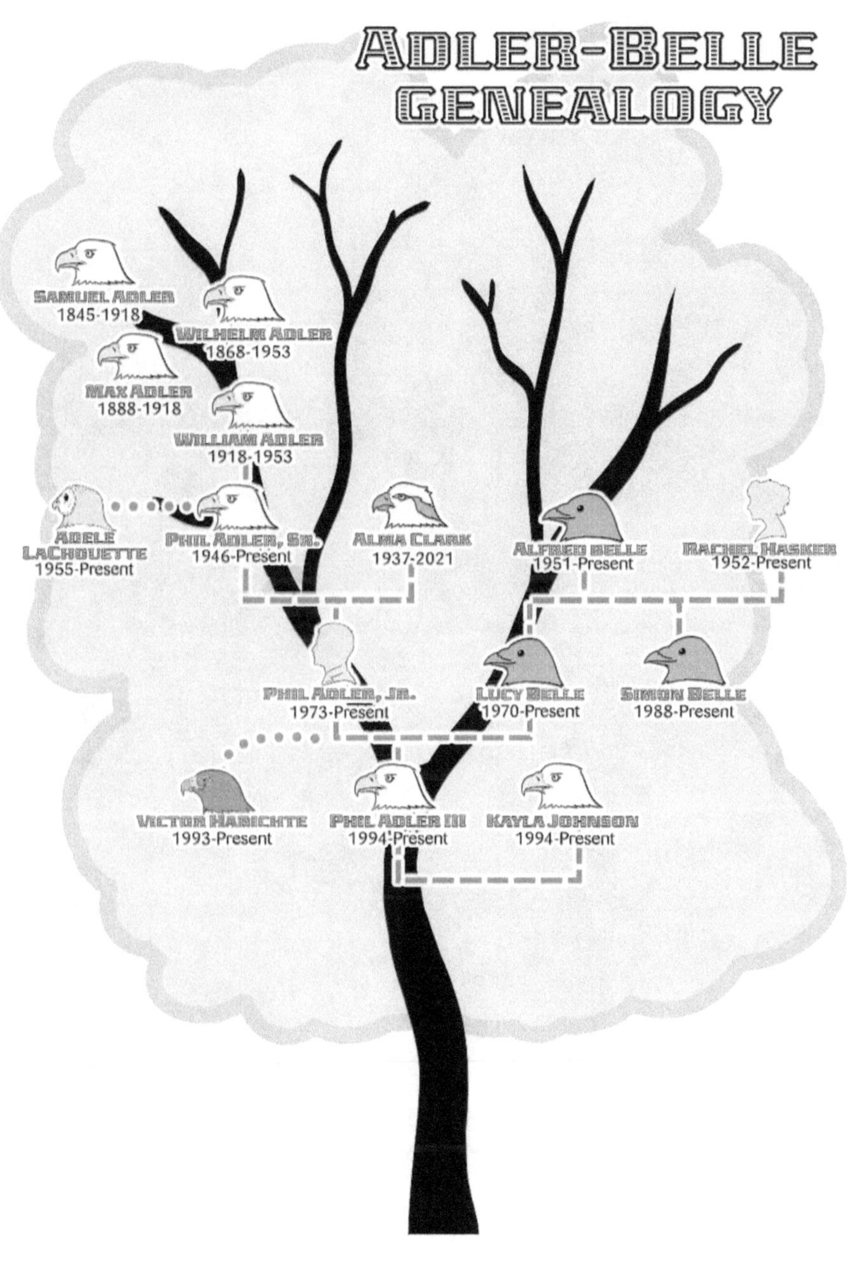
ADLER-BELLE GENEALOGY
SAMUEL ADLER
1845-1918
WILHELM ADLER
1868-1953
MAX ADLER
1888-1918
WILLIAM ADLER
1918-1953
ADELE LaChouette
1955-Present
PHIL ADLER, SR.
1946-Present
ALMA CLARK
1937-2021
ALFRED BELLE
1951-Present
RACHEL HASKER
1952-Present
PHIL ADLER, JR.
1973-Present
LUCY BELLE
1970-Present
SIMON BELLE
1988-Present
VICTOR HABICHTE
1993-Present
PHIL ADLER III
1994-Present
KAYLA JOHNSON
1994-Present

Chapter 1: Violation

A lively, rhythmic roar filtered down through the high white ceiling and blue-green walls of the busy locker room. Speakers around the room blasted out "Throw It Up" by Lil Jon, a song frequently played just before game time to motivate us. But at that moment, I sat in my chair at my wood-framed dressing space, back facing the room, eyes closed, trying to be someplace else for just a little bit.

I'd already suited up in my forest blue and white uniform emblazoned with the logo of the Pennsylvania Bald Eagles, or Baldies, as fans affectionately referred to us. I'd been with the team for over a year, but it was still hard to believe that I'd achieved my childhood dream. I wasn't ashamed to admit that I loved seeing myself in the uniform. I had endured a decade of physical punishment and focus, through high school and college athletics, to earn the privilege to wear it. So, naturally, it was dear to me.

Everyone has their own methods for coping with the excitement and stress just before a game, be it obsessing over their appearance, cracking jokes, or checking their good luck charms. Mine is meditation. I pause and mentally focus before I go into a game. The noisy locker room made this difficult sometimes, but fortunately the chaos was settling down.

Stragglers were getting their last massages, finishing their tape jobs, and making final adjustments to their uniforms. A couple of the guys were bullshitting in the doorway. Some were savoring the last moments of peace they'd have for the next three hours, while others reveled in a surge of pre-game adrenaline. I liked to imagine it was the same nervous calm that paratroopers felt on the morning of D-Day, clinging to their last personal moments before plunging into hours of grueling work that might change the world, and their lives, for better or for worse. Our stakes were never as high as theirs, but we took our jobs seriously, as though we were also heading into battle. There would be no returning to this moment again. No do-overs. Victory and survival to the next game were our only goals.

Without opening my eyes, I lifted the towel from around my neck and pulled it up over my head. I tucked my knees in closer to my chest and rested my elbows against them, while my hands covered my ears. As I entered my meditative state, the cheers of the hyped-up Sunday crowd, throbbing through the ceiling above me, transformed into surging ocean swells and screaming sea birds as I flung myself thousands of miles away.

I was a bald eagle, soaring above dark, rocky sea cliffs topped with firs. It was my favorite location for mental escape—a lonely spot along Oregon's Pacific Coast on a rare sunny day. I carved an invisible path back and forth over a rocky island, the surf crashing far below. The din of gulls, guillemots, and murres swirled around me in an incredible cloud of noise punctuated by the barks of sea lions and the crashing of sparkling green waves. I focused on cutting the perfect bank at just the right time to bring me through the shifting wind to the perfect place above a deep green pool between two jagged rocks. The setting was stunning, but that's not what made it a favorite. I drew strength from this place because it was a memory of a perfect day where everything clicked.

On the lee side of a dark rock the size of a building, I found a wind shear that dropped me like a feathered stone. I used the changing wind direction to slip sideways towards a rising mist of salty droplets. The hands of the wind thrusted me upwards, and I rode them just high enough to peek down into a green, foamy pool, checking if my timing was right. Then I curved my leeward wing and swung back into the shear again, shallower the second time because I wanted to hasten to the next rise on the wind.

It was a half-planned, half-opportunistic, undulating dance with barely any flapping, relying instead on the ambient forces of nature to propel me. It would look lazy to the casual observer, but tide, ocean swells, wind gusts, sun angle, and, especially, presence of my prey, were all being calculated. I could have scavenged, like most bald eagles, if I only needed to eat. But I wanted the best fish!

I rose again, peeked over the clifftop, and saw my golden moment come into reality: a shining salmon lazily swam across a small green patch of upwelling sea. The water glittered with an effervescent swirl of fine bubbles that made the fish feel safe and secure. The tips of my primaries buzzed as I flattened my wings and lowered my head into a determined dive. I passed into the shadow of a cliff and became a dark blur against a background of black basalt. The fish swung lazily into the center of my 'kill zone' — the area in relation to my trajectory where I would have maximum control and could pivot in any direction to alter my momentum to match theirs.

At 100 yards downwind and 40 yards above the water, I pulled in both wings halfway and lowered my curled feet. Small currents of turbulence ruffled the feathers on the back of my wings as I brought them into an intended partial stall that dropped me rapidly. Gulls reeled and squawked, shitting in fear or nipping at me with razor sharp beaks as I busted through their flock. The dark water rushed up towards me like concrete, but I was not afraid. Everything was under control.

I leaned my weight forward, and my trajectory flattened so that I sped across the rippled surface until the fish was only three yards and half a second away. I dropped my feet lower, spread my toes, and thrust my black talons forward! In the final millisecond, the fish jerked in surprise, but it was too late. My wings strained as I ripped the fat salmon out of the water. My eyes sparkled and my spirits soared with the endorphins of accomplishment. I felt every fiber of my churning, pumping flight muscles as I pushed my body, confidently, to its limits.

I climbed back into the sky and admired the glistening fish, which gaped in bewilderment as its watery home dropped away far below. I dodged jealous seabirds and the half-hearted stoop of a juvenile eagle that had hoped to make me drop my prize. I worked hard for that fish, and it would be an excellent meal for me, my wife Kayla, and our friends on shore. No way was I letting go of it! Once clear of the would-be thieves, I adjusted the fish in my grip, and steered for the trees to perch and rest.

It was a favorite memory because patience and practice, preparation and adaptation, paid off perfectly. It gave me focus for the challenges of the day. And after all that work and concentration, that fish was one of the tastiest I'd ever enjoyed. No, it wasn't a daydream. It was real. I made it happen and I lived that moment. I knew that I could make it happen again. And I knew that if I could yank that perfect fish out of the ocean, I could sure as hell catch a football and haul ass to the end zone.

"Guys, time to go!" came a shout in the room. I was jerked out of my memory by the forceful bellow of Ben Dupree as he spun my chair around. I pulled the towel off my head to see him offering a hand.

"Thanks! Guess I checked out pretty good there."

He lifted me up with his thick, black arm effortlessly, and we walked towards the gathering at the center of the room.

"No problem, man. I see you do that every week before a game. Where you check out to anyway?"

Dupree was my best friend on the team, a veteran player

that made me feel at home. There's a lot more to pro-football life than anyone on the outside can imagine, and Dupree, with his five years' experience as a running back, helped me figure it out. We shared some personal things here and there, but given the nature of my unconventional, unbelievable lifestyle away from the game, I had important reasons for keeping the details of my family life private, even from him.

I casually replied, "Oh, just a great fishing trip I had when I was in college. Ya know, one of those perfect moments when everything goes just how you want it to?"

"Fishin'? No shit? Ha ha! That's different. Most guys be thinkin' of the perfect play, the ass they gonna kick, girls they're gonna impress. But, hey, whatever gets you in the zone, man."

"Well, it qualifies as the 'perfect play.' It was a great time."

A shout came from the refreshment area at the end of the locker room. "Mr. Adler! Mr. Adler! Got somethin' new for ya!"

A pimple-faced young man was handing out energy drinks to the players. I didn't recognize the kid, but his eagerness was contagious. I knew the face of an ardent fan and making them smile hadn't grown old for me yet. I walked closer and cupped my hands to invite a pass. The kid chucked it in perfectly.

I chuckled, "Hey, not bad! You're gonna be my replacement someday!"

"Can you sign a can for me too, Mr. Adler?"

"You bet!" I smiled and took the offered Sharpie marker. I scribbled my signature on another can before popping mine open and strolling away. "Thanks!"

I didn't have time to sip and savor it, as there was a prayer circle already forming in the middle of the room. I chugged half of the sugary, lime-berry-melon concoction before I got there. It was the final ritual before we poured into the hallway and trotted out onto the field for the opening of the game. Everyone quieted down and linked hands. We were all from different backgrounds, with different personal lives and inspirations, and even different religions. But the prayer circle was less about religious devotion and more to unite and focus us. Its effect was palpable. As soon as we broke the circle and slapped on our helmets, there would be no going back, so we committed to helping each other succeed in the common goal of victory. Nothing else mattered.

Before I knew it, we were out on the field, awash in the cheers of the crowd. The quiet reverence of the opening anthem passed like a dream, and we won the coin toss. But, as usual, we deferred to the visiting team, this time the Peregrines, for the kickoff. I'd have to wait a while since our defense was up first.

It was a fine October afternoon, with warm sunshine and the smell of autumn in the air. The air wasn't hot, but I felt prickly and sweaty around my collar. It felt out of place since I hadn't even exerted myself yet. It reminded me of the butterflies I had in my first games, so I shrugged the sensation away.

I was a fifth draft pick. Being picked later wasn't from lack of skill. I kicked ass in four years playing college ball with the Penn State Nittany Lions. I proved my potential. But I was on the small end of stature for an average pro football player, being only six feet tall and 175 pounds. On paper, it's hard to stand out in a crowd of skilled guys that all made headlines in their college careers. So, it came down to other statistics when they hadn't seen me play, and I sounded like a shrimp compared to the others.

But luckily for me, Coach "Hatch" Haskins noticed my records and saw a chance for my speed and agility to be an asset. While the big guys churned and burned to clobber me, I bent, dodged, and zipped just out of reach. Teammates chided that I was more like a bird than a man in my moves when I avoided defensive linebackers. If they only knew the truth! It was the bird side of my life that inspired so much of my athletic drive. If you snatch fish from the sea in the presence of hungry, thieving eagles, you learn quickly how to dodge, fake, and hang on to your meal. I often wished I could tell them more about my inspiration, but we werebirds shared our family secrets with very few.

Hatch was my strongest advocate from my first day of practice. He was polite, but impossibly demanding. Sometimes it felt as though he drilled me harder than anyone else on the team and the more I met his expectations, the more he demanded. I wondered whether he hated me or thought I wasn't good enough for the team, but he wasn't insulting or demeaning, so I didn't let myself get discouraged.

I think Hatch wanted, from the start, to hone me into a lean and nimble wide receiver. There had to have been a streak of nostalgia in Hatch. I'd seen the autographed photo of legendary wide-receiver Tommy McDonald hanging in his office. I never asked, but I liked to think he saw something of Tommy in me, and that was why he molded me for the same team position. I did my best not to disappoint him. I studied everything he threw at me. I did the drills, honed my skills, and took everything he said to heart.

My hard work paid off in a game against our in-state rivals, the Pittsburgh Pirates, where I got a lucky break. Our prime wide receiver, Reinhart, pulled a muscle so severely that he had to sit out the third quarter. We were behind, fourteen to twenty.

You can't tune out when you're on the bench. It's a time to observe and learn your opponent's weaknesses. I had studied the Pirates' recent games, so that day I stayed riveted to their defense's performance, looking for any changes in their strategies and movements. I noticed a slight hesitation in Hadley, an outside linebacker, to turn left. I thought it might explain why they had him playing on the right side of the lineup that day. It was probably the ankle he had rolled earlier in the season.

I mentioned it to Hatch and Simmons, our quarterback, as I was called to the field. I was ready to run whatever play they gave me, but I hoped that they would trust me and put me in position to make Hadley turn left. On the first two plays, I did what I was told and swung out on centerline drives that gained little yardage. But Simmons was just buttering their bread. On the third play, he gave me a look we'd already practiced. It meant he was counting on me.

On the snap, Simmons pulled left. The defense took the bait and spread most of their players to the left. I ran up the right, barely missing Hadley's delayed turn to block me, and caught the ball on the run. I hauled ass for thirty-five yards with Hadley and two others five yards behind, but no way could they keep up with this light-footed bird. I ran it into the end zone and made my first pro career touchdown.

It was an awesome feeling to be in just the right place at just the right time. Not by accident, but on purpose. It was a feeling I wanted to have again and again, so I watched every moment of every game, looking for whatever clues might help make that a reality.

In the opening drive of today's game, the Peregrines pushed the football down to our fifteen-yard line, but their offensive petered out before they could score a touchdown. They squandered their last down on a rushing play rather than kick a field goal, so it was time for me to hit the field with the offensive team, staring down eighty-five yards to the end zone. I was going to need my legs plenty today, but I secretly wished I could use my wings!

Like barrels of dynamite, the Peregrines defense lined up in front of us. They were fresh and strong, ready to chew me up if I wasn't quick enough. Simmons didn't want me injured so early in the season, so he advised caution initially and threw me a short pass on the first play. We only made five yards before I was forced to drop and avoid getting crushed by the combined weight of two massive blockers. The next play collapsed after only one yard, and Simmons was almost sacked.

As we reformed on our fourth down, I shook my head, wondering if we could crack their defense today. It was our last chance to extend the drive. We couldn't let it end so soon. There were still several options, but which one would Simmons choose? *Come on and give me an opening this time…*

The ball was hiked, and Simmons faked a toss to the running back, as I maneuvered towards a gap opening up in the swarm of defenders. The fake worked perfectly, and I swept the ball in for a twenty-five-yard run before being forced out of bounds. *Yes! We were moving forward!*

As I trotted back, I felt a tingle in my legs, as though there was energy there itching to be used, but I hadn't pushed myself hard enough to tap it. *I should have been able to get past that cornerback. Why didn't I?* My teammates rewarded me with slaps of appreciation though, including a pound on the back by Dupree.

"Good goin' man! Let's get this drive on!"

I smiled and trotted back to the line, shaking off demons of doubt. We had made the first down and there would be more plays. That was all that mattered there and then. I had to reset and be ready for the next opportunity.

On the next play, I hooked around to the left, but Simmons couldn't find a clear path. He was pushed out of the box and threw the ball away to avoid a sack. No yards gained.

We huddled for only a moment; Simmons slipped us the phrase "skyhook" and said to me, "Let's do that thing we did on your first TD."

I nodded and stepped towards my lineup position. My job would be to run around the mass of men to my right, while Simmons made it look like he was moving the play left, maybe even setting himself up for running it on his own. Everyone else would move left too, as though to help him. I loved this play and was ready to do it, but that strange feeling rippled through my legs again. As we settled into the lineup, the hairs all over my body prickled and my vision flashed white for an instant. I shook my head to clear it.

The only time I normally had these sensations was when I was transforming. But that couldn't be. I wasn't controlling this. I tried pushing it out of my mind.

As I looked back up, Simmons furrowed his eyebrows as if asking: *You okay?*

In response, I winked my eye and nodded to reassure him I was good to go. I told myself: Okay, body, you want to transform right now? Well, you can't. Not in front of all these people. But I'm gonna make you channel every ounce of that energy into hauling ass down this field like a bird in flight to make a goal.

The ball snapped and I ran hard and wide to the right, and that's when the tingling returned like a tidal wave. It swept down my whole body from my forehead to my toes. I felt like I did in my meditation, as if I was no longer a man after a football, but an eagle after prey. There was no crowd or rival team, just a leathery red fish hurtling towards me, and everything was in perfect motion for me to catch it. The human bodies coming at me could have been crashing waves and solid rocks, but that was no barrier to a creature that could fly!

I sprang into the air, channeling all my strength into the jump. Energy surged through my body again, out through my pecs and into my arms. My uniform ripped wide open, and my body pads shot away like bursting buttons on a shirt that was too tight. Huge, brown-feathered wings erupted from my shoulders to complement my arms. My rump exploded through my pants into a broad fan of white tail feathers. My helmet cracked as my face stretched into a beak and white feathers poured out of my scalp. My ankles stretched into large yellow eagle feet, tearing my cleats to shreds.

The sensations were out of place for football, but not new to me. At that moment, I was so engaged in the play that I scarcely noticed and poured everything into seizing my prize and taking it to the goal. I let go of my self-imposed limits, and pushed as far as I knew my body could go. I jumped like I knew I could, and my body obeyed and launched me five yards upwards and five yards forward. The ball slammed into my grasp with a smack!

With a thumping downstroke of my thirty-foot wings, I lifted and turned towards the Peregrines' end zone. My tail spread wide and carved the slow air, as my primaries bent and buzzed under the strain as I picked up speed. All I heard were wind and cheers, like ocean swells, around me, as I pumped my wings down the field towards the goal.

Far beyond the reach of any players, I leveled my wings for a glide into the end zone. The crowd cheered wildly on their feet. I veered around the SkyCam and flared my wings for a landing. Sports photographers bumped into each other at the end zone to get the perfect shot. Suddenly, I snapped back to reality, and I realized what I'd done.

It was too late. I couldn't play this off. I tilted my wings, dumped my airspeed, flapped a couple of times, and landed in a sprint. I trotted to a stop, as my hefty talons tore up chunks of sod.

When I turned around, both teams were standing around watching me. Clearly, nobody knew what to make of my transformation. What was I to do? I hadn't had an accidental transformation since I was a kid. That had been frightening enough in relative privacy. Now I was on live television being watched by millions. I thought for a fleeting moment that I could just pretend it was part of the show.

With one hand, I yanked my busted helmet off and threw it to the ground. With a smirk, I thrust the ball up high and turned slowly around, awash in the battering cheers of the crowd. Photographers ran up close, their shutters clicking and flashes detonating. All I could do was stare back with my big golden eyes, spread my wings, and give a winning smile.

Hatch stood dumbfounded, his mouth hanging open, and every one of the guys on the sidelines pointed at me and muttered to each other. In the stands, the crowd jumped up and down, trampling down the aisles to get a closer look. It was a flood of ecstatic people, and I was concerned that someone could get hurt.

Field personnel shied away, and even my teammates stayed thirty yards back. The crowd believed it to be a realistic stunt, but the field personnel knew it wasn't, and that made them uneasy. I knew it was only a matter of seconds before the crowd sensed their unease and launched into their own panic. And under all that, I was scared too. Scared for whatever just went wrong with me. Scared that I'd ruined everything I'd ever worked for. Scared of what might happen next. Shame swelled inside of me for what I'd done, and my wings sagged. My family's secret had been hidden for generations and I'd blown it wide open in front of the world. It was time to get out of there before it turned ugly.

I gave a salute to the crowd, dropped the ball casually, and leapt into the air. I pumped my wings hard to gain speed and my shadow passed over the players in the middle of the field. The Peregrines' players shouted and ran for cover like mice under a passing hawk, but my teammates alternated between cheering and staring in awe. I thought, for a moment, of returning to the locker room. But with fear in so many eyes, I doubted it would be anything less than an awkward and dangerous situation.

I flapped hard, and circled around the field gaining altitude, before heading out over the Jumbotron at the west end of the field — straight into the brightness of the low afternoon sun. As soon as I cleared the edge of the stadium, I dropped down out of site of the cameras and transformed again into a normal, feral bald eagle. That was the best disguise I could muster for getting away quickly and discreetly.

As I passed over the parking lot, a photo drone zipped up above my tail. I rolled, flared my wings, and grasped a corner of it with my left foot. I rolled back upright and let go, flinging it into a light pole. It crashed with a satisfying crack, and plastic bits rained to the ground.

In minutes I was miles away, skimming the treetops, confident nobody was following me. Out of immediate crisis, the gravity of what just happened flooded over me like cold rain. My eyes misted with tears, and my chest heaved with sorrow. I swallowed hard like I was choking on a frozen fish. Many questions raced in my mind. *What happened and who did this to me? Would I ever see my teammates again? Was I done playing pro ball? And what could I do about it now?*

Chapter 2: Retreat

In the grimy light, three hundred feet above leafy treetops, a cold, spattering rain stung my eyes and forced me to repeatedly flick my semi-transparent nictitating membranes. The clouds were so low that the tops of higher hills, such as Catawissa Mountain, were erased by the soft, gray ceiling. Wispy tendrils streaked down around me, as heavy raindrops pulled the clouds towards the earth. Most of the rain bounced off my feathers, but I was soaked enough that had I stopped flapping, I'd have been chilled to my bones. All I could hear was my breathing, in with the upstroke, out with the downstroke, mixed with the stinging precipitation. I had no phone, no car, not even any clothes. I could have gone home, but Kayla, my wife, wasn't going to be there, and I didn't have a key with me. My best option was Grandpa Adler. I just hoped I could make it there before dark.

Eagles don't see well in the dark, especially when their eyes are half-closed by pelting rain. At last, in the dying light, I saw a distant curl of blue smoke and a warm glow on the rim of a forested ridge. I paused flapping and inhaled the familiar scent of wood smoke and rotting leaves, and closed my eyes as relief washed over my frame. It dawned on me that I'd been flying continuously for two hours. It should have been faster on a decent day, but low ceilings had forced me to change course many times. I was exhausted, both mentally and physically. My emotions were close to spilling, and my heavy heart could have plunged me into the Susquehanna River below.

I opened my eyes again, and the landscape had tilted dramatically to the left. My mind had drifted so much into self-pity, that I was numb to my avian senses, and that is a dangerous place to be in flight. I shook the rain from my face and resumed flapping, shredding my muscles against a stiff breeze that shook the treetops. I crossed the wind shear generated by a ridge line to the west, an invisible flow that undulated like a river washing over a rounded rock. Its only telltale sign was the tumbling of raindrops that danced sharply in my eagle-eyed gaze.

My wings buffeted one last time as I entered the relative calm below the shear. I sighed wearily and set my wings into a long, damp glide that terminated at the grassy knoll in front of my grandfather's cabin. I immediately sagged onto my wings in the wet grass and mud and let the tears flow. Everything I had ever worked for was gone. Years of sweat and tears, bruises and bloodied knees, all for nothing. I buried my beak in the mud and sobbed as the cold penetrated into my bones. I just wanted to die and get swallowed up by the earth. Then I realized I wasn't alone.

A pair of man-sized, yellow hawk feet stood a few feet away, toes half buried in soft mud. I looked up and confirmed it was Victor. His brown speckled breast feathers, creamy white belly and legs, and broad red-tail were dripping wet. Above all that, he wore a wide, hawkish smile, and his reddish-brown eyes conveyed warmth, even in the cold twilight.

He asked, in a squeaky, hawkish voice, "You want to turn yourself into something more manly and walk inside, or do I have to carry you like a gentleman and his falcon?"

I shook my feathers violently to shed the weight of the rainwater, and planted my wings on the ground as I closed my eyes and focused on transforming. My legs and wings started changing first. My feet enlarged, and the scaly, yellow skin of my eagle feet advanced up my shins to just below my knees. I lifted my buttocks and tail, and widened them as my legs plumped to human proportions. My wings divided, starting at the tips, with one pair of wings pressed into the mud and the other lifting and shifting around to closer to my spine. These "backwings," as we called them, were a common feature in a werebird's "anthro," or humanoid-bird hybrid, form although sometimes we also chose to have feathered arms only to facilitate sitting on human furniture or riding in vehicles. As my backwings enlarged, my torso lengthened and widened, and a sound like knuckles cracking under heavy muscle reverberated in my airsac-hollowed core.

The wings I had planted on the ground pulled in their flight feathers, and the naturally simplified bones of their tips divided into four long, yellow fingers and a thumb, all tipped with short black talons. The feathers of my forearms withdrew into the plumping flesh, as large yellow scales, known as scutes, formed on my hands and arms up to my elbows, where they gave way to soft brown feathers. My eagle head enlarged, and the feathers lengthened and widened to maintain proportions with my now six-foot frame. Steam rose from my soggy feathers, and I panted from the great heat of metabolic insanity raging within me. As the transformation completed, I sat in the mud on my hands and knees, weak and spent.

Victor's voice said calmly, "Need a hand?"

I looked up to see Victor offering his scaly, yellow bird-hand. I gripped it and grinned meagerly. He started to pull me up, but I yanked back. He screeched out "Fucker!" in surprise, as he tumbled down into the mud puddle beside me. He twisted nimbly as he fell and wrapped an arm around my throat while his backwings flapped to maintain a superior position on top of me.

I bucked and slopped my feathers in the mud and leaves, but there was no strength left to fight. My muscles burned still, the transformation seemingly only adding to the fatigue I was experiencing. But anger and frustration smoldered inside me, and I yearned for a good fight to let it out.

"Skreeeee!" I pressed hard with my legs and threw Victor's weight far enough forward that he flopped off my back, and we tumbled on to our sides. I punched behind my neck and scored a blow.

Victor cussed out and stabbing pain lit up my right thigh as Victor sank his talons into my flesh. I screeched, and my face slammed into the mud, driven by a fierce blow from his right elbow.

Victor wasn't smiling now. "Do you yield, you ungrateful piece of carrion? Or do I have to make you drink that mud puddle?"

I went limp. "Okay, okay, you win."

Victor released his grip and slowly rose to his knees. I chuckled as he stood up tall and offered his hand down to me again. He smiled and said, "Good. I'd hate to have to ruin your good looks."

I took his warm hand and let him help me up to my feet. He jerked me closer and wrapped his arms around me in a firm, mud-caked hug, his warm beak placed against my nape. "It's gonna be okay, brother."

I lifted my tired arms and hugged him back, pulling energy from my swelling emotions. "Thanks, Vic. I…" My beak squirmed to hold back my emotions. "Sorry for the punch. Not sure what came over me."

Victor chuckled, "You've had a rough day, amigo. It was a pretty weak punch anyway. You get that one for free."

Surrounded in warm, friendly feathers, I couldn't contain my emotions. And there was no need to. Victor was orphaned as barely more than a toddler. Our family adopted him and regardless of different parents, he was always my brother, and we were inseparable since before I could remember.

My body shook, and I sobbed heavily in Victor's embrace. His hands froze in surprise at first, but then he hugged me tighter and rubbed my back as he whispered soothing words that gave me permission to bawl my eyes out. It was both draining and refreshing.

Victor gave no indications that he was uncomfortable or unwilling to stay out in the rain all night if need be. But soon we were both shivering from the cold soak. I released my arms first, and he followed.

A gruff chirp came from the porch of the cabin: "You boys look like drowned chickens. Come on in and dry off! Got a good fire goin'."

It was Grandpa Philip Calvin Adler, Sr., the namesake of both me and my father, or Gramps, as Victor and I referred to him. He sat on a stool on the porch with a wooden pipe clamped in his beak and supported by one hand. The bowl of the pipe glowed briefly, and dimly illuminated his peppered white head plumage, sharp yellow eyes, and hooked eagle beak. A puff of white smoke rolled from the corners.

Vic's smile was warm and wide. "C'mon, brother. Let's get you cleaned up, dried off, and warmed up."

As we trudged up to the porch, Gramps rose from his stool and said, "Good to see ya grandson. Got some a' your favorite fish pie bakin'. We were 'specting you to show."

I wiped a clump of mud from my beak and said, "Thanks, Gramps! I can hardly wait!"

Gramps shook his head, "M-mmm you're filthy! No way you're comin' in here like that! You two go get cleaned up in the Changin' House."

The Changing House was across the yard from the main cabin, tucked under the trees beside the driveway. Any time family gathered at the cabin, Gramps' rules applied: You had to be in avian form, either feral or anthro. It was a multigenerational rule that went all the way back to the late 1700s when the homestead was first settled. And so, the Changing House was your first stop, if you weren't already wearing feathers.

The single-story structure was so much more than its name suggested. It was where we left our secular humanity behind and embraced being werebirds. It offered practical accommodations such as wooden lockers, benches, small rooms for changing clothes in privacy, if so desired, bathrooms, and even showers and a sauna. It was dated and certainly not fancy, reminiscent of a summer camp shower house rather than a bathroom in a modern home, but it provided everything visitors needed to comfortably change out of their clothes and take their avian shapes or reverse the process when they left the mountaintop retreat.

We stopped at the door and roused vigorously to shed as much rain and mud as possible before we went inside. The hot shower helped me feel more like myself again.

In ten minutes, we were back at the covered porch of the cabin. Gramps greeted us and we followed him through a pair of glass-paned French doors into a spacious front room that was the heart of the abode. The room was tall, reaching two stories high to the open wood rafters. It was decorated in well-broken-in leather furniture and end tables made of the twisted limbs of local hardwoods. Gramps loved to work with wood in his shop out back and had made many of the decorations himself. But many others were also inherited with the cabin, such as the old buffalo hide rug on the floor in the center of the room.

To the far left was a crackling fireplace made of round river rocks with a thick plank for the mantelpiece. Above that was an enormous painting of two humanoid bald eagles, one taller than the other, holding taloned hands, obviously in love. The scene was that of a summery green forest with Gramps' cabin in the background. The painting was well over a hundred years old, done in the luminism style typical of the late nineteenth century.

A balcony with a log railing hung above two sides of the living room. Old-fashioned doors with brass knobs opened from the bedrooms onto the balcony and an open wooden staircase led down from the corner of the room to the main floor. A hallway started under the stairs, led along the wall separating the kitchen from the living room, and continued back to, from left to right around the end of the hallway, a master bedroom, a back door, a bathroom, and a back entrance to the kitchen pantry. And finally, to the right of the entry doors, the room extended to include a dining table and a kitchen bar that allowed one to see into the cooking area beyond.

Adele stood at the top of the stairs, smiling down at us. She was a graceful, slim, barn-owlish woman cloaked in pale, golden feathers. Her arms and legs were white along the insides and the color of lightly toasted marshmallow on the outsides. Her round head was covered in reddish-gold feathers, and her owlish face was snow white with a pink beak, half covered in feathers, and two eyes, dark as deep pools of water. She spoke with a velvety feminine tone and a Cajun accent as smooth as a rolling river.

"Phil! You're here!" She glided down the stairs on her dainty owl feet and offered her hand. "We're so glad you came. We were so worried."

"Ma'am, nice to see you again." I took her graceful fingers in mine. They were pink, with small scales interspersed with small pale feathers, just like a barn owl's toes. Her movements were smooth and silent. When the short feathers of her forearm brushed my hand, they were as soft as whispers, and wafted a delicate scent of flowers and forest.

Adele LaChouette was a recent addition to our family. Gramps had met her on a Wander, as we liked to refer to our long trips in feral form. He'd traveled down the Mississippi River, from Minnesota to the Gulf of Mexico, and discovered a family of anthro-owls there that, until then, none of our kin had known about. She visited frequently and it was practically a given that she would be around whenever I stopped in.

I think that Gramps was uncertain about a relationship as Alma, my grandmother, had passed away only a couple of years prior. He even asked me about it one awkward day, probing for my opinion on whether an old patriarch like him should bother with dating. I knew that despite his age, he was a man, or tiercel, with needs of companionship that family and friends couldn't provide, and so I emphatically encouraged him to pursue all that made him happy. And, as far as I was concerned, Adele was a perfect fit for him. As it turned out, she would soon be an invaluable addition to our family.

"You are such a polite bird. Your grandpa has trained you well. But you know you may call me Adele." Adele surveyed the two of us and stepped back. "Mon Deux, but you two are a mess!" She laughed with an owlish churr. "Get yourselves cleaned up, and we'll have dinner ready for you in no time."

"Thank you, Ms. Adele." It was hard for me to not be formal in the presence of such grace.

The warm scent of dinner filled my nares, and I drank it in. We wiped our wet talons on a doormat, and Gramps handed us towels to dry off.

Victor and I gravitated to the warmth of the fireplace, fluffed out our plumage, and sank our talons deep into the dense cozy fur of the buffalo rug. We sipped beers and said little as we stared at the dancing flames. Gramps was sitting at the table across the room by the kitchen with Adele by his side, both seeming to bide their time, expecting something from me. Relaxation brought about by the alcohol, in combination with the maddening scent from the kitchen, awakened my appetite.

Gramps knew the effect his fish pie was having on me. He stated from across the room, "Cawwt these trout ma'self yesturday. Six all t'gether. Nice 'n plump this time a-year. Got the rest smokin' out back too, 'long with some unfortunate deer

I found fresh by the highway whilst flyin' 'bout."

Victor and I turned around, watching that our tails didn't get too close to the flames. I lifted mine with my hands and let the warmth saturate my underfluffies.

"Is it still fishing season, Gramps?"

"For eagles, every day is fishing season." He laughed. "I ain't bought a proper fishin' license in ma life. Ain't 'bout to start." He turned to Victor. "'Sides, ain't like the fish ain't got a sportin' chance. No rod, no reel. No clothes either! Just what nature gave me!" He spread his taloned fingers in the air, as though ready to snatch an imaginary fish.

I shook my head, "Naked fishing. You are shameless, Gramps!"

Gramps took a sip of tea and said, "Hey, I just said no clothes. My feathers concealed my less seemly parts just fine."

Adele chimed in, "I take exception to that. I find nothing unseemly about those parts."

Gramps blushed and Victor giggled.

After a moment, Victor continued, "Few of those licensed fishermen help out the local eagles like you do neither. Seems like proper compensation to me. You got any around these days?"

Victor was referring to the birds that Gramps was always assisting or rescuing. Sometimes he delivered fish and meat to eagles he knew were struggling. He would swoop by in eagle form, drop a fish casually, as if by accident, and then rest nearby, making sure that the intended bird had their full meal without being interrupted by others. Sometimes he rescued injured birds and delivered them to a local wildlife center. The rehabilitators and veterinarians had no idea of the true nature of Gramps' uncanny ability to find and catch the birds, and, of course, he never told them of his secret werebird nature. But his reputation had grown, and many simply referred to him as

"The Eagle Man." It's a title he loved and considered publicly appropriate, since our German surname Adler translates to "Eagle" in English.

"No, thank gawd. Helped out the nesting male down by Halifax a few months back. Got cawt up in some fishin' line, tangled to hell. Shoulda seen the look on his face when I flew up with my pocketknife and cut 'im free! Summertime's pretty quiet gen'rally. But winter's comin' on, so there'll be starvin' youngsters and wayward migrants to help out soon."

As he said this, I found myself fiddling with the label on my beer bottle, far away in my own thoughts.

Gramps glanced over at Victor and said, "I'm gonna check supper. Can I get ya 'nuther?"

Victor nodded, "Looks like Phil has barely touched his, but I'll take another, please. Thanks!"

Gramps rose and walked to the kitchen. Despite his age, his avian hearing was good, so I knew he'd be attentively listening from afar. They knew my mind weighed heavy with the events of the day, but they waited for me to bring it up.

Victor leaned in and put his taloned hand on my forearm. "Wanna talk about what happened today, buddy? Any idea?"

I was ready to open up about it. "I fucked up, I guess."

Victor cocked his head and poised his bottle to his beak as if to drink, but didn't. "You sure about that? If you were twelve, I could understand. But you've had years of perfect control."

"I dunno… I was having these weird sensations. Like tingly feelings, came and went for a while before the big one. I felt no restraint when that happened. Hardly even knew what happened, like in a dream when you suddenly realize you're in public with no pants on."

Victor said with a smile, "You're weird. I'll have you know I always have pants on in my dreams."

I laughed and nudged him mirthfully with an elbow.

Victor pushed back. "Watch the beverage, now." After a brief pause, he added, "Seriously, I've never heard of one of us having that much lapse of control, unless you're young and learning, or old and your mind's going."

Gramps shouted insistently from the kitchen, "You best see Doc, Sonny."

Victor smiled, took a sip from his beer, and stared up at the painting above the fireplace, as if he could fill in the rest of this conversation. In football, I was a valuable asset, which meant that I was constantly medically scrutinized to ensure peak performance. As a result, I had acquired a distaste for medical exams.

However, Doctor Edward Schumacher, better known simply as "Doc," was a different matter. He was well-known among the secret network of werebirds in Pennsylvania, and ran a private clinic in Sunbury, where he saw both werebird and small animal patients, most any time needed. He couldn't transform, but was distantly related through my mother's side, and his fascination with our physiology led him to be trained in both human and veterinary medicine, with a particular interest in birds, of course.

Gramps continued to press, "Could be a legal necessity, y'know? To prove that you weren't unfit when it happened."

I was grumpy about it, but it was sound advice. I grumbled back, "Okay, I'll give him a call."

"Glad you agree. Already took care of it. Called him when you was cleanin' up. We head down to his office right after dinner."

I was too tired to protest, but for good measure, Gramps followed up with, "No backsquawk about this. He's agreed to meet us, and he's on my side and that's that! Now come and sit down for dinner."

The fish pie was warm and satisfying. I devoured my portion with hardly a word. While Gramps, Victor, and Adele jabbered in the kitchen and washed dishes, I sprawled out on one of the leather sofas by the fire and picked up the old landline telephone. I punched in Kayla's cellphone number.

Kayla's mother, Beth, had recently suffered a minor stroke, so she traveled up north to visit her in the hospital and support her father for the past week. The phone rang, and she picked up.

Kayla answered: *Hello. Gramps? Have you heard from Phil?*

I spoke, "Hey, lovebird. It's me."

Phil! I've been trying to reach you! Kayla's voice was full of loving concern. *Are you okay?*

"I'm fine. I didn't have a phone, or I'd have called sooner. I don't know what went wrong, but we're going to see Doc Schumacher in a bit. How's Mama Eagle?"

Kayla's feminine voice came back: *She's doing much better. It'll be a few more days here in the hospital before she can go home, though. But I think dad can take care of things from here. I'm heading back in the morning.*

"It's okay, babe. I sure miss you, but Mama Bird needs you now."

Hon, I can't let you go through this alone. You're a strong tiercel, but you need me. I don't have to remind you how ugly it's gotten before when people found out about our kind. And this time it's millions of people. It's all over the news, the internet... everywhere.

My heart skipped and my stomach sank like a stone in a muddy river. I'd purposely avoided looking at social media and news all evening. I wiped the cold sweat from my brow and propped my head up with my elbows on my knee, slumped over from the weight of everything. I did need her, now more than ever.

Are you still there, Phil?

"Yes... I just... god."

Look, it's gonna be okay. Maybe it's time we all came out, ya know? We're all gonna be behind you one way or the other. You know that, right? You didn't do anything wrong. You didn't hurt anyone.

"I just feel so... powerless! Fuck! One minute, I feel like I can fly through this shitstorm, and the next, I'm spinning out of control like a feather in a storm. And all the time, I feel like I gotta do something, now, but what can I do, ya know?"

You're doing everything you can do right now. Thinking, talking, taking care of yourself. Preparing before you act is a good strategy. It's how you win, right?" She paused and then added, "Remember how we met?

"How could I ever forget?"

Yeah? Well tell me about it. I forgot.

"You know how it goes, silly goose." I smiled wide. I'd played this game with Kayla before.

She chuckled. *Tell me again, handsome. I need reminding.*

"Okay, okay. So, it was our homecoming game. I barely knew you. You were so smart, taking your college prep classes. We barely had any classes together. And you were never one of those chatty popugirl types that would try out for cheerleading or hang all over the jocks. You helped out at the first aid station at games, and the first time I really noticed you was when you cleaned a scrape on my arm and put a Band-Aid on it."

That wasn't just a booboo! You almost needed stitches! Kayla chided.

I smiled again. "I'd have just ignored it, but you insisted we do things right. Who was I to argue if it meant spending a few more minutes with a knockout like you? I don't remember what we talked about exactly, but before I knew it, you were done. Maybe it was your looks too, but I think it was your bedside manner. You put me at ease, talking so calm, talking at my level... not like doctors usually do. And the wrap you put on the dressing had the Bald Eagles' logo on it... like you knew more about me than you let on."

Mhmmm... I could hear the smile in Kayla's voice. Don't stop there! What happened next?

I sat back in the couch again, my shoulders unclenching and my body relaxing as Kayla put me at ease. "You were on the varsity cross-country team, so I figured out where you liked to run and made sure our paths crossed. On our first date, we went canoeing down at Hawk Point. Beautiful fall day, so many colors in the trees, right about this time of year in fact. And we got treated to a bald eagle fishing in the river. I started gabbing about eagles, telling you all about their courtship habits and nesting. Then I got embarrassed, figuring you were a normal girl and didn't care so much about birds. Turns out you knew more than me!" Phil chuckled.

Kayla laughed. *I have to admit, that talk about mating habits was turning me on. You probably thought I had been reading up on birds just to get in your pants!*

"Ah, no, no. Okay, maybe a little! But I didn't care. Okay, actually it was kinda hot. I knew right then that we were made for each other."

Kayla dreamily replied, *It was a magical day, hon.*

"Yeah... it really was."

I wanted to go flying with ya then and there and do some cartwheel displays. Wrap you up in my wings and steal you away before some other broody hen got ya." She sighed, *"But it was a little while longer before we both found out each other's secrets. Funny how that worked out.*

"Yeah. Meant to be."

Don't forget the other part, babe, how we turned the tough times around. Later that season that douchebag... what was his name?

"Kyle."

Yeah, when we were playing Reading. He was an asshole. I wanted to kick him where it counts. You had pretty thick skin, but you finally had enough of his trolling during that late season game. You lost your cool, transformed on the field, and flew the ball in for a touchdown. It was chaos! Refs yelling. Coaches yelling. Our team cheering. The locals booing. You had just turned into an eagle right before their eyes, but they were worried about losing the game. And right in the middle of it all, that jerk making a bigger stink of it.

I stared into the fire, letting Kayla's words bring the memories into clearer focus.

Kayla's voice softened. I was so proud of you. You got right up in that prick's face, in front of the refs and everyone and said, 'Hey, it's just football... I'm here for the fun, take your stinkin' points back!' It just sucked all the wind out of their sails. Their egos deflated. All of 'em shut up, while you picked up your busted gear and walked off the field." She chuckled. "*And then we just went back to playing football like nothing happened.*

"Lucky there weren't as many video-taking cellphones back then. And not many fans that day."

Yeah, well, I wish there had been. Cuz it was beautiful how you handled it. Everyone, even Reading's team, except Kyle, was on your side. That's how it's gonna be this time too. You're special, Phil. You bring people together with what you do, but also by who you are.

I grinned from ear to ear. "I'm so lucky to have you, Kayla. I feel a lot better. I love you."

I love you too, honeybird. I'm gonna be back tomorrow, and we'll kick some tail, together, all right?

"All, right, have a good night, love."

You too. Give Gramps and Victor hugs from me. See ya soon!

As I closed the call, I inhaled deep and full and closed my eyes, and let out a long, relaxed exhale. Things were going to be all right.

Chapter 3: Turn Your Beak and Cough

The streets of Sunbury ran parallel to the river, terraced up the hill to avoid the occasional floods that afflict the region. The rain had stopped, and the dark, wet streets reflected the orange glow of overhead streetlights. We had all changed into our human forms and dressed normally so as to be publicly presentable. Luckily, I was able to scrounge up some work clothes I had left in Gramps' wood shop: Torn jeans, a thread-bare t-shirt, and a pair of beat-up boots. I looked like a scroungy farmer, but Doc wouldn't care. Adele stayed behind at the cabin, awaiting the arrival of her sister, Zoe, who was driving up from New Orleans to visit for a week.

Doc's clinic was on Main Street, situated in a brick building that dated from the 1950s. From the back alley, it was two stories high, but from the street side, it was a single story, unassuming building of light blue concrete blocks with red brick details. We pulled up to the front in Gramps' old Ford pickup and parked. Venetian blinds were closed behind the large front windows, but a dim glow illuminated the room beyond.

We didn't have to knock as Doc met us at the door and unlocked it for us. He said in a gravelly voice, "Hey boys, good to see ya. Come on in!"

Doc was a little over five feet tall with a broad nose, rounded cheeks, and wrinkled eye corners with heavy lids. Thick bushes of snowy hair made up his eyebrows and covered the rest of his head like a nest under construction, brighter white than the lab coat he was wearing. He had a wide smile, and offered a soft, warm hand that he shook kindly when it was grasped.

Doc locked the door behind us. "Senior, you and Victor help yourselves to some coffee in the break room. I think, given the things I gotta ask Phil to do, might be best if we do this privately. We can reconnoiter afterwards, if Phil feels up to it."

Victor had to make a parting remark, "Remember Phil, just relax, and turn your beak and cough when he asks."

Doc chuckled and said, "Very funny, Victor. Keep it up and I'll be checking you up next!"

Victor and Gramps drifted off to the break room while Doc and I stepped into an exam room. He was thorough, grilling me about everything I ate and drank, how well I'd been sleeping, and all my daily habits of late. He had me transform in varying sequences and mixes of anthro and feral forms. I passed all his tests with ease. But he didn't seem discouraged by not finding anything wrong.

He collected blood from my human arm, and another sample from my wing while I was in feral form. As he gently rocked the blood tubes in his fingers to mix them with diluents, he said nonchalantly, "Okay, you can shift back to human form and put your clothes on. I'll meet you in the break room with the others."

In a few minutes, I stepped into the break room to find the three sitting around a circular table in silence, cupping paper cups of coffee in their hands. The room was painted in pale earthy tones and had forest-patterned curtains on the windows. It was a calming getaway for staff.

It was getting late, and everyone was concerned and worn out. Gramps had transformed his head to his bald eagle form he preferred when relaxing.

Doc spoke up, "Care for a cup, Phil?"

"Smells good, but nah, I'm not much of a coffee drinker. I'm hoping to wind down somehow and sleep tonight."

Doc muttered, "Mhmm, good plan."

"So, what's up, Doc?" I realized the unintended Bugs Bunny reference just as Victor snickered.

Doc ignored him and said, "I think someone slipped you a mitogen."

Gramps choked on his sip of coffee.

Victor stared in disbelief. "What the fu--?"

Doc rotated the cup in his hands. "Yeah... I know. Not something that just lands in your food casually. But the symptoms you describe, your total loss of control, and you being healthy and capable in every way now... it's the option that makes the most sense. You mentioned trying out a new energy drink. Perhaps that was the source."

I thought back to the freckled kid in the locker room, just before the game. "Fuck. Yeah." I saw the baffled looks on Gramps and Victor. "There was this new kid handing them out. I even signed one of the cans for him. Half an hour later, I'm exploding on the field."

Victor looked down at the table. "So, someone knew what you were and how to manipulate you. Who the hell are they?"

Gramps' hackles lifted and his sharp eyes brewed with anger. "Boones. That's my bet."

Victor shook his head and exhaled as he calculated what seemed like impossible odds at the moment.

I grunted, "Maybe. But we haven't had trouble with them in years. Why now? Don't they have better things to do? Their grandpa, Earl Boones, is too busy campaigning for US Senate to mess with us right now."

Gramps glared at me. "You'd think so, wouldn't ya? That worthless sack of droppings, Earl Boones, 'been obsessed with you since you was knee-high to a harpy."

Doc leaned back in his squeaky chair and stroked his soft, bare chin.

"Look at me, Phil!" Gramps demanded.

I noticed how much his eyes had paled from golden to almost white in the past few years, belying his advanced age. But they could still focus like lasers, just as they were doing at that moment. His head feathers were fluffed up in displeasure, but I knew he wasn't angry with me.

Knowing he had my undivided attention, Gramps continued, "Remember your first time, hmm? Who just happened to be there, hmm? Coincidence?"

Victor added, "Yeah, we were at the zoo for your birthday."

I swung my gaze in Victor's direction slowly, recalling the event. "Yeah. It was my eighth birthday. I loved birds, so mom and dad took me to the Philadelphia Zoo to see the free-flight raptor show. They arranged for a special falconry experience, and we even went behind the scenes." My eyes lit up at the fond memory. "It was like the best thing in my life up to then. I was little, so I only got to hold a kestrel. And then they let me stand by the target perch they flew their bald eagle to. The wind from its wings and the smell of its feathers were like something warm and familiar. But during one of the flights, when they flew her to the perch, she veered and tried to land on me. She wasn't trying to hurt me, but she scratched my arm a tiny bit and gave me a good shock. I fell over, and when I looked up, the eagle was standing on my chest, staring into my eyes as though it knew me. And as I looked at myself, I realized I was covered with feathers. I thought I was dreaming."

Gramps broke into a contagious laugh, mirth moistening the corners of his eyes. "Yeah, boy, you didn't know wut ya were yet." He chuckled some more. "You thought that eagle had turned you into a friend! You knew your kin could do it but we'd made sure not to get your hopes up. I was so proud of ya. After that, since your daddy couldn't transform, it was up to me to teach ya how to be an iggle."

"It was amazing." I shook my head as more details surfaced in my memory. "The handlers were spooked like deer in the headlights. They freaked. Probably thought mom and dad would sue the shit out of 'em. I was a little upset cuz I thought I'd done something wrong. Hell of a way to discover you're from the freaky side of the family. They gave me an eagle plush—you know the one I keep on my dresser at home. And they bent over backwards to make us happy. Must've really blown their minds."

Victor choked on a giggle.

"But, of course, officially, that never happened. I support their program now and we're all pretty good friends. They still got that eagle, Martha, and they let me hold her sometimes. But anyway, mom and dad covered me up and rushed me out of there as fast as they could. And, yeah, later on they explained to me what I was. But now that you mention it... with all that happened, I tend to forget that there were other people there. Someone was being real mean too, laughing at me, cussing and calling me a freak."

"Yup. Earl Boones was there. He was a supporter of the Philly Zoo's wolf program and was tipped off that we'd be there. He showed up at your party and was ingratiating himself to your folks. Way out of character. Maybe he was hoping to see you change and use it to expose us. Lucky thing, the photographer was out sick that day. 'Course maybe it wasn't just luck." Gramps gave a wink. "The staff was real happy to not say anything about it, since they felt at fault."

"But how did you know, Gramps? Dad didn't have the gene. They didn't think that I did. I was real late in finding the ability to change."

Gramps leaned back in his chair and clicked his finger talons on the table as he smiled. "Oh, I had no doubt. Your affinity for birds, for one thing. Reminded me of me! How in the heck Boones figured it out, I don't know. But his interest was enough for me to pay off the photographer to take the rest of the day off."

Victor cocked his head and looked at Gramps. "What do they care about us? Why go through so much trouble?"

Gramps let out a long, beaky sigh. "Aside from seeing us as freaks of nature or some kind of devils, our family rivalry goes back a long ways. It's not just Hatfield and McCoy-type stuff, one neighbor spittin' on another's name 'cuz of some forgotten insult. Them Boones started out on the wrong side and have made their entire way out of skullduggery 'n greed. They came up here after losin' ev'rything on the side of the Confederates in the Civil War. People were lookin' to rebuild and start fresh. My great-great-grandpa Samuel was taken with a Boones lass. Married 'er and helped her move up. He extended a hand to her kin too, and they followed her up here. Gave 'em a bit a' land out by Bloomsburg. They was in need, and we had plenty of room.

"Unfortunately, that first wife died during childbirthin'. He let her family keep the land. But they didn't remember the hospitality. That land ended up havin' Anthracite coal under it, and soon they was working the locals to the bone minin' it and buyin' up around it. They put in the first rail lines, and some of their family took on the business of forgin' steel in Pittsburgh and shippin' coal elsewheres. Before long, they tried ownin' everything. And they took whatever they could, even from the families that helped 'em out. Later on, in the '20s 'n '30s, we was in their faces helpin' workers unionize. A generation after that and we were gettin' in their way during the civil rights and environmental movements. They're always on the side of greed at the expense of those they deem lesser.

"We Adlers have always managed to do okay, cuz we look to each other and help those around us as much as we can. We werebirds know the value of nature, and care for her like the mother that she is. It's in our blood. And we know what it's like to be judged and harassed for bein' what idiots think is lesser. So, we stand for the rights of others too. Which natch'urly puts us in the way of the Boones when they want to dam up rivers, blow up mountains, or make slaves out of honest folks."

Doc interjected, "I wasn't aware our two families' histories were entwined so far back. Always thought the rivalry was more recent."

Gramps nodded, "Yeah, lots of folks don't know. Hell, I don't even know much for certain. 'Cept that the Boones have had a weird obsession with us for a long time. They know what we are and wants to use it against us if they can. Last episode I recollect was a few years back, when Billy courted Maureen, my daughter Summer's only child."

Victor commented, "More like harassed. He was too crass and stuck-up for the likes of a pure soul like Maureen. She told me she didn't want anything to do with him and made it plain more than once."

Gramps continued, "That's right. But he kept after her until I intervened."

I chuckled, "You could certainly call that an intervention. Gramps left a road-killed deer sitting upright in the driver's seat of Billy's truck when it was parked at a boat launch. Pinned a note to the wheel that said 'Leave Maureen alone or you're next!'"

Doc grinned enough to show the whites of his teeth. "Sounds like a clear enough message."

Gramps didn't laugh. "I meant it. Ya gotta be direct with these thick-headed Boones." He leaned forward and pointed a leathery yellow finger-claw at me. "You sure you don't recognize that fella what gave you the drink?"

"Shit, I didn't catch his name. I just signed a can without any special notation. I remember he had light blue eyes and dark brown curly hair. He was maybe eighteen or nineteen? Lean face and pimples. Lanky. I'd never seen him before. He didn't have a name tag. Wore this white polo with a blue swirl logo over the left side. And, heck, Gramps, it's pro ball. Even if he had told me his name, there's so many people coming and going all the time, I wouldn't have remembered anyhow. It's been all I can do just to get to know my team."

Fatigue was turning my mind to clay. I covered my mouth in a deep yawn and shook my head.

Doc moved forward and rested his elbows and hands on the table, staring at me. "Look, you really should go get some rest. You'll think a lot clearer. If you can't shut your brain down, take a couple diphenhydramine to help you sleep. Or a shot of whiskey. But maybe the best relaxer of all is to think about this family around you. We're all here for you, Phil."

I nodded wearily. "I really appreciate you meeting us here this late."

Doc smiled, "You're one of my favorite patients. And you know I'm always here for the family, no matter what time of day." He stood and set his empty mug in the sink, as he shut off the coffee maker and turned back to us. "I'm going to send your samples out in the morning. It'll take a few days to get results back. I'll be checking for mitogens, performance enhancers, just to cover your legal butt, as well as the usual chemistry and CBC to see that there's no obvious indications of disease, but I expect that to be normal. In the meantime, try to track down the kid that gave you the drink. If you can get a sample of it, we might be able to match its chemical signature to the mitogens we find in your bloodstream, if there are any."

"Thanks, Doc."

Doc added, "You got any idea what the team will do?"

"Not really. For all I know, they might've already fired me. I gotta go down there tomorrow and get my car and phone. I'll probably check in with the coach when I do that."

Doc grunted sleepily, and the conversation died.

We said our goodbyes and goodnights and drove back in sleepy silence. Soon I was back at Gramps' cabin, back in anthro-eagle form, sinking into a nest of soft blankets in an upstairs bedroom. I took Doc's suggestion of a shot of whiskey and then basked in the warm glow and avoided negative thoughts that crowded my attention. I chose to focus on seeing Kayla again tomorrow, and the love and support of my family. I listened to the rain patter on the cedar shake roof until I fell into a deep, dreamless sleep.

Chapter 4: Eagle Legal

The rain had stopped during the night, and the morning sun streamed in through the east windows and lit up the front room of the cabin. As I strode down the creaky staircase, I heard Victor chattering away with Gramps while he cooked breakfast.

Victor set his coffee down as he saw me coming down the steps. "I heard you on the phone a while ago upstairs. What'd your boss say?"

"I couldn't get any higher than Assistant Coach Deans. They said to take a break, a week at least. I'm a valued player, etcetera, etcetera, but there are procedures to go through, and they'd make do without me while it got sorted out. Since 'the incident' happened during gameplay, I guess we have to have a meeting with a National Football Association rep tomorrow."

Victor exclaimed, "A week? Did you tell them it's not your fault?"

"It was hard to know where to start. I told him it was an old, inherited condition, and this was the first time I'd ever lost control. Told him Doc thinks I was drugged. He asked why I didn't stick around to get tested and debriefed. I said I didn't feel safe and didn't think anyone else felt safe. Didn't wanna start a panic or make things worse. Hell, I couldn't stick around. He just said 'yep, yep, okay' and that he'd pass it along. On the other hand, he didn't tell me much at all. It was like he didn't know what to say and wanted to be careful with his words.

When I told him about the kid and the energy drinks, his response was 'Okay, whatever you say, Adler. I'll pass it along. But everybody else seems fine.'"

Gramps walked in and set a plate of sunny-side-up eggs, hash browns, blackberries, and thinly sliced venison on the table before me. "Eat up, sonny. I got us a meetin' with Bill Franklin in an hour."

Victor piped up, "The family lawyer? There ya go!"

The salty, rich aroma made my head feathers fluff and my beak salivate. "Thanks, Gramps. Best thing to wake up to. Where's Adele?"

Gramps replied, "Stayed up cavortin' with her sister all night long, so they're both sleepin' in. 'Course her sis is still on a nocturnal schedule, which is their preference back home. The nights are right lively down there in Louisiana. Even Adele takes a nap here and there, with the shades drawn, tryin' her best to accommodate the Adlers' diurnal schedule."

I nodded as I devoured my breakfast.

Gramps laid a hand on my shoulder. "I knows what yur thinkin. But this ain't the end of things. Franklin's one of us, ya know. He'll know what to do."

Victor winked. "Hell ya! We got enough connections even for the NFA to contend with. Besides, they love ya there. Your fans love ya. They're probably gonna love you even more now that the bird's out of the bag. It's gonna be hard for the NFA to just bury this and cut you off."

"Thanks, Vic. You got a point." Their words helped, more than I could even articulate at the time.

Victor scooted his chair back from the table and rested one foot across his knee to prop up his right hand and coffee cup. He glanced back and forth between Gramps and me. "What do you guys think about doing a little snooping around at the Boones'?"

Gramps set his coffee cup down on the counter carefully, and I stopped chewing my food.

Gramps nodded, "My thoughts 'xactly."

I shook my head, "I dunno, guys. I mean… yeah, I'd love proof on whether they're involved. But if we fuck up and get caught, it could tip our hand and make things worse. Or get someone hurt." I stared at Victor, "I don't want nobody getting busted or killed over me."

Victor snapped his beak. "This ain't just about you, ya big galoot. Affects all of us."

Gramps nodded silently. "Phil's got a point though. Mebbe wait until Franklin advises us."

Victor tipped his cup back and emptied it into his maw. He stood and delivered it to the kitchen sink. As he returned, he paused and said, "Good luck with the lawyer. I've got a couple things to do back at the office. Kayla gonna give you a ride to Philly to get your stuff?"

"Yeah. Gramps'll take me there after the meeting and let me in. Then I'll wait for Kayla, and we'll go on down."

Victor patted my shoulders as he passed behind my chair. "Cool. Give me a buzz later and let me know."

Gramps chimed in, "Listen, boys! Let's all gather back here, say 'round seven? Adele and I will serve up supper, and we can all start makin' plans."

Victor chirped, "Count me in!"

I pushed back from the table and sighed, "Sorry, Gramps, but we got a meeting first thing in the morning with the coach and his bosses. Kayla and I are going to stay down in Philly tonight."

Gramps touched his forehead, "Ah, yes, forgot about that. Tomorrow evenin' then?"

I nodded, "Or sooner. I don't know how long the meeting

will go or what else will come up, but if we can get back sooner, I'll let you know."

"Fair 'nuff."

"Well, I'll see you tonight, Gramps." Victor gave me a mock salute as he opened the door, "And I'll see you tomorrow, sir. Carry on!"

I watched Victor bound across the yard on his oversized bird legs and thought back on his offer to fly into harm's way and spy on the Boones. I would risk everything for Gramps, Victor, or anyone in my family. But when it came to others risking for me, it was a hard pill to swallow. It was a burden I wasn't ready to shoulder, even if they freely offered. I hated the whole shitty mess and, by extension, hated myself for what I was and how it had ruined my career, as if being a werebird was the problem.

A few minutes later, Victor drove by in his white and green Ford pickup with the livery of the Pennsylvania State Department of Forests on the side. It was the vehicle he used for his official duties as a non-game biologist.

As dust followed his departure down the driveway, my thoughts returned to my predicament. If transforming during the game were my fault, why did I lose control? Doc didn't find any intrinsic explanation for it. Maybe he was right and someone had violated me with chemicals and exposed my deepest secret. It cut me to my soul and made me angry, desiring sweet, bloody revenge. But I had just enough self-discipline to see where those thoughts led, so I purposefully exhaled and unclenched my fists.

My thoughts were going nowhere helpful, so I shook my head and jerked myself out of my preoccupation. I returned to the guest room and took my time transforming back to human form. I'd spent so much time in anthro-eagle form the past couple of days that being human felt confined and cold. But it also strengthened the warm realization that being a werebird is an asset, not a liability, if for no other reason than it made me a part of a wonderful and loving family that would not let me face this problem alone. I would never be alone.

Gramps and I arrived at Bill Franklin's office at nine in the morning. It was darken inside as it was normal to be closed on Mondays. But because of our emergency, he had agreed to see us on his day off and had shown us into a bright conference room. Gramps sat next to me at a woodgrain conference table. Aside from the table, the room contained walnut shelves laden with binders and legal reference books.

We were both in human form, though Bill was fully aware of our nature and wouldn't have minded either way. Gramps sported his shock of snow-white hair and thick white eyebrows over his blue eyes and sharp nose. I'd often surmised that a normal person would only be mildly surprised to learn that most of his time was spent in the form of an anthropomorphic bald eagle.

Bill entered the room, dressed in jeans and a Pennsylvania Bald Eagles sweatshirt. He was tall, lean, and dark-skinned with high cheekbones, and wide, expressive eyes. His short, black, curly hair was peppered with gray around the sides, the marks of his human age of forty-four years. His face reminded me of a peregrine falcon, which wasn't far from the truth in his off-time. He carried three cups of coffee and set one down for each of us.

Gramps sipped his coffee. "Mmm, my compliments to the chef."

I made an exception to my usual aversion to coffee and thanked him for the cup. I immediately dumped two sugar packets in and used a stirrer from the table to mix it.

Bill was unfazed at my adulteration of his coffee, and nodded as he made his way to the sun-drenched window. "My secretary, Cindy, keeps us all comfortably caffeinated around here. I'll pass along your compliment." He tugged on the string of the venetian blinds and let them slide down to block out the view. "Gentlemen, I think we can be ourselves here, in private. Don't you?"

Gramps chuckled, "Don't need to ask me twice." Gramps closed his eyes and shook his head, as though shaking off the weight of being human. White feathers erupted through his white hair, and his nose pressed out into a great, yellow beak. His fingers lengthened into yellow, scaled digits with short, black, triangular nails—still eagleish, but more conveniently proportioned for writing and shaking hands. To keep from shredding his clothes, the rest of his body remained mostly human.

Bill spread his arms and lifted his face. He let out a soft screech as feathers sprouted out of his arms with a sound like fluttering canvas. The feathers were brown and fluffy around his shoulders, gradually decreasing in size towards his wrists. Broad flight feathers skewed out from the sides of his upper arms, gray above and reddish-cream below with small, evenly-spaced, dark brown arcs along their length. His hands yellowed, the fingers lengthened, and the nails pressed out into short black talons. A bluish-gray beak and yellow cere replaced his sharp nose, and dark feathers replaced the skin below his eyes. The rest of his facial feathers were pale, except for a hood of earthy red. His eyes darkened as his irises enlarged to fill the entire visible portions. His eyelids yellowed, and the lid margins furrowed while ridges pressed out above them, as they took the form of the piercing gaze of a lanner falcon.

I was caught up in watching Franklin's dramatic transformation, noticing his sequence, which differed from mine. Everyone had their own style, and his was impressive.

Bill softly screeched, "Your turn, brother."

I wasn't in the mood to impress anyone. The crisis and a sleepless night left me feeling little pride or joy in this formality. I just wanted to move on with business, so I nodded and pressed out my massive eagle beak, with a crunch that rattled my eyeballs more than usual. A wave of hot prickles raced from my forehead to my shoulders as I let my feathers erupt from hiding. Warmth washed over my knuckles and the backs of my hands. My fingers plumped and gnarled into sinewy, yellow bird digits tipped with short, but respectable, talons. My eyes enlarged and brightened as my supraorbital ridges pressed out above them. I emitted a single high-pitched eagle chirp that rattled the walls.

Bill's beak corners lifted slightly along with his lower eyelids. The falcon equivalent of a smile. "Splendid. It's been years since I've seen you transform. You have excellent control."

I wasn't expecting an evaluation of my transformation ability. I nodded at the compliment, "Thanks."

Bill took a seat opposite us as he continued, "Yes, excellent control. Very different from what happened yesterday, isn't it?"

I tilted my head at Gramps, who smiled and lifted the coffee mug to his beak.

"Do you know about my family, Phil?" asked Bill.

"Well, no, not really. I've seen you at some of the family meetings, maybe once at a barbecue at Gramps' too. Lovely wife, whose name is slipping my mind. You got a couple kids, a daughter and a son?"

"Her name is Linda and, yes, Alexander and Aya. But I was referring to my ancestry." Bill's slender yellow fingers danced in graceful arcs as he articulated his thoughts. His words were delivered quietly and evenly, requiring close listening, but they bore such keen thoughts, that I found myself holding my breath to hear each one carefully. "My family's genealogy reaches way back to ancient Egypt. My middle name is Horus if you didn't know. It's an ancient surname that has only been recently lost in common use. In all likelihood, we were the living forms of the bird gods that also served as Pharaohs. People revered us, and we used our power for good, mostly, but also for intimidation and power."

My eyes focused on his, and I could see my own reflection in his black orbs. I didn't know where he was going with this, and my impatience probably showed when I flashed my nictitating membranes a little too rapidly.

Bill blinked too and sat back disarmingly. "Society has come a long, long way since then. It takes considerably more than animal magic to serve the needs of a complex society. It will still get you awe and attention, but it's more likely to get you shunned or killed these days. I know you know this. Which is why I know you didn't expose us all on purpose."

I leaned forward, locked eyes, and said firmly, "No sir. I don't take our powers lightly."

"Good. Good. Don't forget that. And never forget that we are all in this together. We are powerful together." Bill extended an angled hand, his elbow on the table. His black eyes remained riveted to mine, inspiring in me a thrill of awe as I imagined tens of thousands worshipping his distant ancestors, ruling proudly as bird deities.

I took his hand in mine and gave it a firm squeeze. "I'm glad you're on my side."

Bill smiled as widely as his falcon visage allowed and nodded affirmatively. He then shifted his gaze and reached for a yellow legal pad and pen. The pad was covered in scribbled notes. He cleared his throat and flipped the pages as he leaned forward.

Bill spoke: "I'm not a sports lawyer, Phil. But as soon as Phil Sr. contacted me last night, I started looking things up. Fortunately, there's plenty of public record of the controversial topics in professional football—almost too much, if you catch my drift. I see no precedent like yours, of course. The National Football Association disciplines players for domestic violence, racial slurs, sexual impropriety, or in-game social justice protests. But due to media awareness and public watchdogging, the Association tends to be very reserved when confronting these issues unless they directly interfere with game play, which has happened in this case."

I nodded. There was nothing too surprising here yet.

Bill continued, "But as we've covered, you didn't do this intentionally. I watched the whole thing as it happened. I've read fan eyewitness comments on social media sites. The controversy should not be about willful misconduct. You didn't take steroids, rough up players, or deflate game balls. Your body did something that was unexpected, but natural, for who, and what, you are. As long as the argument stays focused on that, I think you have the upper hand."

"Mhmmm," Gramps agreed. "These days pro sports can't afford controversy over race, sexism, or, heh, speciesism?"

Franklin nodded. "Pretty much. If you hadn't left on your own, my guess is that they probably would have ushered you out to avoid contact with the other players and the public. They would have wanted to contain the issue. It's a typical corporate response to something extraordinary and potentially controversial. If it conflicts with their interests, they contain the problem, control damage, and find ways to strengthen their position. Do you have a sports lawyer, Phil?"

"Yeah, and I called her this morning. I've barely needed her until now, but she's flying down tonight. We're meeting tomorrow morning, just before we meet with the coaches."

"Good, good. What's her name?"

"Sarah Hollister. She's from the NFAPA—the players' association. She's been with them for ten years and is good at what she does. But it goes without saying that she's never dealt with this sort of thing before. I was wondering, Mr. Franklin, if you could be there too. Maybe you can help her understand us better."

"You bet. Any chance to help an Adler and..." Bill gleamed with excitement, "...a chance to see the Eagle Nest."

Bill was referring to the training complex and stadium in Philadelphia. His eagerness buoyed me up, like I was soaring on a thermal. I smiled, "Thanks a lot! And, sure, you bet! I don't know how long the meeting will go, or if I'll be welcome, but if I can, I'll show you around."

"I understand. I'll get in touch with Sarah if you'll give me her number. We'll go into this as prepared as we can be. I've got to ask, though, what are your goals? Other than keeping your job, of course?"

"Uh, just that, really. What else is there?"

Gramps squinted, "Mmm... ahaaa, I think what Bill's gettin' at is the wider ramifications here. Like Victor said, the 'bird's outta the bag,' now... for all of us, maybe."

Bill nodded, "Exactly. Not only that, but you're suspecting that someone did this for a reason. Was it to expose werebirds everywhere? Or was it strictly personal? If you go forward, standing up for your own rights, you'll be shining a big, big spotlight on all of us, which might be what your secret attacker is wanting. This will change how people see you forever, and the more public it becomes, the more difficult it will be to live a quiet life. They might think of you as 'that bird guy' more than they think of you as a great football player. Are you ready for all of that?"

My guts twisted in knots. I stood and walked to the window, rubbing my chin as I contemplated the question. I was antsy and wanted to fly talons first into this fight for vindication. But I had other people to consider too. I turned around and looked at Bill. "I gave up living a quiet life when I chose football as a career. I don't like to make decisions based on fear. So, yeah, I want to go for it. But Kayla has to weigh in on this too. She's on her way home now."

Gramps nodded. "You know what she'll say, though. She's

a right lady eagle. A real fighter."

I nodded, "Yeah. But she still has to say it. Beyond being married to me, she's also a physical therapist for the team, so whatever I do will affect her career too. And then there's all the other birdfolk to consider. It's gonna require the Family Council's input before we go beyond those with an immediate need to know."

Bill agreed, "Definitely. The way technology, and our dwindling privacy, is going, I think we're bound to be discovered on a larger scale eventually. I would love for my daughters to hold their heads high in a world that lets them be themselves. But I'm not confident that society is quite ready for it. We can already see how unkindly it treats other non-conformers in our society."

Gramps nodded, "Goddamned shame, it is."

Bill nodded, "Have you engaged an investigator yet?"

The question caught me off-guard, as though I were slouching by not having thought of this yet. "No, uh, hadn't gotten that far."

"Mhmm." Bill sat back in his chair and made a thoughtful teepee with his slender falcon fingers. "You need a good PI, and someone that will be respectful of your special background. Someone with good knowledge of the Boones even."

The mention of that name made my stomach churn, like it was time to cast a pellet.

Gramps beat me to the question, "Who are you suggestin'?"

Franklin's falcon eyes locked onto mine. "Robert Boones."

"What?!" Anger surged through my stiffened arms, but Gramps laid a calming hand on me.

Gramps was the voice of calm. "You best 'splain that choice to us, mister. The Boones is likely why we're in this mess. How can one of their own be the best one to protect our interests?"

Bill remained placid, but his voice hardened. "I know it's not a palatable choice, but I've seen Robert's work. He's diligent. He's fair. He's been a detective for the county for a few years now, and his knowledge of local criminal activity, even within his own family, would be difficult to match. As to his deference to his family, he has, voluntarily, turned over information to the DA that led to convictions of other Boones before. Remember Bull Boones' conviction on charges of assault and battery? Robert keeps it on the down-low, but that was his work. And there are others. He moonlights. Here's his number." He slid a business card across the table.

I looked at Gramps, "What do you think?"

He shrugged. "Don't know the man too well, but for a Boones, he's been the least offendin'. Seems upright in his local community dealins'. Can't recall him ever locking horns with us Adlers."

I still hated this idea. "Don't we have anyone in *our* family that's a PI?"

Gramps scratched his hand and looked upwards, as if peering into mental file cabinets. "Don't think so, not 'round here leastways. But I can ask the family network."

Bill squeaked forward in his chair. "Trust me. You can trust him. I can't disclose why, exactly, but I would trust him."

Gramps nodded and winked, "And I trust you."

I added, "I feel I can trust you too, but I'll have to think about this. It's nothing against your integrity. More like I don't know if I could talk to a Boones right now without knocking out some teeth and ending up in jail."

Bill nodded silently.

There was an awkward pause, and I was glad when Gramps interrupted it, "I'll get busy today on arranging an all-families meetin'."

Franklin nodded, "Count the Franklins in. Name the time,

and I'll be there."

"Appreciated, sir. Wouldn't hold it without ya."

Franklin stood and shook my hand, giving me an intense, but friendly falcon stare with his dark eyes. "Hang in there, Phil. We'll get you through this. But for now, if you two don't mind, I have some calls to make and some research to do. We'll meet up again an hour before the meeting tomorrow morning."

Chapter 5: Return to the Nest

After Gramps dropped me off at home, I showered and put on some fresh clothes. I had every intention of being awake and ready to go when Kayla arrived. But my body had other ideas, and I fell asleep on the couch while browsing news stories and historical articles regarding the Boones family. Next thing I knew, two hours had passed, and I was awakened by a long and sensual kiss.

When I opened my eyes, Kayla's sweet face was pressed to mine. It was like a drink of warm, sweet hot chocolate after a blustery winter flight. My hands slid up her arms, pulled her down against my body, and we embraced for several minutes, silent except for our unhurried breathing. My fingers stroked up and down her spine as she played with my short hair.

At last, I broke the silence. "It's so good to have you back, hon. How was your drive?"

Her mild country accent lifted the edges of her words. "It was smooth. It's good to be back. How are you doing?"

"So-so. Man, I did not mean to crash like that." I started to move to get up, but Kayla kept me pinned to the cushions.

"You probably needed it. Can't imagine it's been too easy to sleep."

"Took a long time to fall asleep last night, but I got a good six hours finally. Lots of thinking, lots of flying, lots of changing form yesterday. I guess I needed more rest."

Kayla rose to her feet. "Can I get ya something from the kitchen?"

I admired her for a moment. Her slim body and modest chest rode upon a pair of muscular thighs and legs that could run for miles, kick a flame off a candle, or do other amazing things behind closed doors. Her face was slim, with just enough cheekbone below her brown eyes to accentuate her frequent warm smiles. Her hair was long and straight and brown. Inside her head was a mind as sharp as her talons in eagle form. In her chest beat the heart of an eagle too, full of love but also furious devotion for her own. She was not a Hollywood model of girlish glamour, but she could kick all their asses without contest. She was perfect in my eyes.

Kayla slowly smiled as I gazed dreamily up at her, holding her fingertips. "What?"

"Nothin'. Just fallin' in love all over again." Maybe it was inspired by the heightened emotions of the past twenty-four hours, but I couldn't help myself.

Kayla cocked her head and squeezed my hands. "Love you, my eagle."

"Love you too, honeybird."

"We're gonna get through this, okay? But I guess we better get going if we want to avoid traffic."

I smiled and sighed, "Yeah, you're right. Help me up." I was joking, but before I knew it, Kayla had wrapped my arms across my chest, poised my legs, and, using a special first-responder maneuver, had lifted me to a sitting position and tugged me up to my feet. I immediately hugged her again and gave her a kiss.

Kayla melted for a moment, and her hands slid down my back and gripped my firm buttocks. Her breasts against my chest were soft and round, and desire swelled between us. It was interrupted when her phone buzzed on the table. My mind teetered between ignoring it and making love to my wife right there in the living room or doing the responsible thing and letting her answer it. She pulled her hands back up to my chest, and I released my embrace.

Kayla said, "Sorry, hon, could be dad. I'd better take it."

I ran my hands down her sides and gave her a reassuring wink. "It's okay. I'll get ready to go."

I had to adjust my pants after the arousal, and I was surprised that sex was even an impulse, given that my whole life was collapsing. But like a pinch of salt on food or sunshine on a gloomy day, Kayla had a way of bringing out all the most pleasurable things in my life.

I heard Kayla on the phone as I grabbed a gym bag from the closet. It was her father, but it sounded like he was just making sure she got home and that I was okay. In a few minutes, we were on our way down the highway to Philly.

The radio was still on from Kayla's drive, playing Top Forty hits and noisy commercials. I wanted to have a conversation and it was distracting so I asked Kayla, "Mind if I turn it off for a while and you can tell me about mom?"

She nodded, "Sure, hon."

I was about to switch it off when I heard the name Earl Boones mentioned. It was a short news blurb about the national election that was coming up in a week:

> *According to polls, Republican Earl Boones is likely to unseat incumbent Democrat Jack Nielson for US Senate in next week's election. The race took an abrupt turn in Boones' favor when Nielson collapsed on stage during a press conference three weeks ago with encephalitis of unknown origin. Doctors say his condition is stable although the Senator remains in a coma. This is National Network News...*

I shook my head. "Too bad it wasn't Earl that fell into a coma instead. Hard to believe that asshole might soon be senator."

I switched off the radio and Kayla filled me in on Beth, her mother, and what the doctors expected. Also, how her father, Dane, was dealing with her care. They were both over seventy, Kayla having been a bit of a surprise to her mother, who thought she was too old to have children. I had told her many times that they could both come and live with us when and if the time came that they couldn't take care of themselves. We were fortunate to have a large enough home and, due to a choice between us, we had no children yet. I reminded Kayla of this again and squeezed her hand as she drove us down I-476.

In the quiet that followed, I knew that we should discuss what I would do to defend my career. I told Kayla about Bill Franklin's advice, including the encouragement to contact Robert Boones.

She simply smiled and said, "Hmm."

I was expecting something stronger. "What do you mean 'hmm?' You know something, don't you?"

Kayla looked at me, still smiling, then back at the road. "It's nothing. Well. He had some kind of thing for you in high school, I think."

I raised my palms, "Woah now! I think you're mistaken. We played a little ball together, but he couldn't cut it. He barely lasted one season. Decent runner and a strong arm, but I wasn't interested in him beyond--"

Kayla giggled. "No, silly, not like that! I think he joined the team to hang out with you and be your friend."

I lowered my hands, and my brows knitted in puzzlement. "Aw come on, really?"

Kayla continued, "That was the rumor for a little while, among the girls on the running team anyway. Leslie Boones, Robert's older sister, was on the team, remember?"

I clutched the air with my hands to emphasize my words,

"What the hell is it with these Boones being fascinated with us? Fucking creeping me out!"

Kayla shook her head, "I don't know. But if any of them will tell us, Robert's probably the one. He seems different than the others. The fact that his bitch of a sister called him a weirdo is enough to interest me."

I rolled my eyes, "Good. Maybe you should talk to him."

Kayla smiled at me and cocked her head, "Or we could do it together."

I shifted in my seat, uncomfortable that we were getting closer to actually contacting the guy. But having her there would be a restraining presence. "Do you think you can stop me if I start swinging?"

Kayla slipped on her sunglasses, "If he pisses you off that much, then I'll hold him down for you. Deal?" She looked so badass in those shades.

I chuckled, "Deal. I'll call him up as soon as I get my phone."

"You can use mine."

"No, no. Not just yet. I'm nervous. I want to talk about what we're going to do when we get to the field. I get the feeling it could be tense. If they let you come in with me, can you poke around the refreshment station while I gather my things? We need to find a can of that stuff the kid was handing out. What was it called… Million or Zillion… something like that. It was green and blue with lightning bolts or something. See if you can find some. Grab a couple cans or some empties if that's all there is."

"I'll try."

"Doc says he doesn't need much."

"What are you going to say to Hatch?"

"I doubt he'll be there. You know how it is. The place practically shuts down the day after a game."

"So why is it going to be tense? We should have the run of the place."

"I don't know but, Coach Deans seemed real distant and tense on the phone. Hell, they might just meet me at the door with a box of my stuff and say, 'Get lost!'" I buried my head in my hands, as the worst career-ending thoughts crashed down upon me again. "It could all be over. Just like that…"

"Hatch wouldn't turn his back… I mean those guys love you! Hon, you gotta quit thinking the worse." She gently touched my shoulder, and the butterflies in my stomach fluttered away.

It took almost two and a half hours, but soon we were at Liberty Field, parking beside my classic blue Ford Bronco I'd left there the day before. The gated team lot was practically empty. I didn't have my pass, so I had to check in at the security desk, but there were no hitches, other than everyone staring at me as I signed in. They had questions in their eyes, but silence on their lips, likely ordered by the administration not to discuss the events of the previous day. Their only words were, "You got fifteen minutes, Mr. Adler. Be sure to stop by and check with us on your way out."

I was buoyed by the fact that we had no escort, but my pace slowed as soon as we stepped into the deserted, dimly lit locker room. The final events of my pre-disaster life flooded in.

Kayla asked, "You okay, Phil?"

"Just remembering everything. I remember meditating about my Oregon fishing trip and then telling Dupree about it. We walked over there, to the refreshment table." I pointed to the folding plastic table, still set up, but empty. I walked over and ran my hand along the top. "My last moments of my old life were right here. Mother fucker!" I slammed my fist hard into the top, and the table reverberated.

Kayla clutched my tense shoulders. "Hon, take it easy. Get your stuff. I'll look around."

It didn't take me long to grab my clothes and personal items. One of the items I missed most was my wedding ring. I couldn't wear it in a game, so I always dropped it into the pocket of my pants. I pulled it out and slipped it on, then stuffed my phone and wallet in my pants pockets, and everything else I dumped into the gym bag I'd brought.

As I turned around, Kayla shouted, "Phil! Is this it?" She was holding a can of Zillion.

"Yeah!"

"There's a bunch left on the counter here!"

"Grab a few and jam 'em in this bag. You see a marker there?"

"No, sorry hon. The trash is empty too." She shoved three cans into my bag.

"Too bad. Thought it might be a source of fingerprints or something. But maybe the cans will have some." I zipped up the bag. "Hey, we're lucky we found anything."

I looked around the room. "I hope I'll be back here again soon."

"You will!" Kayla put an arm around my shoulders and guided me towards the door. "C'mon, hon. Let's go get a hotel and something to eat."

I smiled and took her arm in mine. "You got it, babe." As we walked down the hall, arm in arm, I tried to flush the tension and negative thoughts from my mind. I tried to stop thinking about myself. For the past two days, my life had been non-stop about me, me, me. I spoke quietly to her, "You know how wonderful you are to me? Let's forget about this shit tonight. Let's do what you want to do. Let's just be us tonight."

Kayla whispered back, "You read my mind."

I still had one important task to perform, and it was nibbling on my brainstem like a hungry duck nibbling on corn. I knew that if I didn't take care of it, it would paralyze me from completely letting go. And so, after we checked into the hotel and Kayla was taking a shower, I called Robert Boones. I was relieved when I got a voice mailbox instead of his live voice. It was simpler this way, but I still managed to fumble the ball.

"Uh, hi there… Robert. This is Phil Adler." I cleared my throat. "Uh, Bill Franklin suggested I give you a call. We, well I, would like to see about having you investigate a matter of, uh, urgency to us. Please give me a call back. Um, I'll be busy tonight and in some meetings in the morning. Maybe we can meet at Gramps', uh that is, Phil Adler Senior's place, tomorrow afternoon. Or wherever is best for you." I provided my number quickly and ended the awkward call.

I cursed myself for sounding so tentative but, at the same time, was amazed that I was calling *him, a Boones*, at all.

Kayla still managed to hear me and said, "Good bird. Now, silence your phone, I'll silence mine, and we'll have us an evening."

And that's what we did. We took a cab uptown to our favorite steakhouse, then a cocktail and, finally, a peaceful walk along the waterfront on the Schuylkill River Trail. For a few hours, we didn't talk about football or our present dilemma, and when we returned to our room, we melted into each other's arms and made love like it was our second honeymoon.

Chapter 6: Pause and Effect

It was a Tuesday morning, nine o'clock, and I was sitting in a classroom with Coach Hatch and a few "suits," a slang term for the legal and corporate types that rarely got their hands dirty. Kayla was by my right side, resting a reassuring hand on my arm, and my lawyers, Sarah and Bill, were on my left. A brightly lit classroom meant for thirty big guys should have felt spacious, but it was too small for me under these circumstances. I just wanted to fly away, fast.

The suits introduced themselves as Max Petinsky, the team's lawyer, and Percy "Babe" Babbitt, an NFA representative. I fidgeted with my armrest while Hatch opened up the meeting. I couldn't help but feel a painful distance from this man that had, up until now, been easy to approach about any problem, large or small. But at that moment, the four feet of table between us felt like forty yards.

I felt Kayla's hand on my forearm and realized that I was jiggling my knee and biting my lip from tension. I immediately calmed at her touch and flattened my feet on the floor. I should not have drunk a cup of coffee.

After Hatch finished, Babe articulated the NFA's position, which held that Phil had created a major disruption in game play that couldn't be tolerated, whether deliberate or not. If unintentional, under normal circumstances, sitting out the rest of the game would probably be sufficient punishment. If deliberate, it could be grounds for sitting out several games or the rest of the season.

Just an hour before, I'd met with my lawyers, Sarah and Bill, in private. Bill had tried to fill her in about the unusual history of the Adlers, and she had already seen video from Sunday's game. But I took the extra step and demonstrated my abilities to her.

I couldn't completely transform without removing my clothes, but it was enough to slip off my shirt and change my head and upper body and show her my backwings. Her eyes were as big as coasters, and it looked for a moment like she might faint, but after some sips of water and taking a seat, she settled down. She told us that she had a fear of birds, so it was no small thing for her to finally touch my feathers and hands before the meeting was over. Any doubts about the reality of our existence were blown away. I just hoped she wouldn't have nightmares knowing that such fantastic creatures exist.

Sarah responded now to the wall of men on the other side of the table. She started professional and cool. "We need time to investigate this ourselves, gentlemen. And if we don't know exactly what happened, there's no way you can either. But I can assure you that my client did not do this on purpose. Yes, there was a miracle that took place, a power that he and his relatives share, but they take great care to conceal it. It's as much, if not more, in their interest to avoid public displays like this, as it is in yours. We think someone working in close proximity to Phil sabotaged his ability to control his transformations. Phil's physician mentioned a class of substance, known to werebirds as 'mitogens.' These chemicals are detectable through laboratory tests but aren't commonly checked in residue screens since they are not considered performance enhancers. His doctor should have results tomorrow. If he's positive for mitogens, then this could turn into a criminal investigation to find sources in proximity to Mr. Adler on the day the loss of transformational control occurred."

Hatch shifted in his seat and lifted his hand, glancing back at the NFA representative. "Whoa, hold on now. Are you suggesting that one of us did this to him? That's something I flat out deny. No way. Phil's one of our best, and we're in the middle of the season. Makes no sense whatsoever."

Max butted in, "I'm afraid I have to agree with—"

"Wait!" Sarah raised her hands. "Wait... No, we're not blaming anyone, least of all team management. But I think we all have to agree that there are a lot of people around on game day, some of whom could benefit from disrupting the Bald Eagles' game play. We have to keep that possibility open. These substances are not naturally occurring, and known to few people, so if they're present, it suggests intention."

Babe grunted and shuffled some pages in his plump hands. "That's all well and good, but we don't have time to wait for an investigation. We have games to play. You two parties will need to hash out fault on your own. What we need to know is that you'll be ready for the next game. This thing is exploding on the internet, sponsors are hounding us for explanations... advertising contracts." He raised his eyes and looked at Hatch.

Hatch sighed and rolled his eyes. "Yep... our PR and marketing people are freakin' out too."

Babe pursed his lips and fidgeted his thick fingers, as though counting dollars as he glanced at Max. Max cleared his throat, and Sarah took a deep breath, knowing what was coming next.

Max folded his hands on the table. "We think it would be a good idea for Phil to take a break. Sit out a few games while we sort this thing out."

Sarah shook her head as he finished the sentence. "No... this will only make Mr. Adler look guilty of something. He didn't do anything wrong. It wasn't deliberate. You don't punish someone for getting injured or sick, right?"

"But you said it yourself—he lost control. His medical evaluation is not completed yet. There's no way to know yet, for certain, that it won't happen again." Max wagged his head, "The fact is, he created a huge disruption in a way we are simply not prepared to address. We need time to sort this out, but the game has to go on."

Sarah smiled and leaned back, "He didn't 'create' this distraction; someone else did. You need to open this up for investigation. The NFA should pitch in too. Haven't you guys had enough bad publicity for one decade? Every time you squelch the efforts of players to be themselves and share what they believe, it makes you look like thugs. Don't you see that?"

Babe's face reddened and it took him too long to think of a safe answer.

Sarah continued, "Mr. Adler can't help that he's a werebird and he had no choice when he was forced to reveal a very personal part of who he is; a part of him that up until now, for a season and a half, you had no idea existed. Why should Mr. Adler be punished for being what he is, especially when the reveal wasn't even his choice?"

The three men were attentive as Sarah leaned forward on the table. "He's a hard-working, loyal... valuable, member of the team. We're not asking for you to let him play as an eagle, though there's nothing, as far as I see, that would actually make an eagle illegal..."

The men chuckled. I admired her ability to get in their grill and yet get them laughing the next instant.

Sarah turned to me. "Phil, tell them what you told me just a little while ago... the part about why you play."

My heart raced, but it helped to see the subtle smile on Hatch's face. He still believed in me. I cleared my throat and flattened my hands on the table. "Well, Coach Haskins knows this story, about when I was settling in during my first week of practice with the team. I was getting my butt kicked pretty hard. College ball had been rough, but it was always a mixed bag of talent. I'd never gone up against a whole line of the best of the best. I thought I was a goner. But I wasn't about to quit. If I was gonna fail, I was gonna go down swinging. The coaches and veterans didn't blow any sunshine in us rookies' sails either.

"Anyway, one day Coach Haskins had us running drills, and I was faster than everyone else. I was always a good runner and jumper. Then, just out of the blue, he had Pascal chuck balls at us when we weren't expecting it. I was catching everyone of 'em. Hatch was smiling, and I could see a twinkle in his eyes. Ya know, we don't see that often, but you know you've impressed him when it happens."

Haskins shifted in his seat, disguising his broadening grin.

"Like most of these guys, I just want to be the best. I don't need to be a star. I get a high off feeling like I'm pushing my body to the limit, and that I'm right where I'm supposed to be at just the right moment so that we all succeed together. I want *the team* to be the best."

The NFA rep inhaled sharply, an insincere smile on his lips.

Hatch dropped his hand from his mouth and exposed his flushed cheeks. "Don't dismiss it, Percy. It's just like he said. He's never shown anything but excellence and selflessness to me." He turned back to Phil. "Tell me, son, can you keep this under control? Can you promise me that?"

Max leaned in, "And will you submit to testing for narcotics and performance enhancers the day before each game?"

I nodded emphatically, "Absolutely. Is that okay with you, Sarah?"

"Sounds reasonable. You have nothing to hide."

Everyone looked at Percy, who mopped the sweat from his forehead with a handkerchief. "I'll have to consult the higher ups, but I know that there's no way in hell I can get them to let you play again this weekend. Give us at least one week. And we all keep quiet about this to the media while we confer further. Call it medical leave."

Sarah nodded. "Can we call it 'family leave' or something similar? Or be more specific that this is not a mental or physical performance problem? Since we're not giving the public any details, I don't want them filling in the blanks too much. And will you allow access to the club for a private investigation?"

Max nodded, "We'll call it medical, for undisclosed personal reasons, and that we expect him to come back in a couple of weeks."

The meeting broke up shortly after with everyone polite, if not jovial. I shook Hatch's hand and courteously thanked him for his support.

Hatch shook my hand back with a grin and said, "I'm rootin' for ya but, too, we really need ya back in the game. Take care of yourself and your family and let us know if there's anything we can do to help."

I had to ask, "You won't get in trouble from the corporates?"

He winked, "There's limits maybe, but you let me worry 'bout that."

His words buoyed me up like a rising thermal under my wings, and I left the meeting without any doubts that my team supported me. I still had to convince the Association authorities though, and to do that, we had to get to the bottom of how I was forced to transform, who did it, and why.

I was driving north when I called up Gramps to let him know we'd be back soon and could round up at his place in the afternoon. But he had worrying news. Victor hadn't been seen, or heard from, since we both left Gramps' the morning before.

For some years, Victor lived in a small caretaker's home behind Gramps' main cabin. He helped Gramps take care of the property and, since Grandma Alma's passing, kept Gramps company. Unless his biologist duties or camping trips pulled him away, he consistently shared evening meals with Gramps so it was exceptional that he didn't show the previous evening.

Gramps' voice was weak and worried: *He texted later in the day to say he might be late for dinner, but then he never showed and didn't call. I checked his place and tried callin' 'im this mornin', but I ain't been able to raise him by phone or text. You heard from him?*

I moved to the right lane and spoke up for the hands-free microphone clipped to the visor. "No. Hadn't needed to. We weren't supposed to get together until this afternoon. I was going to call him after I talked to you."

Well give it a try, just in case it's on my end.

"You're talking to me just fine, Gramps."

Just please try, as soon as we hang up. Gramps went on. *I'm 'fraid he mighta went off and did what he was talkin' 'bout doin'. You remember what he said when we parted yesterday?*

"Oh shit… yeah. He wanted to fly down and eavesdrop on the Boones."

Yep. Damn, I don't even know which place he woulda' went to.

"Probably Earl's estate or Tommy's ranch, right?"

Mhmm… most likely places to start.

"Did you go over to his house?"

Yep, yep. Nothin' outta place. I'm gonna fly 'round the Boones' places and scour with ma iggle eyes.

"Sounds like a golden idea, Gramps, but please be careful."

For sure, Sonny. I'll take my Z-Phone and give ya updates.

"I'll stop by home and get my harness and Z-Phone too. I'll join you as soon as I can."

A Z-Phone was a tiny cellphone readily available from online shopping sites. It was a basic non-smartphone, but it allowed calls and texts, and it could transmit GPS coordinates, so if one of us was incapacitated, we could track each other down. Simple voice commands made it easy to operate when we were in feral form. We attached them to ourselves with small, lightweight harnesses and some of us used thin neck loops with throat mics pressed against our breast. They concealed well under our feathers and could pick up our voices with less wind interference in flight.

As soon as we hung up, I called Victor's cell phone number, and the call went straight to voicemail. I also called his work phone and left a message, but I was confident he wasn't at work, or he would certainly have replied to Gramps by now. Sometimes he went camping, or on long feral bird adventures, and could be unreachable for a few days. But he wouldn't have split in the midst of everything that was happening and definitely not without telling us. Then again, even going out on his own to snoop on the Boones, without telling us, was strange. I called Gramps and left a message that I couldn't reach Victor either and that I would proceed with our plan. My stomach sank like I swallowed a lead weight. I let it travel down to my foot and pressed the accelerator pedal to the floor.

Chapter 7: Blood and Feathers, Tracks and Fur

Wildfires in the western US burnished the sky with a yellow-orange haze that cast unfocused shadows on the landscape. Under that uncertain sky, I drove my old Bronco as hard and as fast as I dared, while Gramps' words spurred me on.

When I reached home, I grabbed my gear including my Z-Phone and harness for my feral form. Kayla wasn't far behind. I walked up to her driver's door before she shut the engine off. She rolled down her window and wrinkled her brow. She could see the worry in my face. "What's up, hon?"

"Victor's missing. Hasn't been heard from since yesterday, and his truck's not at home."

"Jesus. He went out on his own, didn't he?"

"Maybe. Gramps is out looking." Just then, my phone buzzed in my pocket. I pulled it out and saw it was Gramps calling, so I answered.

Gramps' voice was shaped by a beak, but the urgency came through clearly: *I soared all over the Boones Ranch. I didn't dare get too close, but I saw somethin' that gots me worried. A couple brass shells by the barn. Looked shiny and new from above. Some recent blood 'n feathers out in the pasture too.*

"Oh god... Have you called the wildlife centers?"

Not yet. That's ma next call, though them Boones wouldn't bother takin' him to one, and it'd be a long crawl to the road. 'Course, could still be hidin' someplace nearby undercover.

"Sure as shit he'd be a goner if they found him."

You'd best come up here and help me take a closer look. One of us needs to be a lookout while the other gets down in the grass. How'd things go there anyways?

"Not all bad. Can't play for a while, but the coach and team are all behind me."

Good, good.

"Could be worse. I think Sarah and Bill saved the day. I'll tell ya more later, but we're coming to you now. Where are you?"

Up on River Ridge Road in a stand of pine across from the Boones Ranch driveway. You best be discreet and park a ways off. Don't need to spook 'em, in case they don't already knows we're on to 'em.

"Be there in a jiff!" I hung up and looked back at Kayla. "Gramps found some clues. Can you take me up to Catawissa? I think I should leave my Bronco here… it's too recognizable."

Kayla said, "Sure, no problem."

In twenty minutes, we came to the ideal jumping-off point, a quiet parking area for the Catawissa Creek Nature Preserve. It was about a mile from the Boones Ranch, so it wouldn't be a long flight to get there.

To our shock, Victor's state truck was parked in the corner of the lot under some low trees. We parked next to it and peered inside. The same pants and shirt I had seen him wearing yesterday were wadded up on the seat.

"There's his clothes. He's got to be in feral form. I don't see his Z-Phone or harness, so maybe he has it on him."

I pulled my phone from my pocket and opened the family's tracking app. Victor was offline. "If he's got it on him, it died, or someone turned it off. Damn, I wish this app showed some kind of tracking history."

Kayla stepped back. "I bet his phone is in his pocket. Let me try calling it…"

In a moment, we both heard a buzzing coming from the clothing in the cab.

"His normal cellphone is in the truck! No wonder we haven't been able to reach him. He's definitely out somewhere in bird form."

"Goddammit, Victor, you knucklehead!" I slammed my fist on the hood of his truck. "Come on, babe, help me get out of these clothes and up in the sky!"

We walked up a paved path under the autumn trees. Once up the path a discreet distance, I stopped and looked around more thoroughly, to be sure no one was watching. I took Kayla's hand and led her off the path. We bucked the thick brush for twenty yards until we came to a small, untraveled clearing concealed from the main path. I hastily shed my clothes and handed them to Kayla, as she glanced around to make sure nobody was watching.

Worry and excitement made my voice shake, and my words were punctuated by little wisps of steam in the cool air. I checked my phone one last time. "Shit. Still no reply from that fucker Robert."

Kayla took my phone and bundled it with my clothing. "It's been less than 24 hours. Give the guy a chance."

"Keep an ear to my phone, will ya? If Robert calls, try to set up a meeting with him for as soon as possible?"

"Sure, hon, no problem. How ya getting home?"

"I'll fly home or catch a ride with Gramps, or hopefully Victor, when this is done. Give Gramps a call if Victor turns up someplace. You mind making some calls around to check if anyone found an injured hawk?"

"Sure. I'll start with Susquehanna Wildlife Center, then the DCNR and Game Commissions. Maybe go down our list of local wildlife-friendly vet clinics too."

"Good idea." I grimaced as I yanked off a shoe and sock and put my foot down in the cold, damp leaves. I rubbed my pale bare skin, reduced to only my underwear. I shivered as I bent over and slipped them off too.

Kayla smiled and gave a quiet wolf whistle. "I gotta get you out in the woods more often!"

"Yeah, you like what nature does to me?" I chuckled and grabbed her close in my arms for a kiss. She was warm and soft against me. "Last night was a wild treat."

"Sure was." she said, and gave me another kiss.

"Love you, babe. I'll see you soon."

I backed away from Kayla and poked my eyes about one last time as I prepared to take the plunge into avian form.

"You be careful! And have Gramps call me in two hours—TWO HOURS! If I don't hear from you, I'll be coming after you myself!"

I was already transforming when I replied with a screechy, "I will!"

My body shrank and my vision blurred as my eyes changed shape, then snapped into the high-resolution detail that my eagle eyes delivered. My view parted and tilted to a wider field as my beak emerged and pressed my eyes to the sides of my head. I closed my eyes and concentrated on changing my body into the shape of a natural bald eagle. I let out a long exhale as my chest shrank. A wave of heat ruffled my prickly quills as I shed body mass and my emerging feathers matured. My arms twisted, popped, and then re-fused into wings that erupted with dark brown feathers. My feet shrank and my toes stretched, the skin rippling into yellow scales and black talons sprouted from the tips. White feathers replaced my brown hair, and the final, dramatic touch, punctuated by a sound like sliding paper, was the jutting out of large wing and tail flight feathers.

As I settled into my familiar feral shape, I breathed deeply in and out a few times, re-oxygenating tissues that were strained by the intense mitosis of transformation. I opened my golden eyes, extended my wings, and fluttered my tail, verifying that everything was where, and how, it should be.

Kayla smiled and bent down, giving my soft throat a delicate scratching. "I don't often get to see you do that, hon. You are handsome as a feral." She slid my Z-Phone and harness on over my back and fastened the Velcro strap. Then she leaned forward and gave me a kiss on the tip of my beak. I couldn't kiss back, but I rubbed my beak on her face and gave her a lick on the cheek.

As Kayla stood up and backed away, I turned and shoved up from the ground, beating my wings hard to rise vertically to a branch twenty feet up. A few more hops and flaps, and I exited the forest canopy and flew off to the north.

After two days of meetings, phone calls, and constant worry, it was refreshing to do something strenuously physical. I gulped the cool, crisp air as I beat my wings during the climb. Once at altitude, I stretched my wings and tail in the warm sunshine and let it wash away my tension. I rose to 1200 feet above the ridge—high enough for good scouting, but not attracting too much attention. My wings rocked in a rising thermal, and I was tempted to let it lift me to the cool heavens, away from my problems, but I was anxious to catch up to Gramps and unravel what had become of Victor.

It wasn't long before I spotted another eagle resting in a poplar tree along the highway. I could tell it was Gramps by a characteristic long "v" of white feathers down his neck to his crop. I set my wings into a long glide, and when I got close, I dropped my feet to slow into a steep dip, then tilted my wings, flared, and landed quietly beside him with only a small flap. Normally two eagles landing so close would fill the air with loud chirping calls, but not this time.

I stepped closer to Gramps, and arched my neck as I reconfigured my vocal anatomy. Normally, an eagle's syrinx, the organ in their chest that produces sounds, would be incapable of human speech. But an experienced were-eagle can find ways around that. The result is a high-pitched lilting voice, but it's intelligible.

"Anything new?"

Gramps' eyes seemed paler than usual, and his feathers were slicked tight against his body, conveying worry and stress in bald eagle language. He shook his head slowly and whispered back, "Nothin' good. I saw large paw prints 'round the pasture yonder, where I spotted the blood. Now that you're here, I'll go down and check it out while you keep watch for me."

I nodded and followed him in a short glide down to the pasture-covered hill that lay to the south of the Boones' driveway. We landed on separate fence posts along the asphalt drive. A grove of oaks and elms stood a few hundred feet away down the hill by a red barn. If I were a nosey hawk, that was the cluster of trees I'd have perched in.

On the other side of the oaks was a long, red barn with white trim, and across from that was a four-car garage. A short distance away to the left of this scene, uphill behind the garage, was a massive house with terraced decks that overlooked a private horse arena. The town of Catawissa and a lazy bend of the Susquehanna River lay far below. The Boones also had a larger, ancestral estate, visible a few miles away across the river near Bloomsburg.

The house and garage were clad in green wood siding with various white to sandy shades of marble, limestone, and granite making up the porches and columns around the doors. Numerous peaks and dormers decorated the house and outbuildings, as though the owner had a lot to say to the less-well-off in the valley beyond. Above the door of the barn was a sign that read "Boonedocks." The Boones Ranch was residence to Tommy Boones and his family, including his 25-year-old son, Billy, whose sole occupation seemed to be toady for Earl or living off the family tit.

But on a Tuesday afternoon, there seemed to be nothing much going on except a handyman cleaning the gutters of the house. A black Dodge 1500 pickup truck sat parked in front of the barn and country music played inside.

I nodded to Gramps, and he flew down into the grass in the middle of the hillside pasture. I figured he was checking the bloodstain he'd told me about on the phone. The tall, dry grass concealed him from my perspective, except when he lifted his head occasionally. He seemed to be moving around, and I hoped he was finding more clues. I turned my keen eyes back to the house and barn below.

I made up my mind, years ago, not to trust the Boones. The incident at the zoo when I was a child had left a strong impression on me. Then there were the stories Gramps had told me. And Kevin, one of my nephews, went to school with Billy, and relayed to us what a conceited loudmouth he was. He loved to remind everyone that he was a Boones and that his family had plenty of money. Nothing he did, on his own, was that remarkable. But he threw big parties and drove flashy cars, and that was enough to be popular in high school. I usually tried to steer clear of the Boones, so it made me especially uneasy being here, on their land. But if they had harmed Victor, their ass would be grass.

Gramps' peppery head bobbed about, as he sauntered down the hill in a straight line. A door slammed at the house and Billy walked out, making a beeline for his white Ford F-150 Raptor. He fired it up and backed up to turn around. I had no time to lose. I leapt off the fencepost, flew straight downhill towards the trees, and slid under the nearest bush. It was the shortest route to get out of sight of the driveway.

Gramps heard the boom of the truck's dual exhaust and followed, tight on my tail. We both crashed into the bushes at the same time and rolled into a mass of feathers and strewn leaves, just in time for the truck to clear the tree line and rev loudly as it climbed the hill.

We kissed the dirt, covered in debris, until the truck reached the top of the hill. It didn't slow, stop, or swerve, so it seemed that we weren't spotted. In a moment, the tires screeched as the truck sped off down the highway.

I slowly lifted my head and shook off the leaves.

"That was too close for comfort." Gramps whispered.

"You're telling me, I—" I stopped short, as my eyes caught the familiar shape of a red feather lying in the leaves.

Gramps studied it. "Looks like one of Vic's tail feathers. There's a bit of flesh on the calamus, so it was forcibly removed, not molted." He reached out and picked up a delicate clump of hair with his beak and held it for me to see. It had a bit of skin and dried blood attached.

I cocked my head uncertainly. "Dog hair? Was he attacked by a dog?"

Gramps replied, "Wolf, actually. Huge by the looks of it. I don't know a species we'd have here that's this monstrous big. There's massive tracks in the pasture up yonder too. They were just milling about though, like they was searchin'. But whatever happened, they sure had a tussle here."

My heart sank. "Did he survive?"

He shook his eagle head, "Don't know, sonny. Possibly. There's only a few clumps of small feathers. As you know, that's not enough to kill ya. But there's a pretty good amount of blood in the field, less down here. And what of this wolf hair? It don't make sense to me. I don't see kennels or packs of dogs on the ranch."

Gramps raised his right wing and worked his beak under

his breast feathers to expose the top of a dark brown leather pouch. It was a small bag that he wore slung around his upper body for carrying critical items when he was out and about as an eagle. It was small and colored discreetly enough to not attract attention as he flew. He picked up some hair and feathers from the ground and pressed them into the pouch's opening.

He whispered, "Let's look some more. See if ye can get one of them shiny rifle shells from the yard. But be careful. Sounds like someone's inside the barn."

We spread apart, and I stepped carefully through the shadows to the edge of the barn. Normally I wouldn't have been so concerned for my safety in human form, whether around the Boones or not. I knew how to handle myself. But an eagle is not secure on the ground in a hemmed-in place between the woods and a barn. There was no way out but up, and it would be a steep, and therefore slow, climb to safety. So I slinked along the edge of the barn, suppressing the swagger that eagles naturally have when walking on the ground.

I peered around the front corner and saw the glint of brass in the gravel by the concrete drive. Fortunately, the Dodge pickup was parked close enough to offer good cover, so I looked about and then dashed the remaining ten feet between the barn and the truck.

I picked up one of the cartridges, but as I did so, I noticed two sets of massive wolf-like tracks in the gravel. There was dirt scattered onto the pavement, as though the beasts propelled themselves rapidly into the woods and kicked up gravel behind them.

I gave a low chirp and Gramps came over for a look. He whispered, "See the spacin' of the tracks and the way they kicked up dirt at the back? These wolves were off with purpose, straight towards some other sign in the woods." He nodded his beak towards the woods. "I saw more big dog prints back there too, walking with a man's stride, and there were faint signs of feathers brushin' the ground too."

I wanted to believe that Gramps was telling me tall tales, but this would've been a really weird time for it. "What *are* these tracks? I've never seen dogs this big."

Gramps followed Phil's eyes around the scene and shook his beak. "Definitely wolf but waaay bigger. Man-sized. And not always walking on all fours neither."

"The heck you saying? Werewolves?"

Gramps cocked his head and examined the ground from various angles. "Never met one, personally. But who are we to say it's not possible? I mean, no one would believe there's birdfolk like us either." His eyes returned to the cartridge held in my beak and he delicately took it and tucked it into his pouch.

My hackles prickled with unease. But I didn't want to leave without Victor. "You think Victor's in there?"

"If he's not dead, mebbe."

"God, don't say that! I gotta go in there and look around."

"Keep your voice down! And absolutely not, grandson."

"But he might be dying in there!" I stalked up close to the right front wheel of the truck to peer back around the corner. There was a sharp pain in my tail as Gramps tugged on it and pulled me back.

"Ouch!" I glared at him and lifted my hackles in annoyance.

Gramps sternly retorted, "We gots to be smart about this! There's no way we can get in and outta there without being seen. And we have no way of knowin' who else, or what else, is in there too. But I bet Adele could get in and out tonight without bein' seen. Let's get back to ma place."

Chapter 8: Robert

The sun sank low in the west, casting angled red light across Gramps' porch. Adele and Zoe prepared to leave while Gramps doted over them with concern for their safety. The agreed-to plan was to take them down to the same park I had departed from earlier. Gramps would wait there while the pair flew ahead as feral barn owls. One would sit watch in a tree while the other went into the barn's hay loft and investigated.

"Just stay long enough to confirm he's there, all right? Don't try to bust 'im out or reveal yourself in any way, okay?"

Adele narrowed her owl eyes, "I can handle myself, dear."

"Ooooh I knows ya can, sweet chili pepper." Gramps shook his head emphatically, "Mmm-mmm, no disagreement there. But there's something new and awful about what's goin' on at that ranch. It best be faced as a flock, with family to back us up. But we can't do that 'lessen we knows that Victor's there and what we'll be up against. That's all we need, babe."

Zoe chuckled back, "She's gonna want to gouge all their eyes out if they're harming Victor. I'll try to keep her temper in check!"

The two sisters breathed deeply a couple of times, and then exhaled as their bodies shrank. Their beaks shrank and feathers withdrew such that, for a moment, I saw that their foreheads were flat and triangular their eyes bulged from their sockets. Owls possess an otherworldly appearance under their feathers, with angular head geometry, concavities around their neck and belly, and eyes that are cuffed in blue rings of bone, barely contained in their head. Of course, you see none of that when casually observing them in the wild, but without their shape-giving feathers, as during the mid-phases of transformation, you see the alien-like anatomy all too clearly.

Their arms shrank, in proportion to their bodies, and their soft gold and white wing and tail plumage contracted to the correct size for normal, feral barn owls. Their pink toes shriveled down to the dainty talons and long slim legs that give rodents nightmares. As fluffing her plumage and giving herself a quick inspection, Adele screeched with satisfaction.

They flapped up to the backs of chairs at the table, and Gramps and I slipped their Z-Phone harnesses on. A feral could do this on their own only if they paused and modified their wingtips with digits to operate the fasteners. But it was awkward, so assistance was always appreciated.

Once their phones were checked, they hopped onto Gramps' shoulders and accompanied him to his pickup. In a minute, they fired up and rattled away down the driveway, just as the sun sank below a forested ridge.

Kayla and I watched them go, our hopes riding with them. I would have liked to go, but I had other urgent business. Robert had called back that afternoon, and Kayla had set up a meeting with him at Gramps' at six that evening, which was rapidly approaching.

Kayla put an arm around my shoulders. "You ready for this?"

"Heh, no."

Kayla whispered teasingly, "Remember what I said about him liking you in high school? He even said he looked forward to the meeting."

"Oh god, a fanboy! He was a bit friendlier than I cared for at the time."

"So? Is that so bad?"

"Well… no, I guess not. He wasn't creepy or anything."

"Then what's the problem, other than his family name?"

I grunted, "Ain't that enough?"

"Was he ever mean to you?"

"No, I guess not. I remember he was there at my eighth birthday at the zoo. He wasn't a dick like his grandpa or Tommy. He seemed as stunned, and curious, as I was."

"Maybe that's why he wanted to be your friend. Maybe he looked up to you." I walked towards the Changing House, and Kayla followed, continuing to admonish me. "Give the guy a chance."

"Okay, okay, I'll be nice. But if you see my fists clench, you best hold me back. Right now, it's hard not to want to knock his head off his shoulders."

Kayla and I stepped into the Changing House, switched to our human forms, and dressed ourselves. A few minutes later, I heard a rumbling in the direction of the driveway and looked out to see a 1969 AMC Ambassador crawling carefully around the bend without raising a speck of dust. The car was immaculate, and it was clear the owner didn't want to tarnish her, if he could help it. She was the color of a mountain bluebird and rolled on sparkling chrome wheels, the engine purring like a tiger.

Robert shut down the engine, stepped out, and strode towards us. He was my age, thirty-three, medium-build, and had short dark hair and sunglasses. He wore jeans, a white t-shirt, and a black leather jacket that hung open.

I tried to start on a cordial note. I whistled, "Wow, that's a nice ride!" It was forced, but I had to admit, it *was* a nice car.

As he pocketed his sunglasses he said, "Thanks! I restored her myself."

"No kiddin'?"

"Yeah, a hobby of mine. Helps me clear my head after a long day of work, ya know." He waved to Kayla, who was leaning against the railing of the porch. "How you doing, Kayla?"

Kayla replied, "Not bad until this mess."

"Well, yeah. That goes without saying." Robert shook my hand, "Thanks for calling. I'm sure it was tough."

I squeezed his hand, a little harder than necessary, and released it. "You have no idea."

"Easy there, sport. Don't harm the investigator." Robert opened and closed his hand and shook off the pain.

So far, I wasn't impressed, and I guess it showed. I stood a little too firmly, for just a little too long.

Robert closed the awkward silence, "Eeyeaahh… well, I'm guessing you want to get right down to business?"

Kayla beckoned, "Come on in, boys. Let's sit down and be civilized. Want a shot of whiskey? Or some ice, for your hand, Robert?"

I let Robert lead the way. "Let's save the whiskey for our victory. If you got some coffee, that would be perfect."

We all sat down at the big dining table, and Kayla brought coffee for Robert, who had pulled out a small notepad and pen.

Robert narrowed his eyes and looked sideways at me. "Let's cut through the preamble. I saw what happened to you at the game. In-fucking-credible. Just like that time at your birthday party."

I nodded sternly. "More than you know. The only two times, ever, in my life, that I totally lost control of my transformation ability. I'm waiting for a lab test to come back to prove it, but we're pretty sure someone slipped me a mitogen somehow."

Robert scribbled a moment longer. "Mitogen… what is that,

exactly?"

There was something in Robert's voice that didn't sound completely ignorant of that word. All I saw was a smug asshole who probably knew exactly what happened, and what unspeakable things were being done to Victor. My jaw squirmed and I cracked my knuckles.

Then Kayla laid a hand on my clenched fists on the table. I met her blue-eyed gaze, and suddenly felt ashamed of myself. I was losing control of my anger. I nodded for her to take over.

Kayla answered, "Sorry… this has been a hard couple of days for us. A mitogen is a chemical that encourages cellular mitosis. It facilitates transformation… makes it take over, and you end up in whatever form is prompted by your mental state."

Robert nodded. "Ahaa, I see. Do you know how they roofied you?"

Kayla patted my hands, "Hon? Why don't you go get your gym bag?"

I abruptly slid my chair back loudly and stood up square and tense. Robert straightened up in his chair, and even Kayla looked at me with surprise. I dropped my shoulders and exhaled. "Sorry about that. Fuck… I gotta be honest, Robert… I don't trust you. Nothing personal against you, but I think one of your kin did this, and I don't know that I can trust you to be impartial." My fists closed again and I thought, briefly, of grabbing Robert by the throat and locking him in a room as a hostage to negotiate getting Victor back.

Robert met my gaze evenly, but did nothing with his hands or body to provoke me further. "I'm a professional, and I—"

My fists shook, and I finally slammed them into the table, causing Robert's coffee cup to jump noisily. He jumped in his seat a little too. I clenched my eyes to hold back my emotions and said, "Bill Franklin says you're okay. If there's any doubt, say so now, or so help me, I'll make you regret bein' born if you lie to us. Can we count on you?"

Robert had dropped his pad and pen, stood up, and squared himself up with me across the table. "I take my job seriously, Phil. I've never fucked a client over yet, and I'm not about to start. Everything I do for you is confidential. And, yeah, if it's one of my worthless redneck family members, I'll help ya nab 'em." He firmly offered his hand across the table. "You can shake on that."

I took his hand, mentally prepared to be gentler this time. To my surprise, Robert jerked my hand closer to himself, pulling me off balance, and he smiled. "Does that mean I'm hired?"

I smirked, "It does. What's your fee?"

"Thousand bucks a day, plus expenses."

"You got it!" I shook his hand and released it. I looked to Kayla, "Babe, maybe I need one of those whiskeys after all."

Kayla looked at Robert, "I think that was a victory."

Robert sat back down neatly in his chair with a little smile, "Well then, I'll have one too!"

I walked to the living room and reached into my gym bag. "This little shit was handing out these new energy drinks at the start of the game." I handed Robert a can of Zillion. "I started feeling funny about ten minutes later, then lost control twenty minutes into the game."

Robert held the can by the edges as he studied it. "This was canned by Eastern. See?"

He held the can so that I could read the words Bottled & Distributed by Eastern Beverage Distributors, Inc., Philadelphia, PA.

"So?"

Robert wore a knowing smile. "What did the kid look like?"

"Maybe five feet tall or so. Dark, curly hair... white.

Probably all of nineteen I guess? He wore a blue polo shirt with a swirl on the left breast."

"Mhmm… I got news for you. And, remember, I'm just the messenger. That's one of Tommy Boones' businesses."

I wanted to smash something. "You serious? So, it was a Boones?"

Robert pushed back in his chair, "All know is that the kid worked for them. You gotta have a lab analyze this stuff. And I need to check this for prints. You got a Ziploc bag, Kayla?"

"Sure!" She walked to the kitchen and came back with a baggie.

As Robert slipped the can into the bag, he added, "Doesn't seem like a dumb thing Tommy would do. He wouldn't want to jeopardize his legit business. But there are other Boones goons that work there. Your physical description narrows it down pretty well, but I'll have to do some checking on the DL."

I chuckled at his disparaging, but accurate, label for his family members. I asked, "Down low?"

"Yes. Very quietly. In case you don't know, I'm not exactly on even footing with Earl or his idiots, ever since I put Bull away. He just got out of jail, and I'm sure he'd love to pay his disrespects to me, and the others would cheer him on. All by way of saying that I have as much a need to be discrete about this as you do."

We drank our shots of whiskey, and the heat of it going down relaxed my shoulders. Robert nodded after he drank his shot and commented, "Nice stuff. My compliments to your grandad."

"I'll let him know," Kayla replied.

Robert nodded and said, "You know, I had always hoped our paths would cross again."

I was afraid this moment would come. "Yeah?"

"Yeah. Ever since your transformation at the zoo. And then at that game against Reading. I had a front row seat for that one too. God that was so cool." Robert was smiling wide and shook his head in wonder at the images in his memory. He went on, more excitedly, "And I… I wondered what you ever did with that secret talent of yours."

I looked out the window, not having to fake disinterest in Robert's curiosity. "Well, yeah… we don't really like to talk about those events. And now's not really a good time either." I turned back with an unwelcome glare.

Robert's nod and fading smile conveyed that he got the message. He rolled his eyes, as though second-guessing why he agreed to help such a moody client. He met eyes with Kayla, who looked up from writing a check and smiled awkwardly.

I opened the front door and said, "Thanks for coming over. We appreciate your help. Here's a check to get you started." I held out my hand. "It's been… interesting, to see you again, Robert. We've got some family business to take care of yet tonight, so if you'll excuse us?"

Robert stood, folded up his writing pad, and pocketed it with his pen, looking hurried, but trying not to seem so. "Sure thing. Be in touch tomorrow."

As he drove away a minute later, Kayla asked, "Why didn't you mention Victor?"

"I don't trust him that much. Not yet. I want to hear what Adele finds out before I bring it up with anyone outside of our group. Then I can see if his facts about it match ours."

Chapter 9: Samuel's Account

Kayla and I cuddled on the couch, back in our comfortable anthro-eagle forms, waiting for a call from Gramps. I knew Adele and Zoe wouldn't go into the barn until it was pitch black, but it didn't make the waiting any easier. Kayla lay against me, and I slowly ran my fingers through her crisp, white head feathers as she snoozed. Her eyeballs twitched with saccadic movements under her thinly-feathered white eyelids. She might have been dreaming, or just not fully asleep. Either way, I didn't want to disturb her. The weight and warmth of my loving mate against me succeeded in making me sleepy too.

When my phone rang, we both jolted awake. It was 8:23 p.m., and Gramps was calling.

"Gramps? What's up?"

Victor's in there and he's alive, but not well. Broken wing and very weak. They got 'im crammed in a little airline kennel. No food or water, not that he sounds like he can even stand up or eat or drink right now. Adele says he was unconscious mostly.

"Fucking bastards! Does he know we're coming for him?"

She says she made the werebird sign, and he weakly signed back. So, yes.

Rage blazed in my heart and tears moistened my eyes. I choked out, "Good. Good. Hope he can hang on a bit longer."

Listen, sonny, there's more. She saw them transformin' into wolves to do their patrols. The Boones are werewolves!

"Holy shit… that explains what we saw."

'Splains lots of things, includin' why they're so obsessed with being rivals, possibly. Reminds me of my great grandpa Samuel's war stories 'bout men behavin' like animals. Always assumed it weren't so literal.

"What's the tactical situation like?"

Sounds like just Billy and Hayden watchin' him now. I don't want to go in there with anything but full force in case that changes, given the fact they got the guns, the property rights, and we got the unknowns of fightin' werewolves now.

I was torn. I wanted to charge in, crack heads, and rip Victor out of there right now. But Gramps was right. "Yeah… hard to not just do something, but you're probably right."

We gots to start the contact tree rollin' and gather up a posse. We can't go rollin' in there at night no how. It'll have to be first thing in the morning. You and Kayla call your contacts, I'll call mine, and we'll tell 'em all to meet up here, at the Catawissa Creek Nature Preserve, at 7 a.m. sharp. We'll give out assignments then, but they need to come prepared for a fight, feral or anthro. Got it?

"Will do, Gramps. You guys coming back?"

'Fraid not. Adele and Zoe gonna stay down there and keep watch on Victor all night. Figure I'll hole up here at the truck and relay information as I gets it.

"You need anything?"

Naw, brought me some snacks and cawffee, and I got ma feathers to keep me warm. How'd the meetin' with Robert go?

"He took one look at the Zillion can and told us it, and the kid, were from Tommy Boones' distribution company."

Looks like we're gonna be bustin' down the right door in the mornin', then. We'll get Victor, and maybe some other answers too.

After talking to Gramps, Kayla and I made our calls and texts, and those family members contacted their assigned members. By midnight, we had twenty-eight werebirds committed to showing up in the morning. I was energized and ready for a fight, so much so that I knew it would be impossible to sleep.

Gramps' words about great-great-grandfather Samuel drove me to the bookshelf in the corner of the room. Samuel had been a prolific journal writer and his writings had all been preserved by the family. I stroked my thumb across the old leather-bound spines of his books on the shelf, marked with faded stencils of his initials and the years they covered. I pulled a few from the 1860s, laid them out on the dining table and browsed until I found his entries written during his time as an infantryman for the Union Army during the Civil War. The entries occupied most of one entire journal and included many sketches and scribbles.

One bit of artwork depicted wolves wearing Confederate uniforms, snarling and running through a smoky battlefield. The nearby text was unsteady and wandered on the page, and it was poorly composed as compared to his usual thoughtful style. He was excited and hurried when he wrote it.

It was difficult, but I pieced together that the drawing and notes were from a battle in 1865, late in the war, in Virginia in pursuit of General Lee's crumbling army. They faced a company of Confederates that had stayed behind during a general retreat, and yet, fanatically refused to surrender. Samuel called it a 'delaying action,' the soldiers sacrificing themselves for the army to escape. They were almost completely surrounded, and the Union called for them to surrender, but they refused. Finally, the Union lit a hay field afire to drive them out. But the smoke and dying light of day provided cover for the Confederates to make a dash towards escape.

Despite being in rags and running low on ammunition, the Confederates would not give up before their cadre and wounded were evacuated. Before long, the battle deteriorated into brutal hand-to-hand combat. In the confusion, a pack of massive wolves seemingly materialized out of nowhere. They had no fear of humans and proceeded to ravage the ranks. Some wore scraps of Confederate clothing. All of them were intent on attacking Union men, ripping out their throats and dashing away. It was intense hours of fighting in smoke and flickering light, punctuated by the screams of friends and the ragged growls of fierce beasts…

In the savage confrontation of last night, I feared for my life more times than the sum of all my previous actions. And, I must confess, I revealed my deepest secret, though none but two of the enemy saw it, and one of them dispatched, the other's living in doubt.

I was caught alone and beset by one of the wolves, whose fur was the blackest of soot. I blocked its lunge with my rifle and then plunged my boot knife into its middle. Despite the wound, it continued to fight most powerfully, and we grappled desperately in the bloody mud. I took a vicious wound to my left arm and hand, and then the wolf, which should really be called a beast, for it was so much larger than any wolf I've seen or heard of, latched to my throat with its maw. It tore my flesh and I feared my immediate death, so I changed, and the beast was in such amazement, it fell back on its haunches with an expression that, were it a man and not a beast, I would think it was blinking in wonder. I plunged upon him with my foot talons and crushed his windpipe and did manage to stay atop him with the assistance of my wings.

Whilst the first choked for air, a second beast, a gray wolf with black markings as though he rolled in coal dust, attacked me next. In birdfolk state, I reacted faster and gripped him by the gorge with my hand talons, brought him down, and opened his throat with my beak. The hot blood gushed and sprayed my white feathers crimson as I rode out his death throes, and the beast went still. When I turned back to the first beast, he was drooling blood, gasping and coughing with such a croup, that I believed him gravely wounded. I let him run into the smoke and did not pursue, soon collapsing from my own pain and loss of blood.

This morning, the clouds hang low and gray, smudged with the smoke of burning bodies and straw, and I am sick from the smell and faint from my wounds. I am told that most of the Rebs were killed, only a few surviving to surrender. There were also two wolf-beasts amongst the men, one with hands covered in hair and claws like a dog and massive shoulders somewhere between man and wolf.

I did not see a specimen with slashed throat, so I do not know what became of the first wolf I beset. I curse now that I did not pursue, but, too, in the light of day, I am left wondering how I ever prevailed at all. Surely God's Providence was upon me, for the thing was twice my size. It makes me shudder to think how nearly I came to dying last night, and I am tearfully thankful to be alive. But I fear that the price for living is that wolf-men will haunt my dreams, every night for as long as I draw breath, for the first beast in its departing did cast a hair-raising glimpse upon me. Its gaze was of pure hatred, as though my very soul was an inexcusable affront to him. And perhaps he yet lives.

The beasts were burned with the rest of the animal carcasses, but I am not convinced that was the proper funeral right. They should have been buried with the other Rebs in the mass grave, for I am convinced they were men, like me, who could change at will. Another race with a secret curse to check the influence of our secret blessing on the world…

My feathers stood on end as I finished reading Samuel's account. I flipped ahead to see if there was further mention and, not seeing any, I closed the journal and rubbed the 3 a.m. gravel from my eyes. I wasn't sure that was the best thing to read in preparation for sleep, but it didn't matter, because I could scarcely keep my eyes open. I added another log to the fire, cuddled in with Kayla on the sofa, and finally fell into what I hoped would be dreamless sleep.

Chapter 10: Guns and Poses

Kayla and I left Gramps' cabin an hour and a half before dawn. It would take nearly an hour to make it to the meeting point, and I wanted plenty of time. With Kayla driving, I meditated on my mission to save Victor. In the discipline of football, I'd learned to visualize scenarios before a game and decide on personal goals and limits. It didn't lock me down to pre-determined responses, but it made decisions on the field faster, since I'd already mentally rehearsed them.

The question I asked myself was how far I would go to rescue Victor. No authority would enter the Boones' farm and search their premises for an injured hawk on what would seem like a whimsical report. And the Boones certainly wouldn't fling their doors open to the law, at least not without a search warrant. So, I would have to break the law and trespass, and I had absolutely no problem with that, if it meant saving my friend.

I was also ready for hand-to-talon fighting, if necessary. I knew that they might defend their property with firearms, as well as fists and wolfish jaws. In the eyes of the law, they would have more reason to kill me in self-defense than I had for being there, especially if I was behaving in a threatening manner. But Vic was like a brother to me, and I wouldn't hesitate to risk my life for him, just as he had already done for me.

But would I kill? I took a deep breath and let it out slowly. I recognized that there was a part of me that wanted to get in a scrap. I wanted to hurt the assholes that hurt Victor. I'd never seriously wanted to kill someone before, but in a heated confrontation, it was a real possibility that day. If I found Victor dead, or even nearly so, could I keep myself from beating someone to death or ripping out their throat like Samuel had done? The powerful, deadly impulse was close, and rested like a cold, dark orb in the fore of my skull. It was a pearl of hatred that my brain could not expel, and it was out of place from my usual mental state. Bouts of indignation invited me to touch the cool, smooth curve of that nidus of hatred, but I feared that if I did so, I would be overtaken by it. Human malice combined with the killing instincts of a bird of prey would be a lethal brew. A part of me hoped that a Boones would do something stupid and force me to cave their face in, but I knew it would ruin my life if I allowed myself to go that terrible distance.

I took a long, controlled inhale, resolving to stop myself short of killing unless I, or my friends and family, were in mortal danger. There would be a hard stop, a brick wall, beyond which I would not act unless that barrier was shattered by my enemies. I relaxed and exhaled evenly, embracing a sense of peace and resolution.

When we arrived at the Catawissa Creek Nature Preserve, the sky was turning from black to steely, predawn gray. I found Gramps, Adele, and Zoe gathered by Gramps' truck. I handed Gramps a fresh thermos of coffee.

Gramps smiled. "Mmm, you read my mind, grandson. Thank ye so kindly. Adele and Zoe just arrived from the barn, and were givin' me an update."

Adele told us that Billy and Hayden hung out at the barn all night, taking turns on patrol every so often. Mostly, they drank beer and played video games in the tack room, while Victor lay in a small airline kennel. There were no other guards.

I was bursting to know about Victor's condition. "How was he doing?"

"Not so good, my dear. I think his wing is broken and he is very weak. He was unconscious most of the time. They have him in a small cage with no food or water."

My head feathers flared. "Did you pick up on which asshole shot him?"

Adele nodded, "It was Billy. He saw the Z-Phone on Victor's back and suspected he could be one of us."

I asked, "I wonder why they didn't just finish him off?"

Adele replied, "They want him alive, at least long enough for their grandfather and a vet to visit this morning. They are going to take blood from him and, if he survives, take him to someplace they call 'The Annex.'"

Gramps frowned and cast his eagle eyes downward.

Adele saw his concern and asked, "What is it, dear?"

I was already punching up the word in my phone's web browser. I had to add the word "Boones" before the search results made sense. I came up with BooneTech, Earl's medical research company, who operated a private satellite facility on their family estate.

Gramps said to me, "Remember that little SNAFU with the county a couple years back where Earl dug that big hole on his property and had all the construction goings on?"

I nodded. "Yeah, some kind of private property rights versus zoning. But he won, and they kept going."

Gramps continued, "I flew by there yesterday, lookin' for Vic, and it was all done. Two-story buildin' with 'BooneTech' sign on it. Big green meadow 'round it and a parkin' lot. It's all within his gated estate."

I looked at a few more results on my phone and summed it up, "According to this, and there ain't much here, BooneTech is a private company that does research to cure various genetic illnesses and cancer. Some humanitarian stuff." I wrinkled my brow. "A private lab for medical research? Why so secretive?

And I can't picture Earl giving two shits about kids, or anyone else, with cancer."

A squawky voice behind me chimed in, "He doesn't!"

I turned to see Simon, my uncle on my mom's side. He was a dapper anthro-magpie with a black head and breast, black pointy beak, and white markings on his glossy black backwings. His arm shoulders were draped with white, soft feathers that ended at his elbows in black-scaled forearms and five-fingered hands. He smiled at his beak corners.

Simon held a PhD in evolutionary genetics and was a research professor at Massachusetts Institution of Technology's Biology Department. In his spare time, he had made it a life goal to determine the origin of our unique transformation abilities.

"Uncle! I didn't expect to see you here!" I spread my arms wide and embraced him.

Gramps hugged him, and politely introduced him to Adele and Zoe. As he finished his greetings, he explained, "I was visiting mom at the hospital and heard about the trouble, so I hightailed it down."

I had to ask, "So what's up with Earl then?"

"A lot. I was going to report on this at the next family conference, but it appears we can't wait that long. BooneTech is doing some strange stuff. I think his people might be on the verge of a major discovery."

Gramps said, "I don't like the sound of that. What kind a' discovery?"

"I'm still figuring it out, but here's what I know. I've been reading Cecil Boones' papers, and he's contacted me a couple of times in recent years. We're scientists of different disciplines, but since we have overlapping interests in anthropology, our paths have crossed. I heard from Kayla last night that the Boones are werewolves, right?"

Gramps responded, "Mhmm, that's affirmative."

Adele excitedly added, "I saw Billy and Hayden transform several times overnight. Once, Hayden morphed to a wolf right in front of Victor and lunged at him, almost scaring the life out of him. Then they laughed and teased. It was terrible."

I shook my head. "Fucking assholes. Clearly, they don't give a shit if he knows what they are. They're gonna kill him for sure."

Simon nodded, "The fact that they can transform makes sense of a lot of things. Looking back with that knowledge, I see that Cecil must be investigating our origins too. He might be closer to the truth than I am though. In one of his papers, he described a cover stone from Mesopotamia that featured five animal deities arranged around a circle. He remarked on how it bore an uncanny resemblance to a cave painting in Central America, believed to predate Aztec culture. There were anthropomorphic depictions on it—animals with human characteristics. There was a bird with hooked beak, an alligator, a canid of some kind, a fish, and a felid."

Gramps interrupted, "Birds and wolves in the mix, eh? Sounds familiar."

Simon nodded again. "Right! The similarity between the art pieces was undeniable, but most of the academic community chalked it up to commonalities in origin myths based upon acute familiarity with key vertebrates in their ecosystems. But it's also interesting what he didn't say in that paper. Like what else was found in the Mesopotamian find, particularly underneath the covering stones."

I replied, "Not sure I follow, Uncle."

Simon put a hand on my shoulder and smiled, "The depictions are of these creatures arranged around a circular object with spokes of energy or light. Now what could that circular thingy be?" As I pondered this, Simon opened something on his phone and swiveled it around to show us. On the screen were four dark, blurry photos of a smooth, black sphere with faint markings. "This is from a friend in Customs who pulled some strings on a Freedom of Information Act request. It was imported about five years ago. The eventual destination was redacted, and the importing organization was a trust front, but it came from Cecil's study site in Syria."

Simon swept a finger to the left on the screen, and a second photo, taken from top down, was much clearer. It depicted inscriptions of the five same creatures Simon had just described, arranged around a circular depression.

Gramps asked, "Ancient Mesopotamians? And Incans?"

Simon lowered his phone. "Pre-Incans, yeah. Peoples with no way to possibly communicate with each other from what we know of their technology. But maybe someone else with superior technology helped them."

I scoffed, "What, like Ancient Aliens? Like that show on the History Channel?"

Simon shrugged, "Yeah, I know it sounds crazy, but maybe. Or maybe a pre-existing civilization lost to time. After all, our industrial revolution is barely more than 200 years old, and that's nothing in the picture of total human history, much less life on Earth. I'm running out of other theories. Besides, we take our ability for granted. The rest of the world would call us werebirds aliens or freaks or demons."

I chuckled, "Yeah, I guess when you put it that way." I turned to Gramps. "Werewolves. Space aliens. It's like we're in a cheesy sci-fi movie. I can't think of a more appropriate bunch of bastards to play the part of the werewolves, though. The Boones are perfect for it."

Simon shook his head. "I've been banging my beak against a genetic brick wall for years. Our critical transformation DNA is nowhere to be found in living birds, nor in the few bits of fossil DNA available. And the complexity of the molecular mechanics behind our ability to transform goes way beyond normal evolutionary genetics. It reminds me of our present-day attempts at genetic engineering, fast-tracked a few hundred years. It's elegant and clean, without the extraneous genetic baggage that natural evolution totes along. Ever ask yourself how humans, a species that's maybe 300,000 years old, end up incorporating DNA from a completely different class of animals that evolved long before the first modern humans? That's the question I asked myself, way back in high school, and that's what drove me to devote my life to figuring us out."

During our conversation, the rest of our extended family and friends trickled in, some thirty-two in all. Kayla, as family secretary, recorded all their names, for our history but also for a headcount so we wouldn't accidentally leave anyone behind.

As high lacy clouds took on the first golden streaks of the approaching sun, Gramps closed the conversation by saying, "Thank ya, Simon. We'll have to continue this later. Can ya stay a few days with us? I'm plannin' a family council meetin', and I want ya there if you can swing it."

Simon nodded, "Definitely. Hoped you'd offer."

Gramps called the family to circle around for a briefing and to hand out assignments. Some would go feral, some as humans or anthros, driving to the site and arriving a few minutes behind myself and Gramps. I would be taking the lead, flying up from the rear of the barn to catch them by surprise while Gramps and Adele faced them from the front.

By 6:50 a.m., those that were going as ferals or anthros had stripped, transformed, and prepared. We circled up and took each other's hands in a final moment of quiet reflection, or prayer in the case of some. Gramps sent us on our way by saying, "For family," and we all solemnly agreed.

I broke away and walked towards the roadway. I couldn't go flying around the countryside in anthro form, so I spread my backwings out wide and mentally focused on becoming my feral form. My whole body shrank, and my arms resorbed into my shoulders as my backwings took over. My shoulders popped with a meaty clunk as the two pairs of arm and backwing humeri, the first bone in those limbs, fused into a single pair of wings. My vision blurred and darkened, and I exhaled loudly, almost losing consciousness from the hastened collapse into my smaller form. My lower body compressed, and I hastily expelled a stream of white droppings to make space. My tail bones multiplied, and my tail feathers compacted, my feral tail being more mobile than my anthro form since I was free of obstructing buttocks. I inhaled a body-sized draft of cool, energizing air, letting it fill my airsacs and extend into my pneumatized bones. I was ready.

I pushed off vigorously and flapped up the highway, crossed the Susquehanna River, and continued up a creek drainage that would hook around to the east side of the Boones Ranch. I stayed low to avoid being seen and followed ever-shrinking drainages in the rising terrain until I was tracing a stream barely more than a wet ditch. Then I poured on the power and charged through the air low and fast, staying tight to the stream bottom that I knew led to the small grove of cottonwood trees next to the Boones' barn.

I swiveled in and out of the trees like a slalom skier in an Olympic competition. Instead of kicking up snow, I kicked up flocks of robins and crows that burst into the air as I whipped past, and then scolded me for the intrusion. I pressed my wings hard, my beak and glottis open to pull in the air to fuel and cool my exertion-heated flight muscles as they propelled me at seventy-five miles per hour through the countryside.

It wasn't long before the paddocks and barn came into view. I dropped my legs for rapid deceleration, flared, and landed quietly on the ground behind the barn next to a manure trailer. I stayed close behind the trailer and peeked to make sure nobody was watching. Leaning forward on my breast, I spread my wings on the ground and started the transformation process back to my anthro form.

My wings pulsed and thickened, then separated into two

pairs of half-formed appendages. The front pair feathered out over the upper half, while the distal portions resorbed their feathers and took on scaly yellow skin and thick digits with long, curved talons. The back pair enlarged to become my massive anthro backwings again. My eagle feet enlarged, and my rump pulsed and thickened into the feather-covered thighs of a man, while my tail feathers lengthened. My head simply grew to the size of a man's, but still wore the beak, feathers, and eyes of an eagle.

As intended, the transformation left me lying low on the ground and out of sight. I had arrived in feral form, so I had no clothing. As usual, my feathers covered my privates just fine, but I had also willed the exposed skin of my feet, forearms, and hands to thicken into heavier scales than I might normally wear in casual company. As usual, I also sported thicker muscles than I did in human form. Stronger, taut, and ready for a fight.

I stepped lightly around the trailer, avoiding the crispy autumn leaves, and squatted down low by a fence to eavesdrop for a moment. Earl Boones spoke, his voice smug and patronizing, as if he were reasoning with a child. It was a practiced manner of speech that he had mastered. He chose polite words, but the tone had just enough condescension that if you were an ally, you might be amused, but if you were an enemy, you'd be irritated and uncertain as to the intent of his words.

Earl's voice continued, "I know you don't see birds, Paul, but I ain't askin' ya to do brain surgery on the thing. Just look him over, give him a shot, or whatever he needs to stay alive, and we'll turn him over to some tree huggers for care. I just, ya know, feel sick that he got hurt on my land, and want to do the right thing."

I slipped around the rear barn door and ducked behind some hay bales stored in the first horse stall I came upon. I peeked between the slats and saw a lanky, thirty-something man with a prominent Adam's apple, high cheekbones, and a faded ball cap that matched his green coveralls. He looked like a veterinarian.

The doctor nodded and drawled through a thick mustache. "Well, okay. Won't hurt to take a look. Can you get him out and hold him for me?"

Next to him was Earl, a pink-skinned man standing five feet tall and all of a hundred and sixty pounds with soft blue eyes and hair as white as my eagle head feathers. His cheekbones were as round and rosy as crabapples, and the soft wrinkles at the corners of his eyes lent a misleading mirth to his appearance.

"Sure!" Earl turned and winked at Billy, "Boy, go get the bird."

Hayden leaned his butt against a table littered with empty beer cans and potato chip bags, the spoils of his all-night guarding session with Billy. He was thick in the arms, and had a square jaw and broad neck. His hands were thick from manual labor, and I guessed he was in his mid-twenties.

Billy had brown hair, blue eyes, and a lanky physique. By his appearance, you could believe he was in his early twenties, although he carried the sneer of a rebellious teenager. He was taller than Earl by almost a foot, but if there was a scrap between the two, I'd have wagered on Earl to win despite being three times Billy's age. He slipped on a pair of leather welding gloves and headed towards an airline kennel.

Paul looked up disapprovingly at the dim bulb and scooted a dusty table closer to the light. In a moment, Billy returned with Victor's limp body in his hands. My eagle eyes surveyed every detail. His beak hung open, his tongue stuck to the roof of his mouth from dryness, and his eyes were half open and stared into nothingness. My fists and beak clenched as I resisted the urge to run right in and kick their asses. But I had to wait until the posse arrived and evened the odds.

"Geez, guys, this hawk's had it. Got a towel or something?"

Earl threw a dusty horse blanket on the table and Billy laid Victor down on his back, still restraining his legs, but Victor was not putting up a fight.

Paul shined a light in Victor's eyes. "His eyes still respond, so he's alive." He went about examining Victor further. "His mouth is really dry. There's an open fracture of his left wing looks like." He manipulated the wing a little, and Victor flinched and squeaked. "Looks like it's busted."

Paul straightened up and shook his head, "He's lost a lot of blood. He's in shock. He's severely dehydrated. He's suffering. I think we should just put him down."

"Aww, ain't that a shame..." Earl said, with a practiced veneer of compassion. "Well, can ya take some blood from him first?"

"I've never drawn blood on a bird. And in his state, I'll be lucky to find a vein for giving him a shot of euthanasia drug, much less take blood. Besides, whaddya want that for?"

Earl rolled his eyes up to the ceiling and leaned back on the heels of his cowboy boots. "Oh, I hear that they can have bird flu, right? We'd want to know about that bein' 'round here, right?"

My fists shook and my plumage rustled as I struggled to contain my desire to bust my fists through Earl's big white smile. *But where was our posse?* Victor gazed emptily beyond the walls into a void none but those close to death probably ever face. Suddenly, his wings stretched out and his legs stiffened, as his neck twisted under his wing and his beak gasped for air. It was like the spasms I'd seen Gramps' rescued birds go through when poisoned, or when they were about to die.

Paul said with glum resignation, "Shit, boys, it might be too late. I think he's checking out now."

Earl put a hand to his mouth to hide a grin. He transitioned to a forced cough. "Well, damn, thanks for try—"

Earl was cut short by an eruption of barking dogs and the skidding of tires on gravel. *Finally!* I stood up and risked another peek through the slats.

The men's heads swiveled towards the front of the barn. Earl barked at Billy. "Get out there and see what's goin' on!" He turned to Hayden and snarled, "Git yer lazy ass out back and guard the door!"

Hayden flinched and shrank back, like a puppy before an Alpha wolf. If he had ears or tail, they would've been tucked in as he turned and stalked in my direction. He passed the stall I was hiding in and exited the back of the barn.

Paul's voice was uncertain. "What's goin' on, Mr. Boones?"

Earl spoke to Paul like an impatient father, "Look, son, if that hawk ain't dead, you make it dead. And get us a blood sample one way or the other."

Paul protested, "But — ?"

Earl's voice dropped to a growl, "Dammit! This ain't none of your beeswax. I didn't put you through school to listen to your lip. You know what we are and what we're capable of. You do as your told... or else!" Earl's cowboy boots clomped across the concrete like the rolling of thunder before a storm, as he snatched an enormous pale cowboy hat off a wall hook and headed to the front door.

As soon as Earl was clear of the room and Paul was focused back on Victor, I crept to the back door. I found muttering to himself and smoking a freshly lit cigarette. He didn't hear a thing as I punched him in the back of the head and sent him reeling against the paddock fence. He fell with a thud into the manure.

It was over quick, but damn it felt good to lay him out. I crept back towards Victor. Paul glanced, probably dismissing me as Hayden from the corner of his vision, but followed with a double-take as he realized an enormous eagle-man was coming at him. He shot his hands upwards in surrender and stumbled backwards with eyes as wide as two fresh eggs in a frying pan.

"Woah now! Don't hurt me! I don't know what's going on, but it has nothing to do with me. I'm just the vet."

I held up my finger to my beak in a shushing motion, and whispered just loud enough for him to hear, "I'm just here for Victor. You let me take him, and there'll be no trouble."

I trotted lightly on my eagle toes to the front wall and peeked through a gap in the sliding door. Billy had a double-barreled shotgun leveled at Gramps' head, who stood a dozen feet away. Gramps had his hands spread in his characteristic calming motion, his green wildlife first-aid kit held in one of them.

Gramps spoke calmly, "Woah, now, just settle down, boy. We know you have Victor in there. Ain't no use denyin' it."

Billy sneered, "I don't know what you're talking about, you senile old man!"

Adele walked around the hood of Gramps' pickup, and Billy's eyes shifted to her for a moment, then back to Gramps.

A kettle of eagles and hawks gathered low overhead, circling and tilting in the wind. An enormous white dropping spattered sloppily on Billy's red ball cap. He cussed and wiped the white streaks from his hand to his pants. But he kept the shotgun aimed at Gramps' face. Two more cars pulled down the driveway, and the barrels of the shotgun rose slightly as Billy's confidence wavered.

But Earl was unfazed. He drew a shiny revolver from a holster under his black denim coat. The oddly large piece in the old man's scrawny hands, much like the oversized cowboy hat on his head, gave the perception that he was trying to compensate for something. But Earl's confident expression tempered the comedy of his appearance. His sharp eyes and wide grin said that he wasn't backing down. He proudly cradled the gun in his hands and grinned ear to ear.

"Howdy, Phil, ya old shitbird! What brings ya ta trespassin' on my property?"

Gramps' white head plumage tussled in the breeze, as his sharp eyes stared Earl down. "You got Victor, a hawk, our kin, in there. We ain't leavin' here without him."

Earl chuckled, "I think you're mistaken."

"Nope. We know ya shot him. We know you're torturin' him for some kinda lame-brained scheme of yours. And now we knows what ya really are. Bunch a' wolffolk, the lot of ya."

Earl's expression brightened, and his bright, straight teeth gleamed. "So... took ya this long t' figure it out, eh? You never were too bright." His ten-gallon hat waggled with his mocking tone.

Gramps took a step closer, and Earl cocked his gun. His smile fell and his blue eyes went sharp and cold. "Don't cause a fuss, Phil. Just get back in yer little truck there and get off ma' land. I won't even call the sheriff on ya."

Two cars eased in behind the gathering crowd of werebirds and their doors clicked open. One was a black SUV with tinted windows. A thirty-something brown-skinned man with a bald head, thick neck, and bulging chest muscles stepped out. It was Marshall George, a friend of Mr. Franklin, who ran his own security service.

Marshall stripped off his tank top, flexed his shoulders and glossy, black plumage erupted. His face elongated into a smooth black beak and his dark eyes grew larger. Massive wings unfurled on his back with a ruffly sound. In a moment, he wore the glorious upper body and head of his Northwest Coast raven heritage.

My cousin Ben was with Marshall, wearing a black leather coat and a Phillies cap on his head. He was firmly built and bore the head and smokey plumage of a golden eagle. His thick, yellow hand-claws gripped a baseball bat up that he rested over one shoulder. Ben's sister, Maureen stood next to him, having flown in as a natural golden eagle but then transformed to her anthro form.

The other vehicle was a red Jeep and a pair of young lady anthro magpies, dressed in blue jeans and tank tops, stepped out. They were Judy and Jade Keller, cousins on my mom's side.

Earl's jaw muscles tightened, and his eyes narrowed. "Just try somethin' stupid. Give me an excuse to blow your fuckin' head off." Earl pointed the barrel of his pistol at the sky. "Or I can play some target practice with your friends up there!"

Gramps shook his head slowly. "You got plenty witnesses here now, invited or not. So, I wouldn't do that."

"Well then, just be good 'lil birds and skedaddle on outta here. We're real busy. Got a mare in difficult labor and you're interfering. So go on and get out before I call the cops."

It was a standoff, and Victor didn't have time for this, so I formulated a new plan. I backed up and said to Paul, "Call for help. Make it sound convincing."

Paul cleared his throat and shouted, "Help! I need help in here!"

It worked like a charm. Billy came trotting in through the front door, straight into a wall of darkness. Before his eyes could adjust, I shut them with my fist. He careened into a support post with a slam and collapsed to the deck unconscious as his shotgun clattered beside him. I shook the sting from my fist slowly and clenched and unclenched my fingers. It stung, even with thicker bird scales on my knuckles, but I was satisfied that his head would hurt worse than my hand.

I picked up the shotgun, checked the chambers, and clicked it back shut. It was loaded with slugs.

Paul had Victor bundled in the horse blanket, and handed him to me, saying, "Look, his cousin was here too, just a few minutes ago."

I cracked my knuckles. "Yeah, Hay's taking a nice little nap out back."

Paul smirked. "Serves him right. I'm Dr. Paul Eckert, by the way. Damn, sure is nice to meet ya! Love watchin' you play."

"Yeah, so did I. Hopefully I can again. How's Victor?"

"He has a name? Oh my god... he's one of you!" Paul's jaw slacked, and he stared back at Victor. "Damn! I should've known. This was all so fishy. He's alive, but just barely. He needs fluids and he's got to be in a lot of pain. I can give him some subcutaneous fluids. I don't know much about birds though."

I gingerly scooped up Victor's bundled form from Paul and said, "It's okay. I appreciate it, but I think we better just get him the hell outta here. And, no offense, but we got our own doc that knows us well." I saw Vic's Z-Phone and harness lying nearby too, so I grabbed them.

Paul agreed, "Okay. Sounds like his best chance. So, I suppose it's true then?"

I cocked my eagle head. "How's that?"

Paul's face widened into a starry-eyed grin. "I saw the game on TV. You really did turn into a bird! It wasn't faked. You must be somethin' like the Boones, only bird instead. And this hawk must be your kin. I'm so fuckin' glad I didn't put him down."

I nodded. "Yeah, that makes two of us. Vic's my brother. Tell ya what, let's keep it our little secret, okay?" I reached out and offered Paul my scaly yellow hand.

Paul shook it eagerly. "Sure. And don't tell no one I helped ya either."

I winked. "You got it."

I peeked around the front door. All of our feral members had landed and transformed into anthro forms. They closed in, tightening around Earl and the doorway. There were no human faces to be seen, only a wall of menacing beaks. The two women, Judy and Jade, were a pair of black-billed magpies. Simon stood with them. Marshall wore the luxurious black ruff and stout bill of a raven. Ben wore the face of a golden eagle. And there were a dozen other hawks, eagles, and corvids staring Earl down.

As I stepped out into the sunshine, I noticed a bead of sweat rolling down the back of Earl's red neck. He heard the gravelly scrape of my feet, and a smile grew on his lips. He spoke to me without looking, "Billy, call the sheriff."

C-click!

The sound of the cocking shotgun close behind Earl's right ear made his face drop like he had had a stroke. He opened his hands and widened his arms, letting the pistol swivel barrel-up on his trigger finger.

"Very good, old man. Now just set that pistol down nice and easy on the ground and kick it away."

Earl's shaky hand dropped the piece to the gravel, and he gave it a pathetic kick.

Gramps stooped down and picked up Earl's pistol, opened the cylinder, and dumped the bullets in the dirt. He smiled at Earl's deflated face and flung the pistol into the woods.

I fumed and nodded my head towards Earl, "Vic's still alive, barely, no thanks to this piece of shit!"

Gramps' face changed, his ocular ridges becoming thicker and more menacing as his hackles lifted. His eagle eyes aimed at Earl's face like two loaded cannons, and he hissed and lunged, snapping his beak just short of the old man's nose. Earl yelped, stumbled backwards, and fell into the gravel as his cowboy hat tumbled off. He quickly propped himself up on his elbows and shuffled hastily backwards until he was against the barn door, prepared to take the fight to the next level.

But Gramps just turned to me and took hold of the bundle with Victor inside. He hurled angry words at Earl, "You hurt one of our own! You fired the first shot!"

Earl chuckled through his wide, white smile. "First shot? Heh, where you been?" He shook his head, "You big chickens are way behind on that score."

Gramps kicked gravel in Earl's face, and his smile disappeared.

Gramps shook his head, "You crossed the line. From now on it's just war with you Boones. That's what you want, so that's what you gonna get."

Earl gave a terse smile. "Bring it on, birdbrain!" He shook his head and growled, as a white snout emerged in his face and his teeth sharpened into canines. He snarled with a deep, half-human voice, "You have no fucking idea what we're capable of."

I wanted to blast a hole through his head. That dark, cold orb of hatred in my forebrain throbbed to life again, and it made me even angrier to realize that Earl had pushed me that far. But then a grin crossed my face as I realized how pathetic he looked. He was disarmed, he was crawling in the dirt, and he was threatened enough to expose his well-guarded secret to us. He was too stupid to know how weak he appeared. I stepped forward. It would have been so easy, and satisfying, to simply pounce on him and choke the grin off his face.

Victor squirmed in Gramps' arms. I took a deep breath and coolly exhaled my rage. Instead of pouncing, I jerked the shotgun towards Earl, and he flinched, with his hands before his face. I smiled and cracked open the breech, dumped the shells on the ground at Earl's feet, and chucked it into the bushes.

"C'mon Gramps. This pile a' shit's not worth it. We got Victor. Let's go."

In a few moments, everyone had piled into cars and departed, or transformed into birds and flown away. But I knew it wasn't over. On our way out of there, I thought of the smug expression on Earl's face. It was an expression laced with temporary fear only. What he had done to Victor was nothing less than outrageous, and he seemed supremely confident that no one could call him to account. We had won this battle, and hopefully Victor would survive, but Earl's bigger plans were likely unscathed.

Chapter 11: Hanging by a Thread

A few hours later, we were at Doc's clinic, and I was in human form, leaning against the front of a veterinary intensive care unit cage. Victor lay within, in feral hawk form, unconscious and motionless except for faint breathing. He was a helpless heap of feathers beset all around by the muted sounds of technology. A fan delivered warm air into the chamber, oxygen hissed out of a tube next to his face, and an intravenous pump churned, sending life-restoring blood and fluids into his parched veins. An oximetry clamp on his wing pulsed out his heartbeat and blood oxygen level. The room smelled of bloody feathers and iodine.

My mother, Lucy, sat next to me on a stool while I pressed myself to the transparent acrylic panel that separated me from Victor and his hyperbaric environment. She was a middle-aged woman of medium build with curly, brown hair touched with gray. She had round cheeks and kind facial features around her chestnut eyes. She gently laid her hand on mine.

I said to her, "I want to touch him, mom, to reassure him. But Doc says we can't right now."

She cupped my hand in hers. "You've done plenty, Phil. You saved his life." She kissed my cheek.

Gramps stood at the door, in human form, engaged in quiet conversation with Dr. Schumacher. Doc wore a crisp, white lab coat over blue medical scrubs and his hair was neatly combed — a stark contrast to the rumpled after-hours look he had upon our last encounter.

Doc spoke, "It's best if he stays in bird form for now. For one thing, a bird's healing potential is better. But also, any transformation would probably use up the last of his energy reserves and kill him. I can't use mitostats to halt transformation either, as they will interfere with rebuilding his red blood cells."

Gramps nodded. "Ya figure four or five days and his anemia will get better?"

"Yes. Birds usually build new red blood cells about that fast."

"How 'bout the wing?"

"The bones were exposed, and the flesh was torn up pretty bad, which makes fracture repair real tricky. As you know from your wildlife work, once those bones dry out, which doesn't take long, they just don't heal. And transformation can't fix dead tissue."

Gramps' eyes moistened. "Are ya sayin' he might not fly again?"

Doc looked down at his clipboard. "Possibly. But, really, we gotta give him a few days to stabilize before we can say anything for sure." He glanced back at Victor. "Dealing with open fractures... that's one condition where he'd probably be better off as a human. Once he has the strength, we could have him switch back to human form. Then an orthopedic surgeon could have a crack at fixing him up. Once they get that necrotic tissue out of there, get his arm put back together, I think his werebird physiology could take care of the rest."

Gramps nodded. "Is there anything we can do to help?"

Doc shook his head slowly, "Not much anyone can do for the moment. He's floating on pain meds, he's got antibiotics, packed red blood cells, and fluids going in... oxygen support... it's all I can do for now until he stabilizes."

"I've seen some of your relations pretty seriously banged up before." Doc shook his head, "It always amazes me how well birdfolk heal. So, take heart. His chances are better than an average bird or person." Doc slid Victor's chart into a wall rack and jerked his head towards the hallway. "Come have a cup of coffee with me."

I suspected there was more than just a cup of coffee going down and I wanted to hear what Doc had to say. I turned to Mom, "You wanna stay and keep watch on Victor for a bit?"

She nodded and smiled, "'Course. Bring me a cup though, would you please?"

"You got it."

I followed Gramps and Doc down the hall towards the back of the building. I smelled the roasted aroma before we reached the break room, the same one we had all conferred in just a few days before. The lights were dimmed, and a white noise generator was playing the sound of a babbling brook. Doc switched it off and poured us each a cup of coffee from a glass pot as we sat down.

He gave a little wink as he set a cup in front of me. "You look like you could use it today."

He was right. It smelled warm and delicious, so I smiled and accepted it.

Gramps curled the cup in his weathered hands and looked expectantly at the doctor's face. "Somethin' else you wanted to say?"

The doctor took a sip and leaned back against the counter in his white lab coat. "Yeah... it's about Lucy. Just want to be sure... she's not Vic's biological mother, right?"

Gramps creased his white, bushy eyebrows together. "No, no. He was adopted."

"That's what I recalled, and I wouldn't ask for clarification, but it's important to know. If she was his mother, I'd ask her to transform to feral form and donate blood. We've got some of his previously donated, packed red blood cells in our blood bank. But it'd be nice to have more on standby. Does he have any living relatives around?"

"Not that we knows of. Real sad. His parents was from Indiana and settled at our place in the spare cabin. They was both shot while out teaching Vic to fly in feral form. Poor kid saw it happen. When we found him, he was hiding in the bushes, watchin' and waitin' for them to get back up. Boy was scared speechless for a couple days. Ripped my heart out, it did. He was just yay high in human form." Gramps held a hand a few feet off the ground. "Such a talent for the art of transformin'. Unusual to see our folk able to control it so young. 'Tween me and my departed Amanda, and Phil's folks, he didn't grow up without love." Gramps smiled at me.

"Yeah, we were inseparable. He's my brother from another mother."

Gramps nodded. "Exactly. Family, so far as we're concerned. It's just moments like this that we're reminded otherwise."

Doc tilted his head. "Totally sure? No relatives hereabouts?"

Gramps said back, "Well, we have hawk kin, but none that are direct relations so far as we know." He took a sip of coffee. "You don't suppose you could use blood from another red-tail, could ya?"

Doc shook his head. "Nice thought, but not from a wild bird. For one thing, studies have shown that avian transfusions, while helpful, don't last long in the recipient. But the bigger concern is what would happen with that blood when he transforms. Bird blood carries DNA, unlike mammalian blood. The hawk's DNA wouldn't contain the same transformation genes, so chances are it wouldn't transform. So..."

"Mmm... he would transform but the blood wouldn't."

"Exactly. It would be like giving a person a big dose of bird blood. The immune system would fight it like an infection. Anaphylactic shock and death, most likely. Not pretty."

"Damn."

Doc placed a hand on Gramps' shoulder. "He's got a good chance, even without the transfusion. We'll know more by tomorrow."

Gramps eyes glistened with concern as he nodded.

Doc leaned closer. "Something else. Phil's lab results are in."

I perked up, "Yeah?"

"You were exposed to an unusual polypeptide that fits the profile of a mitogen. The lab is still determining the exact sequence of amino acids. We should be able to use it as a sort of chemical fingerprint. Since these substances aren't common naturally, if we get suspect samples, and find the same signature, it would be airtight proof of tampering."

"Well, you're in luck. We got a couple cans of Zillion. I got one of 'em in the car here now."

"It won't just prove why you transformed but could identify the guilty party. It's a custom compound, so if we found its match in the Boones' possession, that, and some testimony perhaps, should be enough for a court to find them at fault."

It tightened my gut to think of explaining our abilities to a courtroom and, by extension, the world. But, then, that information was already out and beyond our control. I'd do it if it cleared my name.

Gramps must have been having the same mental gymnastics. He stroked his short white chin scruff and looked at me quizzically.

I responded with a shrug, "Maybe we wouldn't have to sue anyone. Maybe it's enough just to establish the connection and threaten action. Settle it all quietly?"

Gramps nodded. "Yes, sounds like the team wants to keep it quiet too."

"But we'd need to get some of the mitogen from the Boones." I shook my head, "That won't be easy."

Gramps chuckled incredulously, "That's an understatement. Sure as shit those Boones are gonna clam up tight after today. You don't think that vet fella would help us, do ya?"

I shrugged, "I don't think he knows anything. He was surprised that Victor was one of us. Other than knowing what the Boones are, I don't think he's involved any deeper."

Gramps asked, "You suppose he's their version of the Doc here?"

Doc chuckled.

I replied, "Maybe. But my impression was more that he was a regular veterinarian, probably bought and paid for by Earl to care for their horses, not their, uh, more doggish needs."

"Doggish?" asked Doc.

I swallowed some coffee. "They're like us, only they turn into wolves."

Doc scrunched his thick, gray eyebrows. "You're pulling my leg."

"Nope! We just found out about it too."

Simon walked into the room and asked, "How's Victor doing?"

Gramps turned to him, "Not good, but Doc says he's got a fightin' chance."

Doc's face brightened, "Hey there, Simon! Haven't seen you in a long time!"

Simon shook Doc's hand, "Yeah, sorry about that, Doc. It's a long ways to come for a checkup!"

Doc shook his head gently, "Speaking of that, you're

overdue. If you're here for a few days, we need to fix that."

I leaned back in my chair and said, "Hey, Simon, I was just explaining to Doc that we were engineered by ancient aliens, or some damn thing."

Gramps looked sternly at me.

Doc chuckled nervously. "For real? I mean, hey, anything seems possible once you know werebirds and werewolves are real."

Simon nodded, "Well, Phil is oversimplifying it. I might just take ya up on your offer of an exam, and I can go over what I know with ya. I think the Boones might be close to figuring out our origins."

Gramps added, "Accordin' to Adele, they wanted to experiment on Victor. We don't quite knows what though. They was goin' t' take blood and take him to a lab of theirs called 'BooneTech Annex.' You know anything 'bout that?"

Doc shook his head, "I know of BooneTech and what they do, above-board at least. They offer commercial lab services, including molecular diagnostics for a variety of pathogens. Cancer screening too."

Simon chuckled, "I wonder if they skim off some of that blood for their own genomic databases too. Sounds like a lovely way to screen the populace for whatever may be of genetic interest to them."

Doc nodded, "You might be onto something there. Obviously illegal but wouldn't be the first time it's happened. I could file a tip with state department of health if you think it's fishy."

Gramps lowered his voice and forced Doc to lean closer. "Be real careful, Doc. I had both barrels of a shotgun and Earl wavin' a pistol around in my face just a little while ago. The Boones is already greedy and ruthless. I don't know where they'll stop to protect something as important as this."

Gramps looked at me and grumbled, "And you shouldn't be flauntin' that information around so casual, sonny. It sounds crazy and it's nothin' to trifle 'bout. Just think if the press got wind of ya sayin' things like that? Shoot, you got plenty problems enough."

I sheepishly replied, "Sorry sir. You're right. Hard to believe, but that doesn't make it untrue. And even if not true, if the Boones believe in it, they'll fight like hell to protect it."

Gramps added, "Speakin' of the Boones going unhinged, I think one of us should stand guard on Victor, if that's okay, Doc?"

Doc nodded. "Overnight?"

Gramps nodded.

Doc rubbed his chin, "Well, we're not really set up for that normally, but I know I can't say 'no' to you Adlers in a situation like this. Sure, why not?"

I was relieved. Truth is, I couldn't see myself leaving Vic alone until he was conscious, at the very least. "I'll stay out of the way. Even make myself useful if I can."

Gramps wasn't done chastising me, "Sonny, you look as ragged as a spawned-out salmon. You need some sleep. Go grab some shuteye. You can take over from me later tonight on the second shift."

"Aww Gramps, I'm okay—"

Gramps snapped his fingers, "Naw, now, just do as I sez. I got the feeling that events are gonna heat up and you're goin' ta need yer rest. I sure ain't gonna last the night, so it'll have to be you standin' watch in the wee hours. 'Sides, Doc sez ain't nothin' likely to change in the next four or five hours."

Doc nodded his head in agreement.

I rubbed my tense neck muscles. "Don't know if I can possibly sleep, but I could use a jog and a shower and some grub at least."

I stopped and peeked at Victor one more time. He was sleeping soundly still and his closed, feathery eyelids reminded me how sleepy I was too. "Hang in there, buddy. You're gonna make it."

Chapter 12: The Not-So-Silver Bullet

I returned to the clinic and relieved Gramps around eight o'clock. He introduced me to Brook, the overnight veterinary technician, and headed back to his cabin for the night.

Brook stood a stocky five-and-a-half feet tall and had straight black hair that hung down to her waist. She was jovial and told me she welcomed the company, as sometimes she got the "creeps" being alone, particularly in the wee hours of the morning.

Nothing much happened through the midnight hours. I sat on a stool next to Victor most of the night and spoke softly to him as he lay unconscious. I helped with a few chores, as it took my mind off Vic and allowed me to stretch. We locked all the doors and shut down most of the lights, except in the hallway and treatment rooms. I swept the hallway and took out the trash. Brook knew who I was but didn't bother me with a lot of questions about football. I got the impression that she didn't follow the game, which was just fine, as I didn't feel much like talking about it.

I nodded off to sleep a few times while watching Victor. Once, when I woke up from a momentary nap, I saw Victor's eyes moving under his feathery eyelids. He opened one a little bit, and the pupil contracted.

"Hey Vic! Are ya in there?"

Victor swallowed with difficulty and widened his eyes.

"Don't talk now. And don't transform. You're hangin' by a thread, buddy. Doc says to stay in bird form a while, okay?"

Victor seemed to nod his head as his eyes closed again, and he sank back into sleep.

I stood up and stretched my arms to the ceiling. Then I touched my toes a couple of times and walked back into the treatment room.

"I think Victor just woke up for a moment."

Brook was seated at a corner workstation with her feet up on the desk and a book in her hands. A radio softly played country music in the corner. "Oh yeah?"

"Yeah. He seemed to understand me telling him to just lie still and not exert himself." I wasn't sure if she knew what Victor was, or what I was for that matter. Doc wasn't in the habit of divulging that information to others casually. We'd already discussed enough of our lives for me to know that she didn't follow football, so I couldn't be sure if she'd heard anything about my accident at last Sunday's game.

"Good advice. Well, nice to hear he might be improving. He's your pet hawk then?"

Hmm, so she doesn't know. "Yeah, yeah. I'm a falconer. I've had Victor for years. He's my best friend."

"What happened to him?"

"Some asshole shot him."

"Oh no! That's terrible!"

"Yeah. It took a couple of days to find him too. And I think the guy is pretty upset that he may be facing charges, so that's why me and Gramps are here keeping an eye on Victor."

"Oh. Yeah, sounds like a good idea."

"Seems like a slow night."

"Yeah, which is a good thing in this business."

"I bet. But how do you keep yourself awake during these

hours?"

"I read a lot. Sometimes I draw or knit if it's really slow. Sometimes watch a movie on my tablet. I got a book here if you need something..." She picked up a dog-eared paperback from the desk and waved it towards me.

Its title was Werewolf Lover. The cover art depicted a hulking, dark wolfman leaning a frail, young woman back in an ardent kiss. I stifled a laugh as the irony hit me. "Nah, no offense, but it doesn't look like my kind of book."

She giggled, "Fair 'nuff. And, yeah, you're not missing anything. The cover makes promises that the pages don't deliver. Got it for a dime at a garage sale, so no big loss I guess."

I thought about how, just a few days ago, I would've rolled my eyes and dismissed that silly book as pure fiction. But now I wondered if the author was related to the Boones. Who better to write cheesy werewolf smut than an actual werewolf?

My thoughts were interrupted when the music on the radio stopped and a news break came on the air.

Senator Nielson has officially dropped out of the race. He remains in a coma with no improvement in condition expected any time soon. With less than a week to go until election time, Republican Earl Boones may be the de facto winner and go on to the US Senate. When asked about the race, Boones commented, "Too bad about Nielson, but Pennsylvania can do better."

I cursed under my breath. "Can you believe that guy?"

Brook hadn't been paying attention to the broadcast. "Who?"

I smirked and said, "Never mind." I didn't feel like a political discussion.

Brook looked at the clock on the wall. "Ah, good. It's 2 a.m. Time for hourly treatments. Thank God, something to do!" She stood, pulled her long hair back behind her head, and adjusted the scrunchy around her ponytail. She stretched her arms and bent down to touch her pink Crocs and picked a downy feather from her pant leg.

She walked over to her only other patient besides Victor—a pug that was soundly sleeping in a stainless-steel wall cage.

"Need any help?"

"Nah, there's just 'lil Buster here. Then I'll check if Victor needs anything." She turned to the sleeping pug. "How ya doin', Buster? Another hour and I'll take you out for a potty break. Then you can have some yummy treats!"

She opened the barred door, and Buster stood and stretched, then sniffed her hand while wiggling his nubby tail. She checked his belly incision and the fit of his Elizabethan collar, the plastic "radar dish" around his neck that kept him from licking his wounds. She let him lick her hand and rubbed his head, then closed the cage door.

"Looks like a good boy."

Brook spoke while she scribbled some notes on a chart hanging on the cage door. "Yeah, but he was naughty. Ate a sock and had to have surgery. Looks like he's gonna be okay though." She hung the chart back up. "Let's have a look at Victor."

I followed her into the ICU. She turned down the oxygen flow and opened the Plexiglas door to Victor's cage with a gentle hiss. She checked his leg catheter and wing bandage. "Can you lift him up while I change the towel under him?"

"Sure!" I slipped my hands under poor Victor. His eyes opened halfway, and he cocked his head slightly. "Hey, buddy." His legs moved slightly, and his tail lifted as he let out a wet dropping onto the towel under him.

Brook giggled. "Perfect timing! Good boy!" She pulled out the towel and laid it on the floor, then slipped a fresh one under him. "There we go, you can set him back down."

As I set him back down, I couldn't help but notice Victor smiling at me as he closed his eyes again. I don't know if that was a look of satisfaction at relieving himself, if he was happy to see me, or if he was just higher than a kite. But I was glad to see him coming around.

Brook admired the artwork on the towel briefly and remarked, "Mostly white urates, just a touch of green, and clear urine. That's good to see. Means his hydration is improving and his kidneys are working. As soon as he's more awake, he can probably start to eat again."

I barely heard her as I was lost in softly petting Victor's head. I was smiling, but there was a tear in my eye. Brook could probably see that there was more than a simple falconer-bird relationship, but I didn't care. It was the first opportunity I'd had to touch Victor since his rescue.

Brook was reluctant to pull me away, but she looked into my eyes and said, "We should probably let the oxygen build up in the cage again."

"Oh yes, sorry... I just wanted to reassure him that things will be fine." I pulled my hands away. "Probably seems silly."

Brook looped the IV line through a small, gasketed notch on the door and resealed the front of the cage. "No, not at all. I think animals understand our emotions. Even birds. You act calm and gentle with them, and they know you mean well."

I smiled and nodded. I'd been on both sides, having been bird, man, and forms in between. And I'd helped Gramps care for sick eagles and hawks many times. Although I could carry most of my human awareness in my bird forms, sometimes I pushed my humanity away and let my man-brain idle in the background. This happened pretty much automatically when I was intent on hunting and there was no space left for philosophizing about my actions. In that state, basic emotions were there but, more prominently, I felt something akin to invisible fibers, connecting me to creatures outside of myself. I reasoned it was nothing metaphysical, just the result of heightened awareness.

But in that mental state, those connections were faintest when it came to encountering humans, as though they were outside the realm of any interest to an eagle. Yet, I could appreciate that in a situation where there was no escape, and no other source of food or comfort, that connection could still be established, even in a bird that had no human consciousness already. Maybe Victor would have more to say about it later when he pulled through.

I replied to Brook, "Thanks for taking such good care of him. I think you're right. He seems relaxed with you. He appreciates your gentle touch."

Brook tossed the dirty towel into a laundry hamper and walked back to the treatment room. "Does he like women? Would I be able to hold him sometime on the glove and get a picture?"

I chuckled and wondered at what I might be committing Victor to doing. I decided I could bear his wrath if it meant he'd be strong enough to protest. "You bet. He loves women. You two will get on famously I bet."

Brook smiled. "All right! It's a date then."

"Good." I felt an awkward silence coming, so I stepped back. "Well, I'm gonna use the restroom and brew up some more coffee. Would you like a cup?"

"No thanks, I've got some tea in my thermos."

"Good, good." I headed to the bathroom, partly because I needed to, but partly to hide briefly. Brook was an attractive young lady, and I was a happily married guy. I essentially just agreed to a date with her and Victor. I hoped she'd understood that it was just a friendly thing. I didn't want her to get any more serious ideas.

I took my time in the bathroom and read a magazine for a little while. The ventilation fan obscured most noises outside the bathroom except for noisy barking by Buster. I finished up and washed my hands. When I opened the door, I heard scuffling and grunting, so I rushed towards the source of the sound and found Brook on the floor of the treatment room. Buster barked and clawed at the door of his cage, trying to get out to help her.

Brook's mouth was duct-taped, and when I dropped to her side, I discovered that her wrists and ankles were secured with zip ties. In her hands she held a pair of tiny bandage scissors and she was trying, unsuccessfully, to cut her ties. She had managed to work a blindfold off one of her eyes. When she saw me, she pled unintelligibly through her gag. I ripped the tape off her mouth, took the scissors from her hand, and cut her ties.

"You okay?" I asked.

"I'm okay. Some guy jumped me and tied me up! He headed out the back. Didn't take drugs or money. But I saw him stuff Victor in a box!"

Just then we heard tearing cardboard, and the fluttering sound of avian transformation. The assailant shouted, "What the f--?" but the explicative was cut short by the meaty sound of a fist slamming into a face. The scuffling intensified, punctuated by an inhuman screech.

"Victor!" I leapt to my feet and tore off down the hall.

Before I got there, a crash sounded in the breakroom, and a barely human, male voice growled, "Fuckin' freak! Time to die!"

Claws scraped on the floor as the pair of creatures wrestled and tumbled into the hallway. Victor was obvious—a birdlike man covered in white and brown feathers with a sharp yellow beak and large brown eyes. His widely spread hand claws and hawk wings were customary, except that one of his wings hung awkwardly, and had shreds of bandage tape dangling from it.

But I'd never seen the likes of the other creature. It hulked, hunched over, and its muscles pulsated in the throes of transformation. Its muscular body sprouted with black fur, shredding and ripping its clothing into tatters. Its arms were somewhere between those of a man and a beast. It savagely barked and shoved Victor so hard that he slammed his back against the wall.

In the momentary pause, the werewolf ripped off the tattered remains of a black ski mask. The man's half transformed face resembled Hayden, the man I'd punched in the back of the head that morning, but I wasn't sure. His face throbbed and stretched into a wolfish muzzle, his eyes darkened, and white and black fur erupted from his face and head. Canine ears arose and black whiskers punctuated his cheeks.

I wasted no time. My tingling skin erupted with feathers, my shirt and pants exploded, and in a few seconds, I'd taken on my muscular anthro form.

The creature snarled, "Fucking Adlers. I was just here for Victor but fuck it! I'm gonna do what grandpa was too chicken-shit to do and kill ya both!"

I hissed back and shouted, "Good to know I didn't just ruin my clothes for nothing then!"

Before I could get a run at him, he charged me and pounded into my chest, driving me back into the treatment room. We bashed into a wall of shelves and sent them flying, scattering broken bottles and medical supplies everywhere. My head hit the tile floor hard enough that my vision sparkled with stars. I'd been tackled worse, but not by a dog. He had me dead to rights, his jaws closing on my throat, when suddenly he was yanked backwards.

I gathered enough wits to thrust my feet into his belly and send him flying backwards. I rolled over and saw that Victor had him by the tail and was dragging him away. The creature yipped and spun, but Victor's right hand shot straight to its throat, and he buried his two-inch claws up to the hilt. I saw his fingers throb as he lengthened his talons deeper into the beast's flesh.

The werewolf gurgled and pummeled Victor with its fists, as blood bubbled from its nostrils. I struggled to my knees in the broken glass, short on breath, from the dazzling slam to the floor. *Not a bad tackle*, I thought, *for an amateur.*

Brook crawled to the ICU desk and reached for her handbag.

The werewolf snapped its massive jaws at Victor, coughing as its blood sprayed out from around Victor's clenched talons in his neck. Victor raged with narrowed, quivering eyes, like a hawk that was cornered and forced to fight for its life.

Finally, I made it to my feet and stumbled towards them. I grabbed the creature from behind and reefed its arms back into a full nelson. Its eyes bulged and it flailed wildly, desperate for air. The three of us collapsed into a blood-smeared heap on the floor, but the werewolf continued kicking clouds of feathers and shreds of flesh from Victor's belly. Victor finally ran out of gas. He shrieked and crumpled to the floor, leaving me to struggle against the werewolf alone.

The werewolf's front was drenched in blood and his movements weakened by the second. He made a sickening sucking sound in his throat and rallied an unnaturally strong kick with his legs that scooted us through the broken glass on the floor.

I grunted and spat words at the creature as I choked it, "Kill us? Why don't you just die first, asshole?"

My eyes caught movement to the side, and it was Brook, standing ten feet away with a revolver in her shaking hands. She cocked the hammer and aimed.

I shouted, "Brook! Shoot him!"

The werewolf jerked his head around, eyes bloodshot and foam spewing from the corners of its mouth. He tensed and wrenched around in my grasp, my talons raking free of his slippery, blood-soaked fur. I was losing control, and it gave him strength. He managed a gurgling growl of pure hate, as he stared down the muzzle of the pistol. He wasn't going to stop until somebody died.

I screeched, "Now Brook!"

Blam!

My ears rang, and a cloud of bright pink flesh misted my face. I fell over, pulled by the beast's weight as it went limp at last.

Brook collapsed slowly to her butt on the floor, and the gun sagged down between her knees, still clutched in her tremoring hands.

I turned my bloody bird face towards her, and she lifted the pistol again.

"Woah, Brook! It's okay! It's me, Phil! All right?"

She nodded.

"This thing is dead. You did good. Just put the gun down now, okay?"

Her breath spasmed as her face contorted into a sob, and her hands dropped to the floor again.

I pushed the body of the werewolf off me and looked at the carnage. I sat in a puddle of blood, feathers, fur, shattered glass, and brains splattered across the floor and wall. I crawled over to Victor.

"Victor? Victor?" I pleaded for signs of life and he inhaled sharply. Somehow, he had managed to transform back to human form. He was pale, unconscious, and his naked body was smeared in blood. He looked like shit, but he was alive. My eyes misted with grateful tears.

I turned to Brook. "Are ya hurt? Brook?"

"No!" she managed between sobs.

"Hey, you did a good thing. That thing was not gonna stop. It was either him or us. We gotta call Doc in. But whatever you do, don't call 911! We don't want the cops to see this. You understand?"

"W-What was that thing? What are you?"

I sat up and leaned against the wall. "I'm Phil Adler, and I'm a werebird, like most of my kin. And Victor, well, he's one too. This other guy, though, well, you just met your first werewolf. I got a pretty good idea who it is, but it's probably better if I don't tell you. Doc Schumacher knows all about us, which is why he let me stay here tonight. But werewolves... until tonight, none of us had ever seen one, except maybe on the cover of a cheesy novel."

Brook gave a sobby chuckle and smiled as she cried.

I asked quietly, "Who taught you to shoot like that? That was dead on."

Brook tearily replied, "Daddy. He gave me this pistol too. Wanted me to be able to defend myself. But I never shot anyone before. Am I gonna be in trouble?"

I rolled to my knees and started to rise to my feet, "You're gonna be fine. It was self-defense. Him or us. And if this is who I think it is, you did the world a favor. But here's the thing: You can't tell anyone about this. No one. He was just a normal guy that broke in, ok? You understand?"

Brook nodded, "Uh-huh. Okay. But I didn't even use a silver bullet."

"Huh?"

"Isn't that what kills werewolves? A silver bullet?"

I turned my face back towards the dark, hairy carcass. "Yeah, that's what movies say. But I guess it's just bullshit."

Chapter 13: Aftermath

The next morning, I sat in a hospital room with Gramps, Kayla, and Simon, while Victor lay unconscious in bed. An IV pump quietly delivered fluids into a catheter in his right arm. His left arm was bandaged and slung across his chest. We were all in our human forms, as was necessary given the coming and going of nurses and doctors with no knowledge of werefolk.

I finished telling the others my account of what happened while Simon shared donuts and coffee with us.

"After that, things are kind of blurry. Man, I'm amazed at how quickly Doc got there along with Cousin Nancy." Nancy was Doc's special nurse that's privy to knowledge of us werebirds. "It's incredible how he can switch from veterinary to human medicine in less time than it takes me to transform. In just a few minutes, we had Victor on a gurney, had a new IV in his arm, gave him a couple shots, and had him on his way here in an ambulance. They came along with him while Brook and I managed to get Hayden, or whoever that was, onto another gurney and down to the basement out of sight."

Kayla remarked, "That poor girl. She'll never be the same."

Gramps asked, "How big was that wolf?"

"Massive and stronger than a guy that size. Probably 300 pounds? It wasn't easy to move him, even with my werebird strength."

"Hayden, eh?"

"That's who it looked like before transforming all the way. I punched his lights out yesterday. Kind of a sucker punch really since he didn't see me coming. He's a scrapper in human form, but not nearly as big and tough as this werewolf. I checked through his clothing, but he was smart enough not to have any identifying items."

I creased my brows and massaged the dull ache behind my temples. Despite a few hours' sleep yesterday, I felt like I hadn't slept in a week. It was probably the frequent transformations, not to mention the nonstop psychological strain of the past couple of days. I was exhausted, and the problems were piling on faster than I could sort them out.

I sighed with defeat. "Maybe I. I think I… Just… should take a leave of absence…"

Gramps and Kayla looked at me like I'd just smothered a kitten.

Kayla slid a hand over my shoulders and rubbed my neck. "You can't do that. I won't let you do that. It'll end all the things you've worked so hard for."

I shook my head. "Victor almost died. I almost died. I can't keep this up. We've got way bigger issues to deal with than my dreams."

Gramps raised his hand for attention, "Son, you're not alone, ya know. We got this. Together."

I covered my face with my hands, "And that's what worries me! The Boones have always been jerks, but not killers. We might not survive this!" I shook my head in bewilderment. "Why the hell are they doing this anyway?"

Gramps responded, "Don't know. I just don't know. I agree, it's not like them to go quite this far. Everything is sayin' to us that somethin' new is brewin'. Maybe Victor can tells us more, when he's able."

Kayla pulled me into a hug. She spoke to the room, "What's

gonna happen to Hayden, or whoever that is?"

Gramps replied, "Don't know. It's up to Doc. Sure sounds like it was Hayden Boones." He shook his head slightly. "Too young to die, even if he's from a family of thugs. I'll watch the news for any reports of missin' persons, in case the Boones ever dare report him bein' gone. Seems like he would'a had help. But I guess they was long gone?"

"It was a while before we checked out the back, but yeah, I didn't see any cars or burnout marks or anything."

Kayla cocked her head in a birdlike gesture of thought, the only giveaway she might be more than human. "Then the Boones might not know if their plan succeeded."

Simon agreed, "Yeah, true. Might not even know Hayden's missing yet, if he and Billy acted on their own."

Gramps sighed, "Mebbe."

My tired consciousness piqued, and I lifted my head from Kayla's shoulder. "Yeah, that's true. I guess that's an advantage for us."

Simon commented, "If they were willing to kill Victor, and you, and they failed, maybe that'll hold up their plans for a bit. We'd better warn all the families about the Boones and the existence of werewolves. For their own protection. The Boones got lucky when Victor fell into their lap. But they seem desperate. Might start attacking us with even more impunity."

I replied somberly, "Yeah, you might be right. This might be heating up to a bigger action against all of our kind."

Gramps mentioned, "I started callin' up the Council a couple days ago. We've decided on an emergency, top-level, in-person meetin' tomorrow night."

My eyes widened. "I don't think there's ever been an emergency eyes-only meeting of the family councils in my lifetime."

Gramps fiddled with the collar of his shirt. "I 'spect not.

First one I've ever called. But these are concernin' times. I'd like you all to be there."

Kayla and Simon replied affirmatively.

I added, "Of course I'll be there." My lack of sleep was making me edgy and agitated. Conversations like this only added to it. "Man, I feel like I got ants crawling in my head, and I wanna punch something real hard right now. I think I'll go for a run and work out some of this restlessness. You guys okay for a while?"

I used Victor's bathroom to change into my running clothes and then hit the streets. I really wanted to go for a strenuous flight, but that wasn't a good idea in town, of course. As I ran, I mulled over the events of the past few days, trying to figure out what the Boones might be up to and why they attacked me, in particular. Simon's suspicions of some breakthrough sounded more and more plausible. *But why take so many risks? And why are they revealing their long-lived family secrets now too? What do they have to gain? It must be big.*

After running for almost an hour, I arrived back at the hospital and stretched. I found a bench in the shade and made a call to check in with Hatch. He was happy to hear from me. There was nothing new to report on the part of the team or the NFA, but they were all sorry I wasn't going to be in the weekend game.

"Sorry I can't be there. I'm doing everything I can to get this shit wrapped up quick though. And I sure appreciate you stickin' your neck out for me at the meeting. Means a lot."

Hatch asked: *How's your investigation going so far?*

"The Doc says my blood work confirms I was poisoned with a mitogen. We're working on establishing the how and who, but we got some good leads. But... you know Victor? My brother?"

Yeah?

"He was checking a lead and got abducted. We had to go on a rescue mission to get him back and he's banged up really bad. Got him in Sunbury Hospital."

Holy shit, Phil. Goddam. I'm sorry to hear this has gotten so extreme. You need some extra security? I could send some of the boys up there and bust some heads.

I chuckled. "Might come to that. But I think we're good for the moment. Only good thing coming out of this is it's really bringing the family together. We got all our brains and muscle coming out on this."

As you know, Phil, we take care of our own. You just let us know if there's anything we can do to help, okay?

"Thanks, Coach. I really appreciate it."

All right. Catch ya later. Give my best to Kayla.

As I wrapped up the call, I spotted Robert Boones walking towards me. He wore blue jeans and a crisp, white button-up shirt, and carried his leather jacket slung over one shoulder. He tipped his sunglasses to the top of his head.

My shoulders tensed. "Well, look who decided to show up! Kayla called you yesterday and we never heard back."

Robert nodded, "Yeah, I got the message. Sorry about that, but there's been some things popping up."

I put my phone in my pocket and tried not to look too skeptical. "Yeah, what kinds of more important things?"

Robert sat down on a bench across from me. "Well, some rednecks getting their skulls thumped and an old man getting assaulted on private property."

Uh oh, I thought. I tried to replace hostility with a cool, curious expression. "Oh yeah? Any serious injuries?"

Robert smirked. "No, just injured pride."

"Oh really? Who did it?"

"They're saying it was you and your grandfather. Had an

officer up there taking a statement."

"I see. Are you here to arrest me?"

"No, it isn't my case. And I doubt they'll arrest you just yet. But somebody's gonna be calling you and asking some questions, I'm sure. You might want to notify your lawyer."

I nodded.

"Something else. Hayden's mom called me up this morning, looking for him. He was supposed to take her to a medical appointment, but never showed up. I'm kind of partial to his mom, since she's my sister."

I looked down at the ground, trying to figure out how I was going to tell Robert that his nephew was dead. "Uh-huh."

"I told her I'm not really in the business of keeping track of Hay, but I called up Billy, since those two are thick as thieves. He sounded suspiciously clueless. He could have just told me he didn't know, but he was too evasive about his and Hay's whereabouts last night. Made me think the two did something stupid."

I put my hands on the bench and leaned forward, averting my eyes as I started, "Look, Robert, I think I know where Hayden is. He tried to kill Victor last night. It didn't go so well."

Robert's lips stiffened. "I see. Is Victor okay?"

If I'd been in my plumage, my hackles would have elevated threateningly. "I guess Earl left that part out of his report, didn't he? Billy shot Victor. They held him a couple of days in their barn and tortured him for some kind of medical experiment put on by Earl."

Robert's hands gripped the front edge of the bench as he leaned forward and demanded, "The hell you saying? That doesn't make any sense. What's that got to do with Hay?"

"Victor was in critical condition in Doc Schumacher's clinic. Someone in a ski mask tried to take him. I think it was Hayden. Victor transformed and got in a scrap with him. Hayden, or whoever he was, turned into a wolf thing. I was there watching over Victor so then I got in the fight too."

Robert's eyes were red with anger. "Yeah?"

"Hayden was trying to kill us. He even said as much. He nearly had me, but the nurse pulled out a handgun and she… well, she shot him. It was self-defense."

Robert looked ready to explode. He raised his voice, "Why didn't you call the cops? Or me?"

"Honestly, we didn't want to have to explain Victor, werebirds, werewolves, or any of that. He was still in wolf form, so it's not like we could hide what he was. It would have opened up a huge can of worms for everyone. As for not contacting you, I was waiting for you to get in touch with me."

Robert cursed and shook his head. "Fuck!" He stood up and pivoted on one foot, sending a powerful sideways kick into a trash can, causing it to bounce against the wall and spill on the ground. The bang turned the heads of some people exiting the nearby doorway. He paced back to me and shouted, "What the hell possessed you guys to go sneaking around Boonedocks? Are you deranged? Why didn't you tell me?"

I stood up and squared off against him, "I wasn't sure I could trust you!"

Robert met me face to face, ready to fight. He nodded at my words and spat out, "Are all you Adlers so stuck up and distrustful?"

I shouted back, "When it comes to the Boones, you bet! Give me one good reason why I should trust you?"

Robert replied, "Cuz you paid me and I'm a professional!"

I relaxed my hands and dropped my voice, "You're right. Truth is, Victor went on his own. He wanted to help so badly that he risked his own life. Took us most of a day to piece it together ourselves."

I had to pause and control my overwhelming emotions

when it came to the subject of Victor. I swallowed and continued, "It was dumb, but the fool did it for me." I met Robert's stare. "But it wasn't enough for them to torture and nearly kill him. They had to bust into the clinic and try to finish the job. Hayden left us no other choice but to stop him." I lowered my voice, "…dead."

Robert sat down and sank his face into his hands, silent for a moment as he absorbed my story. "I hear ya. My god… what am I supposed to tell his mama?" He was on the verge of tears. He looked back at me and punctuated his words with an open hand, "I gotta see the body. To confirm it's him, okay? I can't go to my sister with this until I know for sure, you understand?"

"Yep, I can take you to him." I nodded and sat back down, as Robert pulled a tissue from his pocket and soaked up the moisture from his eyes and blew his nose. Seeing a Boones express such concern for a loved one sapped all the anger out of me. "Hey, man, for what it's worth, sorry it came to this. We weren't looking for a fight. We didn't want anybody to get killed."

Robert nodded, "He used to be a good kid. A smart kid. I took him camping and fishing a few times. His dad split when he was nine, so I helped his mama out when I could. Then he grew up too much and fell in with Billy. God knows all the stupid shit those two were up to. But everyone that follows that kid comes to no good."

I nodded quietly, giving Robert time to compose himself.

Robert folded up the tissue and spoke, "Speaking of Billy's toadies, I have a solid lead on the boy that served you that Zillion."

I perked up, "Oh yeah? Who was it?"

Robert went on, "I think it's Jimmy Naples. He's Billy's cousin and works at Eastern Distributors. If you're up for it, I could use your help to go interview him. But I want to see

Hayden first."

"Come up with me to the room. I need to change clothes and give Doc a call to arrange a visit, okay?"

As we approached the hospital room, I saw that Victor was moving his head and talking weakly with Kayla. A thrill overtook me, and I jogged the last ten yards to the room, exclaiming, "Victor! Buddy! You're up!"

Victor turned and smiled. His face was pale, and his head wobbled when he tried to lift it off the pillow. I bent down and embraced him. He was fragile and puny compared to the robust anthrohawk that almost kicked my ass a few days prior. I gently released him and placed a hand on his chest. "Damn, it's good to see you alive and awake, but don't overdo it, okay?"

He placed his right hand across mine and replied with a whisper, "It's good to see you too."

I sat down next to him, practically in tears. "Need anything? More of those choice drugs?"

"Nah, nah, man, I'm feelin' gooood. Good drugs. Just real tired."

"Yeah, they say you lost a ton of blood. They pumped you up with some, but gotta give you a chance to make your own too."

Victor nodded.

"So, what the fuck, bro? What happened last night?"

Victor nodded at the door where Robert was standing, and his face clouded with uncertainty.

I smirked, "He's okay. He's my private investigator now." I glanced at Robert. "I trust him." I turned back to Victor, "…so you can too."

Victor nodded with a pale smile on his lips.

I showed Robert in and introduced Simon before I shut and locked the door. I looked at the wall phone, wondering if anyone could listen through the speakerphone on it. I was about to just rip it off the wall, but Robert pressed a red button that read "Privacy," and averted my impatient vandalism.

I sat down on a stool close to Victor as he whispered out his account.

"I was up in those cottonwoods by the barn, listening to Billy argue with Earl on his cellphone. Earl was royally pissed off at him for acting on his own. He didn't go into all the details, but Doc was dead-on about it having something to do with mitogen he delivered for Earl. I didn't think he saw me, and he went back inside. Next thing I know, he's comin' out with a rifle. Turns out, he's a pretty good shot."

Victor's heart monitor beeped faster, and a tear rolled down his cheek. "Man, I didn't think I'd ever see you guys again. That fucker Hayden was terrorizin' me when I was lyin' there near dead. I shit myself when I saw him transform into a werewolf. I thought I was a goner. I don't remember nothin' after that, until the fight last night."

I took Victor's hand in mine and said, "Yeah. He won't be terrorizing anybody anymore."

Victor continued, "Those guys in the barn never shut up. They were talking about needing my blood for their cousin Cecil to do somethin' with. 'Bout all I could gather from those dumbasses' conversations was it had somethin' to do with common ancestry, genetics, some mysterious tech that they knew practically nothing about. The way they talked was crazy, like the morons were planning to take over the world. I don't think they expected me to make it out of there, or they wouldn't have been so careless."

Gramps' eyes were wide. "Adele told us somethin' sim'lar."

Victor's eyes brightened, "I saw her. Tell her I'm mighty grateful. She gave me hope. Kept me goin'."

Gramps choked back tears and a proud grin. "I'll pass it along, son."

Victor lifted a shaky hand to wipe his eyes, but I beat him to it and dabbed the corners of his eyes with a tissue, then used it on my own moist eyes.

Victor asked weakly, "What do you suppose it's all about?"

I glanced at Simon, "Simon thinks it might be about some kind of device they got a few years back. Might be some alien thing."

Simon smiled at Victor and stepped up to the side of the bed. "Real good to see ya alive, cousin."

Victor clasped hands with Simon and replied, "Good to see some brains arrived on the scene."

Simon chuckled, "Well, yeah, you know how smart us corvids are. As to the device, it might be a tool of some kind. It's a little hard to tell from the blurry photos I have of it. But maybe they needed your blood to interact with it somehow."

Simon surveyed the faces gathered around Victor's bed, "What do you think about contacting Cecil? I can do it casually, as though following up on his earlier research inquiries."

Robert looked skeptical. "It would tip them off that you know even more than they think you know already."

Gramps agreed, "Mhmm… What do you think about Cecil, Robert?"

Robert shook his head, "Earl owns him, and all of his work. He's one hundred percent employed by BooneTech. I'd never have thought of him being as ruthless as Earl, but if he's willing to experiment on you guys, all bets are off."

Simon added, "But we don't know if that was his choice. All my communication with him has been cordial, collegial, mutually respectful. In professional circles, he's a bit of a cold fish, and none too social. He's likely to tell you you're wrong to your face, even in public settings, and that rubs egos the wrong way. But he doesn't seem like a monster. I think we have little to lose and, potentially, much to gain, if I reach out to him."

Gramps was convinced, "Mhmm… you're right about not much to lose, as we knows so little. Go ahead, Simon, but be real careful. If you guys decide to meet up, don't go alone. We certainly can't afford to lose ya."

Victor smiled at me, "Maybe we are 'all made of star dust?'" He raised his eyebrows and smiled.

"I don't know. I think the Boones came from Uranus, personally." I glanced at Robert, "Present company excepted."

Robert smirked, and Victor gave a chuckle before wincing and clutching his belly. "Oh! Damn, that asshole kicked the shit out of me." He lifted the bedsheet and peered at his abdomen, which was covered in bandages.

Gramps said, "Doc says you got some busted ribs and bruised liver. Damn lucky you didn't fracture your spleen or, well, let's just be glad that didn't happen."

Kayla asked Simon, "Do you think we should go to the authorities about all this? Maybe the military?"

Simon shook my head emphatically, "No way. Sure as heck, if they get involved, they won't tell us anything. Might 'disappear' us and stick us in a lab."

Gramps added, "Yup. Never been any good when regular people learnt of us. I can only guess that alien stuff mixed into it would make it much worse."

Victor nodded. "Having proof of aliens, not to mention working technology, would completely disrupt the balance of control. Religion. Technology. Politics. All on its head."

Gramps spoke, "Yeah, let's just keep all this to ourselves. Only talk about it in person and private. No emails, no calls if we can help it. 'The very least, folks would think us crazy. At worst, could find ourselves gettin' unwanted attention from media or who knows…"

Victor nodded his head. "Sure would be nice if we could get a crack at that device ourselves."

I looked at Robert. "What do you know about this thing?"

He replied, "Nothing. Well, almost nothing. I've heard rumors around family gatherings. Earl and his foundation supposedly working on figuring out how our werewolf abilities work and enhancing them. But it's all kept secret and, amazingly, they manage to keep it mostly under wraps. I certainly didn't know anything about experiments on birds or people, or anything about an alien thingamajig. What were they doing to you at the Ranch?"

Simon chuckled, "Minor correction. We shouldn't be calling this thing alien. It's extraordinary, but that doesn't mean it's extraterrestrial in origin, or even non-human."

Victor cleared his throat and answered Robert, "Nothing. No food. No water. Just watching me die. I guess it took Earl a couple days to get back from some trip, and he didn't trust anyone else to get involved. They were supposed to take me to some other place too." Victor shivered and pulled the blanket up around his neck. "You guys got to me just in the nick of time."

I patted Victor, "Take it easy, buddy. Just rest, okay?"

"Wait, something else… that conversation I was listening to just before I got shot. Mentioned someone named Jimmy and a job well done. Earl was pissed that they used too much mitogen and it was really expensive."

Robert looked at me with a smile and raised his eyebrows in affirmation.

I squeezed Victor's hand, "Thanks, buddy. We got a lead on Jimmy too. Gonna go pay him a visit in a bit. You done good, brother."

"Thanks, again, for gettin' me outta there. And helping me fight that big son-of-a-bitch. I thought I was a goner. Nobody can whip us two brothers though, eh?"

"Yeah, I'd never seen your eyes like that. Talons locked

around his throat. That was some wild shit. I hope I never piss you off like that."

Victor nodded and his smile faded. His lips tensed and his stare hardened. I nodded back. It was unspoken, but I could tell he didn't like thinking about that fight any more than I did. Hopefully neither of us would ever have to fight so desperately for our lives ever again.

Victor looked up at Robert with knitted eyebrows. "Do you know what those bastards were trying to kill me for?"

Robert gave him a straight expression. "I'm not sure about the whole barn episode. But as for last night, it's simple. You knew too much. I don't know what their endgame is, but it must be huge to go to these lengths."

Victor nodded, "Sorry about Hayden. Don't know if you were close. I really didn't want to kill nobody."

Robert cleared his throat, "Thanks. Phil explained it, and I believe him. It was you or Hayden. I think you were the better man."

Victor nodded wearily and closed his eyes. "All right." He looked at me sleepily and said, "Go easy, bro. Let me know what you find out. I'm just gonna take a nap now if that's all right."

Gramps grunted, "It's the anemia. Makes ya tucker out real fast. We best leave ya be. C'mon, folks, let's give him some peace and quiet."

I squeezed Victor's shoulder. "I'll check back later. I'm taking Robert over to see Hayden, if any of the rest of you want to stretch your legs."

Kayla spoke quietly, "You guys go. I'll stay with Vic."

I leaned over and kissed her. "Thanks, Kayla. Can I bring ya anything?"

"Sure, hon. Bring me a sandwich on your way back."

I filed out into the hallway with Robert, Simon, and Gramps, and in a few moments the four of us exited the hospital into the crisp autumn sunlight. Few words were said as we walked the short distance from the hospital to Doc's clinic. Doc met us in his reception room and led us down to the chilly pathology laboratory in the basement. It smelled of wet fur and blood as we entered the room, an off-putting scent that only increased when Doc pulled the sheet back that covered the beast.

Robert approached with his hand over his mouth, his brown eyes flicking over the contorted half-human, half-canine remains, until his stare came to rest on the cloudy eyes and tight-lipped grimace on Hayden's familiar canine face.

"God damn." Robert teared up. "God fucking dammit... That kid started out a sweet boy." He choked and sobbed as he touched Hayden's cold, lifeless paw. "I don't blame y'all for defending yourselves, but I wish he hadn't ended up this way."

Gramps touched Robert's shoulder, "None of us wished it."

I hesitated to say anything, fearing I'd make an awkward remark and worsen Robert's palpable anguish.

Robert pulled a tissue from his pocket and wiped his face. "I was the one that first taught him about transformation. I can still see his young eyes full of the wonder of nature. He loved camping and tracking game..." Robert inhaled abruptly and stifled another sob. "It's Billy and fucking Earl that did this to him. They just used him up and threw him in harm's way. They're fucking animals. And now the only ones that care are his momma and me."

I finally thought of what to say. I stood close to his side and put a hand on his shoulder. "That's not true. We care too."

Robert straightened up and wiped his eyes again. "There's a lot of bad blood between our families. Lot of bad blood." He looked at me with red, moist eyes. "And this isn't gonna help smooth things any."

I replied, "Probably not. But we gotta figure this out or

Hayden won't be the last." I looked him firmly in the eye and said, "Maybe we can put an end to all this together. Save both our families." I held out my hand.

Robert stood, stunned. He shook my hand slowly and solidly. "You got it. I'll do it for what Hay once was, and how I'll always remember him."

Gramps wiped his eyes and reached out to shake Robert's hand too. "It sure would be good to find common ground between our families. Make Hayden's the last wasted life."

Robert looked back at Hayden's corpse. "Somehow, I have to tell his mother. She's worried sick."

I shook my head, "Listen, I can't tell ya what to do, but I gotta be honest and say that I don't like the idea of telling too many people what's going on. Are ya sure it's a good idea to tell her just yet?"

Robert replied, "I trust her. She's my sister, and she'll respect my safety. And I can't let her suffer and hope for her boy, now that he's never coming home. But you guys did the right thing hiding him here. No one else needs to know."

I nodded. "I understand. You need a minute alone here?"

Robert composed himself and wiped his face again. "No, no. I'll step out in a bit and make the call. But me and you have a date with Jimmy soon, and it's a bit of a drive, so I guess we best wrap this up." He turned to Doc, "Can you keep him cool here for a while? Keep him safe and secret?"

Doc replied, "Yes, this is a safe space. Only a few people have access to it, and I trust them all completely. They all know about the Adlers and won't violate our secrecy here."

Robert nodded, "Let me know if there's any issue. I'll get back to you about arrangements for his remains. By the way, do you have photos, video, or other evidence besides the body?"

Doc responded, "Yep. Video of the break-in and attack. I

had my assistant take some photos of him here on the table and some hair, blood, and saliva samples, which will remain here for now."

Robert nodded again, "Speaking strictly as an investigator, be sure to keep off-site backups of any recorded media. I don't know what those assholes could try next. You might want some extra security on hand for a few days."

Doc nodded, "Obviously we have plenty of DNA too, which should still identify him as a Boones, most likely. The DNA doesn't change during transformation, just what parts are expressed. But I'd still need some DNA from his mother or from personal articles to confirm."

Robert quietly added, "Hmm, I guess family consent for testing barely applies here. He died in a form that no coroner would identify, on the surface at least, as Hayden. But no need to cross-check that, Doc. This is Hayden, all right."

"Okay, good enough." Doc replied. "And, sorry for your loss, detective."

"Take good care of him, Doc. You need anything, let me know."

"Appreciated. He's not leaving my custody until you say so."

Robert turned away abruptly, then paused at the door with his hand on the knob and his shoulders held stiffly. "I need to go have a heart-to-heart with Hay's mom. Can you meet me back at the hospital entrance in an hour or so, Phil?"

"Sure thing. I need to shower up and change clothes anyway."

Robert nodded and slipped out the door, letting it close behind him.

As I turned back to Gramps, he was shaking his head with sad eyes and murmured, "Never thought I'd see the day of a Boones bein' friendly, much less helpful, with us."

"Me neither." I replied.

Chapter 14: Jimmy

I found Victor sleeping when I returned to his room, and Kayla was curled up on the couch snoozing too. I quietly showered and changed clothes, before heading down to the front entrance a little early. The sun warmed my shoulders as I stepped outside the hospital entrance.

The team's publicist, Melanie Allen, had left me a message, so I called her back. The furor over my transformation raged on in social media, sportscasts, and late-night talk shows. There were hundreds of requests for interviews, but I couldn't commit to anything since my future was unsettled. She knew all this, but she also saw an opportunity for positive publicity for the team.

Melanie's voice carried the energy of a marching band on speed. *This is a great opportunity for national publicity! Do you have any idea how many fans are pommeling us with questions? They all want to know how you pulled off that stunt!*

"Oh? Is that so? That's... so... cool!" I said with the enthusiasm of a child forced to eat their broccoli.

Melanie paused a moment and asked more slowly and quietly: *So, just, how did you pull that off? And why is everyone so hush-hush about it?*

I tried to picture her world of fast-paced deal-brokering, celebrity schmoozing, show business, and advertising. It was a reality I would no more understand than her being able to understand my family and our secret transformation powers, or the terror of wrestling with a werewolf. And, at that moment, I had little interest in connecting those worlds. Yet, I had to be nice.

I artificially sweetened my voice, "Well, I can't really say. You know magicians never reveal their methods, right?"

Ohh… yeah, right! So, it was just a stunt? It looked so real!

"Look, Melanie, I'm sure the management will have an official statement soon. And I'm really busy taking care of my family right now, okay?"

A rare, brief silence fell over her. *Okay. But, just between you and me, that was incredible. If it somehow doesn't work out to stay with the team, give me a call. I can put you into show business like that!* She snapped her fingers to punctuate herself.

"Oh, okay. Thanks! Well, gotta go now. Talk later, bye!"

I had to get out of that uncomfortable conversation. I was choking on her excited reference to me leaving the team. All my hopes and lifelong dreams were dismissed with a snap of her fingers. She probably had no clue how painful and callus that was, nor how shallow her ambitions sounded to me. I'd be trading my life's story and incredible abilities for being a sideshow freak, popular one day and shunned the next. *No fucking thanks.*

Just as I hung up, Robert pulled up in his gorgeous blue baby. He waved at me, and I walked over, popped open the passenger door, and climbed in. The black leather interior was on par with the outside and smelled warm and clean.

I remarked, "Did I say it before? This is a damn fine ride!"

"You did! But thanks again!" Robert gunned the engine a couple times to punctuate his words.

I shut the door with a heavy, satisfying thud, and the car prowled down the parking lot. As we turned onto the street, Robert punched the gas and squealed off down the street, a childish grin on his face.

"That's hot!" I exclaimed.

Robert answered, "390 gas-guzzling cubic inches. Better be hot."

I asked, "So, you said the other day that you did the work yourself?"

"I did! Most of it, anyway. I got a mechanic buddy that helped some. Got a couple of other cars I'm working on too."

I was honestly impressed. "Cool hobby to have. Damn, Dupree would love to see this."

"Ben Dupree? Bald Eagles running back, Ben Dupree?" Robert said, incredulously.

"Yeah! He's my main buddy on the team and he loves classic muscle cars."

"Well, bring him over sometime. Or hell, I'll drive it there. He can take it for a spin. I'd love to get a photo of him with her."

"Definitely. We'll do it when he comes out for a barbecue sometime." My thoughts drifted to Ben and the team, and a cold pang of uncertainty pulled at my innards. I knew Ben would still be my friend, even if I couldn't play anymore, but it wouldn't be the same.

Robert, sensing the shadow in my soul, changed the subject, "You look tired. Feel free to take a nap if you want."

I sighed and eased the seat back. "I just might do that. Thanks for setting this up, and for driving too."

"Don't mention it. By the way, I didn't want to confront Jimmy at his mom's, that is, Cousin Jenny's, house. So, I got his work schedule at Eastern. We should be able to catch him alone at the end of his shift, and he'll be more cooperative maybe."

I nodded. "Okay."

Robert continued, "And the less others in the family know about this, the better. You feel up to playing the tough guy?"

I cracked my knuckles, "You might have to hold me back."

Robert smirked, "Don't think that I won't. This isn't official business yet, and I don't need complaints of our encounter coming back to bite me in the ass. But we'll play it up like it's an official investigation and scare the fear of God into him."

"I can do that."

"I just hope Earl and the others haven't prepared him for this. By the way, he's got some troubles of his own. Guess who his father is?"

This time I smirked. "Another worthless Boones?"

Robert was quiet.

I apologized, "I'm sorry. That was a cheap shot. I take it back, man. Who is it?"

He nodded, "Apology accepted, but you're not too wrong. His dad is Bull Boones."

"The one you put away for beating his wife?"

"None other. But that wasn't all he did. I'm pretty sure he beat Jimmy too. Certainly wasn't a positive influence. I think that's why Jenny, his mom, distances herself from the family. That, and Earl disowned her after Bull got put away. Bull is a favorite of Earl's. Billy has his hooks into Jimmy now, and probably pulled strings with his dad to get him the distribution job."

"Distribution?"

Robert replied, "Yeah, he drives delivery trucks to all the stores and bars and such."

"Sounds like a responsible job for a nineteen-year-old." I thought back to the kid who gave me the energy drink. "He seemed like a good kid, the few seconds I met him at least. When I signed a can for him, he had a smile about a mile wide."

"I bet! I haven't spent enough time with him in recent years. But there was a time when a bunch of us Boones got together for a Baldy's game in the old man's private box. Jimmy was there, and he knew everything there was to know about football. He's a big fan."

My anger, which had flared when I thought about this kid poisoning me for laughs, cooled a little as I thought about him having his own pressures and problems. Still, what he did was wrong. He basically poisoned me. And he was a Boones with close ties to the worst of the worst. I still had reason to be justifiably angry and wary.

Robert, as if reading my mind, added, "He's not a werewolf like the rest of us, by the way. He didn't inherit the ability. I imagine not all Adlers have your ability too."

I sighed. "Yep. My folks thought it had skipped me until…"

Robert finished my sentence, "…that day at the zoo!"

I grinned. "Yeah. Man, what a trip that was. And what a disaster."

"Mhmm. Earl still tells that story a lot. He loves to gloat when he gets the better of someone."

My smile was gone. "Fucking asshole. Used my birthday party as an excuse to trigger me to transform and embarrass my family. Now his grandson is pulling the same kind of shit." I looked at Robert sternly. "Why do you Boones use each other like that? And why do you hate us Adlers so much that you would treat each other like garbage just for the chance to fuck with us?" I looked back at the road and muttered under my breath, "It's sick."

An awkward silence filled the car, and nothing else was spoken for the next hour and a half as we drove towards Philadelphia. The highway became busier as we approached the suburbs, and soon we passed down uneven streets of cracked pavement bordered by shabby hundred-year-old Victorian houses, corner bars, and old factories of red brick. We pulled off the main street onto a blacktop drive that wound down through an industrial graveyard of tangled rail lines, dilapidated warehouses, and rows of rusty, graffiti-plastered train cars. At last, Robert parked next to a long white building where trucks were continuously backing in or pulling out.

The building resembled an old factory that had been converted, decades ago, into a warehouse, and it was better maintained than most of the boarded-up buildings around it. It had a long, covered loading dock with a dozen trucks backed up to it, varying from semi-truck trailers down to step vans. Forklifts and men with dollies moved stacks of soda and beer in and out of the various vehicles. Some trucks had logos that matched the sign above the loading dock—a blue swirl surrounding the words EBD with "Eastern Beverage Distributors, Inc." in block type under it.

Robert shut off the engine and turned to me. "Jimmy gets off work in a little bit. He walks up this street to catch a bus to go home. I want you to sit in the back. Keep those sunglasses on and put on the hat that's lying on the seat. That way he won't recognize you right away. I'll tell him I have bad news about Hayden and offer him a ride home. Once he's in here, follow my lead. We want to scare him but not give him a heart attack, understand?"

"Sure." I opened the door, flipped the passenger seat forward, and climbed in the back. I put on the hat and laid back as sleepiness overwhelmed me. I tipped the black fedora forward over my eyes and said, "Wake me up when you see him."

But Robert still had things on his mind. "Ya know, if Earl meant to embarrass you at that birthday party, and I don't doubt he did, it didn't have the effect he wanted. 'Least not with me."

"Yeah?"

"Yeah. Not gonna lie, I thought it was really fuckin' cool!"

I tipped the hat back and saw Robert's wide smile in the rear-view mirror.

Robert continued, "That's why I took up football. I knew I

wasn't cut out for it, but it looked like a good chance to be friends with ya."

I acted like I'd never heard Kayla's gossip, "No kidding?"

"It was the only way my folks would let me get anywhere close to ya. It was tough, growing up with this ability and not being able to share it with anyone my age. At least, nobody outside my family that had more than one brain cell. You would've understood."

"Huh. Yeah, I would have. I can imagine that was tough. I was lucky I had Victor to share it all with. Would've been lonely without him."

Robert chuckled. "I even had this silly fantasy, you know, that made sense to a kid, of sharing our family secret with ya and going on crime-fighting adventures together. You know how it is being a kid. Elders tell you what to do and who to stay away from. Makes you want to do just the opposite and prove 'em wrong."

That struck a chord in me, and I laughed, "You'd have probably fit right in with me and Vic. We were looking for wrongs to right all the time. I guess we learned that from Gramps. One time, we scared the shit out of a guy that was poaching deer on Gramps' land. We perched in the treetops and called out to him every time a breeze blew. He didn't know where it was coming from. And we followed him along, in bird form, high up in the treetops, moaning like ghosts, 'We are the guardians of the forest! The protectors of the deer! Death to poachers! Leave now, or diiiieeeee!'"

Robert leaned over the steering wheel, laughing.

I had to continue the story between chuckles, "By the time we were done... he... he was on a full run, crashing through the brush to get back to his car and get the hell out of there... The guy even dropped his gun and didn't look back... it's mounted over Gramps' fireplace!"

Robert laughed till his face was red and he was forced to

sharply inhale. He choked out, "Just think if a big dark wolf had joined in the chase... barking on his heels?... Probably would've shit his pants!"

We were barely able to breathe from all the laughter. But we were interrupted when a delivery truck pulled up alongside the car. Its pneumatic brakes hissed and then it beeped a backup signal as it reversed up to a loading dock.

Robert studied his mirror to identify the driver, and the mirth faded from his face. "Okay, okay, that's our boy. Pull yourself together. Should be just a few minutes."

I couldn't resist letting out a ghostly moan and triggering Robert to bust into restrained laughter through his clenched lips. "S-s-stop it, now."

"All right, all right!" I hadn't laughed that hard in a while and it was just what I needed.

A minute later, Robert craned his neck to look in his right-side mirror. "Shhh, here he comes." He leaned over and rolled down the passenger window as a lithe young man in a gray hoodie walked past. "Hey, Jimmy. It's your Uncle Robert."

Jimmy stopped and turned. He was thick in the arms and chest, just short of six feet tall, and had a pasty white face, blue eyes, and dark curly hair that barely erupted from where the hoodie hugged his forehead. After the briefest of pauses, he smiled and leaned down with his hands on the car door.

He said with a thick Philadelphia accent, "Hey, Unc! How's it goin'? Man, check out the new ride! One a' your projects?"

Robert nodded, "Yeah, yeah. Look, I got bad news. Your cousin Hayden's not doing so good."

"Oh?" replied Jimmy.

Robert pulled the door release handle, "Yeah. Hop in. I'll give you a ride home and tell you about it."

Jimmy's face was clouded as he opened the door and sat down. He glanced briefly back at me but looked away without serious evaluation.

Robert started the engine and pulled away from the curb.

Jimmy asked, "Who's your friend?"

Robert replied, "Someone you know."

"Really?" Jimmy turned around, smiling. As soon as I pulled off the hat and shades, his smile died, and he jerked his face back around to the front.

I reached forward, locked his door, and placed my hand on his shoulder. "What's the matter, Jimmy? You look nervous."

"Oh-oh! H-hi, Mr. Adler. I'm just... in awe! What a cool thing to be in a car with a football star, ya know?"

"Yeah, well, I know what a huge fan you are and just wanted to have a little chat." I squeezed his shoulder firmly, and he whimpered.

Robert cocked his head at Jimmy. "Your cousin Hayden is dead, Jimmy."

"Dead! Dead? Really? But I just saw..." Jimmy's lips flattened, and he looked away.

"Just saw? What, Jimmy? What did you just see?" Robert pressed.

"Nothin."

"You just saw Hay the other day, didn't you? And now he's dead. You were with him, weren't you? You were in on the plan to fuck up Adler's reputation with mitogen, and then you had to help them cover it up, right?"

I gripped his opposite shoulder and let the weight of both of my big hands press him into the seat. I willed a partial transformation, and my body obeyed, emitting a muffled crunch and the moist, papery sound of stretching flesh in my hands. Jimmy heard the sounds and saw my fingers become yellow eagle claws, and he felt the lethal potential of my black talons resting against the skin of his throat. His breath hastened, and his right hand flailed for the door handle.

I pressed my nose against the back of his head and pushed it outward into the smooth, warm hook of an eagle's beak. I chirped with a threatening grate, "Thanks to you, and that stunt you pulled with those other knuckleheads, I'm losing everything I worked hard for. Everything I ever wanted. Only thing left is revenge."

Robert added, "And you morons revealed our family secret, all for a cheap stunt."

Jimmy stiffened as my talons scraped his skin casually. "We did? How?"

"Grandpa's plenty pissed. Billy blames it on you. You're fresh out of friends that'll stick their necks out for you, Jimmy."

Jimmy took spasmodic breaths and I thought he might pee his pants. "Please, Mr. Adler, don't kill me! I didn't do 'nothin!"

In a squeal of rubber, Robert yanked the car onto a side street and raced down behind a boarded-up building. He slammed on the brakes, and the car skidded to a stop on the loose gravel. He growled as his face extended into a gray, toothy wolf snout.

"What are you doing, Uncle Robert? I-I'm on your side! Get this guy's claws outta—"

I ripped Jimmy's hoodie down, softly clamped my beak against his nape, and hissed hot breath down his neck. Jimmy screamed like a rabbit in the talons of a hawk.

Robert spoke flatly, "You broke the code, Jimmy. You let our secret out. That's never happened in two hundred years. I should tear you apart myself, but I have a problem." He glanced at me and said, "Ease off, Phil. Don't kill him in here. Too messy. 'Sides, maybe he'll do the right thing."

Jimmy's eyes were the size of car headlights. "Yeah, man! I'll do the right thing!"

I relaxed my grip and backed my beak away from his neck

a few inches.

Robert smiled, "Adler and I are trying to clean up this mess. He's willing to keep our secret if we give him the mitogen. That's it. He works out a deal, keeps the case private, and gets to play football again. Nice and easy. You just have to get it for us and keep this whole thing quiet. Understand?"

"Yeah! Yeah, I understand." Jimmy's breathing had slowed to a wheeze, and tears welled up in his eyes, as he realized he might live.

Robert pressed, "So where's it at?"

Jimmy took a tight breath, "It's at Uncle Tommy's. Billy still has some."

Robert nodded, "I see. When can you get it?"

Jimmy sputtered out, "T-tomorrow. S-see, Billy promised me a car. I'm picking it up tomorrow night."

Robert's face showed his disbelief. "A car? Are you jivin' me?"

Jimmy shied away from me further, towards the dash. "No sir! See, there was this drawing at work for someone to go to the game and hand out the new Zillion Energy soda. Billy rigged it so I won. I was just the mule. They loaded one can with it and sealed it back up. I marked it so I'd know which one to give Mr. Adler. I didn't want to. I got no beef with you! But Billy promised to give me a car. I need it so I can start night school 'cross town and still make it to work on time. Honest."

I tilted my beak to the side, feeling disgusted with myself.

Robert's face softened momentarily, then hardened again. "You tellin' me you fucked this man's life up, my friend, a guy who's worked hard his whole life for the reputation he has, for a stupid car? Are you serious?"

Jimmy cried, "They gave me some money too, to help me enroll. Here! I have the receipt right here!" He rummaged in his pocket and pulled out a folded yellow slip.

Robert snatched it and unfurled it. The look on his face told me the truth before his voice confirmed it. "Well, whaddya know… eight credits at Montgomery Heights Community College."

"It's why I took this job. Mom can't afford it. I don't want to be a dumbass working nowhere jobs the rest of my life."

My hands and face shrank back to their human shapes with a fleshy sound. Jimmy stared in scared amazement as my face melted back to something he recognized.

Robert growled and flicked the receipt back into Jimmy's lap. His voice was ominous, and his teeth were bared. "Okay, okay, I believe ya. But you're too good a kid to be mixed up with those lowlifes. You know they're just usin' ya, right? Right? They don't give two craps about you and would be perfectly happy if you ended up like your dad."

Jimmy put the receipt back in his pocket and pulled his hoodie back over his head, his eyes averted down at his knees. With a quiet voice he admitted, "Yes sir. I know. But I couldn't turn it down."

Robert looked away, his teeth concealed, his ears relaxed, and his eyes in pain. I couldn't continue the tough guy routine, but I couldn't just blow off his responsibility for fucking up my life either.

I said with a firm voice, "Listen up, Jimmy. You get me some of that mitogen, and I won't press charges. Not only that…" I paused for effect and said, "I'll take care of all your college tuition and books."

Robert stared at me with his canine ears high, as though he heard a rabbit stir in the weeds. With a soft grumble of shifting bone and sliding flesh, his face melted back to that of his human form, still wearing an expression of shock.

Jimmy wiped his tears from his eyes, "No foolin'?"

I smiled, "No foolin'."

"Nahhh… Why would you do that?" His brows were skeptical, as though he figured he was being set up for another debt he'd regret.

I replied, "I dunno, but from what you and your uncle say, you sound like a good kid, normally. And I like the idea of helping a hard-working guy achieve his dream. Maybe show you that not everyone is out to fuck you over. Take your pick."

Jimmy, wiped his face on his sleeve. "Heh, everyone is out to fuck me over. My dad. Billy. Earl. Probably you guys too."

I shook my head, "Not true. Robert cares about you. I'm betting your mom does too. And if you're willing to help fix this, well, then I think you deserve a second chance. But I don't want you doing this if you think you'll get hurt."

Jimmy answered, "Don't worry about that. Billy thinks he's smart, but he's a dumbass. I only play along to stay on his good side. I was planning on catching a bus up there tomorrow night to pick up the car. But maybe I could catch a ride with you guys tonight instead. Sneak the mitogen out of there."

Robert nodded, "Can do."

I punched the back of the passenger seat triumphantly. "Yes! You're the man! I don't need much."

Robert asked, "Where do they keep it?"

"Last I saw, Billy had a small baggy of it stashed in the barn."

I asked, "Can you tell us where? I might be able to have Gramps' girlfriend fly down and fetch it in the middle of the night. That way, there'll be no fuss and no more risk to you."

Jimmy thought hard for a second. "It was stashed in a cigar box, tucked up high on the outside wall in the tack room." He laughed. "Grandpa thinks we used it all up, but Billy stashed some extra away so he could play jokes on kin, or the Adlers, I guess."

I rolled my eyes. "Nice. Well, the only person that'll miss it, then, is Billy, and he won't risk telling anyone."

Robert grinned and nodded in agreement. "Jimmy, I'll need a statement from you as to where this stuff comes from. That's gonna be our insurance. Gives us the option to go legal against Billy and Earl if we fail to get the mitogen. By the way, Jimmy, once you get that car from Billy, don't hang out with him anymore. You know he's trouble, but you don't know the half of it. You will die if you keep runnin' around with him, or your grandpa."

"Just like Hayden, eh?"

"Mhmm." Robert nodded.

I added, "Look, you fucked up taking a shortcut and screwing me over, but I don't think you really knew what you were getting tangled up in. I know it looks like I'm just helping you because you're helping me, but that's not all it is. You got guts, and I want to help you help yourself." I pulled out a business card. "This is my cell number on here. You call me every week, you understand? I want to hear how college is going. And you show me your midterm grades. If you're doing well, I'll pull some strings and get you a better job with the team. Understand?"

Jimmy took the slip of paper with a grin. "I don't know what to say. I never imagined a guy like you would give a shit about Philly lowlife like me."

I responded soberly, "That sounds like your friends Billy and Hay talking."

Robert added, "Or your old man."

I went on, "Don't listen to that shit. They're the lowlifes. They want to keep you down, under control. But you can make your own future you can be proud of. Look at your Uncle Robert here, and what a smart, upstanding man he is."

Robert chuckled.

I went on, "I'm willing to help if you keep on the straight

and level with me."

Jimmy nodded, "Thank you, Mr. Adler. I will! You'll see!"

Robert stared hard at Jimmy. "I hope so. Please don't end up like Hay. Don't. End up. Like Hay. Promise me."

Jimmy was serious. "I won't, I promise. What happened to him anyway?"

I exchanged glances with Robert, and he shook his head the slightest amount. He simply said, "He tried to kill Phil's brother, probably cuz he knew too much, and got himself shot and killed instead."

"Holy shit!" Jimmy looked out the windshield, his eyes wide. "This was supposed to be just a little joke."

"Nobody's laughing now, Jimmy. You help us out, though, and you'll be off the hook. There'll be no reason for either side to involve you anymore."

"I thought you said grandpa was mad. Is he gonna kill me?"

Robert smirked. "Well, I may have exaggerated a bit. He's pissed off at Billy. Billy can't keep a secret for shit. Word is he's been bragging it up. It's just as well if you're on our side. It could turn into a manhunt for Hayden. You got alibis for the past few days?"

"Yeah. Just work and home. I worked all weekend and Monday too. We spiked the drink last Friday night. That's the last time I saw Billy and Hay."

"Okay. Let's go get something to eat and write up that statement."

As we drove back up the street, it sank in just how lucky I'd been. I grew up embraced in a loving family that supported each member, regardless of their talents or choices. There was no reason to stab each other in the back, use each other, or break the law to get what we wanted or needed. We Adlers weren't insanely wealthy, but we'd always stuck together, and were careful enough with our affairs that we'd always had what we needed. More than that, we'd been wealthy in character and trust. I never felt insecure about who I was or who I could rely on.

When I looked at Jimmy, I felt sympathy, not just for him, but for the other Boones that were getting ruined by the likes of Earl and his self-interested henchmen. I hoped I was making the right play. It felt right. Just that morning, I wouldn't have bet anything on a Boones, but by day's end, I was practically adopting one.

Chapter 15: Not a Night for Wolves or Owls

The sun was setting as we arrived back in Sunbury. Robert dropped me off back at the hospital before taking Jimmy over to Boonedocks. Gramps and Adele were chatting with Kayla when I arrived at the room. Victor was sleeping quietly, and though just six or seven hours had gone by, he looked pinker and stronger to me.

I told the others all about the meeting with Jimmy and his promise to help us. When I arrived at the part about the stash of mitogen in the Boones' barn, Adele brightened up.

Adele enthusiastically volunteered, "I will go tonight and get it for you!"

Gramps shook his head. "Sweetie… you're tough as talons, and stealthy as a ghost. But it's too dangerous!"

Adele patted Gramps' chest feathers in firm protest. "Non, non, dear. I am happy t'go. I had no problem getting in and out the other night. And if we wait until the middle of the night, they will not be expecting it."

Gramps grumbled at me, "Couldn't me and you just sneak in there tomorrow and get it? Or maybe Robert?"

Seeing the loving concern in Gramps' eyes was not something I was prepared for. I reviewed the options in my head. Was getting the mitogen worth life and limb? Risking my own life was an easy choice, but could I really ask others to do the same?

Adele reached out a delicate hand and touched my shoulder. I looked into her lovely dark eyes and soft face as she tilted her head in understanding. "My dear, I see it in your eyes. It's difficult sending others to do something dangerous. But I know I can do this. I'm quieter than a mouse, so they won't know I'm there. And nobody else needs to get hurt. I insist that you let me do this for you."

Gramps protested, "Addy..."

She put a finger to his beak, as if to hush him, "Non! This young man made a strong impression on Phil. Enough to open his heart to him. I am going to do this for him."

I blinked and swallowed, pride and thankfulness leaving me speechless. I could see Gramps was doing likewise. He shook his head with tearful eyes and kissed her.

I nodded in gratitude. "It's hard to say no to that. But I insist that Zoe goes along and waits outside in the trees while you go in and get it. Gramps and I can take ya there too, and park at the Nature Preserve, ready to help if there's a problem."

Gramps looked worried for his lovely mate. "If there's any trouble, love, just get the hell out of there. Don't take anyone on. You call the cavalry, okay? Promise me, or we won't do this."

"I will." They snuggled together, and Gramps held her tight.

We decided we'd jump to it at 2 a.m. Gramps and Adele went back to the cabin to rest up, and Kayla and I decided to follow suit and have a few hours alone. We called up Marshall George and he sent his brother Emerson down to watch over Victor while we took a break.

Kayla and I needed the time together. We walked a few blocks downtown and had dinner, then checked into a hotel so we could stay close to Victor. The air was fresh, the food was good, Victor was on the mend, and all the pieces were falling into place for my exoneration. This combination, along with sharing the good times with my mate, put me in a stellar mood. Kayla was feeling it too and when we returned to the hotel, it wasn't long before things became intimate. We transformed to our anthro-eagle selves and made love like a pair of springtime mates, then snuggled in bed and fell into deep, restoring sleep.

Though I only managed four hours of sleep, it felt like eight. I slipped out quietly and left Kayla sleeping while I met Gramps, Adele, and Zoe outside. Low clouds had rolled in, so that once we left town, the night was ink black, except for slivers of gray fog that flashed through our headlight beams as we drove the meandering highway along the Susquehanna River. We swung into the dirt lot of the Catawissa Creek Nature Preserve at 2:30 a.m., and our headlights slashed across the dazzled stares of a family of Canada geese grazing in the dark.

Victor's truck was still parked at the edge of the lot. He had told Gramps where he hid a key so we could drive it back to Gramps' place. Gramps shut off his lights, and we all got out to stretch and prepare.

Adele and Zoe needed privacy to strip and transform, so Gramps and I distracted ourselves with Victor's truck. I reached under the left side of the back bumper, found the magnetic hide-a-key box and pulled it out. I unlocked and opened the door, and the musty smell of feathers and last summer's road dust met my nostrils. I fired up the engine to make sure it was good to go. When we glanced back, the two women were already in their graceful feral barn owl forms. They floated silently up from the ground and landed on a nearby picnic table.

Gramps pet Adele's head, and she rubbed her beak softly against his hand. Gramps' voice was laden with worry, "Please don't take any unnecess'ry risks, okay? Just git the stuff and git back, ya hear?"

Adele's white throat feathers vibrated as she emitted a warbling churr of affection. "I promise. Can you and Phil attach our Z-Phones?"

I fetched the harnesses and phones from the dash of Gramps' truck, and in a couple of minutes, we had them Velcroed in place and switched on. Gramps kissed Adele on the beak, and Zoe giggled, "Don't you two paint a pretty picture! Now let's get going before my heart breaks watching you."

Zoe lifted away and fired off a grating barn owl screech. Adele followed, and the two of them disappeared like white specters into the black gloom. My heart raced. I wanted to go too, but the night was too dark for eagle eyes, and besides, my wings would be too noisy for an operation requiring stealth. But knowing this hardly suppressed my urge to follow.

Gramps and I repositioned the vehicles closer to the road and ready to rush to the rescue if needed. I climbed back into Gramps' truck to keep him company. We spoke quietly in the light from the dashboard, listening to a late night program of soft jazz, and Gramps shared coffee from a thermos. I took some black and found it warm and nourishing.

Gramps guffawed, "Looks like my cawfee has won ya over, eh?"

I nodded. "This stuff ain't bad. Probably habit-forming."

Gramps chuckled. "Oh definitely. With any luck, if you drink it, you'll live as long as me."

A barred owl hooted gently in the distance. I pulled out my smartphone and checked the position of the two women. "They're almost there."

The next fifteen minutes were sheer torture. We watched them arrive near the barn, and could even tell that they split up, but their locations refused to change. Then Adele's location dot disappeared.

"Oh, god!" Gramps started the truck. "Oh, Jesus, no!"

"Hang on! Call her up! I'll call Zoe."

I didn't have to. My phone buzzed and Zoe's raspy owl

voice whispered to me when I answered: *Adele's in trouble! It was a trap!*

My heart sank. "Fuck! Is she okay?"

Meanwhile, Gramps fumbled with his phone, his hands shaking and his eyes tearing up, "She's not answerin'! My sweet Addy ain't answerin'!"

I exclaimed, "Gramps, she can't! She's been caught! They set a trap!"

Zoe's voice came back quietly: *They tied her up and took her in a white pickup. They're driving out now. I'll follow!*

I looked at Gramps as I replied, "You do that, Zoe. I'll be able to follow you, and we can try to head them off, okay? Fly as hard as you can!"

Gramps cried, "Shoulda never agreed to this. Goddammit! I'll never forgive m'self."

I grabbed his hands, "Gramps! Keep your cool! Zoe's on her trail. We can follow her, at least as long as Zoe's wings hold out. But you know as well as I where they'll take her."

"BooneTech."

"Definitely." I pointed east up the road. "And this bridge is on the shortest path between Boonedocks and BooneTech. They're gonna drive right past us!"

"You git in Victor's rig! Let's make us a roadblock!"

I was already bailing out the passenger door. "I'll take the right side so I can hit 'em with the patrol light. You take the left. We'll get right up at the end of the bridge so there's nowhere for them to go but through us. Got it?"

Gramps nodded. "Got it!"

I jumped into Victor's truck and fired it up. In seconds, we were throwing gravel as we tore out of the lot. It took less than a minute to get into position. But the roadway was so wide that even if we parked end to end, we couldn't cover the entire width of the bridge. I checked Zoe's position, and she was only a quarter mile away, in the town of Catawissa on the other side of the bridge. I put my head out the window and looked towards the lights of town. I heard the distant rumble of Billy's Ford Raptor as it rolled down Main Street. A dog barked at the noise.

I shouted over to Gramps, "Here they come! Be ready to pull forward or back if we need to pinch them off or haul ass after them, okay? If they get by, we don't wanna lose 'em!" I snapped on the patrol light and aimed it towards the approaching vehicle.

The Raptor gunned its engine as it left the lower speed limit of town and started across the Susquehanna River bridge. Gramps loaded up his double barrel shotgun and aimed it towards the approaching headlights. At first the truck sped up, but then they slowed down, as though trying to ascertain why trucks were blocking the road. Then I heard shouted curses, and the truck swerved abruptly. The tires squealed, and they slid in a tight one-eighty and sped back towards town.

"Fuck! C'mon Gramps, after 'em!"

Gramps and I spun around and took off after Billy's truck. I checked my phone, and saw that Zoe was holding position up ahead. I shouted into my phone, "Zoe! Are you okay?"

She was panting: *I… I'm okay! I'm at the… end of the bridge!*

"Jump in with Gramps! You can run the shotgun."

As I approached town, I saw a pale owl sitting on the rail. I slowed down and turned on my emergency flashers to get Gramps' attention. He saw Zoe too, and swerved over to let her hop in. I hit the gas to get after Billy.

Fortunately, Catawissa was a sleepy town at three in the morning, but Billy's blaring truck was waking it up. He sped up an empty Main Street, and at the flashing yellow signal of Fourth and Main, he squealed hard left. I shouted to my phone to call Gramps, and in a moment, I heard Zoe answer. I pressed the speakerphone button.

I shouted over the motor, "Tell Gramps to turn around and head to Bloomsburg. Billy's heading for Bloomsburg! You can try to head him off there. Maybe on Route Eleven before he gets to BooneTech! I'll stay on his ass!"

She replied with *Copy that!* And I overheard her relaying the message to Gramps.

In my rearview mirror, Gramps' headlights slowed down and turned off on a side street. Billy's nimble truck sped off ahead of me, doing ninety, and I was having trouble keeping up in the larger, stiffer, slower state truck. As the distance to Billy's taillights grew, I reassured myself with the knowledge that there was only one destination that made sense.

Zoe shouted: *Listen, Phil, there's more! Before they grabbed her, she told me that Jimmy was in there. He was beaten senseless. She couldn't hear a heartbeat so he might be dead.*

If a barn owl couldn't hear a heartbeat, even from across the room, there probably wouldn't be one to hear. I shook my head and pressed the gas pedal to the floor. "Copy that! Let's get these fuckers!"

Route 487 wound up and across a highland of mixed farmlands and residences, and then made a descending left arc back down towards the Susquehanna River. Billy's taillights had become a pair of red dots that I only saw fleetingly when the road straightened out between forested curves. As I dropped down towards the Bloomsburg Bridge, my heart sank as I saw that he was a half a mile ahead of me, already approaching the other side. His truck's taillights brightened and swerved hard to the left.

I shouted into my phone, "He's taking the Fort McClure Road around town. I might lose him! It's up to you now!"

As Zoe shouted, I heard Gramps' engine noisily revving in the background: *We're almost in position!*

I nearly left the road as I skidded hard onto the smaller side street. The road was mostly straight, but trees close along the edges prevented me from getting more than brief glimpses of Billy's taillights, and pretty soon, I didn't see them at all. But I pressed on. I didn't know the roads as well as Billy, but I knew where he was heading. Gramps would slow him down at least.

At last, I came out to the other side, and burned rubber in a hard left turn onto the state highway. I blazed off with the throttle wide open, and in seconds I saw the familiar taillights again, glowing bright as Billy slowed down, his headlights illuminating Gramps' pickup truck parked across the right lane. Then the taillights went dim, and Billy swerved to the left to speed past Gramps.

Gramps peered down his shotgun barrels, aiming low, and a puff of smoke burst out. Billy's truck didn't slow, and I saw puffs of smoke shoot out from the passenger window as they roared past Gramps. By that point, I was only a few hundred feet behind Billy, and I saw that Gramps was okay. He was backing up to get out of my way as I streaked past doing eighty miles per hour.

Gramps had scored a hit! Billy's right back tire smoked and sparked, while the truck shuddered. It slowed Billy down enough that I also had to slow down, and I eased up behind his back bumper. I swiveled the patrol light into Billy's side mirror, and it illuminated the entire cab of his truck. Adele was stuffed in between Billy and a large man in the passenger seat. She was in anthro-owl form, and she swiveled her head back to look at me with eyes full of terror.

The passenger turned too and leaned out of the window. I recognized their square jaw and beefy head. It was Bull Boones. His face bulged, and pointed canine ears rose up from the sides of his head. His forehead shrank, and a muzzle tipped with a black nasal pad emerged in place of his nose. Thick, gray fur erupted from the sides and top of his head, while white fur covered his wolfish snout. His body bulged with muscles and fur that shredded his clothing.

Bull swung a pistol in my direction and fired. My windshield cracked and the back glass shattered. I ducked and swerved but stayed on his tail. The muzzle flashed again but the bullet missed.

Then something incredible happened: Adele lifted up and lunged at Bull, biting him hard in the ass. He hollered and waved his arms as the truck lurched to the left, and his pistol tumbled from his grip onto the right side of the road.

Bull reached inside, grabbed Adele by the throat, and ripped her face from his flank. He punched her in the head several times until she disappeared from view.

I screamed, "Stop it, you fucker!" and sped up. The bull bars on the front of Victor's truck came in handy. I rammed them into the back of Billy's truck, and it swerved abruptly to the left into the oncoming lane, narrowly missing another driver who blared their horn in protest. I swerved to the right to give the car a wide berth, and Billy took advantage of the brief interruption to accelerate. Despite sparks and shreds of tire spewing from his disintegrating right rear wheel, he managed to widen the gap between us.

My heart dropped when I saw the approaching lights of the Boones Estate entrance. Billy slammed on his brakes and abruptly turned left, nearly wiping out the gate house. The guards raised the gate, and Billy limped his truck through the entrance.

I was about to swerve in and through the gate, but the guards were already leveling pistols. I knew I couldn't win this fight, so I mashed the pedal and sped on past. I shouted to Zoe, "Don't stop, it's no use. The guards are ready to shoot. I'm… I'm so fucking sorry…" I broke down crying, "I lost 'em!"

Zoe's voice came back: *I'm going after her!*

I yelled back, "No, it's too dangerous! They know you now!" But I knew it was too late.

Gramps yelled: *Stop, Zoe! Get back here!*

"Gramps! Stop up ahead!"

I pulled over to the side of the road and got out as Gramps eased in behind me. I ran back, opened his driver's door, and pulled him into a tight hug. He sobbed in my arms and cried out, as though someone had ripped out his heart.

I cried back to him, "I'm so sorry, Gramps. I'm so, so sorry."

He replied in a muffled voice, "I knows ya tried, grandson. I knows. And she was so stubborn on doin' this. Oh, my sweet Addy... we can't... we can't let her die in there. We gots to bust her out."

"We will, Gramps! We'll call up the posse and go to war." I wiped my eyes and eased back a bit to look Gramps in the eyes. "I know it's tough, but we gotta hold ourselves together just a bit longer. Jimmy needs our help now too. I'm gonna get Robert on the line and see what to do."

Gramps nodded as I pulled out my phone to dial Robert. "I'm driving back to where Bull dropped his gun. I think you should wait here for Zoe to come back."

For the first time I'd ever seen, Gramps had a dejected, defeated countenance. His features drooped and he looked down at the ground as though lost. It broke my heart more than the threat of losing my career. At that moment, I didn't give a fuck about mitogen or playing football again.

Robert's voice was gravelly and weak as he answered.

I hopped back in Victor's truck. "Sorry to wake you up, Robert, but we got us a major situation here..." I proceeded to tell him the night's events as I drove back up the highway.

Robert was emphatic: *Go back and get that gun before security does, or worse, Bull. If you got a plastic bag, use that to cover your hand, pick it up, wrap it in the bag. Don't touch it with your bare fingers or anything likely to smear the prints, ya got me?*

"Okay, I'm almost there. Rolling past the gatehouse now."

I maintained the speed limit and drove smoothly past, as though minding my own business, while guards picked up pieces of tire rubber and scrubbed off white paint that had adhered to the gate pillars.

"Fuck, they probably saw me. There's no traffic out here, so I'm sure I stuck out like a sore thumb."

Robert rustled around, throwing clothes on and grabbing keys. *Just get the gun, quick as you can, pick it up with a stick in the barrel if you have to, and toss it on the floor. And get the fuck outta there. Meet me up at the Boonedocks, okay? I'm headin' out right now!*

"See ya there!"

I found the tire marks where Billy's truck swerved and Bull dropped his pistol. Luckily, there was a fast-food bag lying on the floor of Vic's truck, so I used that to delicately pick it up, wrap it, and set it on the floor. I sped out of there just as headlights were approaching from the direction of the Boones Estate.

I checked Zoe's location. It looked like she was back at the spot where I'd left Gramps. I called him to check. "Gramps! I got ahold of Robert. He's on his way. We gotta get back up to the Ranch. You got Zoe with you now?"

Gramps sounded like a man with no hope. *Yeah, she's back.*

"Did she see where they took Adele?"

Yeah. They took her to that Annex place. Took her in through a loadin' dock on the side.

"Let me talk to Zoe, Gramps. Head up to the Boonedocks, but don't go back past the Estate. It's crawling with guards now."

Okay, grandson. Here's Zoe.

Zoe sounded like she was in anthro-owl form now, her voice less grating than in feral form. *Hello?*

"I'm so sorry, Zoe."

Zoe sounded congested from crying: *She did it to herself. She insisted on this. It's not your fault, Phil.*

I replied, "We're gonna go full out commando and get her back, okay? She's not gonna die in there. Do me a favor and keep an eye on Gramps. I've never seen him so shattered."

Zoe replied glumly: *He loves my stupid sister so much, yes. His heart is broken. So is mine.*

I groped mentally for the words that would motivate her and Gramps back to the path of hope. "Listen, I'm counting on you two. And so is Adele. I know it's tough to see it, but we're gonna win this. We're gonna get her back and totally fuck Earl in the process. I think that everything we do in the next few days is gonna affect the lives of our people for generations to come. So, stay strong, stay focused, and be careful, okay? I love you both!"

Zoe solemnly replied: *You sound like my sister. She is always so optimistic. She finds the moonlight behind every dark cloud. You are a kind soul, Phil.*

I smiled through my tears. "Meet me up at the Boonedocks as soon as you can."

Copy that.

In a few minutes, we were parked by the gate to the Boones Ranch. It took another twenty before we heard the far-off revving of Robert's AMC, and saw his headlights come up the rise towards us. He downshifted as he rumbled up close to us. He waved his hand for us to follow him down the driveway.

Gramps, Zoe, and I waited by the barn, in human form, while Robert went to the house and retrieved Tommy. Tommy was a moderately overweight man in his late forties, with a bald head rimmed by trimmed black hair on the sides. He was wearing a flannel gown and slippers as he walked towards us with Robert.

Robert introduced us and simply said that we were

concerned about our friend that went missing after being dropped off there.

Robert slid the door open and let Tommy walk in first. It didn't take long to find Jimmy. He was face down in the soiled shavings of a horse stall, not moving. I knelt down with Robert and rolled Jimmy over. His face was completely rearranged with cuts and bruises and caked in clotted blood. Zoe inhaled sharply, and Gramps grimaced as they both turned away.

I tremored with disgust and grief while Robert calmly felt for a pulse. "No pulse. He's dead." He pulled out his phone and dialed.

Tommy exclaimed, "Dear god! What the hell has Billy done this time?"

Robert guffawed. "Whatever the fuck you let Bull and Earl teach him to do." Robert's attention jerked back to his phone as a voice crackled in the earpiece. "Yeah, this is Detective Robert Boones, Columbia County. We got a homicide at 1428 River Ridge Road in Catawissa. Need a coroner and homicide duty officers out here now!"

Over the following hour, more police arrived to assist, and Robert interviewed everyone professionally. Robert contacted his sister, Jenny, and gave her the awful news. The team also documented and confiscated the cigar box resting on a ledge above the table in the tack room, at Robert's specific direction. I watched as they photographed the tiny Ziploc baggy containing a white granular substance within. I provided the gun I'd retrieved from the shoulder of the road too.

Robert encouraged us to tell the full truth, including the details about our transformation abilities. It made it easier that we were speaking with Robert and that most of the world already suspected something unusual was up with me and my family. Robert assured me that it would be some time, and possibly never, that the public would catch wind of our involvement. I tried to let his words reassure and relax me but, truth was, I couldn't relax…we had a battle to plan.

Chapter 16: Madness

Autumn leaves whistled past the busted glass of the abandoned Tastee Freeze. It was at the terminus of a dead-end frontage road that was orphaned when a freeway was pushed through fifty years prior. Brambles and vines had grown up in a green tidal wave, washing over the roof and down the front of the building. Their dried tendrels poked into the dark interior around the edges of boarded-up windows. A faded image of a grinning, freckled boy holding a giant ice cream cone watched us from above the battered, grafitti-covered counter top. I stood in the musty darkness with Simon, watching slanting drops of rain beginning to fall outside.

"You sure he said 1 p.m.? At this old shithole?" I asked Simon.

Simon's voice was edged with irritation at being asked for the third time. "Yes! I even have it here in a text, and he pinned it on Maps. This is the spot. He'll show."

The rainfall increased to a roar on the roof, and soon, trickles and drips splashed sloppily in a corner of the dark room. A soft crack of thunder rolled overhead.

Simon put a hand on my shoulder from behind and asked, "You gonna be okay, cousin?"

I shrugged away from his hand, too grieved and angry over the loss of Jimmy to want any consolation.

Simon persisted, "It's not your fault, Phil."

"Oh really? Wake the fuck up! I'm the guy that bribed the kid to go fetch the mitogen. And he marched right on in there and got killed!" I choked, turned away, and clenched my fists. I wanted to take a swing at anything and beat it to a pulp.

Simon retorted, "You said he was going there anyway. It would've happened with or without your involvement."

I opened my hands slowly and took a ragged breath. "I'm sorry, Simon. I'm tired. I'm disgusted with the Boones. I hate myself. I hate this whole mess of bullshit. Do me a favor and stop trying to make me feel better before I snap and do something I'll really regret!"

I was about to curse Robert again for being late, when I heard footsteps splashing outside. It was him, hunkering under his leather jacket and looking at his phone as he trotted to the door. He slid his jacket down over his shoulders as he entered. His feet scraped on the uneven floor and displaced gritty pieces of broken tile.

"Where were ya?" I said tersely.

Robert's expression was dark. He replied glumly, "Talking to Jimmy's momma."

I bellowed out "Fuuuck!" and picked up one of the empty beer bottles strewn around the floor. I hurled it and it smashed against a far wall. Destroying something felt so good that I hurled another and another in a torrent of cathartic cursing, until no more bottles were in easy reach and I sagged to my knees. It was as though I would never have more than a moment of fleeting peace to recover from wave after crushing wave of adversity. I wanted to give up and go under for good, if that's what it took to have rest. Robert and Simon stayed back and watched in silent numbness, nursing their own shadows of grief.

My anguish was interrupted by the crunch of gravel under tires, barely audible over the pounding rain. I wiped my face with my sleeve and stood back up, recomposing myself. A black Tesla crawled to a stop outside, its wipers beating back and forth as the rain lashed down. But nobody exited for a full minute.

I sniffled and ran my hands hurredly through my disheveled hair saying, "Robert, maybe you should show him a familiar face and bring him in?"

Robert walked to the doorway and looked both ways, then nodded to the car. A thirty-something, tall white man with dark hair stepped out, popping open an umbrella in the process. He slammed the door in a hurry and scurried towards us. In a moment, we were all inside the dimly lit ruins and Cecil shook the rain out of his umbrella and folded it up.

Simon extended a hand. "Cecil, I'm Simon. It's a pleasure to meet you at last."

Cecil's cold, steel-gray eyes darted within angular sockets above his high cheekbones. His nose and cheeks were tan, as though he had recently spent a lot of time in the sun. His thin lips tightened as he shook Simon's hand. "I'm pleased to meet you too, Simon. And thank you for your assistance those months back."

Simon nodded, "And how's that work going for you?"

"Not well, actually. I think I could use more help with it." Cecil's eyes shifted to me. His face was still hard, but I detected the slightest whisper of a smile. He offered his hand to me. "And how are you doing, eagle man?"

My hand faltered in mid-shake. I looked at Cecil, my blood running as cold as the lithe fingers in my grasp. I shook his hand with a firm squeeze and let my skin ripple into thick scales and sharp talons. I said sternly, holding his hand longer than he had bargained for. "Just fine, wolf man."

Cecil's hand transformed into fur and leathery pads of canine flesh in my grasp. He smiled broadly with a mischievous twinkle in his eye. "Good! That's right! Let's not hide who we are. But now's not the time to tear our clothes off and completely resort to our bestial sides, is it?"

I let his hand go and pressed my nose and mouth outwards into a yellow, hooked beak. I tipped my head back and shook my hair like a model in a shampoo commercial, forcing white feathers to flow out from my scalp into the regal headdress of an adult bald eagle. I narrowed my golden eyes, "Speak for yourself. I can meet you halfway, if that's what it takes for you to take us seriously. How about you?"

Cecil nodded to me coolly. "My game exactly." His forehead pulsed and his irises widened into marbled pools of blue and white. His nose widened and slid forward, growing into a toothy snout. White fur sprouted from his skin, and dark whiskers broke to the surface around his pink leathery nose pad.

Simon gave a grating magpie call, and lowered his head. Black feathers rippled out in an instant, and when he lifted his face, his nose and mouth were replaced by a long, chiseled, black beak. His eyes stayed their human size and blue irises for a moment, then widened into dark, shiny orbs, and he blinked white nictitating membranes. He dropped his coat and pulled his shirt off over his head. Even as he made this smooth motion, his skin was dimpling and plumping with new black and white feathers. His forearms thinned and hardened with black scales, as did his fingers.

Robert closed his eyes and tilted his head back. The center of his face swelled and pulsed as it enlarged into the toothy grin of a wolf. As the snout grew to wolf's proportions, white and gray fur and whiskers sprouted, and canine ears rose from the sides of his head with a soft, fleshy sound. His hands, resting in his hips, fluffed with gray and black fur, and his finger joints became knobby and tipped with black claws. As his partial transformation completed, he curled his lips and exposed white fangs. Something in his eyes dulled the ferocity of his toothy grin, and his ears relaxed, as though he was making a conscious effort to be non-threatening.

We faced each other in a circle.

"That's more like it," I said in a chirpy voice. "Now, let's discuss business."

Cecil calmly growled, his voice much lower in his werewolf form, "Indeed. Whatever that may be."

Simon gave a grating squawk, "Drop the theatrics, Cecil. We know about the artifact. Putting it together with our exchanges, I know you've figured out that you need birdfolk to make the thing work. Blood, or preferably, a live, cooperative subject."

I chirped abruptly, "And we know you have Adele!"

Cecil's face went dark, like a stormcloud passing over a picnic on a sunny day. His eyes turned towards the door, then back to me. A smile grew on his toothy face, and his brows knit above his snout in an expression of disdain. "You Adlers. Always so smug and superior. As if we would need you! Ha! Fuck you. I don't have time for this."

Cecil made it two steps to the door, before I barreled into him and slammed him to the ground. He immediately tore his clothes to shreds with erupting muscle and fur and the speed of his complete transformation to werewolf took me by surprise. In a flash, he was a squirming fury of wiry muscle and bristling fur, howling inhumanly and snapping his jaws violently at my limbs and face. I took two jagged bites to my arms before my hand talons siezed his muzzle shut. My feet exploded through my athletic shoes into thick talons, and I wrapped them around Cecil's thighs to bring him under control. Backwings ripped through my shirt and coat, and I flapped them to bring myself up onto Cecil's back and grind his writhing body into the dirty concrete.

I screamed out in ear-splitting eagle chirps, "Stop it! Or so help me I'll snap your neck with my beak!"

Cecil stopped struggling, but continued growling, like a muzzled wild animal.

Robert howled at me, "Don't fucking do it! Or you and me will have a scrap." Robert dropped to all fours, and latched his teeth around Cecils muzzle. "Stop, Cecil! Stop, or I'll help Phil beat you senseless."

Cecil's eyes looked sternly up at Robert, and he growled out, "'Treason has done his worst, and nothing can touch him further!'"

I looked at Robert for an explanation, but his angry eyes flashed with uncertainty too. He barked rabidly at Cecil, but Cecil only whimpered.

To our surprise, Simon laughed loudly and shouted, "You like MacBeth, Cecil?"

Cecil's eyes moved towards Simon, who stood over the three of us.

Simon continued, his calm, unconcerned voice out of place amidst our street fight. "That was MacBeth, right?"

Cecil muttered, "Yes."

Simon nodded, "Oh, excellent! I enjoy MacBeth too, or anything that spotlights struggles between good and evil. Tell me, Cecil, what part of you is dying, and which is coming to life?"

Cecil was silent for a moment, then said, "That depends on what happens here." His brows relaxed and his eyes looked up apologetically at Robert's muzzle. He wagged his bushy wolf tail, and his whole frame softened.

I eased my grip, stepped off of Cecil, and sat on my haunches, my massive white tailfeathers dragging on the floor. I raised my wings and hackles, still ready to spring to lethal action if necessary.

Robert stayed put, his muzzle locked around Cecil's, and the two carried on a wolfish conversation in body language.

Robert growled, "It's time to come together. Our families were meant to be together."

Cecil whimpered back, "Traitor! You know what would happen to you if I told Earl what you've been up to? Fraternizing and confiding with these silly birds!" His voice cracked, and he broke into a barkish giggle.

Robert replied cooly, "I didn't have to tell them. Hayden was a fool and got caught red-handed transforming. Caught on video even. Blame that idiot."

Cecil whined, but it crumbled into a growl at the end, as though Robert's words made him angry.

Robert pressed on, "You know I'm right. You wouldn't come here if you weren't interested in hearing alternatives."

Cecil's body tremored, and he erupted into barking laughter. His handpaws clutched his midsection, and he giggled out, "I can't. I can't. I can't do this anymore."

Robert demanded, "Why are you laughing? What the fuck's wrong with you? You on drugs or something?" He spun around and trapped Cecil under his massive wolf-man body, gripped Cecil's muzzle again in his teeth, and shoved it to the floor.

Cecil's laugh teetered between mirth and agony, and he clutched his face with his paws, as though trying to keep himself from falling apart. He uttered, "You have… no idea… what the crazy old codger... plans to do. You can't stop him." He looked up at Robert with wide pupils, and his eyebrows wrinkled in horror. He shouted, "You can't!"

Robert released his lock on Cecil's snout and barked, "What the fuck are you talking about, Cecil?"

Cecil's stare was blank, and he continued raving, "He's not what you think. You think he's just a greedy asshole. He's more than that. He's sadistic. He's… he's like a demon. Of all the people on Earth to gain access to this unimaginable power… it had to be him. You… you can't hope to stop him. He's been working on this for years. I know because… because I've been there every step of the way."

Robert growled, "We can if we work together."

Cecil nodded. "Yes. There is one thing. Kill me. I think it's the only way."

Robert sat back on the floor and glanced at me and Simon with disbelief.

Cecil went on, "His bid for the US Senate is just the start. He's helped put men in high places. He owns them, and many are our brethren. Getting into power takes money and friends, and he has both. He'll be President in a few years, mark my words!" He giggled again. "And BooneTech." Cecil barked, and scurried free of Robert, into a corner. "You think BooneTech makes cures for childhood cancer? Ha! Maybe, if it's convenient and profitable. It's really about decoding The Orb. It shows us things. It gets inside your mind, if you let it. With what we've learned, we're decades ahead of other biotech firms. We've made drugs that enhance our werewolf abilities. Just imagine yourself four times more powerful and, soon, armed with weapons centuries ahead of what we now have. Unbeatable. Especially when normal humans are subjected to wave after wave of our bioengineered viruses. We're almost there. But we can only unlock the data we need with cooperation from the other clades!"

As Cecil finished his words, his stare turned to Robert, and he emphatically added, "So kill me! I can't do it myself. I've tried! But you could. Do the world a favor!"

I looked at Robert, hardly believing what I was hearing and seeing. I jerked my head towards Cecil, signalling to Robert to comfort his cousin.

Cecil swallowed and choked in emotional distress. "They watch me all the time. They track my phone! I can't... just talking to you... I'll be confined. If I wasn't indispensable, I'd be dead already. So what's the use? You have to kill me."

Robert dropped down to a knee next to Cecil and put a hand on his shoulder. "There's got to be another way."

Cecil shook his head. "I don't think so. Things are moving so fast. And with the new subject, it will be too late in a few days. Maybe a week at most."

I seethed, "That subject is a member of my family, asshole!"

Cecil closed his eyes and shuddered. "She's not a person! She's genetic material. A tool. A Petri dish to BooneTech."

I marched over and seized Cecil by the throat, my talons lengthening and sinking into his flesh.

Cecil sagged in my grip and he moved his tongue, swallowing with difficulty as he choked. He nodded and smiled, relaxing in my grasp, as if giving permission. His eyes bulged and watered, reddening around the edges. I became aware that blows were landing on my arms and head, as Simon and Robert screamed at me to release him. But it wasn't their bludgeoning that stopped me. It was the placid sadness in Cecil's eyes. In those pools of blue and white, I saw through his deception, and my anger cooled. He wanted me to kill him and settle his debt for aiding evil men, but I wouldn't do it.

I relaxed my talons, and Cecil slumped over in a fit of coughing.

Cecil rolled on his side and stared maniacally at me as he raved on, "You fool! You pathetic, stupid bird! Ha! Ha ha! No! You think that parlor trick against you was anything? Ha! That was just a taste of what Earl has in store. And Victor!" Cecil shook his head. "He was just an unexpected opportunity. Not part of the plan. But we would've happily bled him, probed him, and kept him barely alive, whilst breaking his will and forcing him to cooperate, until we had everything we needed."

My hackles elevated, and I wrinkled my brows in barely-contained fury. It took all of my strength to prevent myself from obeying Cecil's death wish.

I heard the metallic click of a semi-automatic pistol being cocked, and looked at Robert. He held his gun at the ready, pointed at Cecil's head. "Hey!" he barked. "Watch your fucking mouth! That's my friend you're provoking. He won't have to kill you, cuz I will!"

Cecil hacked up a blob of bloody phlegm and licked his foamy lips. "Do it then. Just do it. I'm tired of being afraid. Do me a favor and end it. It's your chance to save the world!"

Robert's arms shook, and his finger moved off the guard to the trigger. He was ready to blast Cecil's brains against the grimy floor.

Simon moved in slowly, calmly, and knelt down next to Cecil. He put his arms around the white wolf and pulled him into an embrace. "Shhh. Stop. You're not dying today."

Cecil's eyes swiveled back and forth between Robert and I, as if he were running out of fuel to maintain his charade. Then his arms slowly came up around Simon's chest, and his eyes welled with tears as he peered into the gentle magpie's face. He closed his eyes, sank his handpaws into Simon's fluffy plumage, and sobbed into his breast feathers.

My feathers sagged, and Robert lowered his pistol. I looked incredulously at Robert, as he put his pistol back into his underarm holster. He shook his head as if to agree with me that Simon's selfless interjection was nothing less than a miracle. The rain poured on, punctuated by the sobs of Cecil's pouring tears. Simon rocked him like a distressed child and rubbed his back, milking all of Cecil's angst to the surface.

After a few moments, I nodded to Robert, and we both stepped outside under the soffits of the crumbling restaurant to have a quiet conversation.

"What the fuck was that?" I whispered.

Robert shrugged. "I've never seen him like that. Cecil's usually calm, cool, and collected. Earl's completely broken him."

I pulled my eagle features back in and shrank to human form again. My clothes hung in rags around my limbs and torso. Even my underwear was showing.

Robert shook his head, "See? That's why I took my jacket off."

I scoffed, "Didn't really have time to undress."

I looked into the dark room again, and the two were warmly wrapped around each other, rocking in silent peace.

I turned to Robert, "We need to take him someplace safe. He looks exhausted and crazy. He needs a doctor... or a psychiatrist. Probably both."

Robert nodded, "Mhmm... with what he knows, I got nothing that will be safe. Earl has too many tendrils in our community. You got any ideas?"

I nodded. "We can put him up at Gramps' place."

Robert smiled, "I was hoping you'd say that."

I shook my head, "Believe me, I'm not relishing it. That's been our only retreat lately. But if there's a place that your family has no reach, it's there."

Chapter 17: Paradigm Shift

Cecil was a hot mess. He said nothing but babbling whispers to Simon in the back seat on our way to Gramps' cabin and we practically had to carry him to a guest room.

Doc made a house call and prescribed strict rest along with sedatives. He would have preferred hospitalization and a suicide watch but compromised to committing Cecil to our care, given the extraordinary security concerns. He also set him up an IV and left his nurse, Cousin Nancy, to help us take care of him.

We took shifts watching over Cecil, both to protect him from himself and, in an abundance of caution, guard him against any of his kin that may have attempted to silence him. We also had cousins fly patrols as birds around the property so that the Boones would have a hard time reaching the cabin without being seen.

Gramps was alternately despondent and fidgety. If he wasn't pacing or preparing for the family meeting, he would disappear outside for twenty minutes and come back with red eyes from bawling privately. He was quieter than usual and walked with sagging shoulders. He knew more painfully than anyone that every minute mattered for recovering Adele alive.

It gave us some relief to know that without Cecil, research efforts would be delayed at least. He wasn't the only scientist involved though, and his expertise was not medical, so we couldn't be sure his absence would directly Adele. And there was no way to ask Cecil about anything that first day. Doc assured us that he would be out of touch for most of the first twenty-four hours and admonished us to not bring up anything that would distress him, or it might set him back even further.

My sadness for Jimmy and Adele had transitioned to anger teetering on the edge of a hollow pit of hopelessness. Seeing dejected, defeated faces around me only made it worse.

I tried to cover my grief by snuggling up with Kayla in the living room. It was quiet and cozy, and we were both in our anthro-eagle forms, fully enveloped in each other's fluffy feathers. It helped, but my mind raced too quickly to fully relax. When I pet Kayla's feathers, my hands were too rigid and too quick.

Kayla sensed my consternation and said, "Hon, I'm restless. Wanna go get some exercise?"

My hand stopped playing with her wing feathers, and I smiled a little. "You read my mind. Do you mind?"

Kayla rose to her feet, "Mind? I'm going with you! I need to clear my head."

She stretched her arms up over her head and stretched out her wings. I stood up, wrapped my arms around her mid-section, and pulled her close, and our beaks clicked together.

She playfully smiled and tapped my beak with a finger as she glanced at Gramps, who was pretending not to see us. She whispered, "You think you can catch me?"

I scoffed, "Seriously? Running is my profession."

Kayla's eyes narrowed, "Who said anything about running?"

I cocked my head as Kayla turned and clicked her talons towards the door and the front porch.

"Gramps, we're gonna get some fresh air and clear our heads. You okay for a bit?"

Gramps perked up and nodded. "You kids go have fun. I'll manage."

I stepped out and roused my plumage noisily, shaking dust and bits of down into the breeze. Kayla stretched her hands to the sky and sagged her wings half open in the brilliant sunshine. Her pale gold eyes and smooth yellow beak sparkled. She turned partway towards me, and the afternoon sun accentuated the graceful curves of her trim and muscular body. My heart felt instantly lighter, and I couldn't help but smile in admiration.

I walked towards her, and she spread her wings and bounded a few steps away, teasing me with the words, "Catch me if you can, slowpoke!"

"We can't go flying around as anthros in broad daylight!"

"Who says? The whole world knows what we are. To hell with it. I need to let off some steam!" She spun on her toes and ran towards the cliff edge. With a loud whoosh of wings, she was airborne and lifting into the sunshine.

I shook my head in shock. This was forbidden. It was dangerous. I looked back at the cabin, and Gramps was sitting down on his rocker on the porch, preparing to smoke his pipe. He simply glanced at me and gestured with his pipe at the sky, as if to say *what are you waiting for?*

Kayla's enormous shadow slid across me as she circled overhead. I dropped my inhibitions like a sack of stones and charged into the sky after her. She already had two hundred feet of altitude on me, so I stroked my wings rapidly to catch up. I gulped in the clear, cool autumn air and exhaled hot, salty breath from deep in my airsacs, pushing my avian body to its full potential. My wingtips grabbed the air and pushed it down, as though it were a medium as solid as stairs under my feet. I pressed all my frustrations out through my muscles, into my remiges, and into the sky.

Kayla saw me coming and gave a chortling cackle, sounding

half like a challenge and half like a frisky taunt. She straightened her body and lifted her head, compressing herself into a tight arrow of feathers pointed at the sun. She had the advantage of being lighter than me with almost the same wingspan. The gap between us widened, and she squeakily chittered back at me.

A dark memory wafted across my consciousness, like the distorted shadows cast by a flickering fire. Her chitter reminded me of Cecil's maniacal laughter from that morning. And I remembered Earl's laugh when I was an eight-year-old boy, terrified by the sudden sensation of transforming.

I clenched my beak and frowned with determination. I flapped harder and faster, and forced my primaries to bite the air so hard, they buzzed and strained in the slipstream. I gained on Kayla, and she spun to the right and folded her wings so that she dropped past me as I topped out my ascent. My eyes stayed glued to her feathery frame, and I screeched a loud cry as I rolled to follow her path below me.

Kayla pulled up abruptly into a second climb. My wings shook and my primaries flexed and vibrated, as I rounded out my descent and powered into another climb after her. She squawked and I screamed in reply, a cry of pain as much as an answer to her challenge. I forgot for a moment that Kayla was my wife. Instead, she was a target that I was going to conquer.

I opened my dripping beak and my avian glottis to the size of a softball, maximizing my oxygen delivery. My heart raced, and I poured all my energy into flight. I pulled my arms in to further streamline myself and rocketed up towards Kayla. She saw the seriousness in my expression and taunted me a third time. "Come and get me!"

Kayla folded her left wing, rolled over into inverted flight, and instantly dropped below my trajectory. Once again, my anger and focus on brute strength had clouded my judgment. I overshot her, and she spun gracefully around me, planted her feet on my rump, and pushed off with a giggle.

We spun and dodged like this twice more until my muscles burned and my breath was ragged. My eyes blurred from the lack of oxygen that I was diverting to my flight muscles.

Kayla leveled off above me and chortled down, "You big lunk! You're trying too hard!" She sounded like an opposing defensive player trying to get under my skin. Or a bullying Boones making fun of me.

I leveled off to catch my breath and tilted my wings to carve a wide, lazy circle, letting the red and green autumn landscape tilt and slide below my sharp eyes. I was so confined in my rageful thinking that I hadn't really taken it in until now. I was so focused on Kayla's actions, that I failed to plan my own. I was reacting, not *acting*.

The throbbing in my pectoral muscles lessened, and my breathing slowed enough to close my beak again. Kayla's shadow slid across my back, and I smiled. We locked eyes, but mine narrowed, as a plan hatched in my eagle brain.

I set into a comfortable stride of flapping and aimed towards a bare rock a quarter mile away. The wind was slightly from the northwest, so I expected to hit a rising thermal just to the southeast of the promontory. Soon, I could see the soft rippling of air currents and tiny midges rising up from below. My wings rocked as I entered the edge of the thermal.

Kayla entered the thermal above me. "That's not gonna save you ya know." Her wings rocked and she circled wide, feeling out the strongest parts of the rising current to let it push her upwards.

That's when I eased my plan into effect. I transformed my shoulders subtly and slowly, expecting that Kayla wouldn't notice it easily from above. I fused my arms and back wings into a single set of muscles and feathers and shrank their overall size slightly. She would rely on the thermal to keep herself out of reach, but I planned to use wind and muscle together to advantage.

As her shadow rolled across me again, I pushed into action. I flapped hard straight up behind her, obscured by her own body. When she curved about in her circular path, she suddenly recognized I was not where she expected. Her head darted down and her beak flipped sideways as she locked eyes on my rapidly ascending form.

She faltered and shot her talons outwards towards me. I flared and presented mine in turn, and we seized onto each other's feet. She grinned at me with heavy lids, like an eagle impressed with her choice of mate. I smiled back and chirped victoriously. We hung there in a brief, weightless moment, looking forward to the fall together, just like a courting pair of eagles.

The horizon flipped upside down, and our wings flung backwards from the combination of aerodynamic forces and angular momentum. Then the horizon blurred into a spinning green and blue smear as I stared into the steady eyes of my loving mate. The sunlight and shadow flashed across her lovely white feathers, sharp beak, and soft eyes. Her warm toes were intertwined with mine, and I strained to flex my legs and bring her closer until our breasts and beaks bumped. I opened my beak and tasted hers. The eternal moment opened my eyes to see what I had forgotten was always right in front of me.

I keened softly, "I love you," but it was inaudible in the roaring of wind and fluttering of feathers being blown in non-aerodynamic directions. She mouthed the same words back to me.

Like clockwork, we both released and pushed off each other in instinctual choreography. We folded our wings and twisted our bodies back to a horizontal attitude, before spreading our wings open again and braking into a steep, spiraling glide. We aimed for Gramps' yard, flapped into a landing attitude, and bounced on our anthro-eagle legs to a stop amidst a swirl of autumn leaves.

I altered my form back to my usual anthro appearance, bringing my humanoid arms back to my shoulders and pressing my wings towards my back. I clasped Kayla's yellow eagle hands in mine and faced her as our breathing slowed. We locked our beaks delicately, and then I rubbed mine on the side of hers. I didn't have the words, and neither did she. I stared into my mate's eyes, that glittered in timeless sun sparkles as a breeze swayed the trees.

At last, I quietly said, "Thank you Kayla. You always give me exactly what I need."

She smiled, and her yellow cere blushed faintly. "You complete me too, Phil. Thank you for being my mate."

I squeezed her hands and said, "I had an inspiration."

Kayla smiled. "Oh yeah? My beauty inspired you, did it?"

I stroked her throat fluff. "It always does. But this time it was your playing hard to get. I was like a rookie, going straight at you with brute strength. Wore me out faster, and I was losing the game."

"Uh-huh. You were distracted by anger. Keeping it all in."

I stroked Kayla's breast feathers. "I was. Made me too predictable. We gotta quit letting the Boones control the field. Time for us to call the shots."

Kayla nodded. "That's my tiercel. What's your plan?"

"The old fake and run. Divide those suckers up and go for the prize. I gotta go tell Robert and get him in on this."

I started to pull away, but Kayla held on, and her relaxed eyes told me she wasn't ready to let go yet. I opened my beak and turned it sideways to Kayla's, begging for a kiss. She opened hers, and we touched tongues and sampled each other's hot breath. It was salty and inviting, so we locked beaks together for a moment longer, tasting each other. My hands slid down her sides to her shapely hips and she wrapped her arms around my midsection. We pressed close together for a magical moment, as the wind rustled the orange and red leaves.

I whispered, "Love you, Babe. You never fail to inspire me. Thank you for holding up so well through all of this. I owe you a weekend getaway, just the two of us."

She slowly relaxed her arms and backed her beak away. She smiled her beak corners, and her sharpened eyes added an intimidating edge to the expression. "Something to look forward to. So, let's do it then. Let's finish this. Together."

Chapter 18: War Council

With the help of Gramps, Kayla, Simon, and Robert, we cobbled together a plan to divide Earl's estate guards and draw Bull and Billy out into the open, perhaps even Earl, if we were lucky. We hoped that would provide an opening for busting Adele out. It was a crude plan, but we couldn't refine it further without involving the Family Council.

Years before the internet existed, we Adlers had established our own system of emergency communication. In the beginning, it was aerial couriers that spread the word. When telegraphs, and then telephones, became available, we had contact trees wherein each person down the chain was responsible for contacting a specific set of people until all the involved parties were reached. In recent times, it also included emails and instant messaging lists. So, in a matter of hours, everyone, at whatever tier desired, could be reached. Sensitive information was referred to using short messages with code words to prompt private, in-person meetings. In recent years, the Family Council would get together through a combination of in-person attendance and remote conferencing technologies.

But the information to be presented at this meeting was of the utmost confidentiality and far too sensitive to trust ordinary channels of communication. We faced an emergency that could impact werebirds worldwide. All twenty-one clan heads, or their proxies, from North America would be attending. A few international bird families also responded. All were encouraged to bring their leading minds and toughest fighters, as protocol dictated for such extraordinary circumstances.

The coded message had simply read: "Feathers have fallen. The forest is burning, revealing all. No birds will sing. They shelter at the nest with three dark eggs. Phil Adler Sr." All the recipients knew this was a no-nonsense call to attend to life and death family business, in person, or not at all. In decoded form, the message read: *Family members were in danger and there was a grave threat to all werebirds. It also ordered strict silence and that there would be a meeting at the sender's home in three nights.*

Gramps had sent the message as soon as Victor's abduction was verified by Adele and had set Friday evening as the night to flock. All families had plans in place for immediate execution in the event a message of this nature was received. No one would make light of it or consider anything else of more importance. If they could not come due to illness or distance, they were required to send a proxy. Remote attendance was not allowed, and there were no exceptions.

The last two hours before the meeting, due to start at 7 p.m., were hectic. Kayla helped Gramps in the kitchen and, fortunately, Bill Franklin and his family arrived early with trays of catered food to share. As the afternoon shadows lengthened, more vehicles arrived. Some family members had driven far, and so we accommodated as many as possible in Gramps' cabin, the two small guest cabins in the back of the property, and even in Victor's house, since he was still in the hospital. I found rooms for everyone I could and promised to put some up in our home after the meeting. Thankfully, many had also checked into nearby hotels. Some even planned to roost as ferals in nearby trees if the weather wasn't too harsh, taking the opportunity to return to their roots, as it were.

As the meeting time approached, Gramps sent me around the grounds to make sure everyone made there way to the cabin's living room. My last stop was the Changing House, which had been a busy place that evening but was empty when I passed through. I thoughtfully paused at the entryway to browse the century and a half of personal touches made by my ancestors.

I ran my finger along the wood next to the faded writing above one peg that read "Phil Adler III" in juvenile scrawl. I had written it myself when I was six years old, while dad held me in his arms so I could reach it. It was nothing I hadn't seen before, or even recently, as I tended to visit Gramps regularly, even when our world wasn't coming apart. However, my pensive mood made me acutely nostalgic, and I wanted to wrap myself up in memories and brood on the good times that once existed, long before life careened into its present wreck.

I was jolted by footsteps on the wood porch outside and I found Kayla, in anthro-eagle form, peering through the glass. She smiled at me and opened the door.

"Everyone's inside. Meeting's about to start. Whatcha up to?" Kayla asked.

"Just got a little distracted here on my way back to the cabin." I said.

Her eyes wandered to the wall in front of me. "Ohhh… my cute mate is reminiscing, aren't you?" She said it with a voice of sweet adoration. I loved it when she used that voice, as it reminded me of how she might speak to our own children if we ever had some.

Her eyes wandered along the clapboard wall, plastered with curled-edged photos, yellowed drawings, and faded signatures of Adlers that came and went before us. They represented generations of hopes, dreams, successes, failures, triumphs, and tragedies.

She churred with delight, "I love this picture of you with Gramps."

In that picture, we were both anthro-eagles, and I was holding a small fish while Gramps, who stood beside me, hand on my shoulder, beamed with pride. It was just a small trout, but it was the first one caught with my own eagle feet.

I smirked, "That was a great day. Did I ever tell you who was taking the picture?"

Kayla's eyes lit up, "No. Now that you mention it, I never really thought about it. Was it your dad?"

"No." I replied, "It was Grandma Alma. She was the one that really taught me to fish. Gramps is good, but Grams was the best!"

"Must've been the osprey in her." Kayla said.

I murmured, "For sure."

"It was sad to see her go. But I know she would've loved Adelle and how happy she makes Gramps. Shoot, if her spirit's still around, she'll be right in the fight with us I bet."

I solemnly nodded, "Mhmm."

I delicately stroked the feathers on the side of Kayla's head with the back of my fingers, and she turned her eyes towards mine.

She said, "You know, we're in pretty good company, aren't we? Our families have faced a lot together. We're gonna make it through this too, hon."

My expression darkened. I had to say what was on my mind, here in private. "Kayla… I know you want to be in the fight. And we need everyone, especially birdfolk as capable as you. Just promise me that you won't take any unneeded risks."

Kayla stiffened her posture, but her smile remained. "I'll do whatever needs to be done."

I replied, "It's not that. I know you would give your life for me, or Adele, or anyone here. But I won't be able to fight without knowing that you aren't charging in over your head. We've never been in a fight, much less a war, like this. Just promise me that you'll hang back in reserve until you're needed. It'll really clear my head, okay?"

Kayla nodded solemnly, recognizing the torment raging

inside my soul. I couldn't face the specter of her being abducted like Adele. Or being killed. I would never forgive myself.

"Good." I pressed my forehead to hers and squeezed her hands with mine.

In a few minutes, we stepped through the door into the crowded living room of Gramps' cabin. Gramps stood in front of the stone hearth at the head of the room, a fire crackling behind him. Simon was seated nearby, as was Marshall, in his shiny black raven plumage.

At least sixty werebirds of many different species were present. Most were familiar to me and many had been with us at Victor's rescue. Others were new to me.

A pair of unfamiliar anthro ravens stood on the balcony above, but they bore a resemblance to Marshall. One of them croaked in laughter, their glossy throat feathers vibrating in mirth. Next to the pair of ravens, a great horned owl was chatting with my father, Phil, Jr. A red-and-green rooster perched on the log railing of the balcony next to a lovely red hen, rapidly clucking together in Malay. Ben was in anthro golden eagle form at the top of the stairs, carrying on a bantering conversation with Kayla's bald eagle brother John. The two were forever comparing notes and threatening to have a fishing contest.

On the main floor, Bill Franklin and his wife, Sarah, were in the center of the room, resting on the leather sofa, both wearing their proud lanner falcon plumage. A stately pair of golden eagles were talking with them in a rusty drawl that reminded me of a Texan accent. Three tall Andean condors sat across from them in deep black feathers with white neck ruffs and red-skinned heads. They spoke at a polite, quiet volume in fluent Spanish. Many other eagles, hawks, ravens, and even an enormous seabird that resembled a Laysan albatross, were present, all in anthro forms, creating a backdrop of murmuring noise.

As discussed, Robert was upstairs with Cecil. It was a given that few, if any, in the audience knew of werewolves, and many would know Robert without knowing that he was on our side. We would have to ease the audience into his introduction.

Phil Adler, Jr., my father, saw us enter, and immediately gave a loud shout in our direction. All heads turned to us, and everyone croaked, squawked, and clapped their beaks in appreciation. Gramps let the appreciative cheers roll a moment, then cackled out for everyone to quiet down again.

"Everybody listen now! We'll have time for socializin' after I getchya up to speed. Thank ya kindly for quietin' down and listen' up…" In a few short moments, everyone had settled down, and I gave Kayla a rub on the cheek as I made my way to stand beside Gramps.

Gramps and I laid out all the events of the past week, and the crowd listened attentively. As I came to the murder of Jimmy, abduction of Adele, and the cooperation of Robert and Cecil, there were gasps of astonishment and croaks of uncertainty. I paused short of talking about what Cecil had told us.

A plump and glossy magpie raised a black-and-white feathered arm.

Gramps addressed her, "Misty Blevins, for the benefit of all, state your name and hometown, then go ahead."

Misty replied, "Misty, from Spokane, Washington. What is Victor's medical condition? Is there anything he needs?"

Gramps met her eyes and said, "He was near death when we rescued him, but Doc thinks he's rounded the bend for the better. Still not sure about his wing, or his future ability to fly, but pretty high hopes."

There was a murmuring sigh among the birds.

"Any other questions before we move on?"

Marshall blurted out, "Yeah, when's Phil returnin' to the

game, man? I got money ridin' on the Baldies!"

A cackle of laughter rose along with spattering of clapping bird claws. I smiled and nodded, "It's looking promising for next week. We're waiting on confirmation that the mitogen we recovered from Boonedocks is a match for what poisoned me. If we can do that, I should be back playing by the time we face the Black Cats. I'll do everything I can to not let you down!"

The crowd clapped and voiced approval, but Gramps waved his arms and cut it short.

Gramps went on, "Some of you are probably wonderin' why I'd call a secret council meeting for something that, though dire, seems to be just a local affair. Believe me, if that's all it was, I'd have not bothered you to come all this way. There's even graver matters at stake here, things that will affect us all and, quite possibly, all life as we know it."

I cleared my throat, "Cecil and Robert Boones… are here right now in this house." A swell of concerned grumbles moved through the room.

One of the raven pair on the balcony croaked up first. "How can you be sure that we can trust this Robert?"

Gramps responded, "Just a reminder, folks, state your name and location. A lot of new faces here."

"Oh! 'Scuse me. Jackie Thomas from Oakland, California. So how is it we can trust these particular Boones? Sounds like we can't trust any of 'em!"

Gramps put a hand on my shoulder and spoke reassuringly to the group, "So far as Robert, he's proven he can be trusted by helping Phil get to the bottom of the plot against him, despite it involving his own family. Phil has spent more time with him and could probably add more, but I can tell you this firsthand: I saw Robert's reactions when we took him to see Hay, his nephew, layin' dead on a slab. He was mad. Mad at Earl and his whole family. Nothin' rehearsed or forced about it. He hates what the cancer of greed is doin' to his own."

There were collective nods.

I cleared my throat to get their attention and continued the conversation. "This will come as a surprise, but Robert, and all of the Boones, are werewolves. They're just like us, only they become wolves."

A murmur arose and I held out my hands to calm the crowd. "I know that's a big surprise, but it's looking like we may have a lot in common with the Boones. Let me give you an example. I found this passage in the journal of Samuel Adler, an ancestor who fought in the American Civil War…" I read the pages I had read a few days prior, and every bird listened intently.

As I finished, I looked at Gramps and said, "It's no wonder the Boones have been so fascinated with us. They know more about our common past than we do." I turned to the crowd and continued, "There's more, a lot more. Ever wonder why werebirds are so diverse? I mean, look at us… African roots, Asian roots, Caucasian, Central American. That's just the human side. We turn into ravens, eagles, hawks, osprey, magpies, chickens… the list goes on. And now we know there are wolffolk that otherwise live their human lives just like us. Well, looks like the answer lies in a common origin for all of us.

"Cecil, the broken man we took in today, is the Boones' lead scientist. He's found something, well, that changes everything. Turns out that our special abilities may be the result of genetic engineering. Simon can explain the details better than anyone. But Cecil says that the Boones have a device in their possession that is the key to our origins. It is also the key to knowledge and technology that's, well, far beyond anything in existence on Earth today."

The rooster on the banister crowed out, "Are we talking space aliens?"

Gramps cackled harshly, "Out of order! Please, let him finish speaking, folks!"

I resumed, "Well… yeah, that's one possibility."

The room was silent, but many were looking at each other in disbelief. The rooster chuckled and whispered, "This must be a joke."

I looked up at him and said, "Two people are dead for sure, and Adele is abducted, and possibly dead. Sir, this is no joke."

The rooster compressed his red head plumage, bowed his beak in humble acknowledgement, and said, "I apologize."

One of the condors raised a feathery arm, and Gramps nodded to them. They stood and spoke in a Latin American accent, "Pedro Kolash, Peru. No offense, sir, but this is impossible to accept without proofs. Can we meet these Boones? Can we see this alien machine?"

Gramps nodded up towards Ben, who then disappeared down the upstairs hallway momentarily, and returned with Robert, who was in the gray and black fur of his anthro-wolf form. The room echoed with excited chirps and squawks. As Robert made his way down the stairs and up to the front of the room, some birds shrank from his passing or opened their beaks and flared their head plumage in barely suppressed threat displays.

As Robert walked to the front, I put my arm across his shoulders and hushed the flock with an outstretched hand. "Listen! I trust this man with my life! You'll be trusting yours to him too if you come fight with us tomorrow night." I looked at Pedro. "As for the device, tell them what you know, Simon. Show 'em your pictures."

Simon stood and held out an electronic tablet with a full-screen zoom of the photo he had shared with us previously. He began, "This is what we think it looks like. Cecil is here too, asleep upstairs right now, seriously ill from the stress and strain that Earl subjected him to in his mad rush to complete the decoding of this device. He is literally risking his life to help us."

Simon passed the tablet off to Kayla, who walked around

the room, showing it to everyone, as Simon continued speaking.

"This object, referred to by the Boones as 'The Orb,' was recently imported from an archeological dig in Syria. It's described as a stone sphere, and you can see it's very smooth, like polished marble. The photos are poor, but you can just make out a faint inlaid pattern that focuses around five nodes, each with a different animal figure. These same icons have shown up together in the art of multiple ancient cultures around the world, each separated by thousands of miles of land and ocean. We think that there may be multiple copies of this device, or that it was somehow transported around the world, which seems impossible given the distances, and in some cases, similar times in history when the depictions first appeared.

"This morning, in the throes of a mental breakdown, Cecil told us about needing five clades to cooperate in activating the device. I believe he was referring to the five taxonomic clades represented by the icons on the device. There's a bird with hooked beak. That's us, in case you weren't paying attention." Simon smiled, and a chuckle arose from a few in the audience. "There's also an alligator, a felid, a fish, and a canid. The arrangement implies that you need all five to complete the circle of species that can fully utilize this device.

"See, there are all kinds of similar anthropomorphized animals embedded in the art and stories of cultures around the globe. We need to be reading those stories and admiring that art with new eyes. Some of it is likely inspired by our ancestors and may contain instructions that we need now. But the device is not to be used by any one clade, as Earl is doing. It's engineered to require us to work together. According to Cecil, Earl Boones is using the device, right now, to make unbelievable advances in biotechnology under the guise of BooneTech, his research firm with a private lab located on his estate. I know this sounds crazy, but Cecil says they have ways to make their soldiers larger and more powerful. They are making bioweapons, including the mitogen that caught Phil by surprise, and they have plans to do no less than take over the country, if not beyond, within ten years. The only thing holding them back is cracking that device and playing the cycles of politics."

The rooster on the upper banister raised a wing and crowed, "Khan, Malaysia. Why should we want to cooperate with anyone to activate this device? It sounds dangerous!"

Gasps arose from the top of the stairs, birds parted, and Cecil weakly hobbled towards the edge of the balcony.

Robert shouted, "Cecil! Help him, Ben!"

Ben took Cecil's hand and helped him to the banister as Robert picked his way back through the crowd towards the stairs.

Cecil lifted a hand. "I'm all right, cousin, I'm all right. I have something to say."

Robert held up his handpaws and shouted, "Quiet, please! Cecil would like to speak!"

Cecil cleared his throat, "I've been listening. Simon is a smart bird and speaks the truth. You, Khan, are right. The Orb, or rather its information, is incredibly dangerous. Which is why it must not stay in Earl's hands alone. I know that you are all very concerned for your owl female, Adele. I understand what she means to you. But you must not stop at freeing her. You have to obtain The Orb. Everything else pales in comparison. If Earl keeps it, I guarantee that none of you will live beyond ten years. And you can't go to the military or any human authority about this, or the device will be whisked away, and not properly, and openly, studied like it deserves. It's up to us, working together, to explore it and use it peacefully, as I believe its creators intended."

Simon was smiling, and Cecil met his gaze. "I'm glad you're feeling better, Cecil. Good to see you up and about."

Cecil replied weakly, "Thanks to you… and you." He nodded towards me.

Simon asked, "Who made The Orb, and what do you think their intentions were?"

Cecil nodded slowly. "A very good question. I'm convinced they were extra-terrestrial, given the scope of time and technology required. As far as intent? There are violent episodes in some ancient stories, involving anthropomorphic deities, as the people creating the tales saw them. The stories are undoubtedly colored by superstitious beliefs reacting to the magic-like powers we possess. But by and large, our god-like ancestors were builders of society, not destroyers. I have to think that The Orb, and its companions, if they exist, are meant to teach us and help us in our evolution and technological development. But as I said, they only convey information. In the wrong hands, that information is extremely dangerous."

Cecil slumped closer to the floor, and Ben slung one of his arms under his armpits to help pull Cecil back up. Robert trotted up the stairs to assist.

I directed my voice to Cecil, who looked sleepily back. "Thank you, Cecil. Glad you could pitch in. Rest up. We're surely going to need you tomorrow."

Simon turned to me and asked, "Mind if I go sit with Cecil for a while?"

I nodded, and Simon picked his way across the room, disappearing upstairs with Robert, Ben, and Cecil.

Gramps lifted his hands and said, "We're almost done, folks, and then we can have some refreshments and chat. I'm assigning Phil to be our lead, our General if you will, for the upcoming attack. We've rarely ever had such a rank, but looks like we need one now, and I can think of nobody more suited. I'll turn things over to him for a few more words."

I blushed and hugged Gramps tight for a moment as claps arose from the flock. My father screeched out an eagle-like cheer and other birds joined in with squawks, chirps and bill clatters.

I released Gramps and held up my arms to calm the room. I looked at the excited faces and said, "I won't drag this out. We all need our rest tonight. I'm appointing Marshall and Robert as my captains for two teams. Gramps and Kayla will lead the reserves. There will be other assignments, and some of you will end up on one team or the other. Marshall, please tell us your thoughts."

The tall, thick, glossy raven stood up and looked around. "Marshall George, living right around here, but my ancestors are from the Pacific Northwest. Some of you were with us when that bullshit went down at Earl Boones' house a few days ago. You saw it firsthand. But the rest of you who couldn't be there, I know you would've if you could've. Let me tell you what we saw. Earl has a black heart. He was ready to kill Victor, or any of us that tried to stop him. Had we been a few minutes late, this would be a funeral instead of a strategy meeting. For those who don't know, I saw action in Iraq. Now I run a security business here. We protect some pretty important folks and I'm as tough as they come. I've been shot at many times, took a bullet in the service, so I know how a man's eyes look when they're about to pull the trigger. Earl was ready. Not just that, he was enjoying it. That's rare. He's a dangerous man. It was only thanks to our numbers and Phil's whoop ass, that it didn't get more violent.

"Now Earl's made enemies in his own family too. Strategically, this is the best time to strike. 'Sides, by what Cecil says, it's only a matter of time before they dissect Adele. We can't afford to wait, and I'm on board with all you're laying down, Phil." Marshall sat back in his chair and interlaced his fingers across his lap into a solid mass of black scales.

There were grunts and chirps of agreement from the upper story as Marshall sat back down. Gramps nodded to him. "Thank ya kindly, Marshall, for turnin' out. Gave me a heapin' measure of confidence knowin' you was behind me there. Couldn't have pulled Victor outta there without ya."

I looked around the room at all the beaked faces and continued, "One more thing. Everything you've heard here tonight is strictly confidential. You must not say anything about any of this to anyone outside of this house. Don't even talk about it outdoors. We have owl kin out guarding the property tonight, but it's still possible a Boones could sneak in and be listening with keen wolf ears. And don't drive, fly, or strut by the Boones' properties, or so much as make the impression that anything is out of the ordinary. Adele's fate is in the balance. Your friends and family could die if one shred of this intel slips out. Hell, everyone's future is on the line. There will be a strategy meeting right here tomorrow morning at 9 a.m. sharp. I want each council member's security lead to attend. Any questions?"

Khan lifted a wing and I nodded to him. He squawked, "We are ready to help. My son, Muda, is a skilled fighter. We are not afraid to fight, but I wish we had brought more of our kin with us. Do you know what we're up against?"

I had hoped I might avoid this question, as I didn't have a confident answer yet. I cleared my throat and answered, "I honestly don't know yet and I'm hoping that Cecil can fill us in since he lived and worked on the Boones Estate the past couple of years. But for now, I'm going to assume the worst. As you know, US citizens have nearly unlimited access to firearms, so that's a given. From what Robert tells me, most of Earl's men are not professional security or soldiers, with maybe ten percent having formal training, while the others are hired relatives. They're probably good shots but have limited practice in hand-to-hand or close combat. Certainly, they've never confronted combatants with beaks and wings and talons!" Confident chirps and cackles sounded from the flock. "We also have the advantage of surprise and we're going to attack at multiple fronts at staggered times to draw them apart. My biggest concern is how to penetrate the lab facility. It's a good bet it will have top-notch security measures. Cracking that nut will all depend on what Cecil tell us."

Khan nodded, and silence fell across the room.

Gramps adjourned the meeting, and in a few minutes, the room was alive with conversation. But the tone was palpably muted, as compared to the jovial mood before the meeting. Voices were solemn. Some birds moved outside and fell immediately quiet. With the incredible information fresh in their minds, no one wanted to engage in small talk.

Kayla gathered our house guests and caravanned them to our home for the night. I remained behind, unwilling to be far from Cecil, should he wish to discuss the security of BooneTech. My internal tension wouldn't let me sleep much anyway. I took short eagle naps in the living room and sometimes in a lounge chair we had set up in Cecil's bedroom, taking turns with Robert and Simon, so that at least one of us was always awake at Cecil's side. Some of our other guests carried on quiet conversations at the kitchen bar, well into the small hours of the morning. But at some point, all fell quiet, and I sank into a deep sleep on a sofa in the living room.

Chapter 19: The Calm

A familiar human voice awakened me in the morning. *It was Victor!*

As my eyes came into focus, he smiled down at me, wearing his human face. "Surprise, dumbass!"

I rubbed my eyes and rose to a sitting position on the couch. Victor's face was a healthy pink color, but he stood with a tight, frail posture, leaning on a cane, as though a breeze would knock him down. I stood up, wrapped my arms around him, and gave him a firm hug.

I chirped to him, "Damn, it's good to see you!"

Victor squeaked out, "Hnn! Hey, easy big fella!"

"Oh! Sorry, Vic. You okay?"

Victor stepped back and, in a mock high-pitched voice of a crushed victim, said, "I'll live." I helped him back down onto the couch and sat beside him.

"How'd you get sprung from the hospital?" I asked.

Victor replied, "Doc said my red blood cells were going up, my white blood cells were staying down, and the wounds were healing. He says I could use a few more days there…" Victor shook his head. "But with security concerns, and you needing all the fighting birds you could muster instead of wasting their time guarding me, he thought it would be okay if I came home and Cousin Nancy doted over me."

"It's a relief knowing we'll have Emerson and Ben available

tonight." I wrinkled my brow. "But you can't fight!"

Victor shook his head, "No, you're right, I can't. I sure wish I could. But I'm not there yet, and these mitostats Doc's got me on won't let me transform anyway."

"Mitostats?"

"Yeah, you know, the opposite of what you got. This shit keeps me from doing what my dumb ass wants to do, transform and fix shit the quick way. Feels weird, like I'm missing a hand or a foot."

I chuckled, "Yeah, knucklehead, you're missing your wings!"

Victor nodded, "Doc gave me some mumbo jumbo about strain to my Golgi bodies or mitochondria and, well, it was more than I could remember from cell biology, so I took his word for it. He says in a few days, he'll take me off 'em and have me doing transformation exercises. Might fix up my busted bones, so I won't need surgery." Victor winked towards the door.

I looked over, and saw Doc was standing outside on the porch chatting with Kayla. I looked back at Victor and smiled. "He's the best when it comes to birds. I'd believe him. But I'm not taking you into this fight. Your ass is gonna be planted in bed getting better!"

Victor shook his head. "I'm feeling good. I'm not letting this war be fought without me doing something. Sure, I can't kick wolf butt with ya, but I can still help. With your permission, Herr General…" He recited the honorific with a mocking tone and salute. "I would like to sit tight with Doc in the bird-bulance tonight in case he needs some help."

I'd never heard the term "bird-bulance" before but I surmised he was referring to Doc's specially-outfitted ambulance. It was nice to see Victor's sense of humor was as strong as ever.

I replied, "If Doc says it's okay, I'm fine with that. I know the feeling. I wouldn't let you go alone either."

Victor nodded, and his smile faded a little. "I heard what happened to Jimmy. Cryin' goddamn shame."

I nodded back and avoided eye contact for a moment. I didn't want to think about it too much, as I was pretty sure I'd fall apart. I composed myself and looked at Victor. "Yeah, well, I hope I come across the son-of-a-bitch that killed him. We'll make him wish he'd never touched the kid."

Gramps walked towards us with a cup of coffee and handed it to me as I thanked him.

"What time is it?" I looked at my phone and realized it was almost eight. "How in the world did I sleep so long?"

Victor smarted off, "Woah, you've come a long way. This week's been hell on you, if you're sucking down the coffee like the rest of us mere mortals."

"Yeah, tell me about it." I took a sip and nodded towards the scene at the dining table in the corner of the room. "It's been a week of wonders, but I never imagined I'd see that…" Cecil and Robert were in their werewolf forms, chatting with Simon in anthro-magpie form. Cecil was smiling and chatting, but his canine ears were laid back in social awkwardness.

Victor commented, "Amazing, isn't it? I dunno, bro, but I think I like what I'm seeing. This is our future, isn't it?"

Gramps nodded. "Cecil seems to be comin' round. Mebbe we can have a chat with him now."

I sipped the coffee and nodded. "Mhmm."

As we walked over to the table, I heard what Cecil and Simon were talking about. It was a passionate discussion about the genetics of Pokémon evolutionary biology. By their chuckles and smiles, it was clear that neither were taking it too seriously. Robert looked up at me with a smile on his face, perhaps relieved that someone would rescue him from the nerdy conversation.

I sat down across the table from the trio. "How ya doing, Cecil? You seem to be feeling better today."

Cecil's smile faded, and he cleared his throat. "Yeah, I'm… better. I appreciate what you all are doing here for me. I wouldn't feel safe anyplace else, especially not alone."

Gramps said softly, "Don't mention it, Cecil. It's been a pleasure havin' ya here and gettin' ta know ya. You're welcome anytime."

Robert spoke, "Here's the situation, Cecil. We got a plan to get into the perimeter of the Estate. Thing is, we have no idea how the lab is laid out or where to find Adele. Can you help us?"

Cecil picked up a deck of cards and fidgeted with them, his eyes looking down and his ears back.

Simon met my eyes and understood I needed his help. "Hey, Seece. Look at me." He grasped Cecil's paws gently with his dark avian fingers, and their fidgeting stopped. "You're okay. Nobody's on your case here. We know this isn't easy and you're scared. I can't begin to imagine what it's been like working for Earl. But we're on your side. You won't face this alone anymore. You're part of our family now and we stick together no matter what, understand? We need your help. That's all. You want to help us, right?"

Cecil growled, and his ears pinned back as he showed his fangs. "Don't patronize me... I'm not a child, you pathetic--!"

Cecil's sentence was abruptly ended when Robert viciously barked and lunged at him. Robert shouted, "Stop that bullshit this instant! We are guests!"

I was electrified by the sudden violence of the exchange between the two werewolves.

Cecil panicked, fell out of his chair, and laid on the floor on his back with his tail between his legs. He cowered and whimpered like a puppy, all but peeing on himself in supplication to his superior. With his ears back, he begged, "I'm sorry. I'm sorry. Forgive me, brother. Forgive me, Simon… I'm not myself."

In an instant, Robert was down next to his fallen cousin, licking his ears and hugging him with his forepaws. I looked at Gramps, and he was equally surprised. It was the first time either of us had seen werewolves engage in social interactions, or any Boones show physical affection for another.

Simon swiftly followed Robert's lead and dropped to the floor too, smiling and cooing and rubbing Cecil's chest fur. "It's okay, my friend. It's okay." Cecil licked his magpie hand and looked back up at him with childish glee.

I motioned to Gramps to follow me back outside. Victor came along, and we met Kayla on the porch.

"What the heck was that?" I asked.

Gramps shook his head. "Social hierarchy like a wolf pack, I guess. Gonna be some things to get used to."

I added, "I'm glad we got Robert's level head on our side. I don't like how fast that went from calm to violent, you know what I'm saying?"

Through the window, I saw Robert stand up, smiling, as Simon and Cecil continued rolling around on the floor, wrestling and playing.

As Robert came outside, Kayla asked, "Is that normal?"

Robert responded, "Yeah. Simon wasn't in any real danger. You guys aren't used to how we express ourselves yet, I suppose. Cecil has always been a bit of a hothead, but he's never hurt anyone. He's always obeyed me, though I've had to rough him up a couple times to get my point across."

Gramps cocked his eagle face, casting a narrow gaze at Robert. "I'm begginin' ta' understand you Boones a bit more now. Shouldn't be surprisin' you work things out like wolves.

Tell me sumthin'. How's Earl's demeanor in yer secret family meetins'?"

"Oooh, what you saw in there was nothing compared to the dominance he exerts. You think he's bad as a human, he's a hundred times worse in his role as Alpha."

"So that's why Cecil's so scared," I said.

"Mhmm. In wolf context, letting down your elder, especially your Alpha, is a capital offense. You can be ex-communicated from the pack, or worse. He's not tolerant of failure, particularly when he's invested a lot in you to make you useful, as he has with Cecil."

Dark tendrils of dread arose in my mind that made my beak cold and clammy, like the sour wave of nausea right before an eagle regurgitates a pellet of indigestible matter. "Or betrayal. Like Jimmy. I guess Bull and Billy took a page from Earl's playbook."

Robert nodded. "Yeah, afraid so."

We glanced back inside, and Simon was comforting Cecil on the floor as he cried. The two were in a fluffy embrace of fur and feathers.

I shook my head. "That guy's a mess! What are we gonna do? Everything's riding on him."

Robert nodded towards the window. "I've never seen Cecil take to someone so quickly like he is to Simon. I think Simon's your ace in the hole here. I say just give those guys some space for a while and he'll have Cecil eating from his hand like a lost puppy."

Doc said in a gravelly voice, "I agree. He's already doing so much better. Look, I got things to take care of before tonight. I'll call later to check on Cecil. I'm sure Nancy can take care of him in the meantime. By the way, what time did you want me ready to roll tonight?"

I replied, "We're jumping off from here at 1 am."

Doc rubbed his face with one hand. "I'm gettin' too old for this shit, but you can count on me. First time having to face a combat situation like this as a civilian. I'll have the ambulance ready, and Nancy will be standing by with me, just down the road from the Boones Estate."

I shook his hand, "Thanks, Doc. I really hope we don't need ya, but we'll all feel better having you close by."

Victor took Doc aside to pitch his assistant proposal, while I grabbed Kayla by the hand and led her into the driveway. The weather was unseasonably warm for an early November day, and seeing her dappled in the sunshine made it feel like it was spring already. She was still in human form, as she hadn't made it to the changing house yet. I didn't give her a chance to change her form, as I hugged her tight to me, lifted her from the ground, and spun her around. She planted a kiss on my smooth beak.

"How's my mate?" I asked.

Kayla rubbed her fingers on my lower beak while admiring my white plumage and golden eyes. "Doing fine. Missed you last night though."

"Me too." I leaned forward and fished for another kiss, which Kayla rewarded warmly. I hugged her and whispered, "This'll all be over very soon. I promise, love. Then you and I can get back to normal, okay?"

She nodded and squeezed me back. "Heck, I don't mind a change of pace. And we're probably spending more time together now than we normally do during game season. I'm just worried that you won't come through this in one piece. I… I couldn't stand losing you, love."

I knew better than to blow sunshine up her feathers. "I can't sugar coat this and expect you to buy it, can I?"

Kayla's voice cracked with worry, "Those rednecks are gonna have guns and who-knows-what. I know you have to get Adele out of there. I'm all for it. But just… don't die, dammit."

"Hey, we got a pretty good arsenal too, ya know. And they won't be expecting us. And we got Cecil. With him on our side, we have Earl's nuts in a vice. Robert says that most of Earl's goons are caught between fear of their master and feeling powerful in their 'tacticool' gear, but few are looking to die for his cause. Might even be able to walk out of there peacefully, if any of them have a shred of sense left."

Kayla nodded and pulled closer to me.

I continued reassuring her, "And Tommy, well Robert says that Jimmy's murder hit him hard. He thinks it was Bull and not Billy that did it. But whatever the case, he's helping us with our diversion tonight. And we got, well, all kinds of weapons." I backed away slightly and locked eyes with Kayla, hoping she could see how determined I was to live the rest of my life with her. "Not a minute goes by when we're apart that I don't notice it. I'll be doing everything I can to get back to you in one piece, okay?"

She wiped her teary eyes with a hand, and I pulled her close to me again, tucking her head under my throat feathers. I cradled her head with my right hand and comforted her for as long as I could to make sure she knew she was the most important thing in the world to me.

Soon it was time for our strategy meeting, and by then, Cecil had recovered more of his wits. I don't know if it was the rest and time that helped, or the realization that he was not alone, but as the meeting wore on through the first hour, he became more and more animated. His insights into security practices at the Estate and the unique knowledge of its underground complex reassured us that we weren't going into battle unprepared.

When we broke from the meeting, as the others returned to their families and teams, I had a private moment with Cecil on Gramps' porch. The sky was clouding up, and the air cooling off, as the predicted weather front moved in. It would be a damp night, but not particularly stormy.

I sat down in an Adirondack chair next to Cecil and commented, "Looks like the Fates are on our side tonight. The weather should be perfect cover. Hard to fly very high, but they won't see us coming."

Cecil smirked and remarked coldly, "The Fates are a myth."

I chuckled and reassured him, "I know, Cecil. I didn't mean it literally."

His white canine snout, which had been pointing at the swirling leaves in the yard, swiveled in my direction and he fixed his icy blue eyes on mine. His ears relaxed and he smiled, "Sorry. As you might have guessed, I mostly work alone." He chuckled dismissively.

I leaned my beak into my fingers and said, "Hey, you're doing pretty good for a quiet guy that's never been around a flock of noisy birds before. There's hardly a calm moment around here, even when we're not going to war."

Cecil nodded and gazed up at the congealing puffs of gray cloud. "The moisture will hide your scent too. But be aware that my kin see really well in the dark. It's wise that you have an owl as your lead scout."

I shook my head, "I am glad for it too. And damned if I could keep Zoe from volunteering anyway. Can't blame her."

"No. Certainly not. I'd do the same for my sister." Cecil's gaze had returned to contemplating the ground.

I wanted to ask Cecil about his motivations to help us but thought better of it. The guy had been through a lot, and was just putting himself back together, so why upset him now? Turns out, he was ready to talk about it anyway.

Cecil stared straight ahead and said, "I know what you're probably wondering. Why am I turning on my family? Am I correct?"

I drummed my talons on the wooden armrests of the chair,

and it creaked as I adjusted my posture.

Cecil resumed, "It's a fair question any intelligent person would ask. Even Simon asked, and I think it helped pull me back to reality."

I picked absent-mindedly at a small crack in the armrest. "Simon has a way of disarming people, getting them to open up. He's a good guy."

Cecil's gaze lifted to the rustling treetops, and he closed his eyes. "That's an understatement. He's... well, he's just wonderful. I'm so glad to know him now. Only wish I'd gotten to know him sooner."

I watched Cecil look into the sky with his bluish wolf eyes. It was a longing stare, and I couldn't decide if he were wishing things had worked out this way sooner, or dreaming of good things that would yet come to pass. "Well, Simon sure seems to like you. He's a likable guy but, well, I think he has a special interest in you, and not just because you can help us."

Cecil glanced sideways at the space just before my talons on the porch floor, and a subtle smile came to his muzzle and eyes. "Even after the terrible things I've done?"

I stopped picking at the armrest and caught Cecil's gaze. "Definitely. He's about the most forgiving soul I know, next to Kayla of course, who puts up with me day in and day out." We both snickered for a moment.

Cecil continued, "You're a lucky fellow, Phil. Lovely family, solid friends, and a good mate." His smile turned into a subtle frown. "Nothing like our dumpster fire of a family."

I wasn't sure what to say for a moment, and Cecil filled the silence, "That's why I'm doing this. Everything Earl does is for himself. He makes it seem like it's for the benefit of all of us, but I'm close to the top, and I don't like what I see. It's not a pretty picture."

I shook my head dismissively, "That can change. In fact, I'm looking forward to seeing it. Heck, you of all people should know that we're all part of the same family. We just... forgot. And now we must relearn it. No matter what happens tonight, I hope you and Robert will continue to feel welcome here. I hope our families can grow back together again."

Cecil nodded and quietly said, "I hope so too. I really hope so. Regardless, I don't care if I survive tonight. The hell I've been through and the things I was prepared to do..." He shook his head. "I have to set things right."

Something knotted in the pit of my stomach. "Look, Cecil... I mean it when I say that you're one of us now. We've got your back. You're going to make it out of this. I gotta know, though, are you sure you're up to this? Can we depend on you too?"

Cecil turned and looked at me with a mix of pain and determination in his eyes, as though walking off a sprained ankle. "You can. I won't let anything happen to Simon..." he winced and looked back to the ground, "...or any of us, of course."

I nodded. "And what if you see your relatives hurt or worse? Or what if Earl shows up?"

Cecil's jaw firmed and his ears stood tall. "I'm ready for that. I'm betting on that happening." He looked at me with head cocked slightly, "What about you?"

I clasped my talons together. "Funny you should ask. I have this habit of thinking about what my goals and limits are before a major confrontation. Kinda helps keep me between the rails, so to speak."

Cecil nodded. "It's not exactly the same, but that exercise reminds me of the Ulysses Clause. Willful decision making before you're in a situation where your ability to make decisions may be compromised."

"Exactly!" I replied. "Keeps my temper in check. But I gotta say... well, I'm not proud of this..."

Cecil looked at me, expectantly. "Go on. Please."

I looked Cecil in the eyes. It wasn't easy to say it out loud, but I could tell he was earnestly interested. "Ever since this whole business started a week ago, I've felt this darkness growing inside. Something terrible and destructive. Not like other times when I just wanted to beat a team or an opponent or push past my own limits."

"Revenge," Cecil said, coldly.

I nodded. "It really took hold when I saw how brutally Jimmy was murdered. Maybe by his own dad even. God, I want to just beat the asshole that did that. Beat them without mercy, just like they did to Jimmy. Even if they beg for me to stop. And rip their fucking head off." My beak blushed and my hackles rose as I vocalized what I was feeling.

"You blame yourself for his death, don't you?"

I clenched my fists. "I do. He was trying to retrieve a sample of mitogen for me after all. Fuck. I'd rather he was alive and going to college than my stupid name getting cleared. Feels like the only way I can feel better is to take it out on the heartless asshole that beat him to death. I hate this feeling."

"Look, Bull is a major, major asshole. Convicted criminal. And jail did nothing to change who he is. I'm pretty sure he's the one that murdered Jimmy. His own son." Cecil shook his head. "And I've had to put up with him at the Annex, since he's been on the security team after his release from prison. Parole be damned, Earl gave him guns and responsibility immediately. He has to die. It's the only thing that will stop him."

I relaxed my fists. "Seems we both have some baggage to check at the door, then. So, I've been telling myself, over and over, I won't kill anyone unless I have to. If it's them or the life of my loved ones, the choice is clear. You should do that too."

Cecil nodded darkly and looked away. "Maybe you're right."

"Believe me, it's saved my bacon plenty of times. Kept me from going off on an emotional rampage and regretting it later. Took me a while to learn that lesson, though."

Cecil leaned back and looked at the sky again. I felt like I'd lost his attention somehow.

After an awkward pause, I nodded and smiled. "Simon, huh?" I reached out and gently shoved a hand against his shoulder.

Cecil cringed his ears flat and smiled sheepishly, and we both chuckled.

I chided further, "Hey, brother, I won't say a thing to anyone, but you have my blessing. And I know he likes you too."

Just then, Simon came out of the cabin in his sleek black and white plumage, holding a mug of warm tea out for Cecil.

I rose from my chair and scooted it closer to Cecil's. "I was just leaving, Simon. Here! I warmed up a seat for ya."

Simon thanked me and I winked secretly to Cecil as he took the cup of tea. His smile was a mile wide.

I went back inside the house and found Kayla sitting on the sofa with her back to the porch looking at her phone. She had missed the scene outside. I met her eyes with a smile on my beak, warmed by the secret knowledge of Cecil's feelings for Simon.

"What? Why are you smiling?" she asked, with her own smile growing.

"Let's go for a walk."

She grinned. "How about a flight instead?"

I took her clawed hands in mine and helped her to her feet. "You're on!"

Gramps said something about the weather, as he played cards and drank coffee with Zoe at the table. I knew it was useless, but said it anyway, "Gramps, you should lay off the coffee and get some rest for tonight."

"I could say the same to you, Sonny. Truth is, I couldn't sleep right now if my life depended on it. Neither could you."

I nodded. "Mhmm… well, give it a try anyway. Kayla and I are gonna go for a soar."

"You kids have fun."

Soon we were out back, behind the cabin, on the edge of the wooded canyon that ran beside Gramps' place. We hugged close, our beaks in each other's ear feathers, for a warm, familiar moment.

Kayla whispered, "Let's go feral."

I nodded and whispered back, "Sounds perfect."

She took my hands in hers, laced our fingers together, and started her transformation. Her face and head narrowed, and her body shrank with a fleshy sound.

I followed her lead, keeping pace as we changed together. I focused on the loving face of my mate, barely aware of the warming in my bones or the fleshy ripples under my plumage. My toes sank into the leafy soil, and my perspective dropped until I was only a couple of feet tall, the typical stature of a male bald eagle, and slightly lower than that of Kayla, since female birds of prey are larger than males.

Kayla's eyes brimmed with adoration as they changed from the dark irises of her human eyes to the pale gold of those of an eagle. Her obvious love made my spirit soar without leaving the ground. When our transformation ended, we stood with our beaks touching and our wingtips intertwined.

I stepped back, and we turned and took to the sky together, gained altitude, and entered the updraft of a southwesterly breeze. We swung back and forth across the rising air, never more than a wingspan apart. Her beak and eyes glowed bright as sunshine to me, despite the overcast, and we flew together for an hour or more, in the tight formation of a mated pair, solid against the uncertain clouds gathering around us.

Chapter 20: Showdown

November drizzle fell quietly out of the inky night sky in silky curtains, filtering down through the bright beam of a security lamp. Under the light, in a stone gatehouse, a lone, black-uniformed security guard sat working on Sudoku puzzles. The window was open, and a staticky AM talk radio host pontificated in the background, interrupted occasionally by the crackling voices of guards speaking to each other on their handheld radios.

I'd been perched in feral eagle form in an oak, forty yards away, for half an hour. It was around 2:30 in the morning, but I was wide awake. My eagle vision was not great in the dark, and getting to the tree had been difficult, aided only by the security light at the gate and the dim accent lights along the brick perimeter wall that isolated Earl's private estate from the rest of the world.

Behind the roadside brick wall was a wrought iron fence topped with razor wire, plus a narrow, treeless patrol zone that ran along the entire border of the property, some two square miles tucked in a bend of the Susquehanna River. We couldn't have chosen a better night weather-wise, as the heavy mist evened the odds between wolf senses and the poor night vision of all but the owls in our family. We were going to get Adele out and, if possible, take possession of The Orb.

Zoe had flown in ahead of everyone and was charged with surveilling BooneTech, located a mile to the southeast. From high up in the tree, I could make out the white glow of the security lights where it was located. I watched and waited for her signal that the coast was clear.

The most glaring weaknesses to the security of Earl's estate were access from the sky and from the Susquehanna River that wound along the eastern border. Gramps and Kayla were gathered there with the reserves of our forces, a flock of over a hundred of our birdfolk kin perched in the trees across the river to the east. A small, forested island provided cover for a jetboat, which stood by as an alternate escape route for Cecil, Robert, and any other family members that became injured and unable to fly.

My skin stayed warm and dry under my thick layer of down and contour feathers, the rain simply coalescing into larger drops and dribbling off my back and head. I was anxious and becoming impatient, wondering if Adele was having trouble.

I contemplated speaking into my Z-Phone to check on her, when it suddenly buzzed. I peered at the dim display to see a message from Zoe to everyone saying: *ZOE SAYS GO.*

The security guard was unfazed for a few minutes, still working steadily on his puzzles, but when he had finished one, he looked over his security screens, and noticed something was amiss. However, his perplexed look was interrupted, right on cue, by the approach of headlights.

Cecil's Tesla pulled up quietly to the gate house, and the guard walked out to meet him.

"Good morning, Dr. Boones. Burning the midnight oil?"

"Yes, yes. Coming back from a few days' break and couldn't sleep. I'm eager to get back to it."

The guard nodded and peered around the inside of the car with his flashlight, pausing when the beam illuminated Robert's face. "Mr. Robert. Don't see you here often, especially at this time of night. May I ask your business?"

Cecil spoke with a dismissive chuckle, stressing syllables awkwardly, like a typewriter with sticky keys. "Uh, he found Hayden for us. He's a detective, you know. So... he had to come along. We're taking Hayden's body to the lab."

"I'm sorry, Doctor, but you know I can't let anyone new in without prior authorization."

Robert interrupted by holding up his billfold to show his badge. "Hey, no problem, Rehnquist, I understand. I guess you'll just have to call the old man and let him know. And believe me, he'll definitely want to know. In the middle of the fuckin' night."

The guard winced and adjusted his hat, clearly hedging at the thought of disturbing his caloric master.

Robert leaned over and smiled. "You must be bored out of your mind. Wanna see the body before you call Earl?"

Rehnquist shrugged. "Okay, sure."

Robert exited the passenger door and walked around to the back of the car. The guard joined him there. Robert slapped the trunk twice and said, "He was in werewolf form at the time. Shot through the face, so it's pretty messy. Naturally, he's in a body bag, though. Open her up, Sees!"

The hatch popped open, and Robert swung it upwards to reveal Simon in anthro-magpie form leaning back with both hands on a TASER pistol aimed straight at Rehnquist. Before he could react, Simon fired into his chest, and the portly man collapsed to the wet pavement, jiggling and tremoring while the gun continued clicking rapid-fire bolts of electricity.

"Nice shot, Simon!" Cecil offered a hand to help him out of the trunk.

Simon breathed rapidly, with his hands shaking as he offered the TASER back to Robert. "Oh man, that was scary fun!" He leaned down, hands on his knees, catching his excited breath.

"Good work. Help me tape him up." Robert looked up towards me in the tree. "Any day now, Featherhead!"

I circled down from the tree and flared to a landing on the wet pavement. My body and head enlarged, and my wings melted into feathered and scaled humanoid arms as I assumed my anthro-eagle form. I kept my backwings unformed to make it easier to get in and out of Cecil's car.

In a few minutes, we had Rehnquist duct-taped and stowed in the trunk. Doc had provided a dose of tranquilizer, which we injected into the man's thigh before slamming the trunk shut.

Simon waved a flashlight towards some trees across the road, and two magpies glided down towards us. They were Scott and Cindy, Simon's brother and sister. In mid-flight, their bodies and wings enlarged, so that by the time they touched down, they were half the size of humans. Their feathers pulled into their bodies, and soft bony crunches emanated from their legs and arms as they reconfigured into those of a man and woman, stark naked except for feathers they left in place to conceal their lower bodies.

Simon grinned his beak corners and chucked a gym bag at the woman. "You look cold, sis! Here, have some clothes!"

Cindy smirked as she caught the bag and headed for the shadows to change. In a moment, the two came back, dressed in uniforms of the same style that Rehnquist wore.

We checked the systems in the guard shack and grabbed Rehnquist's radio off the counter. Robert briefed them, "Remember, open the gate for anyone. Just wave 'em through. In a few minutes, all hell's gonna break loose, and normal protocol will fall apart, so don't be afraid to improvise and act the part. I don't want you two getting shot, so don't piss any Boones' off, okay? Gimme status checks every half hour too."

Cindy and Scott nodded, and Scott said, "Yeah, we got this. Good luck!"

I punched a text into my Z-Phone: *LIGHT UP*. This was the

signal for our second team, five miles away at the Boonedocks, to swing into action.

Cecil and Robert climbed back into Cecil's car, I got in the back next to Simon, and we rolled into the compound, taking a right at a fork in the road marked "BooneTech." The well-manicured, paved road meandered through the forest to the south.

Robert turned and looked over his seat at me. In his right hand, he offered me a black semi-automatic pistol. "I want you to carry this." His eyes were full of serious concern. "I trust you know how to use it?"

I met his gaze and nodded as I took the weapon. "Can't grow up around here without some experience with guns." I studied the pistol, found the safety, and checked the chamber and magazine. Then I glanced down at myself and held the gun awkwardly. "Hey, smart guy, just where do I carry this—in my cloaca?" Having transformed from feral to anthro forms, I had no clothing. I was perched in a squatting position on the back seat in nothing but my feathers.

Simon's dark magpie beak flicked downward, his eyes looking at something below my hands.

Robert's eyes looked downward too, and I shifted my hands to cover my crotch as my beak blushed. "What are you pervs looking at?"

Robert chuckled as he turned his eyes back to the roadway. "The holster on the floor, you prude!"

Simon snickered and broke into a beaky laugh.

Cecil joined in his laughter, and the mood lightened for all of us. The holster slipped on over my left arm easily and clipped under my right arm. I could tell it was going to allow my wings to protrude from my back without impinging them.

As I finished snugging up the holster, we approached a large, grassy clearing.

Up ahead, across the tall grass, was a rectangular, two-story white building with large, dark windows arranged in two stripes, one for each floor. A flagpole stood in a circular driveway space in front of the building and a sign above the main entrance bore the word "BooneTech" in glowing white letters beside a stylized blue strand of DNA.

As we approached, we passed a paved square in front of a green metal building. In the center of the pavement was a white circle with an "H" in the middle, and the building had a wide hangar door that was closed. Nearby, an orange windsock hung limply in the rain.

We pulled around to the side of the main building and Cecil was about to park in his accustomed spot, but Robert interrupted him and said, "Back her in close to the door and point the nose out. If we're in a hurry, we don't want to have to turn around."

Cecil nodded nervously and complied.

Robert gripped his shoulder and smiled. "Relax, Cecil. You're doin' great."

We all exited the car and started towards the door when an owlish screech sounded from above. We peered upwards to see Zoe squatting on the roof, her owl toes curled over the metal drip edge. She was in anthro owl form, with her wings draped out like a poncho, keeping her pale, speckled arms and legs dry as she crouched there. Her mottled amber head, nape, and back plumage softened the edges of her frontal paleness. Her white barn owl facial disc was locked on us like a satellite dish, and her eyes were narrowed. Although I couldn't see her mouth corners, her eyes told me she was happy to see us.

It was the first time I'd seen Zoe in anthro form at night, in her element, and I was impressed. She belonged to the dark gloom every bit as much as an angel belonged in ethereal glory and puffy clouds. Zoe's feminine voice was heavy with her Cajun accent as she said, "Cameras here are taken care of.

There's a white pickup with two wolf guards, a pair in a Polaris 4-wheeler that drive the perimeter every thirty minutes, and I came across at least two feral wolves with radio collars. Right now, the Polaris is on patrol down by the river, and I hear the truck on the northern perimeter heading west."

I looked at Robert. "Might be heading back to the guard shack."

Robert nodded to Zoe, "Thanks. There's a lot more holed up at the guest houses, they just don't know we're here yet. Z-Phone us if they come this way. Stay safe."

Rehnquist's radio crackled to life with a series of beeps and an announcement in a clear female voice: *All pack, all pack, high alert, high alert. Situation at Boonedocks. Squads Almond Joy and Butterfinger remain on site, all others to rally point Alpha. Roll out in five minutes. This is not a drill.* The message repeated.

Robert smiled at us, "That's our cue!"

Zoe's head flipped about, focusing on various sounds in the distance. "I hear a lot of activity at the mansion."

Robert replied, "I bet you do! That's their rally point. We better get going."

Zoe said, "Good luck!" and she stood and spread her huge, pale wings. Her claws scraped on the roof as she turned and flapped away silently into the night.

Cecil's wide eyes froze on the space where Zoe had disappeared. My guess is he hadn't expected her to be so graceful in the air.

Robert smirked. "Cecil?" When this failed to get his attention, Robert nudged him.

Cecil jolted and dismissively replied, "Oh! Yes, let's get going, shall we?" He fished into his pockets and produced an RF key fob. He waved the fob over a black sensor and entered a code on a keypad. The door clicked, and Cecil opened it slightly.

Robert held up five fingers and whispered, "Give Sees and I five minutes. We'll take care of the guard and come back to get you."

I moved to the corner of the building and pulled Simon into the shadows with me. The door shut quietly behind them, and we waited. Those five minutes felt like an hour while listening to only the patter of the rain in the gutters and sounds of our hushed breathing. In the distance, engines roared to life, and vehicles sped away towards the main entrance, then screamed up the highway. The radio in Simon's hand crackled, and growly canine voices chattered above the din of revving engines.

Voice one: *What are we charging into?*

Voice two: *The Adlers are burnin' the place down. Got Tommy and Cecil. Gonna kill 'em if we don't surrender our hostage.*

Voice one: *Hostage? What hostage?*

Voice two: *I don't know but be ready for a shootin' match! Awoooo!*

Earl barked over the airwaves: *There is no hostage! They're desperate and crazy! Don't ask questions, assholes, just do what you're told! You pluck every last one of those pigeons! Thousand bucks for every bird freak's head you bring to me.*

Silence returned, and I pulled out the pistol that Robert had given me. It was a Glock 20 in tactical black. I checked the action and let it clack forward, loading a bullet into the chamber. I verified the safety switch was on. I was accustomed to relying on wings and agility in hand-to-hand fights or tearing into prey with claws and beak instead of shooting it from a distance. But Robert equipped me well—a hard-punching weapon that could stop an angry werewolf if I found myself in tight quarters or confronted with gunfire.

I silently resolved that I would only use it if someone else pulled a gun and there was too much space to close the distance quickly. In a moment like that, my claws and wings wouldn't be enough to protect myself or my loved ones. It was a simple choice.

Simon looked nervously at me, his breath steaming through his nasal bristles. I put a comforting hand on his back, smiled, and nodded reassuringly. His shoulders relaxed a fraction and he nodded back. No words were spoken, but we knew we could rely on each other.

The door clicked and squeaked open. Cecil appeared and peered into the darkness towards us. "Phil?" he loudly whispered.

I whispered back, "Here!"

Cecil turned towards us and motioned for us to follow, so we trailed him through the doors and into a modest freight elevator lobby. There were black rubber streaks on the floor and scuffed paint on the concrete walls from parcels being shoved in and out of the elevators or into the adjoining freight bay. A black plastic security camera blister was centered above the door. A segmented LED display above the doors confirmed that the car was on our floor.

Cecil waved his key fob over sensor, punched a code into an adjoining keypad, and the doors opened. Once inside, he let the doors close and used his fob and code again. He didn't need to press a floor button, as the elevator started its descent immediately. In fact, the panel only showed positive numbers, as though the sub levels were secret to most personnel.

I felt like Ethan Hunt in a Mission Impossible movie. Cecil admired our expressions of wonder and gestured at the floor indicator that read "S1." He said proudly, his eyes twinkling, "Kind of cool, eh? Like a spy movie? See, no need for floor commands, since my clearance means only one destination —"

I smothered Cecil's gesticulating hands with my own. "I get the idea. How'd it go down there?"

Cecil blinked his wolf eyes and said, "Fine, fine, all clear." Then Cecil's ears pricked up, and he diverted his gaze downward.

Then I heard it too. The sound of a shot fired. I shoved Simon against the wall and yelled, "Move to the sides!"

The doors slid open, and a blue wisp of cordite vapor wafted in from the hallway. A shotgun blast hit the back of the elevator, and lead BBs bounced all around us. I dropped down to my knees and pressed behind the right side of the door opening, while Simon and Cecil clung to the opposite wall. Cecil was in a fetal position against the corner, barking and howling and losing his mind. Simon hugged tight to him and looked at me for direction.

I slammed the door close button, but it wouldn't respond. Then I realized that an alarm was blaring and emergency lights were flashing. I yelled to Simon, "The buttons won't work! I think it's locked out!"

Oddly enough, the firing had stopped when Cecil started howling. I peeked around the edge of the door just enough to see that a straight concrete hallway lay beyond, a perfect bottleneck for would-be infiltrators like us. Beyond the first few yards, all was obscured by smoke and flashing lights.

"Keep howling, Cecil! I think you got their attention!" I cupped my hands around my beak, "Hey! You idiots! We're on your side!"

A growling voice shouted back, "Come out! Hands up where I can see 'em. One false move, and I'll blow your heads off!"

I recognized the voice. "Well whaddya know? It's Bull! …Shit!"

Cecil stopped howling, and his ears perked up. The alarm stopped and I heard Robert coughing in the background. *Good, he's alive.*

Cecil looked straight at me with the same calm, confident look he had shown when I first met him at the secret meeting just days ago, moments before he had lost his mind. He pushed Simon away and pulled a small inhaler, dangling on a neck chain, from his shirt opening. He pressed it to his lips and inhaled deeply, and slowly stood up as his muscles rippled.

He was starting from his anthro form, so his face was already that of a wolf. But his skull pulsed, widened, and enlarged to twice its usual dimensions. His body throbbed and expanded, emanating with moist sounds, gurgles, and squelches of organs rearranging, the dull thud of bones unjoining and rejoining, and the ripping sound of thick fur bursting from his skin and tearing his clothing to shreds. I'd seen him in his anthro form in recent days, but this was different. He grew taller and thicker, his back and shoulders hunched over with monstrous, taut sinews that tremored and rippled. He roared a twisted howl, blowing steaming breath through a snout contorted in pain or ecstasy, it was difficult to tell which. His fists shot upward and shattered the overhead light fixtures in a shower of sparks, leaving us in shadow.

Another shotgun blast fired and ricocheted off the wall, pelting us with fragments of lead and concrete. Cecil looked down at me, his eyes furrowed in anger. I yanked out my pistol, not sure if Cecil was still on my side, but he held up a thick, gnarled paw to stop me. His cobalt eyes softened, and his muzzle opened in a toothy grin, as he pointed at the gun and gestured for me to give it to him.

Cecil winked and whispered, "Trust me."

I relinquished the pistol into Cecil's paw, and he motioned for us to stand up. He barked down the hallway, "It's okay, Bull. It's your cousin, Cecil! I got the birds right here, so put your goddamm gun away!"

Bull shouted back, "Yeah? Bout god damn time you showed up. The Old Man's been shittin' bricks wonderin' where you were! Come forward!"

Cecil shouted again, "You put your gun down? Better not

fucking shoot me, or Earl will be gnawing on your bones!"

Bull grumbled, "Yeah, gun's down. You're clear!"

"Okay, I'm bringin' 'em out!" Cecil barked. He ushered us in front of himself and held his hands up high with the gun in one hand. The smoke had thinned, but still clung near the ceiling, swirling around Cecil's massive white wolf head.

A wide, high desk blocked the center of the room, and there were strong double doors to the rear and an overhead security camera pod. To one side sat the furry bulk of a werewolf, slumped and motionless in a chair. A gray and white werewolf hulked beside the security desk, a shotgun hanging down in his relaxed right hand. Before I knew what was happening, Cecil's arm came down, and the gun banged right over my head. Bull's forehead erupted in a geyser of blood, and he fell with a heavy thud like a furry sack of potatoes.

My ears ringing, I suddenly found myself two yards away, crouching over Simon, hackles raised, ears ringing, and mantling him like a hen protecting her chicks. Time caught up, and I realized that it was over. Cecil stood over Bull, laughing triumphantly. He fired again into the corpse before Robert shouted, "Cecil! Stop! I'm pretty sure he's dead!"

"You okay?" I asked Simon.

He nodded his magpie beak and stood up from where I'd pulled him down.

I turned to Cecil and asked, "Hey! Are you alright?"

Cecil's blue eyes were moist above his toothy grin and his right eye twitched. I'd watched him flirt with insanity the past two days, but there was more there now, like a man clamoring up from a caved-in mine and seeing the light of day again. There was certainly adrenaline, but I believe he also tremored from his months of despondency turning to hope and vindication.

"Cecil?"

"I'm fine, Phil," he said plainly, with a quivering voice. His shaky paw turned the gun around and offered it to me handle-first. "I'm fine."

I took the pistol and looked at the growing pool of blood around Bull's shattered head.

Cecil continued, "You know what a disgusting monster he was." He looked me in the eyes and said with a cool, even voice, "The things he did to his own child. To me. The piece of shit deserved that bullet a long time ago. It needed to be done, and I fucking did it." After a thoughtful pause he added, "Let's finish this."

Robert slowly lifted himself up, coughing and holding his muzzle in pain. "Fuck!"

I rushed over to him and helped him stand. "You okay? Are you shot?" I tipped his furry face back in the overhead lighting to have a better look. There was blood pooling in his canine nares. He winced and pushed my hands back.

"I'll live. In case you didn't know it, the worst place to strike a werewolf is the end of the muzzle. Jeezus, that HURTS!"

Simon came over, holding Robert's pistol, and handed it to him.

Robert went on, "I was tying up that asshole when 'Bang!' Bull came up behind me and knocked my lights out. Thanks, Cecil. I guess those lessons I gave you years ago came in handy."

Cecil nodded and gave a friendly whine, which seemed out of place coming from the muzzle of a huge, hulking canine.

Robert blinked. "Uh, how'd you—?"

"Get so big? Yes, well, we've learned a thing of two from The Orb. Let's just say we didn't make that mitogen just for a practical joke on birdfolk."

"Does Earl know that trick?" I asked.

"He does. And he has one of these too, the only other one that exists so far. It's concentrated mitogen, along with some other substances to smooth out the ride."

I asked, "What would happen if I—?"

"I dunno. Probably something similar. But let's find out later. With the alarms activated, we gotta hurry." Cecil grabbed the blood-spattered shotgun from Bull's hand and swung it like a club at a camera pod on the ceiling, shattering it and sending the pieces flying. His massive legs sent him up and over the large desk as easily a kid hopping over a crack in the sidewalk.

His right paw shriveled into a human hand again as he crouched down at the keypad on a shiny steel door. He swiped his finger and punched in a code. I heard a mechanical click, and he pulled the door open.

We followed Cecil a short distance down a corridor and came to a hallway that branched right and left. Straight ahead were a pair of glass doors with a security lock. Beyond was a dark room with a single shaft of illumination shining down on a dark, smooth sphere resting on a pedestal.

I paused and stared at it. "So that's the source of all this trouble?"

Simon pressed his face to the glass, his magpie eyes swiveling up and down, scanning the alien object. "My gods! Incredible! You've got to let me in there to see it!"

I chuckled. "Later! How about we go find Adele first?"

Cecil had already swiped his finger and opened the door. "Take a look, Simon, while we go on!"

Simon nodded excitedly and started through the door.

I shook my head. "Bad idea to split up. But give me the radio at least."

Cecil handed the Boones' radio to me and slipped away through the door.

The radio crackled faintly and I turned it up: *Response One. Arrived Boonedocks. This is a nothingburger.*

Robert asked me, "Is that singing I hear in the background?"

Female Dispatcher: *What is the situation?*

Voice One: *Looks like a god damn family cookout. Tommy, Darla, bunch of birds, and half the Pennsylvania Bald Eagles team singing songs and roasting marshmallows.*

I replied to Robert with a chuckle, "Operation Kumbaya is a success!"

Female Dispatcher: *Old man says to get your asses back here pronto.*

Response One: *Roger, on our way!*

I rolled my eyes in relief. "Damn! that worked like a charm. Nobody hurt, no fuss, and the Boones look like the fools they are, present company excepted."

Robert smiled. "Thanks! Let's hope the roadblocks on the bridges hold."

We followed Cecil down the hall to the left and around a corner. He took us through a secure door, through a small room with restraints and padded walls, and finally through another secure door into a hallway with rows of small, orange-painted, steel doors with tiny windows. I'd never been to jail, but anyone would recognize that it was not a place built for people that wanted to be there.

Cecil wasted no time in walking straight to the first cell. A light was on and Adele was inside, in anthro-owl form, crumpled in the fetal position on the floor. I pounded on the door, and she stirred slightly. Then I noticed bloody claw marks, a torn-up mattress, and a broken chair.

Cecil pressed a button on an intercom and said to me, "Talk now," as he fumbled with keys.

"Adele! It's Phil! We're here to bust you out!" I turned to Cecil. "You have all this fancy electronic security shit and you still use keys for this?"

Cecil shrugged. "I guess Earl's an old fart and doesn't trust computers for everything."

Adele moved and lifted her head up from under her hunched form. She was wearing a leather hood over her head and her arms were shackled behind her back. Her backwings were tethered in leather straps and Velcro. Her motions were erratic, and she was drooling. She chirped slowly and tried to stand but fell on her side.

"What in the hell did they do to her?"

Cecil frantically tried another key. "Sedation."

"She's a firecracker. I hope she gave them some pain for their trouble." I shouted into the intercom, "Hang on, Adele! Just about got you out!"

The lock clicked, and Cecil slid the door aside. In an instant, I crouched over Adele and worked on her restraints.

"We're getting you outta here! Hold still while I get ya loose!"

Adele fought and screeched unintelligibly. She was unhinged, and I was afraid of hurting her.

I shouted, "Hold still, Adele! Robert, help me!"

Adele swung her beak at me and missed by a mile, but I got the message that she was not herself. I changed tactics and grabbed the top knot of the hood. I yanked the braces open and pulled the hood off. She shook her head and jolted back against the wall with beak open, feathers erect, and hissing ferociously. Her face was streaked with dried blood from her nares, and her left eyelids were purple and swollen almost shut.

I said in a gentle voice, "Shhh, dear. It's me, Phil. Your future grandson-in-law, Phil. See? I'm an eagle."

She mumbled my words back and blinked her nictitating membranes slowly, her dark pupils fluctuating wildly as she tried to bring me into focus. "Phhill? Is that you?"

"Yeah, Adele, it's me. I'm gonna take the cuffs off, okay? Is that okay?"

"Uh-huhh... Phil? Is that really you? Senior, orrr grandson?"

I worked on the Velcro and straps, answering, "Phil, the third, dear. But Gramps is outside. Got the whole posse here for ya. No way were we leaving you in this nightmare. Can you walk?" I worked on the leather foot bags that kept her eagle feet balled and disarmed.

"Uh-huh. Will walk... outta here for damn ssurre."

I got the last of the restraints off and supported her by the armpits as I hoisted her up. She extended her toes and chirped in pain. Her talons were bloody and split, and one had degloved entirely, completely exposing the glistening red nail bed underneath.

I set her down on the bed. "Lie down here a sec, hon. I'm going to pick you up fireman style and carry you outta here, okay?"

She grated back in her barn owl voice, "Okay. Ces clébards ne peuvent pas me retenir ici!"

I chuckled. "Oui, oui! I don't know what you're saying, but I agree!"

She chortled and smiled. "Now I know it's you." Tears glistened in her eyes. "I thought I was..."

"You're safe now." I hoisted her up in my arms. "Wow, you're light as a feather! Wrap your arms around my neck."

We pushed out the small door into the hallway. When Adele saw the massive bulk of Cecil in the hallway, with a smaller werewolf beside him, she hissed and scrambled in my arms, digging her claws into my neck.

"Easy! Easy! Easy, dear. It's just Cecil! He's a good guy! And this is Robert. The last two good Boones left."

"Boones?"

"Yeah, you remember. Like us, only wolves, not birds. Easy, girl, relax the talons."

She relaxed her claws, but her owl head stayed locked on to Cecil and Robert the whole way as we traced our steps back to where we left Simon. When we arrived back at the laboratory, the lights were all on, but Simon and The Orb were gone. Magpie feathers littered the floor of the lab and hallway creating a path back towards the security station.

I couldn't believe it. "Fuck! We never should have left him. Get the door open!"

Cecil opened the door to the lab and we poured in, looking around and calling after Simon, but no reply was heard.

Cecil growled, "Damn! Fucking Earl must've watched the whole thing, just waiting for us to go for Adele before slipping out with The Orb."

Robert barked, "He's escaping then?"

Cecil nodded his head. "Probably to one of the other facilities. And he has Simon as a fresh study subject."

I added, "Or to coerce into deciphering the device."

Earl's voice crackled on the radio: *Where the hell's my security? Converge on the hangar!*

Response One: *Response One here! Roadblock at the Cat bridge. Heading for the Bloomsburg bridge.*

Earl barked ferociously: *Goddammit all to hell, you run those fuckers over or swim your asses back here! I don't care what you do but get back here now!*

Response One: *Roger Wilco.*

I yanked my Z-Phone out and spoke a text message: "Patrol, status?"

Then I noticed that there was no signal indication. "Shit. Probably can't transmit through all this concrete. How'd the radio work?"

Robert replied, "Probably got repeaters in here."

Cecil started up the hallway towards the front of the complex. "Hurry! His pilot and helicopter are just across the parking lot. He's probably gonna fly 'em out of here, so this is our only chance to stop 'em!"

When we reached the security lobby, Cecil ran to a steel door beside the elevator marked "Emergency Use Only" and rammed the crash bar. Alarms blared back to life and lights strobed. Beyond the door, we ran down a short hallway and up a zig-zagging metal stairway in a concrete shaft three stories tall. Robert ran ahead, and I was right on his wolf tail with Adele in my arms. He busted through the door at the top of the stairs, and we spilled out into the dark night not far from the freight entrance we had used earlier.

Across the grass to the west, the hangar doors were open and a cherry red Airbus AS350B3 helicopter sat on a self-propelled helicopter landing dolly. Its corner markers flashed, and it emitted soft beeps, as it crept the chopper towards the center of the helipad. A mid-thirties, dark-haired man dressed in a blue Nomex flight suit stood nearby operating the remote control for the dolly.

A massive gray beast of a werewolf with thick, bulging limbs stood on Simon with one foot, while another smaller, sand-colored werewolf struggled to strap Simon's feet and hands together behind his back.

The gray werewolf howled at us and shouted at the pilot, "Good enough! Get us the hell out of here!"

The man obeyed and hurriedly worked at removing the red straps that secured the tips of the chopper's rotors.

Earl pressed his foot down firmly on Simon, who squirmed and jabbed his beak frantically at whatever soft flesh he could reach. As it turned out, his beak found Billy's face. Billy yipped sharply and lurched back in searing pain, letting go of Simon's hands to grasp his bleeding nose.

Robert shouted, "Tell everyone to converge here!" He took off running, transforming on the go.

I chirped into my Z-Phone, "Rescue two to all, converge on BooneTech!"

I eased Adele down to the ground and exclaimed, "Cecil!" I handed him my gun, "Protect her! Get to the car and get out of here!"

Cecil grasped my arm and met my gaze with his ears laid back. His eyes were uncharacteristically timid for such a huge predator. "Be careful. That's Earl. He's got everything to lose. It's a fight to the death, him or you!"

I nodded. "Thanks, Sees. I understand."

I took off on a run, but I knew I would need my wings again, so I pushed them out in a muffled crunch of growing bone and muscle and the papery sliding of massive feathers.

Lashed with verbal abuse from Earl, eyes watering, and nose bleeding profusely through his fingers, Billy struggled to get back to his feet. He shakily prepared to give Simon an injection with a syringe. Robert, in feral wolf form at a full gallop, slammed into him, and the two skidded across the pavement.

As Earl watched Robert and Billy fight, Simon stabbed him in the leg with his beak. But the massive werewolf was unfazed. He looked down with a sadistic grin and cocked his leg back. He kicked Simon's chest, then his head, repeatedly slamming his beak against the pavement until he lay quiet, his feathers ruffling in the misty breeze.

Earl opened his steaming maw in a wide, toothy smile and turned his muzzle left and right to project an unearthly howl that echoed like a spooky siren far and wide into the night. I powered through the air like a 175-pound feathered missile right towards him, my beak corners bent down in determination. I jutted my feet forward and spread my toes in a deadly phalanx of sharp talons.

My legs were straight and drilled my full weight into Earl's chest as my talons sank deep. I flapped my wings and bent my legs as he toppled over, then sprang off again. I was perfectly balanced and controlled, blessed with the agility of a top athlete and an aerial predator. Earl was not. My eagle eyes saw every detail as his wolfish body slammed the pavement, back first then his head, flesh rippling from the impact. In those fractions of a second, his smile was gone, and his eyes stared in cold shock, belying the uncertainty he normally concealed behind a smug grin. It was the look of one realizing they had grossly miscalculated. I sped out of reach and landed nimbly ten yards away on the other side.

I breathed easily, while Earl puffed steamy breath from his maw and rolled over onto his chest before slowly lifting himself again. Blood streamed down his chest, staining his fur crimson.

Earl lifted an inhaler from a neck chain to his lips and took a deep inhale. He coughed and doubled over as his shoulders and back bulged and swelled into knots of thick muscle. His werewolf paws throbbed into massive mitts of fur and claws, and his head doubled in size as his ferocious teeth stretched his vicious smile to monstrous dimensions. He let out a long and bloody howl, clenched his fists, and launched a series of brutal kicks into Simon's limp, fluffy body, causing white and black feathers to whirl away in the wind.

Earl stared and laughed with his brows furrowed in disgust, proudly jeering, "C'mon, sport! You were cocky when you had a scatter gun at my back. Just try and stop me now!"

To the side, Billy gave a choking cry of pain as Robert sank teeth into his furred throat. Robert growled horribly, and his whole body shook with the fury of his flesh-rending attack. Billy's limbs thrashed the wet pavement, and his muzzle opened and closed as he tried in vain to swallow another breath of life-giving air.

I ran three strides and took flight straight at Earl again. As my feet left the ground, Earl pulled his legs in to leap up at me, but his massive size didn't give him greater speed. As he left the ground, I snapped a barrel roll around him and planted my foot talons firmly in his hindquarters, while my finger talons latched into his neck. He nearly fell over, but I flapped to keep us upright as his thick arms flailed.

Earl howled in pain as my talons penetrated his neck and ass. We tumbled to the ground, and Earl thrashed and rolled like a crocodile, trying to scrape me off his back or crush me under his bulk. I opened and closed my right hand rapidly, like an owl kneading its talons into its prey, searching for contact with a critical organ that would steal life the quickest. But I couldn't find his jugular under his thick werewolf hide, and his throat was too broad to choke with my hands.

I adjusted my feet and sank them with all my strength into his flanks, urging my talons to grow longer, until they found and punctured his kidneys and lungs. Earl grunted and squealed a fear-laden cry that experienced predators know all too well. It was the panicked shriek of mortal terror uttered when prey sees its end approaching. It heralds a desperate and dangerous moment. When you're losing everything, you will fight with absolutely everything, until you can't fight anymore.

He howled and doubled over. I'd found a vulnerability, and I could tell by his ragged panting that he was feeling the cold, draining feeling of internal hemorrhage.

My avian instincts were at the fore and wanted the struggle to stop as quickly as possible. Behind that layer, my human mind tasted the bitterness of another useless, and avoidable, death. I quivered in deadlock, wrapped around my wounded prey, and whispered, "It could've been different. Our families share the same ancestors. Our futures are together. But you will not see any future now."

Earl tensed and grunted with a wheeze, then spat words out like venom. "Go fuck yourself, freak!" He laughed and then coughed, staining his broad, toothy smile with bright red blood from deep in his lungs.

A chorus of howls sounded all around us, joining in a single strong note that prickled the feathers down my back. Earl grunted, "Looks like the tables have turned on ya, sport!"

From out of the dark mist, wolves and werewolves of many shades ran towards us, yipping, howling, and barking so much, that it was difficult to count them. The pack of furry figures closed in and completely encircled us. Adele and Cecil were pulled from his car and pressed ahead of the closing pack.

Adele shrieked as a white and gray werewolf struck her face with its broad paw. It wrapped its arms around her from behind and pressed its teeth to her neck.

Another nearby werewolf barked, "Stop! Let Earl go! Or say goodbye to this tasty female!"

I glanced at Robert, who was slowly rising to his feet, his fur rippling as he transformed back to werewolf form. His muzzle and whole front were stained in red, and he breathed raggedly. Billy lay at his feet, motionless in a wide steaming puddle as dark as ink in the dim light.

Earl continued laughing derisively in between coughs and grunts of pain. My avian instincts bade me to rip his throat out before he had the chance to turn and kill me, and my human desire to protect my loved ones and avenge my friends urged me to rub him out and make the world better. But I knew they wouldn't hesitate to kill Adele if I finished Earl right now.

I disengaged my talons and pushed off Earl's rump, sprang into the air, and landed on the rotor mast of the helicopter. It quivered and rocked, and the pilot shuffled back away from it. Earl rose, slowly, to his feet, grasping at his flanks and breathing raggedly. He glared at me with destruction in his dark wolfish eyes and grinned a bloody smile.

Earl growled at a nearby werewolf, "Becky! Take the traitors and that bitch owl back to the lab. Chris…" He coughed and spat a blob of blood on the ground, "Change of plans. I'm busted up. Gonna need you to take me directly to the hospital in Catawissa. But first, let's clear the vermin off your bird." He pointed at me and bellowed, "Would someone please blow that shitbird's head off?!"

My heart pounded in my ears, and my beak went cold. I could have dived or flown, but neither seemed promising. The action on a dozen pistols, shotguns, and rifles sounded as werewolves all around took steady aim.

Earl mock-saluted and said, "Adios, freak! Fire!"

Suddenly, a chorus of caws and shrieks punctuated the night sky to the east, and my heart soared. The unsettled murmurs of werewolves, and the clicking of more weapons, arose from the furry throng. I wasted no time, diving down at the closest werewolf. Guns flashed, and a slug tore through the feathers of my left wing, missing flesh. My talons struck full force into the chest of my foe, and I felt her ribs crack as we slammed into the ground together. I grabbed her gun and brandished it like a club, striking the muzzle of the first wolf that closed in on me.

Robert was right about hitting the end of the muzzle; the wolf spun and limped off, howling in anguish. Teeth flashed as another wolf bit into my right forearm. I pressed the shotgun to its throat and pulled the trigger, dropping it in a misty shower of meat and blood.

Meanwhile, a patter of gunfire rained down from the sky on the others. Two fell and howled on the ground while their comrades shot wildly into the sky at the avian shapes that darted in the mist. One shot found its mark and I heard the chirp of an golden eagle as Ben fell limply from the sky and crumpled into the tall grass.

On the north edge of the tarmac, a cluster of wolves yipped

in pain and thudded to the ground as arrows whistled through the air. A small chorus of inhuman owlish shrieks arose from the nearby trees, and arrows zipped out of the dark branches. Two wolves yelped fearfully and charged off into the night while their comrades yowled in pain. Others fired guns blindly, unaided by muzzle flashes from their opponents. Another rain of arrows thudded into their targets and the gunfire diminished abruptly as frantic howls took over the chorus of battle.

The breech-loading shotgun was empty, and I swung it wildly, barely keeping the werewolves at bay. They circled and snarled and snapped their jaws, like a pack closing in on a caribou calf, just waiting for an opening to spring in and bring me down.

They were too close for me to hope to jump into flight, so I kept up my desperate stalemate, striking blows with the stock of the gun, or slashing fur from those that got closer. At last, one succeeded in grasping me, and then another, and then they all closed in and latched onto my legs. They slammed me down to the ground on my back. I was strong, but my light avian body was no match for the bulk of three werewolves pressing down on me and clutching my throat.

One of them, a red-hued wolf with a grizzled face, growled, "You're dead meat, pal! We're gonna pluck and gut you like a chicken, alive!"

Then I saw the loveliest sight in my life. Out of the darkness above me, my lovely Kayla, in anthro-eagle form, with her wings spread wide, came floating down. Her talons were out, and her eyes locked with laser focus onto the back of the head of the wolf that was taunting me.

Mammalian reactions are slow, and he barely had time to furrow his brow and say, "What the fuck you looking at?" before Kayla's thick eagle feet crashed into his skull. She didn't stop, letting her wings tilt and divert her momentum forward as her talons shredded through the wolfman's flesh, and she swiveled back into the sky.

The red wolf screamed, and his flesh hung in strips from his face and head, obscuring his vision with blood. He rolled around on the ground, grasping at his face to hold the flesh together, while the others jumped away in panic and horror. I lost no time flapping my wings to bring my feet back into the air. I sank my talons into the chest of the nearest werewolf. He lost his balance and fell backwards, giving me the clearance and momentum to take wing and follow my mate into the air.

As I sailed clear, I heard one of the werewolves shout, "Fuck this! Every wolf for himself!" They fled for the tree line as three anthro-ravens croaked out cries of war, and strained their whistling wings after them.

As I reached Kayla, I playfully nipped at her tail, and she flipped over in flight and briefly grasped my talons, spinning us in one quick spiral before breaking apart in laughter.

"Perfect timing, hon! Couldn't have been better —"

A bullet whizzed by, followed by the crack of a pistol shot. We both looked down and saw the flash of a gun in Earl's hands, followed by a hollow, wet thump, like a ripe pumpkin dropped on pavement. Kayla screeched and faltered, clutching at her breast.

I wrapped my arms around her and screamed, "Hold on! Hold on!" I couldn't lift the both of us, so I aimed at the soft, tall grass and flapped with all my might to slow our fall. Our wings flailed, ruffled, and stalled, but I wouldn't let her go. I rode with her all the way down until we struck the grass and tumbled to a stop, crumpled in each other's feathers.

"Oh god! Kayla! Kayla?" I searched her feathers for the source of blood that was trickling down her wing. She heaved and panted steamy eagle breath into the air. Her head rolled back, her eyes darted around for my face, and she grimaced and squeaked with the pathetic cry of an eagle in pain and shock.

"Don't struggle, Kayla. You're gonna be okay." My eyes

blurred with tears, as I fought to suppress the fear that she was dying. My fingers found the hole in her right breast near the keel. I had no cloth to make a bandage, nor first-aid kit, so I simply stuffed a finger in the hole. She tensed and screeched.

I yelled out, "Medic! Doc! Gramps!"

All was a dance of crazy shadows, some furry, some feathery, some armed with guns, others with knives, teeth, or claws. Nobody seemed to notice us there in the dark, bloody grass, amidst the macabre sound of gunshots, ripping flesh, howling wolves, and screeching birds.

In my focus on Kayla, I didn't notice Gramps drop down out of the air next to us. He shined a small flashlight in Kayla's face, and her pupils constricted. "Darlin', open your beak."

Kayla's eyes were wide with mortal fear as she allowed Gramps to gently her mouth and check around.

Victor hobbled up as fast as he could and said, "Help's here, Phil. Doc's on his way."

Gramps spoke calmly, "No blood in your glottis. You just lie still, girl, you're gonna make it. Ol' Doc Adler is here. Victor, see if you kin lift 'er legs. Gots to keep 'er from goin' into shock."

Victor obeyed, while Gramps pulled a dressing from a satchel slung under his left arm. He flicked his arm and unfurled the large, white dressing, like a seasoned battle medic. He clasped my bloody fingers, which were still pressed into Kayla's wound, and looked me in the eyes with a comforting nod. I relaxed and pulled my fingers back so he could stuff a wad of Gelfoam into the puncture and cover it with the dressing. I helped him tilt and lift Kayla's torso, while he wrapped the dressing around her chest. She groaned and screeched with each movement.

I choked on my tears, my heart breaking to see her in pain. "Can't we give her something for the pain?"

Gramps nodded, "Doc will be here in two shakes of an eagle tail."

Kayla nodded her beak and made an affirmative squeak.

Gramps muttered to me low while he tied the dressing, "'Twas a long way for a pistol shot. No exit wound. Not spittin' blood. I think it stopped at her sternum. Damn sure hurts, but she won't die."

I stared into Kayla's eyes and whispered, "You hear that, love? Hang in there, my eagle warrior. You're gonna be okay!"

I said to Gramps, "Adele's okay. Beat up, drugged, but she sounded like herself."

Gramps sighed, "Thank ya, Sonny. Best news to these old ears."

Across the pasture, the helicopter's turbines whirred to life. It was only a hundred yards away, but it might as well have been miles for all I cared at that moment. All that mattered to me now was in my arms.

Victor said, "Looks like Earl's takin' off!"

Kayla's brows furrowed in pain, but her pupils were pinned, and her eyelids creased in admiration. It was an eagle's affection for her mate. She gripped my hand in hers and squeaked, "Go, Love."

The chopper's engine ticked and blurted with a hollow pop as the combustion chambers flamed to life. The blades sped faster. The wolves were defending the helipad and Earl was in the helicopter, urging his pilot to take off. A patter of gunfire rang out and I saw muzzle flashes from the werewolves around the helicopter and from the tall grass. Another werewolf fell and his two remaining comrades lifted their paws in surrender. As the helicopter lifted into the air, Earl stuck his wolfish arm out the window, and fired repeatedly into the grass, kicking up the shriveling cry of a wounded golden eagle.

Victor looked at me with his peppered brown eyes wide.

"He's gonna get away, Phil! I'd go after him if it weren't for this!" he said, as he gestured to his arm cast. "It's up to you!"

I looked at Gramps and he nodded. "We got this, grandson."

Kayla raised her voice in painful spasms, "Love. Go… Finish it."

I leaned down and tapped my beak to hers. "Love you, mate. I'll be right back!"

The helicopter kicked up a swirling cloud of feathers and compressed mist as it sluggishly climbed into the humid air. A massive, white-furred figure was clinging onto the skid of the helicopter, rocking it back and forth as it pulled him off his feet.

Cecil! You crazy son of bitch! I thought to myself. But Earl aimed downward, and more shots rang out. Cecil fell with a yip, crumpling to the pavement. The helicopter wheeled around, its rotors rattling loudly as it transitioned to forward flight and lifted over the trees.

I broke into a run and then into flight, skidding to a stop on the pavement seconds later. Cecil was alive but his right hand was mangled from gunshot. Robert was holding it up for him and shouting for someone to grab the first-aid kit from the hangar.

Cecil winced and said, "Fucker shot my hand!"

"Better than your head! Now, give me your inhaler!"

"What for?" Cecil's eyes widened. "You're not gonna… But we haven't tested it on birds…"

I slipped off my sidearm holster and shouted, "There's no time like the present, right?"

Cecil tugged on the inhaler at his breast and snapped the beaded necklace holding it. He tossed it to me and shouted with a grin, "Give 'em hell!"

I smiled and exhaled, then took a deep breath while

squeezing the inhaler. It was like inhaling fire. I doubled over, my sensitive avian lungs foaming and tingling within me. The air tore out of my mouth, and I couldn't inhale again. It was worse than getting the wind knocked out of me during my first season of varsity football. I feared I'd made a fatal mistake.

My vision blurred and my muscles relaxed, as what felt like molten lava coursed through my arteries. My heart fluttered and I fell to my knees, then crumpled to the ground. I tried to take a breath, but my entire body was flaccid and paralyzed.

In the blurry ether, Cecil gripped my hand and shouted in distant muffled barks, "Hang on! The paralysis passes!"

My bones burned, as cells multiplied at insane rates and expanded to many times their normal dimensions. I felt my now limp muscles stretch and burn as they swelled. My skin tightened and prickled with new, larger feathers. Tingling heat radiated out of my tail, as the existing feathers jutted out to enormous proportions.

Then the heat reached my mind. A writhing sensation, like electrified worms, gyrated in the confines of my eagle cranium, followed by a headache so sharp that I feared my brain was splitting in two. At last, muscle control returned, and I inhaled violently, and screeched out a ragged scream as starbursts and fireworks exploded behind my clenched eyes.

As quickly as the pain had seized me, it ebbed and washed away, leaving me panting and euphoric, like erupting to the surface of the water after a deep dive. I opened my tear-blurred eyes and appreciated a wider, larger view before me. As my vision cleared, I saw Cecil smiling at me and chuckling. "Quite the fucking rush, am I right?" He held out a hand to help me back up.

The pain and muscle tension were gone, and so I took his hand and stood up. I was a few heads higher than Cecil's uber-werewolf posture now, easily twelve feet tall. I looked at my massive bulk, spread my wings, and turned around.

I could still make out the clattering of helicopter rotors clear in the distance, and the flash of aviation anti-collision lights reflected off the orange glow of low clouds. I realized that less than a minute had gone by, but it had seemed much longer.

Cecil gave a whistle of appreciation. "My money's on you! Now go get 'em!"

I chucked the inhaler back into Cecil's hands and nodded. "Thanks! Here goes!" I jumped into the air and shoved down with my huge wings. My wingtips slapped the pavement, and I touched my toes down again lightly as I lifted my wings and pulled them down again. A werewolf barked in terror and ran from before me. My larger mass accelerated more slowly than either my anthro or feral forms, but I felt no end to the power surging in my pecs. A few more strokes later, and I was two hundred feet high and still gaining speed.

My nictitating membranes flashed in the stinging mist as I accelerated casually past the speed that would have normally been a strain to achieve. Through slashes of mist and pelting raindrops, I flapped harder until I found the limits of my new muscles and bulkier shape. Fortunately, that limit was faster than the helicopter that groped its way along under low clouds.

As I approached the helicopter, I was jolted by violent rotor wash. The vortices tumbled me upside down briefly before I regained control and climbed higher to stay above the wake. I'd never dared to dawdle in the air around operating aircraft before, so I was uncertain about how to approach it without getting slammed around by turbulence or chopped into confetti.

I took position directly above the helicopter, judging that they had no idea I was there. I thought about simply following them to their destination, but my mind was made up that Earl could not survive this night and I couldn't risk a confrontation in public view. I maneuvered to the right, staying high and just ahead, then rolled right sharply to tumble around the reach of the helicopter's blades. I spread my arms and legs and slipped back under the whooshing rotors aiming for the right forward door.

I barely managed to grasp the chopper's right skid, and my talons latched on tight. I swung under the belly of the helicopter, and my momentum, in combination with my flapping wings, tilted the whole machine almost ninety degrees on its side. The wash was tremendous, and my eardrums popped in the violent chop. I couldn't hope to overpower the helicopter, but upsetting its aerodynamics was enough. We fell a hundred feet, and the landscape tilted as the pilot yawed hard to the right and dropped the nose, diving out of the brief spin. We checked our descent a mere hundred feet above the treetops. The tree canopy gave way to water, as we slipped across the riverbank and out over the dark ribbon of the Susquehanna. The glow of Catawissa shone through the mist a couple miles away.

With the helicopter level again, I reached with my hands to grasp the skid my toes were wrapped around. I clambered up onto it and slammed my fist into the Plexiglas of the door, cracking it like an egg. Earl grinned wide as he pressed the muzzle of his pistol to the window. He pulled the trigger, but it only clicked. Earl's smile dropped like he'd had a stroke.

I punched my fist through the window, breaking the plastic into shards, which my hand talons raked away like thin ice. Earl tried to back away, but his seat restraints stopped him. He fumbled for the buckles just as my right arm thrust in and my hand closed on his furry throat. My huge fingers found his windpipe this time, and I squeezed until I could feel his carotid arteries throbbing under my fingertips.

The pilot had his hands too full of controls to help his boss. He banked the machine abruptly left and right, back and forth, trying to shake me free, but each aggressive maneuver dropped us lower towards the water, and it was clear that we couldn't spare any more altitude. He finally leveled out and concentrated on maintaining level flight.

Earl finally succeeded in unlatching his harness, and the buckle ends clattered to the deck. His massive, uber-werewolf eyes showed their white sclera as he strained to direct his gaze at me. I pulled his head inexorably towards the door, and he tried to speak, but his windpipe was crushed shut. His left arm whipped about, clutching a heavy leather bag, as he grinned a winner's smile. It was The Orb, and he intended to chuck it into the river with his dying breath.

Suddenly a dark beak lurched from the back seat and latched onto the bag. Simon's arms and legs were bound, but not his beak. Earl's expression changed from victory to cold horror, as the bag ripped free from his grasp.

The helicopter banked right again, giving me just the break I needed, and I tugged hard. Soft meat rent asunder in Earl's neck, and blood sprayed the windscreen as I dragged him through the shattered window and released him into the void. He fell away into the darkness in a shower of crimson rain and splashed into the river. And that was it. No thrashing limbs or bobbing head followed. Only the silently rolling, dark waters.

I clung to the door frame as the pilot stared at me in pale horror. I pressed my eagle face inside the window and studied Simon lying back, panting, the leather bag still grasped firmly in his beak.

I shouted to the pilot, "Don't look so scared! I'm not after you. Now turn around and take us back!"

In a few minutes, we approached the Boones Estate hangar. Werewolves and humans were seated on the ground in rows, with more being led to the assemblage, their arms secured behind their backs. Doc's ambulance was parked on the driveway, near where I had left Kayla and Gramps.

I let go and glided down to the tarmac ahead of the chopper. I spread my arms to gesture to the others to make room for the helicopter as it landed and powered down.

I shouted, "Anyone with a knife, get over to the chopper and cut Simon loose!"

A raven voice croaked out, "Got it!" as he trotted towards the helicopter.

I walked towards Robert, who was still in werewolf form. He grabbed my arm and pulled me close in a brief victory. "Damn glad to see you make it back. I don't see Earl. What happened?"

"He's dead. Fell in the river."

"You sure?"

"I ripped his throat out and he went straight to the bottom. No way he survived that."

Robert's brows creased and his mouth corners drooped with sadness. "Thirteen dead, that we know of, including five of your kin. Kayla's doing fine."

I had to ask, "I saw Ben go down. Please tell me…"

Robert shook his head somberly.

I looked down and then away, trying to stave off grief for a few more clear-headed minutes. Recomposing myself, I looked at Robert, searching for the words to say. He spoke first.

"Well done, brother. Well done."

I nodded. "Yeah. I… Oh god." I spasmed for breath as the adrenaline subsided just enough for the horrors of the fight to well up inside me like muddy floodwaters and overwhelm my emotions.

Robert stepped closer and wrapped his wolf arms around me. I spread my arms uncertainly as he hugged me tight. Robert had risked everything for me and my kin. For the first time, I saw him not only as a friend, but truly as a brother. I hugged him back, and tears blurred my vision.

"Hey, brother, we did it." I said as I gave him a squeeze, "Thank you."

Robert nodded silently.

After a moment, I fetched Simon from the helicopter and picked him up in my massive, uber-werebird arms. As I carried him towards the ambulance, I stopped by Cecil who stood with a semi-automatic rifle guarding a row of werewolf prisoners.

Cecil swiveled his rifle and slung it over his shoulder as he reached out to touch Simon. "Simon! Are you okay?"

Simon smiled at his beak corners and reached out dreamily to touch Cecil's muzzle. "I've been better. I'll live."

I said, "I'm taking him to Doc now. But you better take this…" I leaned my face down and let Cecil take the leather bag that was slung around my neck.

Cecil opened the bag and rolled the stony Orb into his paw. The faint markings glowed softly, and I gasped in surprise.

Cecil smiled, "It's okay. It glows in the presence of werefolk."

Simon softly touched it and it glowed brighter and his hand jumped. "Woah, that was weird. I saw something in my head."

Cecil chuckled, "Good! I guess that means it works with bird brains too!"

Simon smirked weakly. His sparkling eyes looked up at Cecil's and he said, "I can't wait to explore it with you."

Cecil's eyes misted with affection, "Me too. But you take care of yourself now, okay? This will be here when you're ready. I promise I won't make a move on it without you."

Simon nodded and gripped Cecil's forearm warmly.

As we moved on towards the ambulance, dozens of beaks and wolf muzzles turned towards me, seeking direction. Some faces were clouded with heartbreak, others numbed by exhaustion and trauma, and a few wore smiles of triumph. My face lit up when I saw my love on a stretcher, alive and warm and reaching for a hug. That was the sweetest hug of my life.

Chapter 21: Epilogue

I was in the locker room again, geared up for my first game since returning to active player status. It was mid-November, and the pre-Thanksgiving fervor for football was palpable in the throbbing crowd noise filtering through concrete above us. I tried covering my head with a towel and meditatively retreating to my favorite fishing hole, but there was still too much baggage in my head to make that mental trip easy. In most ways, though, it was a good excitement.

I didn't have to hide what I was anymore. Sure, people still had plenty of questions, but one of the first things I did upon returning was show the team and staff how transformation worked. I wanted no more secrets between us, and the team was supportive, particularly after our lawyers pointed out that anything less would be discrimination. But barring legal issues, once Hatch and the rest of the staff learned more about my abilities, they were genuinely curious and encouraging. We were all a family, after all, and whether a team member was celebrating the birth of a child, the death of a loved one, or the revelation of a unique talent, we all came out in support of each other.

The NFA had jumped on board too, ostensibly under the guise of celebrating diversity, but I was certain that the real reason was because of the potential my abilities had for boosting viewership. And from all the hype that was going on in the stadium, I had no doubts that their financiers were salivating by the bucket.

Although none of the recovered cans of Zillion were positive for mitogen, the substance recovered from Boonedocks was a perfect match for what Doc had detected in my bloodstream, and that sealed the deal in terms of convincing management that I was fit to return. After all, so long as I stay away from mitogens, something which can be monitored for, then I'd be in full control of my transformations. But I made it clear that I was not a spectacle for their profit or the amusement of a crowd. While playing official NFA football, I would stay in human form, and it was up to me when or whether I shared my transformation ability with the public outside of game time.

Soon, we were circled up for the pre-game prayer and then lined up in the tunnel to jog out to the playing field. The crowd was especially boisterous that day as they chanted out the team's victory song. I think I had more butterflies in my stomach than I did during my first game with the team. Finally, it was time, and we broke out of the tunnel into the open air just as the crowd sang the last lines and erupted in cheers.

I was in the rear half of the column, and as I emerged, the announcer bellowed, "Give a special Bald Eagles' 'welcome back' to our wide receiver, Double-Aught, Phillll Adlerrrrr!" The crowd rose to their feet, and their voices lifted into a deafening roar.

As we lined up on the field for the opening ceremonies, the announcer continued, "We're so glad to have you back, Adler! That was some exit a few weeks ago, and I'm sure the crowd would love to see a repeat performance!"

I was reluctant to fuel the crowd into that expectation, but Dupree slapped my shoulder and shouted, "Give 'em some love."

I stepped forward and turned, waving my arm. The Jumbotron lit up with an animation of a flying eagle superimposed with lyrics to the team victory song, and the crowd cheered along, "Fly, Eagles, fly! Fight! Fight! Fight! And

Fly to Victoryyy!"

As they sang, I turned and took the arms of Dupree and Hansen and lifted them high. To me, at that moment, the team mattered most. They had been there for me in my hour of dire need, and now we were there for each other doing what we loved and aiming to win.

The crowd hushed for the Star-Spangled Banner, and soon we were playing ball. The rest of the game went with no further mention of the events of two weeks before. The NFA and the team wanted to put the incident behind them as gracefully as possible, without an obvious cover-up. I agreed. It respected the intelligence of the fans, as they would not easily forget what had happened.

We played the game aggressively, tasting the weakness in Jacksonville's defense, and soundly beat the Black Cats twenty-eight to seven. I did my part by completing several passes that day and scored one of our four touchdowns.

Afterwards, we mixed with reporters in the hallway outside the locker room. I'd expected a swarm of questions about my transformation incident, and I wasn't sure I was ready to answer all of them, so I hoped to avoid interviews.

That all changed when Melanie Allen, our energetic publicist, surrounded by reporters, locked her eyes on me. She waved me over and I obeyed. As I stepped in front of a camera and a sports reporter turned to me with a microphone, she whispered in my ear, "Lawyers say what you do outside of game time is none of their business, as long as you don't name the NFA in any of it."

"Really? You want me to…?" I asked.

She replied with a nod, "If you want. I can't tell you to, but if it were me, I'd show it off!"

The reporter turned to me and said, "Hey, Adler! Nice touchdown today! How's it feel to be back with the team?"

I smiled as I hugged my helmet to my side. "It's great! I missed the guys and the fans. It's good to be back!" I'd rarely been snagged in the post-game press gauntlet before. In the past it had always rattled me, but today I was calm. I added, "And, in a way, I never left them. We were in touch all the time. Coach Hatch, and great guys like Dupree, really came through and helped us out."

The reporter replied, "Looks like you hit the ground running too, instead of, shall we say, flying? The NFA called your absence 'medical leave,' but it seemed to your fans that it had something to do with the incident during the game a couple of weeks ago. We also have it under good authority that you had a bit of a family emergency. So, what's the story?"

I hadn't expected a question like that. I asked blankly, "My family?"

The reporter pressed on, "Yeah! How are they doing?"

The personal nature of the question touched me in a place that was still tender. But it was a golden opportunity to publicly voice something special that had taken root in my soul. The concept of joining families with the Boones and other wolffolk was still a fragile, delicate sprout of an idea, barely formed. But I believed it could become a strongly rooted tree that would strengthen us, and perhaps even all mankind. Of course, I couldn't divulge all of that just yet.

I smiled calmly and replied, "We're doing better than ever. I can't tell you all the details, but there was some loss in my extended family." I looked at the camera, and a wave of solemn pride swelled behind my eyes. "Family, be they by blood or by choice, are the most important thing any of us has. Sometimes you gotta drop everything to help out those that matter the most to you. The team has received tons of fan mail, and I gotta say that the outpouring of love and concern has been, well, overwhelming. From myself, my family, and the team, thanks to you all."

The reporter smiled back, "Good to hear. And I gotta ask this, because I know your fans are all dying to know: What was that wild stunt all about anyway?"

I chuckled. "Oh, well it was just…" I had prepared myself to tell white lies and bluff my way through the inevitable questions, but that had chafed at my conscience. I wasn't eager to become the topic of further public scrutiny, but lying about it would be insulting to fans. 'The bird was out of the bag' now, so why pretend?

I grinned wide. "Well, it wasn't a stunt. It wasn't supposed to happen, as it's something I keep personal and private. But, well, I've got some big news for everyone. I'm a werebird, and there are generations of us all around the world."

The reporter was stunned speechless for a moment, finally uttering, "Uh, what's a were… bird?"

"Hey, they say a picture's worth a thousand words, right? So how about I just show ya?" I backed away and the reporter made space, with an expression that said he had no idea what was about to happen.

Dupree was nearby, so I tossed my helmet to him, and leaned forward in ready posture, focusing my eyes on the camera and its glaring light. I had practiced transforming all my life, often rehearsing what I thought would be the most dramatic way to show someone new to the experience, if I was ever allowed to reveal myself. At last, I could do it for real.

My backwings rose first, ripping my jersey and body pads to shreds, as they shot upwards and outwards and feathers exploded from them like origami coming to life. There were shouts and gasps as the crowd cleared away abruptly. The reporter's mouth fell open, and his eyes grew as wide as headlights.

Next, I pushed my beak forward from my face, and my eyes moved to the sides, as white feathers burst out of my face and neck and draped down over my upper chest. In my sharp eagle vision, I saw that no one was fainting yet, although some had screamed and ran away. Most were just watching in awe and silence. So, I continued.

I flexed my arms at my sides, and my muscles bulged, tearing the remains of my tattered jersey, and I quickly forced brown feathers to erupt from my upper arms, chest, and belly to cover my skin. My forearms and hands enlarged and rippled with yellow scutes like armor-plating, and my nails lengthened and thickened into black talons, shredding through my gloves. My feet exploded from my cleats into the thick, scaly claws of an eagle, and I pulled down the back of my pants to allow my large white tail to unfurl and flex into full size.

As I completed the transformation, I blinked my nictitating membranes at the reporter and stepped closer. I was a couple of feet taller now, and the man's hands were shaking. I said in a deep chirp, "Hey, it's okay, really. We're not monsters. We're not freaks of nature. We're the same as normal people, just with this talent that we've always kept private. We've been around a very long time, helping people and helping birds. We'll have a lot more to share in the months ahead but, well, I guess it falls on me now to represent all of us. Our enemies forced me to transform during the game. They wanted the revelation to destroy us. But I'm betting that the public can handle the truth and together we'll make the world better for everyone."

I reached out to Dupree. He was grinning from ear to ear, and I pulled him in closer for a brotherly hug, as I took the helmet from his hands. "This guy, right here, and all my teammates. Love you guys, glad to be back and to be myself. And Kayla! My wife. Couldn't have come through any of this without her. Love you, Babe!"

I turned away, Dupree under my arm, and we walked down the hallway, with my teammates crowding in and following us, leaving the reporter and cameraman speechless.

I meant every word, but there was so much more going on

inside including fears and uncertainties of being open to the world. I managed to keep it all pushed to the back of my mind while I was playing or drown it out with the euphoria of showing off for the team or the fans. A new chapter in my life, and in the history of humanity, was opening, and though it was new and a little scary, I reassured myself it would be a positive change in the long run.

After the dark and bloody night of the battle with Earl, I didn't see Robert, Cecil, Simon, or even Victor or Gramps for over a week. Football season is a busy time, and I'd fallen behind. Consequently, I had to endure a whirlwind of catching up, and I spent most of my time at the stadium. Kayla and I stayed at a hotel nearby to eliminate the commute. Honestly, it was good to throw myself back into football and apply myself physically for a little while, as opposed to stewing in shock and loss. In the evenings, I reflected on recent events and tried to find meaning to the tragic losses. Kayla and I took walks and talked about it too, and I am so thankful that she was there.

But as much as I tried to move on, sometimes the events of that night crashed back in on me without warning, particularly the harrowing memories of the final fight with Earl. I had dreams of Earl's pistol muzzle pressed against the helicopter window, point-blank aimed at my beak, the dark barrel of the gun glinting in the strobe light. But instead of being empty, the gun fired. The muzzle flashed and I heard a distant, disembodied bang. My body jolted, as though electrified, and my energy drained away. Earl grinned victoriously as I tumbled helplessly backwards into darkness, and I'd wake up in a cold sweat, my skin prickled with partially emerged feathers.

Even in waking, for several weeks, not a day went by that I didn't recall that near-fatal moment in a sudden vivid flash of sights and sensations. The recollection would be stirred by something ordinary, like rain pattering on a windshield, or hearing the whupping of a distant helicopter. My skin went cold, and my heart fluttered as though I were enveloped in the clammy clutches of Earl's ghost reaching out of the waters to haunt my existence.

Of course, I couldn't talk to anyone but family about those events. And so, being too busy with work to visit anyone else, it fell on Kayla to listen. And she had her own trauma to share with me—memories of being struck from the air and watching my blurry, anguished face as I stuffed my fingers in the gushing hole in her chest. She told me that her worst fear was not seeing me again, or that I might not be able to let her go and finish what needed to be done.

Her injury was just as Gramps had predicted. In anthro-eagle form, her broad sternum, thickened for the attachment of flight muscles, had stopped the slow-moving bullet from hitting anything vital. But it was a very close call. Doc removed the bullet, and after a night in his clinic and a few more days at home in anthro form, she was able to transform back to human form again without risk. Within a couple of weeks, she was back at work with our medical team.

In our nightly conversations, she gave me good advice that kept me from diving into self-absorbed despair during my episodes of post-traumatic distress. She taught me to let the scene play out until it moved on to the good memories that followed. The warmth of Robert's hug after the battle. Kayla's gentle hands and her loving smile in the clinic after surgery. The affectionate exchange between Simon and Cecil. The reassuring hugs of Gramps, Adele, and Victor. The love in those memories pulled me through the pain and left me feeling solemnly thankful to be able to enjoy time with the good people in my life. Their love makes all the difference in the world.

On a fine Sunday in late November, the veterans of the battle, and some of our immediate family members, gathered on the Boones Estate for a memorial service. The dead had been cremated, and on that day we remembered them and interred their ashes in a family crypt on a quiet hill near the

Susquehanna River amidst a celebration of their lives. Even if their lives ended on a questionable note, at some point in their existence, they were all cherished by someone.

Oaks blazed in orange, yellow, and red, and the Susquehanna River, deep blue in the afternoon sunshine, flowed by quietly under a backdrop of colorful ridges that marched to the east. Wind gently tossed the boughs and created a steady flurry of colorful leaves.

When Robert organized the service, I refused his invitation initially. I was worried that to his kin, my presence might seem disingenuous at best or insulting at worst. After all, my family and I had killed many of their loved ones. I thought it was too soon.

But Robert reminded me that he had also killed his brethren. And that honorable killing had been a part of pack culture since before recorded memory. It was sometimes necessary, and extolled, when pack leaders were killed after they lost their way and threatened the well-being and stability of the family. He was certain that, in time, Earl's death would be seen similarly.

The Boones were just one of dozens of family packs scattered around the world. It had fallen to Robert and Cecil to meet with their elders, the Council of Packs, and tell the complete story of what had happened. They shared the secret of The Orb and their efforts to utilize its knowledge.

Robert and Cecil were exonerated by the Council. And so, Robert pressed me to attend. He said, "If I can be there, you can be there. It takes balls to be there. They'll respect that. They already respect that you were saving the lives of your own family. If there's anything we Boones understand, it's that family is all that matters. Sometimes it drives us to do stupid, terrible things even. But in the defense of my family, few knew the sum of what Earl was up to."

I responded, "Come on, really? Are you sure they weren't just playing dumb so as not to get their hands bloody?"

Robert nodded. "Yeah, maybe one or two. It's possible. But maybe that's not all bad. They're gonna keep quiet, be more agreeable, not make waves. Gives us some latitude to do wild things, like combining our families' interests."

"Oh? How so?"

"How about you and me being in charge of security, for starters? Cross-training, sports, hunting trips together. It's not like we're going to war, but I think we could learn a lot from each other. And it would unite us to a common purpose. Wolffolk, as masters of the ground, and birdfolk, as masters of the sky. We could accomplish a lot with our combined abilities."

I nodded. "I suppose that's what the creators of The Orb wanted, isn't it?"

"Seems that way. Cecil and Simon say it requires cooperation of the clades, operating it simultaneously, to unlock all it contains. We won't know its full potential until we involve all the clades. Sounds like a lesson in unity to me."

I'd finally acquiesced to his request to attend, and soon, there I was, standing with the sun on my wings before a crowd of two hundred wolf faces, a few humans, and a hundred familiar bird faces. A wide gamut of colors of feathers and fur and flesh stood before me, listening patiently to my solemn words. There was no priest, for the wolfkind, like us, were not particularly inclined to spiritualism. Centuries of religious persecution had seen to that.

I had written some remarks down, and so I pulled the page out from my jacket pocket and started reading.

"Thank you, everyone... wolfkind, birdkind, humankind, for coming today... and for allowing me to speak." The crinkled paper in my hands rustled in a gentle breeze, and a blue jay called out in the forest below. I swallowed and exhaled, then said, "To hell with the notes."

I crumpled the paper up and stuffed it back in my pocket

and paused to gather my emotions. From my other pocket I pulled out a can of Zillion with my signature across its side. It was the same can I'd signed for Jimmy. Jenny had found it in his possessions and passed it on to me. I set it down on the podium before me and awkwardly wiped a tear from my eye.

"First, I want to tell you about Jimmy. He was a dedicated young man… who looked up to me. He wanted to go to college, but he didn't have the money. His mom couldn't afford it. His dad abused and abandoned him. Somehow, though, he believed in himself enough that he was going to work hard and achieve good things. But some bad eggs offered him a shortcut and, well, I can understand why he took it. He had no idea it was going to be a deadly plot. He didn't want to hurt anyone. He was a good kid and I wish him no ill. I wish he was here with us today.

That crowd is gone now. A week ago, I would've sworn that no Boones could be trusted. But Jimmy showed me that's not the case at all. Robert and Cecil changed my perspective too. Turns out, you've got some really good eggs in your pack."

A somber cluster of howls went up from the wolfish faces in the crowd.

"The most important thing I have to say, is that I love my family. And my family just got a whole lot bigger. Wolf or bird or human, we're all brothers and sisters. It's our family. Turns out we are all related if you go far enough back. And we need each other in order to go forward and improve ourselves. Our designers, and I can't think of a better term, are speaking to us now, in the design of The Orb, telling us that we need each other. We'll be stronger together than we've ever been apart. Honor the memories of our lost and loved by sharing stories of their lives, and sharing the burdens of our hearts, with each other. Honor them further by building upon their sacrifice and making a better future together." I touched the can and concluded, "For Jimmy."

Soon, anyone with words was invited to speak, and perhaps a dozen rose to the occasion and expressed sorrow, respect, heartbreak, and hope. Tommy expressed regret for not following his son's activities with Earl more closely. He regretted the loss of Jimmy too and pledged to see to the needs of his mother. Bull's mother described the hope she had had for her son, and her sorrow for the damage he had caused. Robert recalled young Hayden's keen tracking and hunting abilities, and his love for the lore and lifestyle of a free wolf.

When the list of wolf dead was read, all joined in howls, as the sun slipped below the hills. As each of the avian names was read, a close relation released a feather from the deceased and let it float away on the breeze. The evening air lifted them high above the golden forest, towards the river below, and back to the sky, the water, and the earth, to be integrated into future living things, and so, to never really die.

After the solemn ceremony, a party was held to celebrate the lives of the lost and the new future our families would share. It wasn't all smooth. One heated argument broke out, and Cecil surprised us by barking down the two near-combatants. He was growing into his role as the new Alpha.

After Earl's death, two key proceedings took place. First, was an accounting of Earl's wealth and the desires he laid out in his Last Will and Testament. Second, there was the matter of transferring the leadership of the Boones family pack. The two issues were intertwined, but while the former was a public, legal process, the latter was subject only to age-old family by-laws.

In the case of the first, a charter drawn up generations before restricted inheritance to only those assets earned directly by the most recent heir. None of the land or ancestral property could be divided or sold without the unanimous agreement of the Council of Packs and proceeds from those assets could only be distributed to the entire family, including extended members. The same applied to other ancestral lands around the world.

This had effectively discouraged grabs of wealth for generations.

Earl's Will divided his considerable personal wealth among his offspring. Owning and running his many enterprises fell to Tommy, his second son, and the one with the most business acumen. A large endowment was left for ongoing "medical and anthropological research," a philanthropic cover for BooneTech and its clandestine efforts in genetic research and deciphering The Orb. Cecil Boones was named in legal documents as the permanent head of the committee managing the endowment and all research concerns.

The second issue, selecting the next Alpha to lead the Boones pack, proved to be more complicated. The departed could not strictly pick their successor, although their opinion did have weight. Earl had listed Cecil as his preferred candidate, since he was his eldest son, and because of his "loyalty and scruples."

Cecil had stifled a tear-filled laugh at this phrase. His heart was broken, barely held together by a brilliant mind. On one hand, he had been party to a system that was poised to perform incredibly unethical research. People had died to protect that new and heinous system. The guilt and pressure of it nearly drove him insane. But, on the other hand, when he broke ranks, he betrayed his own father, who had placed his highest trust in him. Cecil had told us of how Earl had been brutally tough on him. He often doubted his own worth in his father's eyes. But those simple, sweet words praising his "loyalty and scruples" cast away all doubt, even if only revealed posthumously. Now he had to try to reconcile the love of a man who could do such unspeakable evil.

Nobody else in the Boones family knew a thing about operating The Orb. Cecil had shown the device to the Council of Packs and explained how it required the help of werebirds, and that he would oversee combining our efforts. He was undeniably necessary and, therefore, safe in his position for now. For the time being, no one would challenge Cecil's status, but Robert explained to me that that could change if he couldn't demonstrate strong leadership. Robert was confident that Cecil would rise to the occasion, and I was beginning to share that feeling too.

And then there was the device itself. Simon took a leave of absence from MIT to join Cecil at the laboratory. It was a treasure to see the two work and play together, as if they had been brothers their whole lives. They shared the same nerdy interests, spoke the same language of science, and their different areas of study complemented each other so that they thought as one mind. They were rarely apart; Simon having taken up residence at the Boones Estate during the past week.

As part of the evening festivities, our combined family councils were summoned to a momentous occasion—the first activation of The Orb using birdfolk and wolffolk samples. As the party continued on into the evening, a select group of invitees, including Kayla and I, made our way to the BooneTech Annex building.

Kayla and I chose to walk along the dimly lit forest paths to the site, and soon we came to the grassy pasture that had been a bloody battlefield only a couple of weeks before. As we traversed the clearing, I passed scars in the earth and stray feathers caught in the dry grass stems. But nature had erased most of the traces of carnage, and no casual observer would have guessed that an epic fight had happened there.

As we passed the hangar, I felt drawn to the helicopter. I walked around it, and studied it quietly, sending Kayla on ahead while I lingered for a few minutes alone.

The shattered Plexiglas window and bloodied passenger seat had been replaced. I studied every inch of the side, as if trying to prove to myself that my memories were real and not merely dreams. My avian eyes could see no traces of blood, but there were scratches on the skids and belly from my talons.

As I sat on my haunches, studying the scrapes, the pilot came out of an office at the back and walked to the old refrigerator in the corner. Beer bottles clinked, and the door shut as he walked towards me. I stood up quickly and backed away from the chopper as he approached.

"Uh, sorry, just admiring," I said.

"No worries, you're fine. I'm Chris Hadlock, the pilot. Earl was my grandpa." He held out a bottle of beer in one hand and had an open one in his other.

"Yeah, I recognize you." I took the beer and nodded, quietly replying, "Thanks."

Chris watched me open the bottle and said, "Don't take this the wrong way, cuz you look a little different now than the last time I saw ya, but you must be Phil, right?"

I replied, "Yeah, Phil Adler the Third."

"Play for the Bald Eagles?"

"Uh-huh, that's me."

Chris reached out with his bottle and clinked it to mine before taking a swallow. I followed suit.

Chris asked, "You saw the scratches, didn't ya?"

I stood silent, emotions churning at the back of my throat.

Chris walked to the helicopter and ran his fingers down one of the scratches. "Let me tell ya, that was one hell of a bird strike."

I met his relaxed gaze with wide eyes. My heart pounded in my chest, and my hand holding the beer bottle shook slightly.

Chris leaned against the chopper with one hand and said, "Quite the bloody mess. Scared the living shit out of me. Fuckin' Earl. I told him a million times to put his harness on." Chris held up his beer bottle to his faintly smiling lips, preparing to take a sip. "Old fool never listened."

I played along with the indirect discussion of what we both

knew had happened. I cleared my throat and took another drink and said, "Shame. Must've been a hell of a shame. You must really regret it."

Chris shook his head slowly. "No, not really."

The scratches tugged at my eyes like tentacles pulling me back to that harrowing night. Chris' voice snapped me back to the present.

Chris said, "He was asking for it, if you ask me."

I was numb as I said, "Excuse me?"

Chris shrugged. "Physics are bound to catch up with the careless. Safety is no accident, ya know. He was asking for it if you ask me. Never know when a bird strike could happen."

I nodded. "I guess so."

Robert and Gramps walked around the corner, chatting as they looked inside the hangar. They saw me and quieted briefly, then resumed walking.

"Thanks for the beer," I told Chris.

He smiled. "Don't mention it. Stop by again sometime. I'd love to talk about flying with someone that really knows how to fly."

I exhaled and shook my head, blinking my eyes to clear the bad memories. I put on a smile and said, "Sounds good," then shook his hand and made my way to catch up with the others.

Like the rest of the Boones, Chris had a vested interest in keeping the family secrets and was able to make up a convincing story for the authorities. The official version was that Earl's death was a tragic accident, having fallen out of his helicopter after a bird strike and having removed his recommended safety harness. The circumstances were plausible to the authorities, after they examined the helicopter and the National Transportation Safety Board interviewed Chris.

Dragging the Susquehanna River for the body proved fruitless, although the partial remains of a large wolf were discovered, consisting of only a severely decomposed leg. The discovery made local headlines and a national tabloid, being touted as proof of the fabled dog men who were sporadically reported in the region since the late nineteenth century. But as is commonly the case with such sensational news, the incident was quickly pushed to the back of public consciousness.

Ahead of me on the way to the laboratory, Gramps and Robert chatted about the politics of our two families, trading notes on how best to bring "the strays into the fold," as Gramps put it. There were bound to be distrustful kin on both sides, so long had our families been at odds. But that was before we knew that the Boones had a similar gift of transformation. And very few had been aware that our origins were the same. Gramps advocated bringing the detractors down here to see the device for themselves. Robert nodded and agreed.

In a few minutes, we were in the elevator descending to the secret sublevel. As the doors opened, my thoughts completely derailed. There was no smoke, no gunfire, no bodies. But for a fraction of a second, I saw the carnage again. Then I realized Gramps and Robert were both looking at me in silence.

I replied to their stares, "Oh, sorry. Guess I was somewhere else for a second."

Robert put a hand on my shoulder. "I know what you mean, Phil."

Gramps nodded his beak solemnly and said, "You boys take your time," and walked off down the hallway.

Robert put his arm over my shoulders and led me forward behind Gramps' swishing tail. Robert had been back here since the battle, but I had not. The arm of my comrade, my brother, was reassuring.

Robert remarked, "This place is gonna give me the creeps for a long time. Glad you're here with me."

I guffawed. "Shit. Likewise. Had it bad there for a second. But don't get me wrong. I'm glad to be back here and I'm excited to see this thing work."

In a few minutes, we joined a group of birdfolk and werewolves in the laboratory. The room was moodily dim, except for the bright track lighting that illuminated The Orb. The charcoal-dark, smooth sphere sat perched on a custom-made cradle atop a marble plinth. Around the plinth was a circular marble bench.

It was decided that the heads of both families would be the first to activate The Orb together, attended with their leadership councils. The council members were already there, assembled in groups on each side. While the social distance between our families was decreasing, there was still a tendency for us to group with our kind.

Cecil greeted us, and everyone clapped briefly. He addressed the room with his white wolfish muzzle and sapphire eyes, "Please, Phil Sr., young Phil, and Robert, come forward with me. Everyone else, please form a circle and join hands. It's clear from the alien inscriptions that whomever our creators were, they wanted us to be united in this adventure."

The crowd of forty shuffled and muttered pleasant greetings as they obeyed Cecil's request. Robert and I crowded in close to The Orb, and the markings that had been barely discernable suddenly glowed with golden light. In this illuminated state, the markings were clear and finely detailed. Each animal clade rune was surrounded by encircling lines that branched, radiated, and reconnected, like artful circuitry, across the surface.

I remarked to Robert, "There it goes again! Cecil says it does when it's close to werefolk."

Cecil smiled and nodded, "The more that are present, the stronger it glows."

I reached out to touch it, but Cecil stopped me, "Careful. If you touch it, it may transmit things straight to your mind."

I asked, "What kinds of things?"

Cecil grinned. "Depends on what questions you have. As far as I can tell, it's not harmful, but it can be deeply unsettling if you're not prepared."

I looked back at the glowing Orb, wanting to take that plunge, but this was not my moment. I withdrew my hand and said to Robert, "Maybe you and I can take a turn after the others?"

Robert shook his head quietly, "Not sure I'm ready to have my brain probed. I kind of like having just me in here." He tapped his own head with a finger.

Victor quipped, "It would starve if it tried to feed off Phil's brain!"

I smirked and retorted, "And the scary things in your head would chase aliens away forever."

Cecil barked, "Quiet! Please respect the occasion." He sat down on the marble bench and said, "Please, Phil Senior, take a seat here next to me."

Gramps obeyed and Robert and I took positions behind the two. Simon motioned for all to crowd in close around the four of us and he took a seat to the left of Cecil and smiled reassuringly as he grasped his left hand.

Cecil continued, "I honestly don't know what new things will happen when we activate it with our two clades together, but please don't panic. Just ride it out. I have every confidence that it will be enriching. I've connected with it many times, and I'm still alive and well."

Robert guffawed, "I seem to remember you going a bit crazy."

Cecil's expression flattened, "The Orb had nothing to do with that! Not directly anyway. It was stress—"

Gramps held up a hand and cut them both off, "Boys! If you don't mind, I'd like to go through with this. I trust ye, Cecil. And 'sides, not much left to scramble in my ol' noggin' anyways."

Robert nodded to Cecil, "Sorry, Sees. Go ahead."

Cecil spoke to the room, "We'll start by pricking each of their fingers to form a drop of blood and then they touch the respective clade runes. Keep your finger in contact. Don't worry if you feel faint, everyone is close by and can help you."

Cecil smiled and held out a small plastic device towards Gramps. "Mr. Adler, here is the lancet. You'll hardly feel a thing."

"That's the same line I give to my bird patients. Oh!" Gramps said as he winced from the tiny stab to his leathery yellow bird finger.

Cecil changed needle cartridges and applied it to his own wolf finger. The lancet snapped. "Hold up your finger, sir."

They held up their fingers and each had a healthy drop of blood on their fingertip. A werewolf documentarian snapped a picture with a camera. Another held a video camera up over the crowd to catch the moment in motion.

"And here we go."

Gramps and Cecil pressed their fingers down onto their respective runes and the concentric rings around each glowed blue, as the eyes of Robert and Gramps closed. There were no flashing lights, no beeps or bloops, just silence, as the two smiled in unison.

Glossary

Anemia: Deficiency of red blood cells.

Alulla: A moveable digit, analogous to a thumb, on the wing of a bird which prevents stalling at low speeds or high angles of attack.

Angle of Attack: The angle of an airfoil (the chord) relative to the slipstream of air.

Anthro: Refers to having a humanoid form. In the case of werefolk, it's a blending of their human and animal traits. Usually they have hand-like forearm appendages, the feet, head, and tail most resemble their feral form, and in the case of birds, they usually have large wings on their back. Werefolk can control the anthro or feral expression of individual parts of their body to create combinations that are convenient for a variety of circumstances.

Attitude (flight dynamics): Describes the orientation of an airframe (or bird) in three-dimensional space. In simplest terms, it usually refers specifically to whether the nose is tipped upwards or downwards, which alters how well the wings produce lift at various airspeeds.

Backwings: A pair of wings located behind the shoulders of werebirds in their anthro form. They are usually capable of flight.

Cere: The soft, fleshy region at the base of the upper beak surrounding the nares (nostrils).

Clade: A general term for a taxonomic grouping of biological life. In the case of this story, it's a mix of Class (Aves) and Family (Canids).

Cloaca: The common collection organ in birds, amphibians, and reptiles, for fecal matter and urine/urates. It also contains the openings to the reproductive tracts (oviduct in females, seminal ducts in males). The outer opening is referred to as the vent.

Crop: An expansion of the esophagus, located at the base of the neck, which stores food prior to digestion.

Feral: The natural form of a werebird's wild counterpart species. So, in the case of an anthro bald eagle, it's the form that looks exactly like a wild bald eagle.

Hallux: The back toe of a bird of prey.

Mitogen: A substance that encourages, or forces, transformation to the form dictated by the mental state of the wereperson.

Mitostat: A substance that blocks a wereperson's ability to transform.

Stall (flight dynamics): The state of such high angle of attack of an airfoil relative to the direction of airflow, that the slipstream separates from the surface of the airfoil and it ceases to produce lift.

Subcutaneous fluids: Fluids delivered between the muscle and skin layers. It's a common method of restoring hydration in animals.

Supraorbital ridge: The semi-flexible ridge located above the eyes of birds of prey.

Underfluffies: A colloquial term to describe the fluffy semiplumes located under the tail of anthro and feral birds.

Werefolk/Werebird/Werewolf/Wereperson: Humans that possess the ability to change into birds, wolves, or other animal species.

About the Author

I'm Hal Aetus and I live in Milwaukee, Wisconsin with my husband, Colin. I grew up in Washington State and have also lived in Alaska. I am a veterinarian specializing in avian medicine and surgery and I particularly enjoy assisting wildlife. I spend much of my time in remote settings lending my skills to field research & conservation efforts.

My interest in writing and creative arts began as a child but went on the back burner for a couple of decades as I attended college and began my career. In 2013 I discovered the furry fandom and was inspired to write fiction and take up digital art. My art and stories focus on avian characters.

I'm also a private pilot with instrument, land, & sea ratings. My unifying passion in life has always been birds and anything bird-related.

Thanks for joining me on my journey through art and writing. If you enjoy my works, leave a positive review on GoodReads.com, Amazon.com, or just tell a friend! Check out my website at aetusart.com for current social media contacts so you can stay up to date on my new releases.

Also By Hal Aetus

I hope you liked The Adler Chronicles. If you did, you'll love my other books…

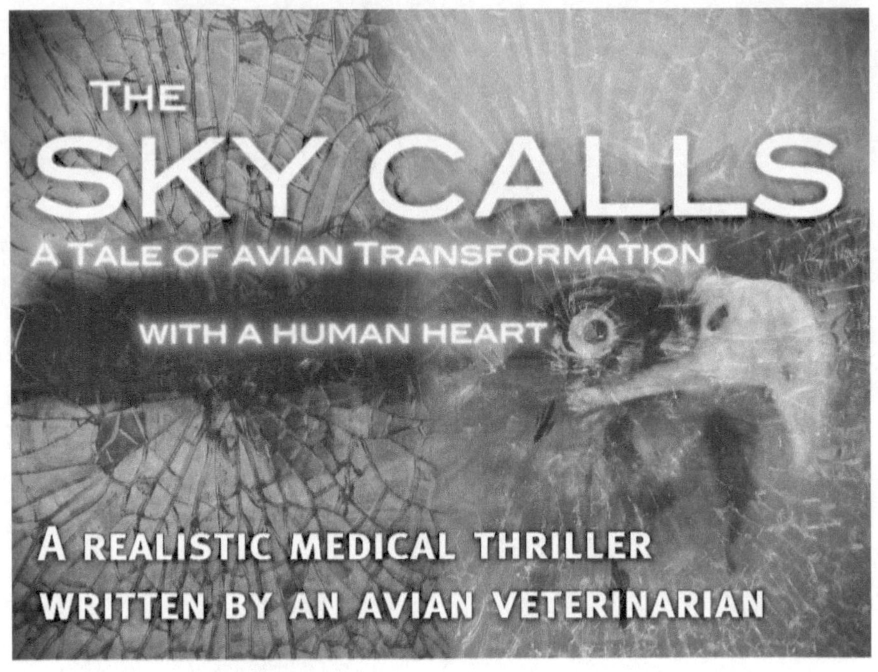

The Sky Calls

Available on Amazon or at

aetusart.com/the-sky-calls

When terminal cancer strikes in mid-life, David Geraki has to make tough choices. He chooses a radical, experimental genetic therapy that saves his life but destroys his humanity as he gradually turns into an eagle. With the help of his lifelong friend, he must hold on to what's left of himself, accept what he's become, and ultimately fight for his freedom to exist.

Whiterock, due out in 2024!
Follow Along at aetusart.com/whiterock

Hundreds of years in the future, humanity is gone and Volatalia, a new avian nation, has arisen from the ashes to become the crowning achievement of the Avian Age. Tristan, a barn owl, and Pepro, a bald eagle, embark on a journey to the town of Whiterock in aid of their mentor, Kor, a grizzled but kind-hearted raven blacksmith, who is commissioned to create rings for a pair bonding the likes of which has never been seen. Soon they meet, Nyx, a peregrine falcon, and Perry, a broken-hearted Laysan albatross. Their simple mission becomes dreadfully complicated as they are pulled apart by forces that seek power and a return to an ancient order. Their love for each other may be the only thing that can hold them together but it may not be enough to save their country.